"Frightening . . . k

"Will leave your hea
nonstop. . . . Just wl⸺⸺ ⸺ver, the
action ratchets up aga⸺ ⸺ up until the final
shot has been fired."

—*The Kansas City Star*

"In her first contemporary suspense thriller, Garwood explodes out of the narrative gate. . . ."

—*Publishers Weekly*

"Engrossing . . . addictive . . . by turns explosive and unpredictable. . . . You cheer for the good guys and are glad when the bad guys get caught. . . . [Garwood] has found a niche for herself in contemporary romantic fiction."

—*The Anniston Star* (AL)

"Moves rapidly to a shattering climax. . . . The frank sensuality of the love scenes is sure to please."

—*Kirkus Reviews*

"Julie Garwood takes her unique voice and talent and moves into the contemporary genre. *Heartbreaker* establishes that Ms. Garwood has quite a flair for intrigue and suspense!"

—*Romantic Times*

"A heart-thumper."

—*The Ottawa Citizen*

"Garwood employs all the senses, creating vivid characterizations and unexpected twists and turns."

—*BookPage*

Books by Julie Garwood

Gentle Warrior
Rebellious Desire
Honor's Splendor
The Lion's Lady
The Bride
Guardian Angel
The Gift
The Prize
The Secret
Castles
Saving Grace
Prince Charming
For the Roses
The Wedding
Come the Spring
Ransom
Heartbreaker
Mercy

The Rose Trilogy
One Pink Rose
One White Rose
One Red Rose

Published by POCKET BOOKS

JULIE GARWOOD

THE WEDDING

POCKET STAR BOOKS

New York   London   Toronto   Sydney

The sale of this book without its cover is unauthorized. If you purchased this book without a cover, you should be aware that it was reported to the publisher as "unsold and destroyed." Neither the author nor the publisher has received payment for the sale of this "stripped book."

This book is a work of fiction. Names, characters, places and incidents are products of the author's imagination or are used fictitiously. Any resemblance to actual events or locales or persons, living or dead, is entirely coincidental.

A Pocket Star Book published by
POCKET BOOKS, a division of Simon & Schuster, Inc.
1230 Avenue of the Americas, New York, NY 10020

Copyright © 1996 by Julie Garwood

All rights reserved, including the right to reproduce this book or portions thereof in any form whatsoever. For information address Pocket Books, 1230 Avenue of the Americas, New York, NY 10020

ISBN -13: 978-0-671-87100-0
ISBN -10   0-671-87100-5

First Pocket Books printing April 1997

27 26 25 24 23

POCKET STAR BOOKS and colophon are registered trademarks of Simon & Schuster, Inc.

Cover design by Dale C. Verzaal

Manufactured in the United States of America

For information regarding special discounts for bulk purchases, please contact Simon & Schuster Special Sales at 1-800-456-6798 or business@simonandschuster.com.

For my sister and dear friend,
Mary Kathleen Murphy McGuire

Prologue

The Highlands, Scotland, 1103

Donald MacAlister didn't die easy. The old man fought to stay alive with every ounce of strength and every pound of stubbornness he possessed. Though he should have welcomed death as an end to the terrible pain and anguish he was enduring, he wouldn't give in to his suffering yet, for there was still the most important legacy of all to pass down before he could close his eyes and rest.

His legacy was hate. The laird was consumed by hatred for his enemy. He needed to see his son burn with the fever for revenge, and until he was certain the boy understood the importance of righting the terrible wrong done this dark day, he would continue to fight death. And so he clung to life and to his son's hand, so small and fragile in his big, leathery one, his black eyes boring into those of his only living heir, while the old man instructed him in his sacred duty.

"Avenge me, Connor MacAlister. Take my hatred into your heart, protect it, nurture it, and when you've grown older and stronger, use my sword to slay my enemies. I cannot die in peace until you've given me your word you'll avenge this evil deed done to me and mine. Promise me, boy."

1

"Yes, Father," Connor fervently vowed. "I will avenge you."

"Do you burn with the fever for revenge?"

"I do."

Donald nodded with contentment. He was finally at peace, and if he lived long enough to give his son directions for his future, that was all well and good; but if the next breath he drew were to be his last, that would be acceptable to him too, because he knew his son would find a way to do what he must. Connor had already proven to be highly intelligent, and his father had complete faith in him.

'Twas a pity Donald MacAlister wouldn't be around to see his son grow into manhood, but with a broken leg and a fair-sized hole near his belly, he knew how foolish it was to wish for impossible things. God was proving merciful, however. The pain had eased considerably in the past few minutes, and a blessed numbness was stealing up from his feet to his knees.

"Father, give me the names of the men who did this to you."

" 'Twas the Kaerns who attacked. They came down from the north and from too far away to want our land. They're blood related to the MacNares, though, and I've a suspicion their laird had a hand in this evil. MacNare's always been a greedy one. He'll never be content. You'd best kill him before he causes you trouble, or his lust for more land will bring him to your doorstep. Don't act in haste," he cautioned. "Neither the Kaerns nor the MacNares are cunning enough to have planned this boldness. They must have acted under directions from another. I don't know who the traitor is, but you'll find out. 'Tis my feeling the enemy hails from within."

"One of our own betrayed you?" Connor was stunned by the possibility.

"Since yesterday eve when they attacked, I've been considering that possibility. The Kaerns came in through passages only my followers knew about. They never would have found the entrances without direction. There's a traitor all right, and it will be your duty to ferret him out. He's one of us, Connor, of that I'm certain. God willing, he's singing the death rattle even now on my own battlefield.

You'll bide your time until you have all the names. Then wreak vengeance upon all of those still living. Consider killing their sons as well, boy."

"I will, Father. I'll destroy all of them."

Donald's grip on his son's hand tightened. "This be my final lesson to you. Watch me die and learn how to live as a warrior. When you leave me, go to the path in the forest. Angus waits there to give you instructions for your immediate future."

The laird waited until his son nodded his agreement before speaking again. "Look around you and tell me what you see. Is it all gone?"

Connor stared at the destruction surrounding him, silently weeping with anguish. The stench of burning wood and fresh blood made his stomach lurch.

"The keep is in ruins, but I'll rebuild."

"Aye, you will. You must make your fortress invincible. Learn from my mistakes, Connor."

"I will make my keep stronger."

"What of my loyal men?"

"Most are dead."

The despair in the boy's voice washed over the laird, and he immediately tried to reassure him. "Their sons will come back. They'll wear your colors and claim your name. They'll follow you as their fathers followed me. The time draws near for you to leave. Wrap a cloth tight around and around your injury to stem the blood before you stand, or more will be lost with each step you take. Do it now while I rest beside you."

Connor hurried to obey his father's command, though he didn't believe his injury was significant enough to merit protection. Most of the blood covering his body was from his father's wounds, not his own.

"You'll have a scar to remind you of this black day," Donald predicted.

"I need no reminder. I won't forget."

"No, you won't forget. Does it pain you?"

"No."

Donald grunted with approval. The boy had never been a complainer, a fact his father found most pleasing. He had all the makings of a mighty warrior.

3

"How old are you, boy?"

"Nine or ten years now," he answered.

"I'm thinking you might be older or younger. Your size tells me you're still a boy, but your eyes have turned into those of a man. I see the bright fire of fury there, and I am pleased by you."

"I could take you with me."

"You will not drag a dead man behind you."

"Do your injuries pain you, Father?"

" 'Tis the truth I don't feel anything now. I seem to have gone numb. A blessed way to die, I'm thinking. Some men would not be as fortunate."

"I would stay with you if you . . ."

"You'll leave when I command you to leave," his father ordered. "You'll save yourself so you'll be able to keep your promises to me. The enemy has left, but make no mistake, they'll come back to finish it."

"We have time, Father. The sun is still high, and the enemy dragged your barrels of wine with them. They'll be too thick-headed to come back before morning."

"Then you may linger a moment more," his father conceded.

"Will Angus send me to Euphemia to tell her what happened?"

"He will not. You will not tell that woman anything."

"But she's your wife."

"My second wife," he corrected. "Never trust a woman, Connor. 'Tis foolhardy to do so. Euphemia will find out what happened when she returns with her son, Raen. I want you to be well away from here by then. I won't have you trained by her relatives. They're all leeches."

Connor nodded so his father would know he understood, and then asked, "Did you trust my mother?"

Donald heard the worry in his son's voice and thought it was probably his duty to give him a kind remembrance of his mother. Still, the boy needed to hear the truth, and for that reason, he didn't soften his answer, but spoke from his heart.

"I did trust her, and anguish was the result. I loved your mother. She was my own sweet, bonny Isabelle, and how was I repaid for my generosity? She up and died on me, that's how, breaking my heart and leaving me desolate. Learn from my folly and save yourself the heartache. I never should have married again—I realize that now—but I am a practical man above all else, and I knew I needed heirs to follow after me in the event something foul happened to you. Still, it was a mistake. Euphemia already had one son from her past marriage, and one child was all she was capable of carrying. She did try though."

Donald paused to gather his thoughts before continuing. "I couldn't love Euphemia, or any other woman. How could I, after what my own sweet Isabelle had done to me? Still, I shouldn't have ignored your stepmother. It wasn't her fault I couldn't care about her. You must try to make up for my wrong. Try to honor her and put up with her pampered son. Remember, your first loyalty must be to your own."

"I'll remember. Where will Angus send me? There is time for you to tell me," he persisted. He was deliberately stalling so that he would have a few more minutes with his father. "Angus could have been killed before he reached the forest."

"It would not matter. Do you think I would entrust such important orders to only one man? I'm not foolish. I told others what was to be done."

"Let me hear the command from my laird."

Donald relented. "There's only one man I trust, and you must go to him. Tell him what took place here today."

"Do I tell him everything you have told me?"

"Yes."

"Do I trust him?"

"You do," he replied. "He'll know what's to be done. You must seek his protection first, then order him to train you in his image. Demand your right, boy. Pledge that you'll be his brother until the day you die. He won't fail you. Go now. Go to Alec Kincaid."

Connor was stunned by the order. "He's your hated enemy, Father. You cannot mean to send me to him."

"I do mean to," his father replied in a hard, unyielding voice. "Alec Kincaid has become the most powerful force in all the Highlands. He's also a good and honorable man, and you need his strength."

Connor was still having difficulty accepting the duty his

father had just thrust upon him. He couldn't stop himself from making another protest.

"But you warred against him."

Donald surprised his son by smiling. " 'Tis the truth I did. My heart wasn't in the fight, though. Kincaid knew that. I tested him sorely and am proud to say I was the nagging thorn in his side. Our lands connect to the east, and so it was a natural inclination of mine to take some of his. He wouldn't let me have it, of course. Still, he understood. Had he not, all of us would be dead by now."

"He is that powerful?"

"He is. Be sure to show him my sword. Leave the blood upon the blade so Kincaid will see it."

"Father, none of the MacAlisters will follow me if I go to their enemy."

"You will do as I command," his father said. "You're too young to understand, and so you must trust my judgment. I want your promise that you will go to Kincaid now."

"Yes, Father."

Donald nodded. "The time has come for you to bid me good-bye. We've dallied long enough, and I've put off dying for as long as I dare. Even now I can feel myself slipping into sleep."

Connor tried, but he couldn't seem to make himself let go of his father's hand.

"I will miss you," he whispered.

"And I, you."

"I love you, Father."

"Warriors do not speak of such feelings. I love you too, son, but I won't be telling you so."

He squeezed Connor's hand as a way of softening his rebuke, and finally closed his eyes. He was ready to let death have him, for he had seen the fire burning bright in Connor's eyes, and he knew he would be avenged. What more could a father ask?

Donald MacAlister died a few minutes later, still clinging to his son's hand. He died as he had lived, with honor, dignity, and on his own stubborn terms.

Connor lingered by his father's side for as long as he could, until he heard someone whispering to him from behind. He turned to see a young soldier struggling to sit up.

Connor couldn't remember his name, and from the distance separating them, he couldn't tell how serious his injuries were. He motioned to the soldier to stay where he was, then turned back to his father. He picked up the sword resting on his chest, bowed his head in prayer for his father's soul, and then crawled away, clutching the treasured sword to his heart. He eased over hot, glowing embers that blistered his arms and the bloody remains of friends, which made his eyes fill with tears.

He finally reached the man who had called out to him and discovered the soldier wasn't fully grown up, after all. Why, he couldn't be more than two or three years older than Connor.

Thankfully, he remembered the soldier's name before reaching him. "Crispin, I thought you dead. Roll onto your back so I may tend your injuries, or you will surely die."

"There isn't time. They came here to kill both your father and you, Connor. Aye, that was their purpose. I heard one of the bastards boast of it to another. Leave before they come back and realize they've failed."

"The enemy rests now. They won't come back until the wine they drink wears off. Do as I command you to do."

Crispin slowly rolled over, visibly grimacing over the pain the movement caused.

"Is your father dead?"

"Yes," Connor answered. "He lived long enough to tell me what I must do. He died in peace."

Crispin began to weep. "My laird is dead."

"Nay, Crispin. Your laird kneels before you."

Connor wouldn't allow him to argue with him, or laugh over his boast, but gave him duty upon duty while he bandaged him. He told the soldier how he could help to repay their enemy for this atrocity, and when Connor was finished binding his wound, he had given the soldier something more powerful than anguish to fill his mind and his heart. He had given him hope.

Although it was difficult because of his size, Connor eventually dragged Crispin to safety. He hid him away in the forest, well-protected by thick branches, and went back to the destruction twice more to drag out two others. One was Angus, the loyal soldier to whom his father had entrusted the duty of instructing his son. The other was a boy Connor's age called Quinlan, who had only just arrived to begin his training the week before. His injuries were severe, and he was in such pain, he begged to be left alone. Connor was deaf to his pleas.

"I decide when you die, Quinlan, not you."

The boy stopped struggling and even tried to help.

Connor desperately wanted to go back again and again to search for more, but the enemy had decided to return before nightfall, and even now he could see the shadows their horses made on the rise below. He knew he couldn't chance being discovered. He still needed enough time to remove the trail he'd made. He immediately set about doing just that, and once he was satisfied the three he'd hidden away would not be found, he promised to bring help and ordered them to stay alive.

He was finally ready to do his father's bidding. He rode his faithful mount half the distance to Kincaid land, but when he reached the steep ledges, he left the horse behind and climbed over the rock so that he could shorten the way.

Once he reached the flats again, he began to run. He moved over the land with the speed of a young buck for short spurts, and when exhaustion made his legs too weak to continue the grueling pace, he used his father's sword and scabbard as his cane and slowed to a walk until he was able to regain his strength again. He wasn't very strong yet, but his determination was that of ten grown men. He would not fail his father.

Connor felt nothing now, not the cold or the pain or the terrible loss. His mind was focused on one thought. He had to get to Alec Kincaid. Pledging his loyalty to the laird was the first step he must take to fulfill his father's wishes, and Connor wouldn't let anyone or anything stop him.

He lost track of time, and darkness was fast approaching. The sky was bright now with hundreds of orange streaks from the sun's too-quick descent behind the twin peaks directly ahead of him, but in a few minutes, those brilliant banners would also be gone. His desperation mounted with each step he took. He had to reach Kincaid before night closed in on him because he knew he would never be able to find his way in the dark. If he continued in darkness, he ran the risk of going in circles, or worse, backtracking the distance he'd already covered.

He could not fail. He started running again. He thought he was close to the border between his father's land and Kincaid's, yet he couldn't be absolutely certain. And then he heard shouts to halt from soldiers running toward him, but in his confusion he thought the enemy had chased him down and meant to kill him before he could keep his promises to his father. He staggered on until he couldn't take another step.

Dear God, he'd failed. He hadn't even begun yet and now he had failed. Kincaid was the beginning of his future, but Connor wasn't even strong enough to get to him.

"Can you speak, lad? Can you tell us what happened to you? You're covered in blood."

The soldiers surrounding him were all wearing Kincaid's colors. As that fact registered in Connor's mind, his legs gave out, and he went down hard on his knees. He wanted to close his eyes for just a moment, but he didn't dare. Not yet. He couldn't sleep until he had spoken to Kincaid. He needed to tell him what happened. . . . He could trust him. . . . He must . . .

He shook his head, trying to clear his thoughts, and then took a deep breath, threw back his head, and shouted, "Take me to my brother."

"Who is your brother, lad?" one of the sentries asked.

"By my father's command, from this day forward Alec Kincaid is my brother. He will not deny me."

It was all right to close his eyes now. He had fulfilled the first of his father's demands. The rest would come as soon as he had spoken to Kincaid. He would tell him where he'd hidden the injured soldiers, command that he go and get them . . . and he would tell his brother so much more . . .

Connor's last thought before he lost consciousness gave him peace. His father would be avenged.

And so it began.

Chapter

1

England, 1108

*I*t wasn't love at first sight.

Lady Brenna didn't want to be presented to company. She had far more important things to do with her day. Her nursemaid, a dour-faced woman with God-fearing ways and clumped-together, protruding front teeth, wouldn't listen to her arguments, however. With the determination of a hedgehog, she cornered Brenna in the back of the stables and then lunged forward. Never one to let an opportunity or a little girl slip past her, the nursemaid lectured her charge all the way up the hill and across the muddy courtyard.

"Quit your squirming, Brenna. I'm stronger than you are, and I'm not about to let go. You've lost your shoes again, haven't you? And don't dare lie to me. I can see your stockings peeking out. Why are you dragging that bridle behind you?"

Brenna lifted her shoulders in a shrug. "I forgot to put it back."

"Drop it this minute. You're always forgetting, and do you know why?"

"I don't pay attention to what I'm doing, like you tell me to, Elspeth."

"You don't pay attention to anything I tell you, and that's a fact. You're more trouble than all the others put together.

11

Your older brothers and sisters have never given me a moment's worry. Even your baby sister knows how to behave herself, and she's still sucking on her fingers and wetting herself. I'm warning you, Brenna, if you don't change your ways and give your parents a little peace, God himself will have to stop his important work and come down here to talk to you. Just how are you going to feel about that? You don't like it much when your papa has to sit you down on his knee and talk to you about your shameful behavior, now do you?"

"No, Elspeth. I surely don't like it. I try to behave. I really do."

She peeked up to see if the nursemaid believed she was contrite. She wasn't, of course, because she really didn't think she'd done anything wrong, but Elspeth wouldn't understand.

"Don't you bat those big blue eyes at me, young lady. I don't believe you're the least bit sincere. Lord, but you smell. What have you gotten into?"

Brenna lowered her head and kept quiet. She'd been chasing after the piglets just an hour before, until the tanner put their mama back in the pen, and Brenna's peculiar stench was just a small price to pay for all the fun she'd had.

Her torture had only just begun. Even though she had had a bath just a week before, she was bathed again, and in the middle of the day, of all times. She was scrubbed from head to toes, and so thoroughly she had to cry about it. Elspeth wasn't at all sympathetic to her wails, and Brenna eventually got tired of crying. She barely struggled at all while Elspeth dressed her in a blue gown and too-tight matching slippers. Her cheeks were pinched hard for color, her white-blond tangles were brushed into curls, and she was then dragged back down to the hall. She would have to pass her mother's inspection before she could be left alone.

Her oldest sister, Matilda, was already seated at the table with her mother. Cook was there too, going over supper arrangements with her mistress.

"I don't want to meet no company today, Mama. It's sorely wearisome for me."

Elspeth came up behind her and poked her in her

shoulder. "Hush now. You mustn't complain. God doesn't like women who complain."

"Papa complains all the time, and God likes him just fine," Brenna announced. "That's why Papa's so big. Only God is bigger than he is."

"Where did you hear such nonsense?"

"Papa told me so. I want to go outside now. I won't run after the piglets again. I promise."

"You're staying right where I can keep my eye on you. You're going to behave yourself today. If you don't, you know what will happen to you, don't you?"

Brenna pointed to the ground. "I'll have to go down there." She dutifully repeated the threat she'd heard over and over again.

The little girl didn't have any idea what was "down there"; she only knew it was awful and she didn't want to go there. According to Elspeth, if Brenna didn't change her sorry ways, she was never going to get into heaven, and just about everyone, including her family, wanted to go there.

She knew exactly where heaven was because her papa had given her exact directions. It was right on the other side of the sky.

She thought she might like it, but really didn't care. Only one thing was important to her now. She wasn't about to be left behind again. She still had nightmares at least once a week over what her mama referred to as the "unfortunate" incidents. The terrifying memories were still lurking in the back of her mind, where everyone knew all little girls tucked away their worries, just waiting for the right opportunity to jump out in the dark and scare her. Her screams would wake her sister, of course. While Elspeth was busy soothing baby Faith, Brenna would drag her blanket to her parents' chamber. When her papa was away from home doing important work the king could give only to someone as trustworthy and loyal as he was, she'd sneak into the big bed and cuddle up next to her mama, and when her papa was home, she'd sleep on the cold floor right next to Courage, his beautiful silver-handled sword Mama swore he loved almost as much as his children. Brenna felt safest when her papa was there because his loud snores always lulled her back to sleep. Demons didn't try to crawl in through the window and nightmares about being left behind didn't visit her when she was with her parents. Those horrors wouldn't dare.

"Please tell Brenna to keep her mouth shut when company arrives, Mother," Matilda requested. "She shouts every word. She does it on purpose. When will she stop the vile habit?"

"Soon, dear, soon," her mother replied almost absent-mindedly.

Brenna edged closer to her sister. Matilda was bossy by nature, but now that their brothers were away learning how to be as important to their king as their papa, her condition had worsened. She was becoming as bothersome as Elspeth.

"You're a pain in the arse, Mattie."

Her mother heard the remark. "Brenna, you will not use such common language again. Do you understand me?"

"Yes, Mama, but Papa says his arse is paining him all the time. It aches something fierce, it does."

Her mother closed her eyes. "Don't sass me, child."

Brenna's shoulders slumped. She tried to look pitiful. "Mama, I'm sorely weary of everybody telling me what to do all the time. Doesn't anybody like me?"

Her mother wasn't in the mood to placate her daughter. She waved her hand toward the cluster of chairs on the opposite side of the hall.

"Go and sit down, Brenna. Do not say another word until you are given permission to speak. Do it now."

The little girl dragged her feet as she crossed the hall.

"Don't make her sit there all alone too long, Mother. The unfortunate incidents have made her difficult. Papa says it's going to take her time to recover."

Mattie was defending her. Brenna wasn't surprised by the show of loyalty. It was her sister's duty to watch out for her while her brothers were away. But it made Brenna angry that Mattie had brought up the unmentionable. She knew how much Brenna hated being reminded of what had happened to her.

"Yes, dear," her mother replied. "Time and patience."

Mattie let out a loud sigh. "Really, Mother, how can you be so calm about it? Have you no guilt? Even I can understand forgetting one of your children on a single occasion, but twice? It's a wonder the child lets you out of her sight."

Elspeth moved forward to offer her opinion. "'Tis my fear you'll never catch a husband for that one, mi'lady."

Brenna put her hands over her ears. She hated it when the nursemaid referred to her as "that one." She wasn't one of the piglets, after all.

"I'll catch a husband by myself," Brenna shouted.

Joan walked into the hall in time to hear her sister's boast.

"What have you done this time, Brenna?"

"Nothing."

"Then why are you sitting all by yourself? You're usually squeezed up next to Mother, talking her ears off. Tell me what you've done. I promise I won't lecture you."

"I sassed Mama. Did Papa catch your husband for you, Joan?"

"Catch a husband?" she asked. She didn't laugh for fear of hurting Brenna's tender feelings, but she couldn't stop herself from smiling.

"I suppose he did," she admitted.

"Did you help?"

"No. I'll meet my husband on the day I marry him."

"Aren't you scared he's ugly?" Brenna whispered.

"What he looks like won't matter. Papa assures me it's a strong alliance," Joan whispered in response.

"Is that good?"

"Oh, yes. Our king has given his approval."

"Rachel says you have to love your husband with your whole heart."

"That's only a foolish wish. When she's old enough, she's going to marry a man named MacNare, and Rachel's never met him. He doesn't even live in England, but Father isn't concerned about that. He was swayed by promises and gifts MacNare gave him."

"Elspeth says Papa won't ever find anyone for me. She says Papa's too busy for the likes of me. I have to catch one by myself. Will you help me?"

Joan smiled. "I can see this is worrying you. I'll be happy to help."

"How do I get one?"

Joan pretended to consider the matter for a long minute before she answered.

"I imagine you select the man you want and then you ask

him to marry you. If he lives far away, then you must send a messenger to him. Yes, that would be how you would do it. You know, Brenna, Papa would be unhappy to hear us talking like this. It is his duty to find someone for you. Why are we whispering?"

"Mama told me not to talk."

Joan burst into laughter. The noise alerted Elspeth, who immediately rushed over.

"Please don't encourage her, Lady Joan. Brenna, you were told to keep quiet. Doesn't that mouth of yours ever rest?"

"I'm sorry, Elspeth."

The nursemaid snorted in disbelief. "No, you're not sorry." She moved closer, wagged her finger in front of Brenna's face, and then said, "One of these days God's going to march in here and lecture you sound, young lady. Mark my words. You'll be sorry then. He doesn't like little girls who sass."

Elspeth finally left her alone, and Brenna fell asleep waiting for company to arrive. Her sister Rachel shook her awake and pulled her along to stand with her older sisters.

Brenna hid behind Rachel's back until her name was called and she was dragged out for display. She was suddenly feeling too shy to look up at the company, and as soon as her papa finished bragging about her, she moved behind her sister again.

None of the strangers paid any attention to her, and so she decided to sneak out of the hall while everyone was ignoring her. She turned around, took one step toward the entrance, and then came to a quick stop.

Three giants came through the door. She was too stunned to move. The one in the middle was taller than the other two and held her interest the longest. She watched him closely, and when her parents hurried forward to greet the newcomers, she realized he was even bigger than her own papa.

She grabbed hold of Rachel's hand and started tugging. Her sister took a long time to look down.

"What is it?" she whispered.

"He isn't God, is he?" she asked, pointing to the dark-haired guest.

Rachel rolled her eyes heavenward. "No, he most certainly isn't God."

"Did Papa lie to me? He told me only God is bigger than he is, Rachel."

"No, Papa didn't lie. He was just teasing you. That's all. You don't need to be afraid."

Brenna was thoroughly relieved. Papa hadn't deceived her, after all, and God hadn't bothered to come down from heaven to lecture her. There was still time for her to change what Elspeth told her was her sinful life.

Her papa drew her attention when he let out a bellow of laughter. She smiled because he was having such a fine time, and then she turned to look at the middle one again. She'd been told time and again that it was rude to stare, but she didn't pay any attention to her mother's rule now. The giant mesmerized her, and she wanted to remember everything she could about him.

He must have felt her staring at him, though, because he suddenly turned and looked directly at her.

Brenna decided to make her papa proud of her and behave like a proper young lady. She grabbed a fistful of her skirt, hiked it up to her knees, and then bent down to curtsy. She promptly lost her balance and almost hit her head against the floor, but she was quick enough to lean back so she could land on her bottom.

She stood back up, remembered to let go of her skirts, and then peeked up at the stranger to see what he thought about her newly acquired skill.

The giant smiled at her.

As soon as he looked away, she squeezed herself up against Rachel's backside again.

"I'm going to marry him," she whispered.

Rachel smiled. "That's nice."

Brenna solemnly nodded. Yes, it was nice.

Now all she had to do was ask.

Papa let his daughters leave the hall a few minutes later. Brenna waited until everyone else had gone upstairs, then ran back outside. She was determined to catch one of the piglets today so she would finally have a pet of her very own. She would have preferred a pup, but Papa had let her older brothers and sisters have them all, and none were left for her, and she meant to right his terrible wrong by taking one of the piglets.

Luck was on her side. The piglets' mama had once again left the pen and was now sleeping in a mud pool on the far side of the stables halfway down the hill. Brenna tried not to make any noise, but she slipped in the mud and made a loud splatter anyway. The babies must have worn their mama out. She didn't even lift her head or open her eyes. Brenna heard the loud squeak of the front doors being opened next, but when no one shouted at her, she was certain she hadn't been seen.

The piglets made her task easy, for they had rolled themselves into little balls and were sleeping on top of each other. Brenna scooped one into the hem of her skirts, wrapped it up tight, and then clutched it against her chest. She thought to run to the kitchens and hide her prize there, and she was sure she would have succeeded with her plan, if her new pet hadn't made such a fuss about it all.

Brenna didn't realize her jeopardy until she was outside the pen and heard a horrible noise coming toward her. Pigs weren't supposed to fly, but the enraged mama seemed to be doing just that. Her head was down, her feet were moving faster than a bolt of lightning, and her intent was clearly issued with an ear-shattering squeal that sounded like the devil himself rising out of the bowels of hell to get her.

Brenna opened her mouth and let out a wail every bit as worthy as her predator's. Too terrified to think, she ran in circles, around and around the pen, her hair flying every which way, mud splattering everywhere, clutching her piglet in her arms as she screamed over and over again for her papa to come and save her.

The sight that befell her parents was horrifying. Their sweet little angel was covered with mud and running around like a hen without her head.

Everyone started running at the same time. Papa didn't rescue her, for he had neither the speed nor the stride; the giant who had smiled at her did. And just in the nick of time.

The mama's snout tripped her, and just as Brenna was being pitched to the ground, she felt herself being lifted high into the air. She squeezed her eyes shut, remembered to stop screaming, and then looked around again. She was still in his arms, yet on the opposite side of the fence a fair distance away from the pen. She couldn't imagine how he'd been able to jump over the obstacle.

Chaos surrounded them. Everyone was running toward her. Her papa was the last one to reach the fence. He was still panting when she heard him ask his company if they knew what had caused the animal to attack his dear little Faith.

Brenna wasn't offended. Papa was always getting their names confused. He'd remember by nightfall though, and from the look in his eyes, she knew what would happen then. She'd spend a good hour sitting on his knobby knees while he scolded her. She didn't even want to think about what her punishment would be if he discovered what she had hidden in her skirts. She fervently hoped he never found out.

She knew her savior could feel her pet wiggling between them, and she finally gathered enough courage to look up at him to see what he was going to do about it. He looked surprised, and when the piglet let out another squeal, he smiled.

She was so happy he wasn't angry, she smiled back before she could remember to be shy.

One of his friends stepped closer to the fence. "Connor, is everything all right?" He turned to answer. Brenna stopped him by putting her hand on the side of his face and nudging him back to her again. She whispered her plea then. He must not have heard her, because he leaned down closer until their foreheads were almost touching.

"Don't tell."

The giant suddenly threw his head back and roared with laughter. She told him to hush, but that only made him laugh all the more. He didn't tell on her, though, and once he'd put her back down, she was able to run past her papa before he could grab hold of her.

"Come back here, Brenna."

She pretended she didn't hear him and continued on. It wasn't until she was safely hidden under the kitchen table, with her new baby sleeping in her lap, that she realized she'd forgotten to ask the man to marry her. She wasn't discouraged. She would ask him tomorrow, and if he told her no, she would come up with another plan. One way or another, she meant to catch him and save her papa the trouble.

Chapter
2

Scotland, 1119

He wore war paint to his wedding.

Connor MacAlister's mood was just as grim as the dark
blue paint smeared across his face and arms. The laird
wasn't happy about the duty he'd taken on, but he was an
honorable man, and he would do whatever was required to
gain justice.

Connor had vengeance on his mind and in his heart;
though, in truth, he didn't think he was unusual. Every
Highlander worth his sword was vengeful. It was simply the
way things were.

Five soldiers rode with their laird. The men were also
finely turned out for battle, but their collective mood was
much lighter, because none of them was going to be saddled
with an English bride for the rest of his days.

Quinlan, the first-in-command, rode beside his laird. The
warrior was almost Connor's equal in height, but he wasn't
quite as muscular through his shoulders, upper arms, and
thighs and, therefore, didn't measure up to Connor's
strength. That wasn't the reason Quinlan had stayed on with
the MacAlister clan, however. It was Connor's intelligence,
his relentless thirst for justice, and his unwavering leader-
ship abilities that kept the warrior by his side. As his loyal
follower, Quinlan would give his life to keep his laird safe.

Connor had already saved him once, and Quinlan knew his laird would willingly do so again and again, regardless of the risk. The other men felt the same way Quinlan did, for Connor treated all of his followers as valuable members of his family.

Quinlan wasn't just a loyal follower; he was also a close friend, and like all the other MacAlisters, he too embraced his grudges, stroking them like lovers for years and years if need be, until he could find a way to right a wrong done to him or his family.

"It isn't too late to change your mind," Quinlan remarked. "There are other ways to retaliate against MacNare on my father's behalf."

"No. I've already sent word to my stepmother that I am taking a bride, and nothing you can say to me will make me change my mind."

"Do you think Euphemia will finally come back then?"

"Probably not," Connor answered. "She finds it too difficult to return to our land since my father was taken from her. She mourns his passing even to this day."

"What about Alec? Your brother ordered you to end this feud, and you gave him your word to do just that."

"Yes, and this will be my last insult. It will surely pain MacNare for a long, long time. I'll have to be content with that. You know how hungry the pig is for an alliance with the English. We'll use his greed to our advantage. Remember, friend, he shamed and humiliated your family."

"And we warred against him for his treachery."

"It wasn't enough," Connor decreed. "When I'm finished, your father will be able to hold his head up again. He'll be vindicated."

Quinlan suddenly laughed. "I'm thinking God had a hand in this, Connor. We didn't know until this morning the name of the daughter you meant to take. Do you remember her yet?"

"She wasn't easy to forget. Besides, I now have a better reason to give to Alec. That is more important to me."

"Your brother's going to be furious all the same."

"No, he'll be pleased once I make him realize the English-woman betrothed herself to me long ago."

"And what will you tell him?"

21

"The truth. She did ask me to marry her. You haven't forgotten that fact. You laughed for a week."

Quinlan nodded. "She asked you three times, but I would remind you that was years ago. She will surely have forgotten."

Connor smiled. "Will that matter?"

Lady Brenna was suddenly overcome with the eerie sensation that someone or something was watching her. She was kneeling by the side of a shallow stream, drying her face and her hands with her embroidered cloth, when she felt a presence behind her.

She didn't make any quick movements. She knew better than to jump up and run back to camp. If a wild boar or worse were close by, any sudden actions would only draw more attention to herself.

She pulled her dagger free and slowly turned as she stood up, bracing herself for what might be lurking in the dark underbrush.

There wasn't anything there. She waited several minutes for the threat to present itself, and still nothing moved. The only sound she heard was the loud thundering of her own heartbeat.

It had been foolish for her to walk so far away from where her father's men had made the nooning camp. If anything happened, she had no one to blame but herself, and if she hadn't been so desperate for a moment alone, she would have thought more about the possible consequences. She still would have gone in search of privacy, of course, but she would have taken the necessary precautions and carried her bow and arrows.

Had she left her instincts at home? She thought she must have because she still felt she was being watched, and that didn't make a bit of sense to her.

Brenna decided she was just being foolish. If someone or something was there, she would have heard him or it approaching long before now. Papa had often told her how exceptional her hearing was, and wasn't it a fact that he often boasted to his friends that she could hear the first leaf of autumn falling on a field of battle? Of course, this was an exaggeration. Still, there was some truth in what he said. She usually did hear every little sound.

But she didn't hear anything now. Brenna decided she was simply overwrought. The journey had been difficult for her, and she was tuckered out. Yes, that was it. Fatigue had to be the reason she was imagining threats that weren't there.

Laird MacNare. Heaven save her, every minute she had to spare, her mind turned to thoughts of her future husband. Then she usually threw up. She was thankful she hadn't eaten today, knowing she'd be doubled over now if she had. Granted, she had never met the man and could be jumping to all the wrong conclusions. He might be quite pleasant. All those horrible stories about him could be exaggerations. Lord, she fervently hoped so. She didn't want to be married to a cruel man, couldn't even begin to imagine what it would be like, and, oh, how she'd tried to dissuade her father from making such a choice for her. He wouldn't listen to any of her arguments, but then he rarely did.

He'd been terribly cold in the way he'd told her, too. He shook her awake in the middle of the night, informed her of his decision, and then ordered her to help her mother and the maids prepare her baggage. She would leave for the Lowlands of Scotland at first light. The explanation he gave her on his way out the doorway wasn't comforting. The marriage would help her father extend his fingers into Scotland, and since the king had decided Rachel should marry one of his favored barons, Haynesworth would give Brenna to MacNare. What was implied but not said was more painful for her to bear: her father loved her, aye, but he loved power and influence more.

And gifts as well, she thought. MacNare had sweetened the kettle by adding more treasures. Granted, the king didn't know about the betrothal and was sure to be angry, but her father didn't seem overly concerned. Greed filled his heart, leaving little room for caution or fear.

Once she'd stopped crying, her mother had tried to give her advice. She suggested Brenna quit worrying. Everything was bound to turn out all right, providing her daughter learned to get along, and let go of her childish dreams.

Thinking about her parents was making her homesick. She couldn't understand why, given the fact that they had forced her into this unwelcome marriage. Yet, she wanted to go back home. She missed everyone, even her old, cranky nursemaid, who was still bossing everyone around.

Enough of this self-pity. She knew she'd be weeping like a baby if she didn't stop. Her future was determined, and only God would be able to change her fate.

Her father's soldiers were probably anxious to be on their way. She thought they might already be on MacNare land, but she knew they still had a good full day's ride ahead of them before they reached his fortress.

Brenna hastily tried to repair her braid. The thing had fallen apart while she was bending over the water washing her face. She started to refashion the braid, then changed her mind. What did she care what she looked like when she met the laird? She pulled the ribbon free, threaded her fingers through her hair, and, in the process, dropped both her dagger and her ribbon.

She had just picked up her dagger when she heard an abrupt shout from Harold, the soldier in charge of her escort.

She picked up her skirts and went running back toward the camp to find out what was wrong. Her lady's maid, Beatrice, intercepted her. The heavyset woman came barreling down the narrow path, grabbed hold of Brenna's arm, and tried to keep on going. The look of terror in Beatrice's eyes sent chills of dread down Brenna's spine.

"Run, mi'lady," she screamed. "We've been attacked by demons. Hide yourself before it's too late. The savages are going to kill the soldiers, but it's you they're wanting most of all. You mustn't let them find you. Hurry now."

"Who are they?" Brenna demanded in a frightened whisper.

"Outcasts I'm thinking, so many I couldn't keep count, and all with blue faces and demon eyes. They're as big as Satan himself. One has already boasted to kill Harold first if he doesn't tell him where you hide."

"Harold won't tell."

"He did tell, he did," she cried out, bobbing her head up and down for emphasis. "He threw his sword down and was giving them your whereabouts when I saw my chance to run. Your father's men will still die. The heathens only wait now for their leader to join them, and then the butchering is sure to begin. They'll drink their blood and eat their flesh."

Beatrice panted with her hysteria. In an attempt to get her mistress to move, she tightened her hold on Brenna's arm, drawing blood as her nails dug deep into skin.

Brenna struggled to get away from the woman. "The soldiers were still alive when you left?" she asked.

"Aye, but it's only a matter of time before they're killed. For the love of God, run."

"I can't leave the soldiers. Go, save yourself."

"Are you daft?"

"If they want me, perhaps they'll listen to my pleas and let Father's soldiers leave. It's a poor substitution, one life for twelve. I know it's foolhardy, but I must try."

"You'll die for your stupidity," she muttered as she shoved Brenna out of her way and ran on into the forest.

Panic-stricken, Brenna wanted to follow her maid, but couldn't. It took all of her courage not to give in to the lure, because if the maid was telling the truth, Brenna knew she could well die in just a few minutes. Dear God, she was scared. Dying required bravery, a noble quality she suddenly feared she'd left at home, but she couldn't let Harold and the others die because of her own cowardice. Even though it was a remote possibility that she would be able to persuade the demons to let the soldiers leave, she had to try to save them, no matter how frightened she was.

She hurried toward the clearing and began her final prayer to God. She didn't waste precious time asking forgiveness for each transgression. It would have taken her a month to get them all remembered, categorized, and confessed, and so she lumped them all together and simply begged for absolution for the lot. She finished her supplication with the request that He please give her enough cunning to find a way to keep on living.

Then she started chanting. "Oh Lord, Oh Lord, Oh Lord."

By the time she reached the curve in the broken path just outside the campsite, she was trembling so fiercely, she could barely stand up straight. She remembered the dagger she still held in her right hand, hid it behind her back beneath a fold in her gown, and forced herself to take a deep breath.

It was going to be extremely difficult to get the savages to listen to a woman. If she stammered or looked afraid, any chance she might have would be lost. She had to be bold, she told herself. Fearless.

She was finally ready. She kept up her chant to God to please help her get out of this, and if He wasn't in the mood to let her live any longer, then couldn't He please make her death quick? She tucked in the word *painless* every other second, and all of her pleas were squeezed into "Oh Lord, Oh Lord, Oh Lord." In her heart she was certain God understood what she was asking.

They were waiting for her. She wanted to faint when she saw them. She heard several long, indrawn breaths, knew the heathens had made the sounds, and while the sight of her apparently stunned them—the looks on their faces indicated as much—such a reaction didn't make sense. They'd obviously been waiting for her to appear, because they were all facing her when she walked into their lair.

They weren't too many to count. Beatrice had exaggerated about their number. There were only five savages, standing in a half-circle behind her father's soldiers. Still, the five were enough to make her knees start quaking and her stomach lurch.

She barely spared the outcasts more than a glance, as her first concern was for her soldiers. Harold and the others were down on their knees in the center of the clearing. Their heads were bowed, and their hands were clasped behind their backs, yet when she moved closer, she could see none of them had been tied. She looked them over to ascertain the extent of their injuries and was surprised, and relieved, to see they looked as fit as ever.

She had to force herself to look up at the outcasts again. Lord, they were a sight for future nightmares. They weren't demons, though. No, no, they were just men, she thought a little frantically. Very large men. Beatrice had also called them savages, and Brenna was in full agreement with that assessment. 'Twas the truth it seemed to be the only thing the crazed woman had gotten right. Yes, savages. The description fit, given that they had blue paint smeared on their faces. Adorning themselves in such a strange fashion must have been part of some ancient ritual. She wondered if human sacrifice was another ritual they followed, and immediately she blocked the horrible thought.

Their garments were also primitive, yet familiar to her. They wore muted brown and yellow and green wool plaids. Their knees were bare, and their feet were covered in elk boots, laced together with leather strips above their calves.

They were Scots. Could they be enemies of Laird MacNare? They were trespassing on his land now. Were they going to kill her as some sort of repayment for the sins of her future husband?

She didn't like the idea of dying for a man she'd never met, but then she really didn't like the notion of dying in any case, she reminded herself. Did the reason really matter?

Why didn't they speak to her? She felt as though they'd been staring at her for at least an hour, yet knew probably just a minute or two had actually passed.

Fearless, she ordered herself. I must be fearless.

Oh Lord, Oh Lord, Oh Lord . . .

"I am Lady Brenna."

She waited for someone to attack her. No one moved. And then, just as she was about to demand that they tell her their intentions and be quick about it, the Scots surprised the breath right out of her. As one, they dropped to their knees, put their hands over their hearts, and bowed their heads to her. Their united show of respect stunned her. No, no, not respect, she thought. Weren't they mocking her? God's truth, she couldn't tell.

She waited until all of them had regained their feet before trying to locate the leader so she could address him. None of them was giving her hints. The blue paint made for more confusion. Their faces were like masks with their grim expressions.

She settled on the biggest of the lot, a dark-haired warrior with gray eyes. She stared directly at him, willing him to speak to her, but he didn't say a word.

Oh, Lord, Oh, Lord . . .

"Why won't you speak to me?"

The one she'd been staring at suddenly smiled at her. "We were waiting, mi'lady," he explained in a deep, forceful voice.

She frowned over his half-given answer. Since he'd spoken in Gaelic, she decided to accommodate him. She and her sisters had conquered the language at her father's nagging insistence, and she was thankful he'd gotten his way. This outcast's dialect was certainly different from what she'd learned, but she was still able to catch enough to understand what he was saying to her.

"Waiting for what?" she asked in Gaelic.

The Scot looked surprised. He was quick to hide his reaction by staring into the distance.

"We were waiting for you to finish your prayer."

"My prayer?" she asked, thoroughly confused.

"You seem to have gotten stuck on the beginning, lass. Couldn't you remember the rest of it?" another Scot asked her.

"Oh, Lord, Oh, Lord . . ."

"There she goes again," yet another warrior whispered.

Good God Almighty, she'd been praying out loud.

"I was praying for patience," she announced with as much dignity as she could summon. "Who are you?"

"MacAlister's men."

"The name means nothing to me. Should I know him?"

A warrior with a rather nasty-looking scar across his brow and down one side of his nose stepped forward.

"You know our laird very well, mi'lady."

"You are mistaken, sir."

"Please call me by my name, mi'lady. It's Owen, and I would be honored if you would."

She was having extreme difficulty understanding why the heathen was being so outrageously polite to her, given her horrific situation. Were they going to kill her or not?

"Very well, I shall call you Owen."

The warrior looked thrilled by her acquiescence, but she felt like throwing her hands up in despair. "Owen, are you going to kill me and my father's loyal soldiers?"

They all seemed taken aback by her question. The one with the gray eyes answered her. "Nay, Lady Brenna. We would never harm you. Each of us has just vowed to protect you until the day we die."

The other warriors quickly nodded agreement.

They were out of their minds, she decided then and there. "Why in heaven's name would you want to protect me?"

"Because of our laird," Owen answered.

They were determined to talk about their leader, which was all well and good because she really wasn't able to pay attention to a word they said now. She was overcome by blissful relief. If Gray Eyes had told her the truth, no one was going to die, and all of her fears had been for naught. Thank you, God.

She wasn't about to celebrate just yet, however, because the intruders still hadn't explained why they had come here. They didn't look the sort to be paying a social call, and she knew she would have to find out their real motive before she could ever hope to figure out a way to get them to leave.

She'd best stay on her guard, while she tried to get some answers.

"I know you're Scots," she began, surprised her own voice sounded so weak. "But exactly where in Scotland do you call home?"

Gray Eyes looked appalled. "My name is Quinlan, mi'lady, and we don't consider ourselves Scots. We're Highlanders."

The other men nodded their agreement.

She had just learned an interesting fact. Highlanders didn't want to let go of the old, dusty habits of their ancestors. The way these men were dressed, in such primitive attire, was an indication, and if she hadn't been so rattled, she would have realized how they felt before she'd tried to address them.

She couldn't imagine anyone having such a backward attitude, but she wasn't going to make them angry by telling them so. If they wanted to be savages, she certainly didn't care.

"You are Highlanders. Thank you, Quinlan, for taking the time to instruct me."

He inclined his head to her. "I would thank you, mi'lady, for seeking instruction from your humble follower."

She let out a loud sigh of frustration. "Please don't take offense, but I really don't want you to follow me anywhere."

He smiled at her.

"You aren't planning to leave anytime soon, are you?" She sounded pitiful.

His eyes sparkled devilishly. "Nay, mi'lady, we aren't."

"You really don't remember our laird?" Owen asked.

"Why would I remember him? I've never even met the man."

"You asked him to marry you."

"You are mistaken, Owen. I did no such thing."

"But, mi'lady, I was told you asked him three times."

"Three times? I asked him . . ."

She suddenly stopped. Three times. Good God, he couldn't be talking about . . . She shook her head in disbelief. No, no, that was years ago, and he couldn't possibly know what she'd foolishly done.

Only Joan knew about her plan to find a husband, and she would never have told anyone outside of the family. Brenna didn't have an actual recollection of proposing—she'd been too young at the time to remember it now—but her sister had told her the story so many times, she felt as though it had happened only yesterday. Like any sister, Joan had delighted in tormenting Brenna about her outrageous behavior. She especially loved to linger over the part about the piglet.

Why Brenna had wanted to catch her own husband or steal a pig to raise as her own pet she couldn't guess now, and the only excuse she could come up with was that she had been very, very young.

"It happened a long time ago, mi'lady," Owen said.

They knew. How they'd found out was beyond her comprehension, but then she was so rattled, she could barely think straight at all.

"This man denied my request . . . didn't he?"

Quinlan shook his head. "Twice he sent back his refusal, but it's our understanding you're still waiting to hear his answer to your last proposal."

"I am not waiting to hear his answer." Her voice was emphatic.

"It would seem to us that you are," Owen insisted.

Neither man appeared to be teasing her. Honest to God, they looked sincere.

What in thunder was she going to do?

"I keep waiting for you to laugh, but you aren't going to, are you, Quinlan?"

He didn't bother to answer her. In fact, all of them were quite content to stand there talking to her. Their behavior was most peculiar. These warriors didn't seem the sort to want to linger anywhere, but they were lingering now. Were they waiting for something to happen, and if so, what?

Brenna didn't like having to be patient. She had the sinking feeling she wasn't going to find out their plans until they felt like explaining, though.

She refused to believe they had come all this way just to remind her of a proposal she'd made years ago, and they couldn't possibly expect her to honor it now. She didn't believe their nonsense about being her humble followers either.

Though it was probably foolhardy, she decided to catch them in their lie.

"You have said you are my humble followers. Were you telling the truth, Quinlan?"

The warrior looked over her head, into the forest, before he answered. He smiled too.

"I am here to protect you and serve you, mi'lady. We all are."

She smiled back. "Then you will do as I bid you to do?"

"Of course."

"All right, then. I bid you to leave."

He didn't move. She wasn't the least bit surprised.

"I cannot help but notice you're still here, Quinlan. Did you perchance misunderstand me?"

The giant looked as though he was about to laugh. He shook his head and said, "I cannot serve you if I leave you. Surely you understand."

She surely didn't understand. She was about to ask him if she could leave without worry he'd follow her, but Owen interrupted her with yet another reminder.

"Mi'lady, about your proposal . . ."

"Are we back to that?"

Owen nodded. "You did ask," he stubbornly insisted.

"Yes, I did ask. I have since changed my mind. Is this man still alive? He must be terribly old by now. Did he send you to me?"

Quinlan answered. "He did."

"Where is he?"

Quinlan smiled at her again. The others were grinning too.

"He's standing right behind me, isn't he?" She thought her nervousness had kept her from hearing him.

Every one of the heathens nodded. "All the while?" she whispered.

"Only just now," Quinlan answered.

And that was why they'd all been waiting. She should have realized. If she hadn't been so busy trying to figure out a way to get them to leave, she would have considered the possibility that their leader might come along.

She didn't want to turn around, of course, but pride prevented her from trying to run. Tightening her hold on her dagger, she braced herself for what she was going to see, and finally turned.

Oh, yes, he'd been right behind her, all right. How could she not have known? The warrior was as tall as a pine tree. If she reached out, she could pinch him. She stared at his massive chest, suddenly too worried to look up. His size was staggering. Why, the top of her head didn't even reach his chin. He stood just a foot or two away from her, and when she took an instinctive step back, he took a step forward.

She really was going to have to look at his face, she told herself. He'd see it as a sign of cowardice if she didn't. Trying to run away would probably give him a hint of how intimidating his size was to her, and why, oh, why, couldn't she find any gumption? She had some just a few minutes ago.

Connor was just running out of patience when she looked directly into his eyes. His own reaction surprised him. The force of her beauty made his breath catch in the back of his throat. He'd thought her pretty when he was watching her by the stream, muttering to herself while she tugged on her braid to get her ribbon undone, but he hadn't taken the time to observe how truly beautiful she was. He hadn't been close enough, or curious enough.

The woman really was exquisite. He couldn't seem to stop staring at her now. The power of her beauty captivated him, and he suddenly realized he wasn't any better than his men. He'd been furious when he'd seen how besotted they were, and now, he admitted, he was in much the same condition.

How could he not have noticed such perfection? Her skin was flawless; her eyes were a clear, sparkling color of blue, and her rosy, full mouth made him want to think about all the erotic pleasures she could give him. As soon as he realized what he was doing, he turned his gaze to her forehead so that he could regain his concentration.

It took him a little longer to remember how to breathe again. His discipline finally came to his aid, and even though he knew she would be a tantalizing danger to his peace of mind, he was still extremely pleased with her. Her bonny looks would make the sting in his insult all the more painful for such a shallow pig as MacNare to endure. Beautiful women were hard to come by in England, or so he'd heard, and this rare treasure had all but fallen into his lap.

It really had been disgustingly easy. None of her soldiers offered the least resistance. He didn't even have to make a fist. He simply walked into their camp, commanded them to kneel, and, by all that was holy, they knelt. Meek as lambs they were, and just as cowardly. Several of the weaklings even tossed their weapons away.

Only one soldier had made an attempt, halfhearted as it was, to shout a warning to his mistress. Connor heard the sound while he was keeping watch over Lady Brenna to make certain no harm came to her while she lingered by the stream, but one of his own men—Quinlan, no doubt—silenced the soldier. Lady Brenna also heard the noise, and that was precisely when she dropped her ribbon and her cloth and started back to camp. Curiosity made her hurry, but after the other Englishwoman grabbed hold of her and filled her head with outrageous tales about demons, it took true courage for her to continue on.

He knew she believed she was running toward her own death. The look of fear on her face indicated as much. One life for twelve. Weren't those her exact words? Connor had been thoroughly confused by her behavior. She was Haynesworth's daughter, wasn't she? Yet, she wasn't like any of the English he'd ever known. In all his years of battles, he'd never witnessed a single act of true courage by any of the English . . . until today. He thought about mentioning that remarkable fact to her, then changed his mind. He didn't believe it would be a good idea to talk to her just yet. The woman was going to have to get past her fear of him before she would be able to understand a word he said. Aye, silence was prudent now.

He clasped his hands behind his back and patiently waited for her to get hold of herself. He wondered if she still believed he was a demon. The look in her eyes suggested she might, and it took a good deal of restraint not to smile, so ludicrous was the notion.

She really was going to have to become accustomed to being around him. Hell, he planned to bed her that evening, but he wasn't going to tell her his plan now. She was going to be his wife, no matter how long it took him to get her to agree in front of the priest. If necessary, he would waste the rest of the day waiting for her to calm down enough to listen to him.

Brenna was determined to hide her fear and thought she'd been successful thus far. She couldn't tell if he was a handsome devil or an ugly-as-sin one. She couldn't quite get past the blue paint to notice. She certainly noticed his eyes, though, but only because they were the color of darkness and as warm and soothing as a fist coming her way. His bone structure appeared to be intact. He had a straight nose, high cheekbones, and a hard-looking mouth. His hair was overly long, almost shoulder length, and the color of night. Odd, but it appeared to be clean.

She didn't have any idea how long she'd been staring up at him, and she certainly didn't notice any movement on his part, yet suddenly his hand was on top of hers. She stupidly looked down as he pulled her hand out from behind her back, and watched him gently pry her dagger away from her fingers.

She assumed he'd either keep the weapon or toss it away to show her his obvious physical superiority, and she was, therefore, astonished when he replaced the dagger in the leather sheath she wore hooked to the ornate belt draped around the tilt of her hips.

"Thank you," she whispered before she could stop herself.

What in thunder was the matter with her? Why was she thanking him? He'd just scared the curl out of her hair. Shouldn't she be giving him a blistering for the terror he'd caused her?

Lord, she was out of her mind if she thought she could give him a piece of her mind. How could she shout at him when she couldn't even find her voice? Besides, her little dagger wouldn't have done him any real harm. That was probably the reason he let her keep it. The strength radiating from the giant suggested he wouldn't even flinch if she tried to injure him.

But, the giant wasn't a god or a demon. He was just a man, very primitive and frightening, yet still just a man. Besides, anyone with a pinch of sense knew women were smarter than men. Her mother had shared that bit of wisdom with her daughters on many occasions, although never in the presence of their father. Mother was always honest, sometimes to a fault. She was also very kind and would, therefore, never say anything that would hurt any man's feelings.

Brenna wasn't going to follow her mother's example. She would try to be a little kind, but she wouldn't be completely honest. She'd never get out of this mess if she told the truth.

"I don't remember you."

He shrugged. He obviously didn't care if she remembered him or not.

"There seems to be a misunderstanding," she began again. "I wasn't waiting for you to answer my proposal." Her voice sounded stronger now.

"I was just a child back then. Surely you haven't been considering my request all these many years." Didn't the man have anything better to think about? "Your men were jesting with me, weren't they?"

He shook his head. Her throat began to ache with her need to shout at him. Apparently he was as demented as his followers, though far less convivial. How was she ever going to get through to him?

Her father would kill her if he ever found out about her marriage proposals. The thought actually worried her for a second or two before she realized how ridiculous it was. Papa would have to get in line to do her in, behind the stone-silent warrior, his followers . . . and MacNare. Good God, she'd forgotten about him. MacNare was bound to be furious when he found out about his intended bride's audacity.

Brenna could see only one way out of her predicament. She had to find a way to make the barbarian understand.

"I have to leave now. Laird MacNare might not be understanding if I'm late. He's supposed to be sending an escort to meet me. I wouldn't want to see any of you harmed because of a little misunderstanding."

The outcast suddenly reached out and took hold of her. His big hands settled on her shoulders in a firm grip, a silent message, she supposed, that she wasn't going anywhere until he was ready to let her. He wasn't hurting her though, and in fact, he was being extremely gentle.

She frowned up at him while she tried to make sense out of the madness surrounding her.

"Your arrival here has absolutely nothing to do with the proposals I sent, isn't that right? You have another motive in mind."

Nothing. Not a word, not a nod, not even a blink. Was she talking to a tree?

She could feel the heat building in her face, knew frustration was the reason for her blush, and let out a thoroughly loud, unladylike sigh that sounded very like a groan.

"All right, we will assume you're here because of my proposals. As I explained to you just a minute ago, I don't remember meeting you. One of my sisters knew all about my foolishness. She told me I'd been worrying about never finding a husband, though I doubt I even understood what husbands were for, and so to ease my worry, Joan told me what to do. She never supposed I'd go through with the plan; but now that I think about it, this is my father's fault because he told me he'd never be able to find any man who would put up with me, and it's your fault too, sir, because you smiled at me. I truly don't remember anything else about our meeting, just your smile. I'll always remember that. In England, you must understand, proper ladies do not ask gentlemen to marry them. It just isn't done," she added in a near shout. "As God is my witness, I really don't have enough strength left in me to go through this explanation again."

"What did you say to the messenger, mi'lady? Do you remember the exact words of your last proposal?" She recognized Quinlan's voice behind her.

How in thunder could she possibly remember? Hadn't any of them been listening?

She couldn't turn to face Quinlan because their leader still had hold of her, and he didn't seem to be the least bit inclined to let go.

"I probably said, 'Will you marry me?'"

Connor smiled. He pulled her toward him, lowered his head, and kissed her just long enough to stun her.

He lifted his head then, looked into her eyes, and finally spoke to her.

"Yes, Brenna. I will marry you."

Chapter 3

The man was clearly demented. He was determined to marry her. Her thoughts about marrying him seemed inconsequential to him. God only knew, she tried everything but physical force to get him to be reasonable. She argued, she pleaded, she prayed.

And all for naught. She had to resort to unladylike measures next. She stomped her foot down hard on top of his to get her point across. He didn't even flinch. She doubled over from the searing pain shooting up from her instep and had to take hold of his arm so she wouldn't completely disgrace herself and fall to the ground. Thankfully, it didn't take her more than a minute or two to regain what pitiful threads of dignity she had left and let go of him. Then she started all over again. She was quite proud of herself, really. She never once raised her voice as she calmly listed at least a hundred valid reasons why they couldn't possibly marry. She might as well have been talking to the wind. The barbarian didn't appear to be the least bit swayed. She wasn't even certain if he was still breathing. He simply listened to her with his arms folded across his chest and a you're-boring-me-into-a-trance look on his face, and when she ran out of dire consequences he would suffer as a result of his insanity, she calmly took hold of her hand and started dragging her behind him toward the horses.

Saints be enraged, she had to get out of this mess. She tried to think of a plan, pleading for God's help all the while, of course. Her thoughts and prayers were interrupted when Quinlan called out to him.

"What is it?"

Quinlan motioned to the English soldiers.

The Highlander didn't need time to mull the matter over. He didn't even bother to stop, but called the obscene order over his shoulder.

"Kill them."

"No." She screamed the denial in a voice that shook with terror.

He was astonished by her reaction. "No?"

"No," she cried out again.

"Why not?"

Dear God, what kind of man would ask such a question? He was finally giving her his full attention, however. He turned to her and patiently waited for her to answer him.

She noticed he didn't let go of her hand. "They're defenseless," she began. "You took their weapons away."

"No, I didn't take their weapons away. They threw them down when we walked into camp. Tell me why they should live," he said in a voice that sounded quite pleasant given the circumstances. "What is their primary duty? Their only duty? Their sacred duty?"

She could tell he was beginning to get angry. His voice had hardened with each question he asked. He was also squeezing her fingers so hard they hurt. "Their primary duty is to defend."

He relaxed his hold. "And who do they defend?" he demanded.

"The king first and always, then the baron to whom they've given their pledge of fealty."

"And?" he prodded.

Too late, she realized where he was headed. God help her, she couldn't come up with a quick way to change direction.

"Me."

"And did they?"

"What they did or didn't do isn't your concern."

39

"It is my concern," he corrected. "Those men have no honor. They deserve to die."

"Such a decision isn't yours to make."

"Of course it is," he replied. "You're going to be my wife."

"So you say."

"So I know," he snapped, his voice as hard as sleet now. "I cannot allow such cowards to live."

"There is another reason you cannot kill them," she stammered. Please, God, help me think of one, she thought. She bowed her head and stared down at the ground while she frantically tried to think of something clever to persuade him.

"I'm waiting."

So was she, but God apparently wasn't in the mood to be helpful. "You won't understand," she whispered.

"What won't I understand?"

"If you kill my father's soldiers, I couldn't possibly marry you."

"Is that so?"

He sounded to her as if he wanted to laugh. She looked up to see whether he was smiling and was thankful she'd been wrong. He looked just as somber and mean as before.

"Yes, that is so. I told you you wouldn't understand. If you weren't a heathen . . ."

"I'm not a heathen."

She didn't believe him. The man was smeared with paint, after all. Only pagans would follow such ungodly rituals.

Connor had wasted enough of his time discussing the matter. He looked at Quinlan, fully intending to tell him to let the soldiers leave, though certainly not because of her weak protests. No, it was the fear he'd caused her that made him change his mind. Fear had its place, especially in the hearts of his enemies, but it would be wrong for a wife to fear her husband.

She wouldn't give him time to be magnanimous. "Wait," she cried out. "Is it important for you to marry me?"

He shrugged. She translated the rude action to mean, yes, it was important. "And you are unwilling to explain your reasons?"

"I need not explain myself to you."

"I think perhaps I'd best explain my intentions to you, though," she replied. "And then I believe you'll understand. If you aren't a heathen, how are you going to get me to marry you? Will you simply announce to your family and friends that you have taken a wife? Or will there be a ceremony with a priest to hear our vows and bless our union?"

"There will be a priest."

She frowned. "A priest in good standing with the church?"

He smiled then. He simply couldn't stop himself. Lord, she was suspicious. "A priest in good standing," he promised.

Victory was suddenly within her grasp. She said a quick prayer in thanksgiving to God for helping her, promised to get down on her knees later to beg His forgiveness because she'd believed He hadn't listened to her plea for assistance, and then said, "Exactly how do you plan to get me to repeat my vows in front of this man of God?"

"You will."

"Will I?"

She had him there. She couldn't possibly know how important it was for her to agree to marry him. He wasn't worried about the behavior of the priest or Brenna during the actual ceremony. He could be intimidating when he needed to be. It was Alec Kincaid who gave him pause. Connor was already standing on trembling ground with his brother, and if Brenna let Alec know she hadn't agreed, there would be hell to pay. He could deal with that, but if Alec wanted the pig MacNare to have her, Connor would have to go against him.

She was pleased to see his smile disappear. "Now I think you understand," she said. "I would like you to let the soldiers leave unharmed. Let them go to Laird MacNare or back to my father."

The innocent woman actually thought she was saving their lives. Connor knew better. MacNare would surely torture the men before he disposed of them, and although her father probably wouldn't be as twisted with his punishment, Connor assumed he would still kill them because they had dishonored him.

41

"And if I agree to this difficult bargain?" he asked, trying to keep his amusement out of his voice. "You'll accept this marriage? I want your agreement and your acceptance."

"There's a difference?"

"There is," he replied. "In time, you'll understand."

"Do you expect me to give you my promise without knowing exactly what it is I'm promising?"

"Do you expect me to let twelve cowards live when they poison the air I breathe?"

He was frowning at her now, and she couldn't help but worry he might be changing his mind. She decided not to press her good fortune. She had just won an important victory, hadn't she?

Still, she didn't feel like celebrating. "I'll agree and I'll accept."

"You have a kind heart."

She was astonished by his compliment. "Thank you."

"It wasn't praise," he snapped. "I want you to rid yourself of such a weakness."

He'd rendered her speechless. How could she possibly argue with such opinions?

His followers were just as odd as their leader. When they were ordered to let the soldiers leave unharmed, they didn't even try to hide their disappointment. They pouted like babies. She glared at the Highlanders while she was being pulled along by their leader. Quinlan had the gall to smile back at her.

The man she had just promised to accept didn't speak to her again until they were well away from the others.

"Brenna?"

"Yes?"

"I'm not always going to be this pleasant."

She could tell he was serious, but still she wanted to laugh until she cried. She was fast losing her control and forced herself to calm down. She needed to stay clearheaded so she could figure a way to get out of this nightmare.

Oh, Lord, what had she gotten herself into?

Damn it all, none of this was her fault. She knew the truth, though she doubted anyone in her family would understand, especially her father. On her way out the door to go to MacNare, hadn't she threatened to do something rash? Papa was surely going to think she'd done just that.

"If my father blames me for this marriage, you're going to have to set him straight. I didn't plan this, and you're going to tell him so. Promise me you will."

He didn't answer her. She knew he'd heard every word, though, because she'd shamelessly raised her voice. "Promise me," she demanded again.

He lifted her onto her horse, and while that was very thoughtful of him indeed, she didn't thank him.

She grabbed his hand as he let go of her waist. "Promise me?" she asked yet again.

"'Tis doubtful you'll ever see your family again. Your concern is foolish."

He thought he was very reasonable.

She thought he was deliberately cruel. Tears filled her eyes over the very idea that she might not see her family again.

She pushed his hand away. "I will see them again. You cannot expect me to . . . Didn't your mother ever tell you it's rude to walk away from someone when she's talking to you?"

Connor couldn't believe what he'd just heard. She had actually criticized him. No one had ever spoken to him with such open disapproval before, and a woman addressing him in such a fashion was simply beyond his comprehension.

Honest to God, he didn't know how to react. If she were a man, he knew exactly what he would do, of course, but she wasn't a man, and that made his dilemma confusing. Brenna certainly wasn't like any of the women he'd known. Most avoided him, and those who had more courage kept their heads lowered and their bearing humble in his presence.

His reaction to Brenna was bewildering. She made him feel like smiling, even when she was frowning at him. In truth, she was such a refreshing change from all of the others, he couldn't even begin to imagine her cowering before him, and though her bizarre behavior pleased him, he knew it would be a mistake to let her think she could always get away with such defiance. It would be a poor beginning at best. He was going to be her laird, and she needed to understand exactly what that meant. Appreciation would come later. He decided to be understanding now, so he put his hand on her thigh, gently squeezed, and stared into her eyes.

"You don't understand yet, and for that reason, I will be patient with you."

"Exactly what don't I understand?"

"Your position in my household. Soon you'll learn to value the great honor I've bestowed on you by marrying you."

Her eyes turned a deep violet blue. Lord, she was pretty when she was angry.

"I will?" she asked.

"You will."

She put her hand on top of his and began to squeeze. She wasn't at all gentle.

"Perhaps you should bestow this great honor on someone who does understand," she suggested.

He ignored her remark and continued on with his explanation. "Until you learn to appreciate the gift I've given you, I expect you to voice your opinions only when you are asked to do so. I cannot tolerate insolence. Now give me your promise."

She was neither impressed nor intimidated by his gruff commands. A woman could only take so much, after all, and she'd just about reached her limit. Surely she would wake up from this nightmare any moment now.

"I may never voice my opinions?" she asked.

"When others who follow me are present, you may not," he qualified. "When we are alone, you may do whatever you wish."

"I wish to go home."

"That isn't possible."

She let out a sigh. Home meant facing her father, and until someone explained the truth to him, she honestly didn't think she wanted to see him again.

"I'll give you my promise just as soon as you promise you'll explain to my father."

"I won't ever bend to you."

"Nor I, to you."

He ignored her outrageous boast. "However, because you're so obviously afraid of me and fear your future, I've decided to make this one exception. If I ever see your father, I'll explain what happened."

She wanted clarification. "But you won't go into detail about the proposals. Even though I was just a child, Father still might not understand."

"I won't mention your proposals."

Her smile was radiant. "Thank you."

He pointedly looked down at her hand resting on top of his. In her gratitude, she was now patting him.

He couldn't resist teasing her. "It isn't appropriate for you to show me your affection in front of the English soldiers."

She snatched her hand away. "I was not showing you affection."

"Aye, you were."

He liked having the last word. She saw him smile as he turned away from her. What a twisted sense of humor he had. Were all the people who lived in the Highlands as strange as this one? Brenna fervently hoped not. How in heaven's name was she ever going to get along with such peculiar people?

Good Lord, she was already thinking about a future with the barbarian. What was happening to her? She should be trying to think of a way to get away from him instead of wondering what it would be like to live with him.

Her reaction to him was most puzzling. She'd felt relief and true appreciation when he'd promised to speak to her father, and yet she had absolutely no reason to trust he would keep his word.

There was only one possible reason for her odd behavior, she decided. Her mind had snapped. "He's made me as addled as Beatrice . . . Good God, Beatrice . . ."

She'd forgotten all about her lady's maid. The poor woman was probably quivering with terror in the bushes somewhere.

Brenna dismounted and went running back to her father's soldiers. They were standing now, silently replacing their weapons. None of them would look at her when she called out to them, and so she moved closer.

Quinlan intercepted her by blocking her path. He didn't touch her, just stood in her way so she couldn't take another step. The other Highlanders had also moved forward to put themselves between her and her father's men.

If she hadn't known better, she would have believed they were actually trying to protect her from her very own escort. The idea was too ludicrous to consider, however, and she decided that they were simply being rude.

"I would like to speak to my father's soldiers."

Quinlan shook his head. "Your laird wouldn't like it."

He wasn't her laird; she was English, for the love of God and king, but she knew she wouldn't get what she wanted if she argued with him. She needed his cooperation, not his anger.

"I doubt your laird will mind at all," she said. "I'll only take a minute. I promise."

Quinlan reluctantly gave in. He moved to her side, clasped his hands behind his back, and said, "You may speak to them from here."

She didn't waste any time. "Harold, please don't forget Beatrice. She's hiding near the stream. I would appreciate it if you would take her back home."

Although Harold wouldn't look at her, he did nod agreement.

"Will you tell my parents not to worry?"

Harold mumbled something under his breath she couldn't quite make out. She tried to move closer so she could hear his whisper, but Quinlan put his arm out to stop her.

She gave the Highlander a good frown to let him know what she thought of his high-handed behavior and then turned back to Harold once again.

"What did you say?" she asked. "I couldn't quite hear you."

The soldier finally looked at her. "Your father will go to war over this atrocity, mi'lady. That is what I said."

Her heart felt as though it had just dropped into her shoes.

"No, no, he mustn't go to war over me. Make him understand, Harold."

She stopped when she heard the panic in her voice, took a deep breath, and then whispered, "I won't have anyone fighting because of me. Tell my father I wanted this marriage. I asked the Highlander to come for me."

"You wanted to marry MacNare?" Harold asked, obviously misunderstanding.

"No, no, I never wanted MacNare. I wanted . . ."

Dear God, she was so flustered, she couldn't remember the laird's name. "I wanted . . ."

She gave Quinlan a frantic look. "What is the name of your laird?" she whispered.

"Connor MacAlister."

"MacAlister," she called out. "I wanted MacAlister. Please remind my father he met my future husband a long time ago."

"It's time to leave, mi'lady," Quinlan advised, for he'd just spotted Connor watching from the edge of the clearing. The laird didn't look at all pleased with what he was seeing.

"One last request," she pleaded.

She didn't give Quinlan time to argue with her. "Harold, tell my father not to come after me. I want him to celebrate my . . ."

"Your what, mi'lady?"

She could barely get the words out without choking. "My happiness."

She ran back to her horse and was already settled in the saddle by the time Connor reached her side. He sat atop a huge black stallion that looked as mean as his master.

She made the mistake of looking up, and promptly dropped her reins in reaction to the anger she saw in his eyes. She quickly lowered her head and pretended to be terribly busy getting comfortable so he wouldn't know she was deliberately trying to shield herself from his temper.

He wasn't about to be ignored. Did she actually want him to believe she was trying to protect him from her father's wrath? The thought was both insulting and laughable.

He forced his mount closer until Brenna's leg was pressed tight against his, and then demanded her full attention by taking hold of her chin and forcing her to look at him.

"Why?"

She knew what he was asking and didn't even try to pretend she didn't. "War means death," she answered.

He shrugged. "For some men it does," he agreed.

"Even one man would be too many," she explained. "I don't want anyone to fight because of me. Father has a large army, but it would be a hardship and a nuisance for him to come after me. He would insist on leading his soldiers, and I cannot help but worry you might . . ."

"I might what?"

"Kill him."

He was appeased. She wished she had the strength in her to push him off his horse. He was a proud and arrogant man, and she had used both flaws to her benefit by letting him assume she believed he would be the superior warrior on the battlefield. While it was true that he was physically superior—because he was younger, bigger, and obviously stronger—her father would make up for the differences by having staggering numbers on his side. It would be a slaughter, all right, and Connor MacAlister would probably end up on the bottom of the pile of wounded.

Why had she lied to Harold, then? Honest to heaven, she didn't know. She had just sealed her fate with her father, because she knew that as soon as his vassal gave him her message, he would go into a rage. He wouldn't be at all reasonable or bother to take the time to think it through and realize she couldn't possibly have planned this trickery. Not only did she not have the heart for it, she hadn't had the time.

Papa was going to blame her, and then he would turn his back on her and never acknowledge her as his daughter again. But he would stay alive to hate her. And no one would die.

"I will not inconvenience my father. However, upon reflection, I realize my own wishes won't matter. Laird MacNare is sending an escort to meet me, and I'm certain his men will kill the lot of you. I expect they should be here any moment now."

"No, they won't be coming after you."

He sounded terribly certain. It would take too much effort to argue, and she was simply too worn out to worry any longer. Her heartache for her family was so intense, she could barely keep herself from bursting into tears.

Unfortunately, she was given a long time to feel sorry for

herself. They left the clearing a minute later, and no one spoke to her again until late that evening. She was squeezed in between two stone-faced warriors who didn't even glance her way. Gilly, her sweet-tempered mare, didn't like the closeness any more than she did.

Connor was nowhere to be seen. He'd disappeared ahead of the rest of them more than an hour before and still hadn't returned.

Conversation would have broken the monotony, but no one was in the mood to accommodate her. After observing them for a little while, she realized they were fully occupied seeing to their protection, constantly searching the forest for a possible threat.

As peculiar as it was to admit, she was eventually comforted by their vigilance. Her backside was taking quite a pounding, and she tried to do as her mother had often instructed and offer her misery up to heaven for all the poor lost souls bound for hell. She didn't understand how her pain would help them find their way, of course, but rules were rules, and so she decided to try to follow them.

Yes, she could suffer discomfort. Penance for past sins would do her soul good. Gilly shouldn't have to suffer, though. Her mare began to slow her gait the higher they climbed up the steep hills. The horse had been neither bred nor conditioned for such a vigorous journey. The poor thing was all worn out and was being pushed beyond her limits.

Brenna wasn't certain whom she should ask to stop. Connor would have been her first choice, of course, but he wasn't there, and she'd have to shout her demand in the hope he might hear her.

She didn't think it would be a good idea to make a sound now. The serious expressions on the soldiers' faces and their visible tension indicated they were traveling through hostile territory.

She found herself wondering if Connor had any friends. After thinking the matter over for several minutes, she concluded he didn't. He had only himself to blame, of course. The laird had all the winning ways of a wounded bear on the attack.

The comparison made her smile. Then she remembered poor Gilly. She decided to speak to Quinlan about her

49

concern and reached over to touch his arm to gain his attention.

He reacted as though she'd pinched him. Jerking his arm away, he turned to frown at her for bothering him. Before she could whisper her worry, he motioned for her to keep silent by putting his hand to his mouth. She quickly pointed to Gilly.

The warrior wasn't blind. Surely he could see how lathered and labored her horse was.

Quinlan didn't acknowledge her concern. He simply nudged his horse into a gallop and rode ahead. She watched him until he disappeared into the trees.

She wasn't left unprotected, however. As soon as Quinlan left his position, another warrior moved forward to take his place.

And on they continued. She was wearing out. She assumed Quinlan had gone to get Connor, but the two men were taking forever to come back. She closed her eyes for what was surely just a minute or two, and when she next looked around, Connor was beside her, lifting her onto his lap. Too tired to push him away, her last thought before she fell asleep was that she would make certain she didn't lean back or press against him.

She awakened drooling all over the man. In her sleep she had turned toward him, wound her arms around his waist until her fingers were splayed against his warm skin, and somehow wiggled her way up higher onto his lap. Her face was pressed against the base of his throat. The heat radiating from him warmed her far more thoroughly than a dozen thick woolen blankets. It felt wonderful.

It was also humiliating. Her mouth was open against his skin, which made her behavior all the more disgusting. Thankfully, she remembered Gilly and was able to put her own embarrassment aside. How much longer could her horse go on before collapsing? Brenna tried to pull away from Connor and demand they stop before her mare injured herself, but he put his arm around her waist and forced her to stay where she was.

She pinched him to get his attention. He retaliated by squeezing the breath right out of her, a silent order to behave herself, no doubt, and if she'd been able to look up at his face, she was certain she would have seen him scowling. The man didn't do much of anything else.

She was mistaken. Connor was smiling, for he was vastly amused by her boldness. He knew he intimidated her; he'd seen the worry in her eyes, more than once he was sorry to admit, and yet she'd pinched him. What a contrary woman she was. If she feared him, why did she try to provoke him? He'd have to get around to asking her that very question someday, when he didn't have more important matters on his mind.

She had just made up her mind to start screaming like a demented woman, but was saved from disgracing herself in the nick of time. Connor finally decided to stop for the night. She was so thankful, she forgot to give him a piece of her mind because of the ordeal he'd put Gilly through. It was going to take the gentle mare a good week of pampering to recover.

Connor dismounted first before turning to assist her. He caught her as she was sliding down the stallion's side.

"You don't use a saddle."

"None of us use saddles."

She skirted her way around him and went running to her horse. Her legs screamed with each step she took, and she could only imagine Gilly's discomfort. She noticed her own saddle was missing, assumed one of his men had removed it for her, and was thankful for that much consideration.

Connor wouldn't let her see to Gilly's comforts. He assigned that duty to Owen, the soldier with the scarred face and a smile she thought was actually quite enchanting. She pestered him with instructions for her mare's care, thanked him for his help, and then watched like a worried mama while he led Gilly over to a spot where the moonlight wasn't barred by the trees. Her horse was cooperating, a sure sign she was up to mischief, for several times in the past she'd taken nips out of unsuspecting groomers. Brenna called out a warning and then went in search of her baggage.

The glen Connor had chosen for their respite was completely surrounded by thick forest. The ground cover and the trees were vibrant with hues of brown and green, and dabbled here and there were purple-tipped flowers just waking from winter's sleep. A canopy of thick golden green branches arched high above her. Streamers of fading light filtering down through the trees gave sufficient illumination for the short walk to the lake that, Quinlan had explained, cut through the southern tip.

Brenna was given sufficient privacy to see to her needs. After ten minutes had passed, Connor decided she'd had enough time alone and went to get her. He found her kneeling over her satchel, muttering to herself while she searched through her possessions. Several articles of clothing littered the ground around her.

She wasn't really paying attention to what she was doing. Her mind was on the problem of coming up with a plan to get out of this mess. Thankfully, time was on her side, she thought, and surely, once she'd gotten her wits about her, she'd figure something out.

Connor, towering over her, waited for her to notice him. He gave up after a few minutes and handed her the washcloth he'd picked up hours before.

"Were you searching for this?"

"Yes, thank you," she answered almost absentmindedly. "I must have dropped it only a moment ago, or I would have noticed. I'm very observant."

He didn't correct her. He didn't give her the blue ribbon she'd also left by the stream hours ago, either. He decided to keep the thing a little longer, as a reminder that he had indeed taken a wife. He was bound to forget such an insignificant detail.

"Wash your face, Brenna. Your mouth is covered in paint."

She straightened up so quickly, she almost toppled over backward. "I don't paint my face." She was horrified by the very idea. Only women on their way to hell would do such a pagan thing.

"It's my paint."

"How did I get paint . . . ? I remember now. Just after you tricked me into asking you to marry me again, you said you would, and then you kissed me without asking permission."

"Yes," he agreed, just to get her moving. In his opinion, the brief touch of his mouth against hers didn't qualify as a kiss, it had been a symbolic gesture, nothing more.

"The priest is waiting for us. Hurry and finish."

She couldn't believe what she was hearing. She bounded to her feet. "Now? The priest is waiting now? Why is he waiting?"

Connor was thoroughly puzzled by her behavior. She acted as though she'd just had the wind knocked out of her. "He's here to get it done," he explained.

She demanded specifics. "Get what done?"

"You couldn't have forgotten so soon," he replied in exasperation. "The wedding."

"Now?" she cried out again. "You want to marry me now?"

She ran her fingers through her hair, then started wringing her hands together, and, dear God, she knew she was shouting at him, but she couldn't seem to make herself stop. Connor was so chillingly calm about it all. He had to be out of his mind if he thought she could possibly marry him right now.

"What did you expect?"

She was too stunned to come up with an answer. "What did I expect? I expected time."

"Time for what?"

Time to come up with a way out of this nightmare, she wanted to scream.

"Time for you to . . . to take me to your home. Yes, that's what I expected. I need time to plan a proper wedding."

"Then I've saved you the trouble. You may thank me later."

"And time for you to come to your senses," she blurted out.

"I know what I'm doing."

She suddenly felt light-headed and realized that, for the first time in her life, she was about to swoon. She turned around and went to the edge of the lake to sit down. Closing her eyes, she tried to think of a plan while the world spun out of control around her. Yes, she needed a plan. Any plan. She was in such a panic, her mind wouldn't cooperate. She would greet the priest, yes, of course she would greet him, and she would talk to him, explaining that she would be happy to share her meal with him tonight and let him get a good rest. He could marry her to the bear first thing in the morning. She would strongly suggest, even beg if she had to, that he wait a little longer, a month or two or ten, because the sacrament of marriage was a serious undertaking after all, and then if Connor still didn't realize his mistake, she'd begin work on her wedding gown.

Connor was quickly running out of patience. Now what was she doing? Honest to God, a man could take only so much, and her resistance was becoming downright bothersome. He decided to take matters, and Brenna, into his own hands. He took hold of her cloth, dipped it into the water, and squatted down in front of her. Before she could scoot away, he took hold of her chin and scrubbed her face for her.

He wasn't gentle. Her face was bright red when he finished, and he didn't know if he'd been too rough on her delicate skin or if she was blushing.

"Let's get it done," he ordered.

He lifted her to her feet and literally pulled her along behind him.

"I finally understand. I'm dead, aren't I? I died of fright when I first saw you, and now I'm suffering for my sins. God, I wasn't that bad, was I?"

Connor pretended to ignore her rantings, and it took all he had to hide his smile. Lord, she was emotional. She wasn't crying, though. The priest would believe she'd been coerced into the marriage if she wept throughout the ceremony. Granted, she had been coerced, but he didn't want Father Sinclair to know it. There was also the fact that Connor didn't particularly like to be around women who wept all the time. They made him nervous, and given his choice, he'd take an angry wife over a weeping one any day of the week.

Brenna wasn't in the mood to cry. She felt like killing someone, and Connor was her first choice. And what kind of sinful attitude was that for her to take to her wedding? She was about to enter into holy matrimony, for the love of God.

Her wedding. It wasn't going to be at all like the wedding she'd planned in her daydreams during sewing lessons. She'd expected to be married in her father's chapel, surrounded by family and friends. What she was getting was a group of ill-mannered warriors and a priest who didn't look old enought to have finished his training.

Pride kept her from making a scene. Because everyone was watching her approach, she moved forward to walk by Connor's side, and as soon as she reached the priest, she lifted the hem of her skirts and made a formal curtsy.

"Shall we begin?" the priest said after casting a worried glance up at Connor's face.

"Now?" she cried out.

Connor let out a loud sigh. "Will you stop saying that?"

"Is something wrong with now?" the priest asked, his confusion obvious. He addressed his question to Connor and dared to frown up at him. "I must tell you, Laird, it displeases me to see you come to this sacrament dressed in war paint. I'll have to give my accounting to my superiors as well as Alec Kincaid. What will I say to them?"

"Say whatever you want to say, Father. My brother, at least, will understand."

The priest nodded. "Very well. Mi'lady, do you come here of your own free will? Do you agree to marry Laird Connor MacAlister?"

Everyone stared at her while she contemplated her answer. She had given her word, God help her, and her father's soldiers had all been breathing when they'd left her, which meant Connor had kept his part of the bargain. It was now her turn.

The priest wasn't at all concerned about the bride's confusion. He was used to nervous brides, of course, for he had already married a fair number of couples in his short while as an ordained priest and had learned to expect just about anything.

"The priest is waiting for your answer, Brenna," Connor reminded her in a voice that held a threatening tone.

"Aye, he's waiting, lass," Quinlan blurted out, though he deliberately kept his voice soothing in the hope of calming her down.

She finally gave in to the inevitable. "Yes, Father, of course, but . . ."

"You must say the words, mi'lady. The church requires that I hear you acknowledge that you marry Connor MacAlister of your own free will."

"Now?"

"Brenna, I swear to you that if I hear that word again . . ." Connor began.

Frantic, Brenna finally remembered the pitiful little plan she'd come up with.

"Father, we haven't been properly introduced. I don't even know your name. I should, shouldn't I? I thought we would share our evening meal together, and you and I could get to know each other, and then you could get a long rest, and tomorrow we would go to your chapel, and if you don't have a chapel, then we could keep on going until we found one, and you would instruct me so that I would be prepared for this joyful sacrament, and I . . ."

She suddenly went completely still. "War paint, Father? Did you say war paint? Connor MacAlister's wearing war paint to my wedding?"

She didn't mean to shout at the priest, but honest to God, her endurance was gone. She simply couldn't take anything more. She didn't care who lived and who died, even if she were the one slain. Only one thing mattered to her now. The war paint.

She turned her wrath on Connor. She was so furious with him, tears filled her eyes. "I won't have it."

The priest's mouth dropped open. He'd never heard anyone speak to Laird MacAlister in such a manner, except Alec Kincaid, of course—but he could speak to him any way he chose—and for a slip of a woman to show such open hostility was both astonishing and courageous. If he lived through this ordeal, he must remember every word he had just heard so he could repeat the tale to his friends.

Connor intended to put the fear of God into her to get her to calm down, but the tears swayed him. Why the war paint upset her was beyond his understanding, but upset she was, and he knew he wouldn't get the ceremony over and done with until he found a way to make her cooperate.

Lord, she was a nuisance.

"Brenna, you will not raise your voice to me." He deliberately tried to sound reasonable. Mean, but reasonable too.

"You will not wear war paint to our wedding."

Honest to God, she sounded as mean as he did. He couldn't help but be impressed. "I want to get this done."

She let go of his arm and crossed her arms in front of her. "We'll wait."

"If you think . . ."

"I won't ever ask anything more of you."

Damn it all, she looked as if she was about to start wailing. Didn't she realize she was about to become his wife? It was an honor, not a death sentence.

His bride didn't seem to understand, however. One of them was going to have to be reasonable, and he guessed it would have to be his duty.

"This really matters to you?"

She couldn't believe he needed to ask such a ridiculous question. The sacrament of matrimony was a blessed event, everyone knew that, and coming to a priest dressed for war insulted God, the church, the priest and her.

"It's very important to me."

"All right then, but this is the last time I'll ever concede to your demands."

Connor paused to glare at his followers when he noticed they were all nodding agreement. Then he turned back to his reluctant bride. "Have I made myself clear?"

"You have, and I am most appreciative."

She suddenly felt like smiling, but she maintained her somber expression until Connor walked away from her. He let out a sigh that sounded like a deep growl. She did smile then; she couldn't help herself. For the first time in a long, long while, she didn't feel afraid of her future, but then her mind had already snapped, she reminded herself, and she couldn't be reasonable about anything now. Connor was cooperating, which meant he wasn't a complete barbarian. It wasn't much to base a marriage on, but she was going to be stuck with the man for the rest of her life, and she was a desperate woman, after all. She would take what she could get, even if it was just a single thread of hope.

She kept on smiling until she remembered the blue-faced pagans who rode with the groom.

She was frowning with indignation by the time she turned to them. "Were you expecting to attend the wedding?"

She didn't have to say anything more. Quinlan and the others bowed to her before hurrying to catch up with their laird.

They didn't balk the way Connor had. Several, in fact, glanced back to smile. They seemed to want to accommodate her. She didn't dare trust any of them, of course, and she decided to follow along, just to make certain they didn't change their minds at the last minute. She believed they'd done just that when they all lined up along the edge of the bank and stood there procrastinating while they talked to one another.

Because she'd been so concerned about important matters, it hadn't occurred to her that the men would have to remove their clothes before entering the water. Admittedly, she'd been too occupied gloating over her insignificant little victory to think about anything else.

Their belts fell to the ground first. She came to a dead stop and closed her eyes. She still wasn't fast enough, for she saw every one of their naked backsides before they disappeared into the lake below.

Their laughter followed. She didn't mind, even though she was certain they had known all the while that she was there and were now laughing at her.

The priest came up behind her. "We haven't been introduced, mi'lady. My name is Father Kevin Sinclair, son of Angus Sinclair of the Neatherhills."

"It's a pleasure to meet you, Father. My name is Brenna. My father is Baron Haynesworth, though I doubt you've ever heard of him. I come from England."

"I had already surmised as much."

"My clothing and my speech are both sure indications, aren't they?"

"Yes, they are," he agreed with a smile she thought was as charming as his brogue.

The priest radiated warmth and kindness, and for the first time in a long while, she began to relax.

"I must compliment you, Lady Brenna. Your command of our language is quite remarkable for a beginner."

"But, Father, I've been studying Gaelic for years."

Horrified, he stammered out a hasty apology. "Do forgive me. I meant to praise you, not insult you."

"I wasn't offended, just surprised," she assured him.

His smile returned. "Did you know you alternate between both languages when you're angry?"

"No, I didn't know. When did you notice this peculiar behavior?"

"When the war paint irritated you. I was also irritated, but not for long. The way you stood up to Connor impressed me . . . and him, I would wager. I don't believe anyone has ever spoken to him before with such passion and fury. It was something to see, all right."

"I shouldn't have been difficult. It wasn't ladylike, and I do know better. My temper got the best of me and is a fault I must try to overcome. If there were time, I would beg you to hear my confession before I married."

"I would be happy to make the time, mi'lady."

"Then there is a chapel close-by?"

"We have few chapels here, but as long as we don't face each other while you confess, the rules of the church will be guarded."

The priest was already wearing the stole he used to hear confessions. The tasseled strip of material was draped around his shoulders. As soon as they reached the clearing, he pulled the ends loose from the rope belt he wore around the waist of his brown robe and turned to find a suitable spot.

He finally settled on a tree stump, sat down, and then instructed Brenna to kneel on the ground beside him.

She bowed her head and closed her eyes. He stared across the clearing, made the sign of the cross with a wide sweep of his hand, and told her to begin.

She quickly listed her transgressions, and when she was finished, she began to ask him questions in an attempt to stall the inevitable.

"Is it sinful for me to fear my future? I don't know Connor very well. He frightens me, Father. Am I being foolish?"

The priest wasn't about to admit that Connor terrified him. He wasn't ashamed of his reaction, as everyone he knew felt much the same way. Still, he was supposed to offer solace, and telling her the truth would only make her more fearful.

"I don't know him very well either, but I have heard enough about his background to understand why he's such a hard man. His father died when he was very young, and he was then raised by Alec Kincaid, who finished what his father had begun. The two men consider themselves to be brothers."

"I'm certain I shall like his brother," she whispered, hoping to God she was right.

The priest was just as certain she'd be terrified of him. Lord knew, he was, though he didn't think it would do her any good to hear him admit it. "I have never felt the need to guard my words in his presence or walk twenty paces behind him. Age has taught Kincaid to listen before he retaliates—at least, that is what I've been told—and for that reason he doesn't intimidate me the way . . ."

"The way Connor does?"

"Now, lass, don't try to guess what I'm going to say. The way the men I was with reacted to Connor made me . . . catch their caution. Try to remember that God will look after you. His plans are often too complicated for us to understand."

Was she supposed to be comforted by his comments? If so, why did she want to weep?

"I will be all alone, Father," she whispered.

"Nay, lass, you won't be alone. God will be with you, and I shall be close-by. I've been assigned to serve Laird Kincaid, for his confessor passed on three months ago, and there is a great need of my services in the region. I will never be too busy to serve you, mi'lady, and if you should ever need me, all you have to do is ask."

His promise comforted her, and she quickly assured him that she would welcome his friendship and his counsel.

Connor and his men watched from a short distance away. Quinlan paced throughout the wait. Connor leaned against a tree with his arms folded across his chest and a hard frown on his face.

"It doesn't appear they'll be finished anytime soon," Quinlan remarked. "I think we should go ahead and eat. It's been a long day."

"We wait, no matter how long it takes. Honest to God, my

patience is gone. No one can have that many sins. Hell, she hasn't lived long enough."

"Perhaps she's confessing some of your sins," Quinlan suggested with a grin. "If that be true, we could be here a full month."

The warrior was so amused over his own jest, he laughed out loud. The sound drew a frown of disapproval from Father Sinclair.

"Laird, could your lady be having second thoughts?" Owen asked. "She might even be deliberately taking her time."

Quinlan rolled his eyes heavenward. "Of course she's taking her time."

After a few more minutes, Sinclair finished. He was about to give Brenna absolution when she stopped him.

"May I ask one last question?"

She was wringing her hands together while she waited for his reply. Sinclair noticed the action and hurried to calm her. "You may have all the time you require. I'm in no hurry."

"Are they watching us? They are, aren't they?"

"Yes, they're watching."

"I've kept my eyes closed as you instructed, but I know Connor's frowning, isn't he?"

"Why, he's barely paying us any attention at all," the priest lied.

She let out a sigh. "I will make the best of it. I'm determined to be a good wife. Thank you, Father, for your instruction. I appreciate the time you've given me. I'm finished now."

Father Sinclair tucked the ends of the stole under his belt once again and finally stood up. He turned to assist Brenna, but he needn't have bothered. Connor was already by his bride's side, pulling her up toward him.

"Would you be wanting to confess your sins, Laird?"

"No."

His frown made Father Sinclair flinch. He hastily walked away, using the pretense of greeting the men.

Connor wasn't aware of how abrupt he'd sounded. He kept his attention directed on Brenna while he waited for her to look up at him. He thought he'd scare a little consideration into the woman. God only knew, he'd feel better once he'd given in to the childish urge, and he would have done just that, if she hadn't looked up at him with such a surprised expression on her face.

"Connor, you're not homely."

"Why do I need to hear this?"

"You don't, but I felt like telling you. It doesn't matter. Homely or not, I still would marry you. When I make a promise, I keep it. I'd like you to promise me something too."

"No."

Her eyes widened in disbelief. "But you haven't even heard my request yet. How can you say no?"

"The priest's waiting."

She forced herself to be patient because there were more important concerns to address now. "Once the priest has blessed the marriage, will you please explain why you are determined to marry me and no other?"

He didn't see any harm in satisfying her curiosity, though he found it odd that she would be interested in knowing his reasons. "Yes," he agreed. "Are you always going to be this stubborn and willful?"

"I didn't realize I was." She hurried to change the subject before he found something else about her to criticize. "Thank you for allowing Father Sinclair to hear my confession. He and I both appreciate your patience."

He looked surprised by her gratitude. "Our priests are the most powerful men in all the Highlands, lass. I would not dare to interrupt, even if I'd wanted to."

She noticed the priest was waving to them and put her hand on Connor's arm. "Father would like to get started. Are you ready? I confess I'm very nervous," she added in a whisper.

"There isn't any need to be nervous. You will stop it at once."

"I will?" she asked, wondering how in heaven's name she could possibly manage that feat.

"Yes, you will, because you will finally realize you'll be much better served with me. No woman in her right mind would want to be married to the pig MacNare."

He sounded as though he knew what he was talking about. She decided to believe him for the simple reason that she really didn't have any other choice. She did wish she had some of his confidence, though, and wanted to lean into his side just to be close to his strength. She didn't give in to her urge, however, because she thought it would make her appear weak to him, and she wasn't weak at all. No, no, she was just nervous. That was all.

As soon as she realized everyone was staring at her, she forced a smile and straightened her shoulders. "I hope I don't make a mess of my vows. I haven't had time to think about what I should say to you. I was wondering . . ."

"No, we aren't going to wait. You'll do fine."

"But I . . ."

Responding to the worry he heard in her voice, he reassured her again before she could get even more worked up. "It will be over and done with before you know it."

She knew he thought she was talking about the ceremony, and she didn't correct him now. She had been concerned about making a muck of her vows, but she knew she'd get them said one way or another. It was the future that still made her apprehensive. It was all so irrevocable. Connor was an unknown. So was MacNare, she reminded herself. Wouldn't she have been apprehensive with him as well?

She stared straight ahead and stood where she was for a full minute without saying another word while she once again considered all the ramifications of what she was about to do.

In the end, she decided she would have to put her destiny in God's hands.

"There's no going back now, Connor MacAlister."

He nodded, for he'd heard the conviction in her voice and knew her mind was finally made up. "Nay, lass, there isn't."

She walked ahead of him now, her head high, her determination strong. "This had better be simple."

It would be simple, for he believed she had finally come to her senses and was going to be reasonable.

He should have known better.

Chapter 4

Nothing was ever simple with the woman. They were eventually married, but honest to God, it took forever to get from the beginning of the ceremony to the end. His bride was entirely responsible, of course. She became so obviously distraught during the priest's long-winded dissertation on the merits of the holy sacrament of matrimony, she simply couldn't stand still. Connor forced himself to be patient and didn't get the least bit angry, or even disgruntled.

He did get dizzy, though. So did all the others. Two of his men had to close their eyes so they could maintain their balance. Sinclair was in much the same condition, and all because he made the mistake of trying to keep up with the bride.

It all started out simply enough. When the priest instructed the couple to stand side by side and face him, Brenna hurried to obey. She seemed eager to cooperate, and Connor naturally assumed she was in as much of a hurry as he was to get it done.

He really should have known better.

"Laird, if your followers would form a half-circle behind you, they may all be witnesses to this joyful event."

"There, now," he said once the men were where he

thought they should be. "Lady Brenna, are you ready to begin?"

"Yes, Father."

The priest smiled. "You look radiant, lass," he whispered. He simply couldn't stop himself from blurting out a bit of praise, but he was quick to catch the men's frowns of disapproval, remembering then that Highlanders were known to be prickly about their women being given any attention by other men, and he realized too late that the peculiarity must also extend to men of the cloth.

He hurried to repair the damage he might have done. "Your bride realizes her good fortune, Laird, and that is why she looks radiant. I meant only to remark upon that fact."

Connor couldn't imagine why the priest had suddenly become so agitated. He nodded just to placate him so he would proceed with his duty of blessing the union.

Sinclair cleared his throat, made the sign of the cross, and then began his sermon on the responsibilities each would accept once they were truly husband and wife.

Brenna started out looking serene and somewhat relaxed with her hands down at her sides. Connor quickly tired of listening to the priest. She hung on to the man's every word. When she started shifting from foot to foot, Connor thought she was as bored as he was. Then she started wringing her hands together, a telltale indication that trouble was coming.

"Lady Brenna, please turn to your laird while you proclaim your vows."

She didn't hesitate in complying with the instruction, but Connor saw the panic in her eyes the second she looked up at him. The color had left her face, and he hoped to God she wouldn't faint before the priest finished.

He waited for her to speak, but after a long minute of silence, he decided he would. He made quick work of the duty with a brisk promise to protect and honor her.

Several of his men grunted their approval.

It didn't take him any time at all. It took her the rest of the evening.

"It's your turn now, lass," the priest coaxed when she remained silent. "You must proclaim your vows. Your hesitation makes me think you might be changing your mind. Could that be true?"

She frantically shook her head. "I mean to marry him, Father. I am searching for just the right words," she explained. "It's important that I get it right."

Those were the last coherent words she spoke for a long, long while. She started pacing while she worried over each and every word she would say. She circled the priest several times, then widened her circle to include all of them. No one was left guessing what she was thinking about, because she spoke each confusing thought out loud as she paced. Connor knew she wasn't aware of what she was doing, and as soon as he gave up watching her, he stopped being dizzy.

Around and around she went, until Sinclair was visibly reeling from turning so she would have his full attention. She explained she, too, meant to protect and honor Connor, just as he had promised her, but unlike the man she was marrying, she felt the need to expound at length upon those two vows with one qualification after another; yet she never quite finished any one thought.

It was apparent she wasn't going to stop until she had it all worked out, and Connor didn't even try to intervene. He relaxed his stance, folded his arms across his chest, and closed his eyes.

The priest thought the laird looked bored, but every once in a while a quick smile would appear on his face, and Sinclair knew Connor had found something amusing in what his bride was saying.

She finally stopped. Connor opened his eyes then, and honest to heaven, he almost laughed out loud. His gentle bride was now standing next to the priest looking quite pleased with herself.

Sinclair seized the opportunity. He latched on to her arm to keep from falling over, but even after the dizziness left him, he didn't let go of her. He meant to keep her from taking another evening stroll.

"Are you finished, lass?" he asked.

"Yes, Father."

Sinclair cast the laird a bewildered look. "Did she get her vows said, then?"

"Would you like me to repeat them, Father?" she asked.

Everyone but Connor shouted no at the same time. She was so startled by their enthusiastic reply, her eyes widened and she took a quick step back.

The priest was the only one who felt the need to apologize. "Do forgive me for raising my voice to you, dear lady. I can't imagine what came over me. I'm certain your laird will answer my question."

Connor wouldn't give her time to protest. He held her gaze steady while he summarized her promises.

"She will honor me, protect me, obey me only when she believes I'm being reasonable—but I shouldn't hold out hope that that day will ever come—try to love me before she's an old woman, and I'd better get it straight in my mind that she will respect me until or unless I do something to prove I'm not worthy, and God save me then. Have I left anything out, Brenna?"

"Nay, Connor," she answered. "You made better sense out of my vows than I did."

The priest paused to mop the sweat from his brow, for the task of getting the couple married had already proven to be a most strenuous undertaking. He then tried to figure out how he could bless them with the bride standing a foot behind him and the groom a good distance ahead of him. He finally gave up on the dilemma, waved his hand about in a wide arc, and ended up blessing everyone.

"You are now man and wife," he announced.

He waited for the resounding cheer to end before suggesting to the laird that he might wish to kiss his bride. He then wondered which one would go to the other. It was the bride's responsibility to go back to her husband's side, of course, but she was still looking quite dazed by it all, and Sinclair doubted she was capable of realizing her duty.

She surprised him, however. She seemed to come to her senses and hurried back to Connor.

The priest was so blissfully relieved the ordeal was finally over and the laird hadn't gotten angry enough to injure the sweet lass's feelings, he added a second blessing just for the two of them.

Connor leaned down to give her a proper kiss and put his hands on her waist to keep her from pulling away from him.

She didn't resist him. In fact, she put her arms around his

neck and met him halfway. The look on her face made him think the angels must be smiling, for it was filled with such joy. Was she happy, then? Connor stared into her eyes while he tried to figure out this dramatic turnabout.

She was about to remind him of his duty when he kissed her. She felt the warmth of his mouth on top of hers for the barest of seconds before he lifted his head and told his men they could eat their supper.

The kiss was nice enough for her to want another, and since Connor was still holding on to her, she thought he might feel the same way.

She was mistaken, however. He gave her his full attention for an altogether different reason. "Now it's going to get simple. Isn't that so, Brenna?"

Though she wasn't at all certain what he was asking her, she agreed just to make him happy. "Yes, it will. I'm going to be a good wife, Connor."

He didn't look as if he believed her, but she wasn't offended by his attitude. In time he would realize how fortunate he was to have married her.

"There aren't going to be any more complications, are there?"

"No more complications," she agreed. "Will you try to be a good husband?"

He shrugged an answer. She decided he meant he would and deliberately thanked him so he would know he had just agreed.

"What happens now?" she asked.

"Are you hungry?"

"Yes."

"Then we eat."

He finally let go of her. She thanked the priest and invited him to dine with them. Sinclair declined the offer, explaining that because the moon was bright enough, he felt it was his duty to ride to his father's home and spend the night there.

She tried not to feel as though she'd just been abandoned by an old friend. She held her smile, thanked him again, and then stood where she was until he'd taken his leave.

Connor never left her side. She turned to him and, only

then, realized she'd taken hold of his hand. She let go immediately and followed him across the clearing.

His men hadn't waited for them. So much for a proper wedding feast, she thought to herself. The Highlanders weren't even sitting down while they ate. They stood in a circle around a jagged boulder, laughing and talking while they enjoyed their food. One of them had placed the supper on a coarse cloth draped over the top of the stone.

It was a dismal affair at best. The second she joined them, a thick silence fell over the group. None of the men would look directly at her either, which only increased her awkwardness.

She felt like a leper. How she wished she could go back home for supper. She pictured her family seated at the great long table, smiling and jesting with one another while they shared their meal. There would be pigeon and fish and perhaps some leftover mutton stew too, and there were always fruit tarts.

Brenna knew she'd soon be wallowing in self-pity if she didn't stop thinking about people she loved and cherished and begin to concentrate on the present. She was hungry, she reminded herself, and if she didn't eat something now, she probably wouldn't get another chance until tomorrow.

Unfortunately, there wasn't much of a variety for her to choose from. There was yellowed cheese, brown bread, and oat cakes. The Highlanders hadn't left any room for her, so she squeezed in between Connor and Quinlan. Her husband hadn't bothered to introduce the rest of the men to her yet. Because she didn't know if it would be considered proper for her to ask their names, she followed their example and didn't speak to any of them. She kept her attention centered on the food and tried not to think about how miserable she felt.

The oat cakes tasted bitter. She wrinkled her nose and took a large drink of water to rid the taste from her mouth, and then, because it would have been unladylike for her to put the remainder back or throw it away, she made herself finish it.

She was so nervous, she took another one before she realized what she was doing. She had to eat the thing, of course, and odd, but the taste did improve considerably, especially when she added a piece of sweetened bread to it.

Brenna didn't notice when the others finished. She ate four large helpings before her hunger was appeased. When she looked up to find out what was going to happen next, she found she had an audience intently watching her.

She was taken aback by their attention . . . and their smiles. "Is something wrong?"

Quinlan answered with a quick shake of his head. "Would you like the rest of the bread? There's one last oat cake as well. You're welcome to it, mi'lady."

Brenna nodded. "If no one else wants it," she agreed. She took the remaining bread and cake, broke both in half and offered some to Connor first, and after he refused, she offered it to the other soldiers.

Everyone declined. They continued to stare intently at her while she ate the food, and she found she didn't like being the center of attention any more than she appreciated being completely ignored.

"Whom should I thank for this food?" she asked when she'd finished.

No one answered her, but several of the men shrugged indifference. Their grins were beginning to bother her. She felt as though she were the only one not included in some jest.

She thought about telling the men it was damned rude to gawk, but quickly changed her mind. She shouldn't be using words like *damn* anyway, she reminded herself, or she'd end up with a day's fast as penance. She couldn't think of anything more atrocious.

"Please tell me why you're smiling," she requested.

"You've impressed the men," Connor answered.

"How have I impressed them?" she asked, pleased that Connor had finally spoken to her.

She straightened her shoulders and waited for the compliment. They'd probably noticed how she'd joined right in, and had been impressed with her because she'd tried to become one of them. Perhaps, too, they'd finally realized how polite she was being. Yes, they'd surely noticed her proper behavior.

"You ate more than Quinlan. In fact, you ate more than all the men."

It wasn't the answer she'd expected. Telling a lady she'd eaten more than a soldier wasn't a compliment; it was an insult. Didn't he understand that? "Quinlan and the others must not have been very hungry," she argued in her defense. "Besides, how much I ate shouldn't be impressive . . . or noticed by anyone.".

He smiled. Lord, he was really quite attractive when he wasn't glaring at her. "We think it is."

She could feel herself blushing. She considered lying so they wouldn't think she was a glutton or a pig, then decided to be honest instead. She was going to have to eat with the rude barbarians again and again, after all, and they'd surely notice if she lied now and then ate until she was full at the next meal.

"I didn't eat as much as usual," she finally admitted.

"You sometimes eat more, mi'lady?" a soldier asked.

He looked incredulous. She gave him a reproving look to let him know what she thought of his behavior. " 'Tis the truth I do."

Quinlan was the first to laugh. The others quickly followed his sinful example. Her embarrassment intensified, of course, and she desperately tried to think of a way to turn their attention away from her eating habits.

None of them was ready to change the topic, however.

"Isn't it a fine, spring evening?" she asked.

"Do you eat more when you're nervous?" Quinlan asked.

What an odd question. "No," she answered.

The rude men all laughed again. She waited for them to quiet down before once again trying to change the subject.

"Connor, will you introduce me to your soldiers?"

"They'll introduce themselves."

She already knew Owen and Quinlan by name, of course, and when she looked at the other three warriors, they each told her their names.

Aeden was the thinnest of the group, though he still wouldn't be considered puny by an Englishman's measure, she supposed, and Donald was the name of the soldier with the big brown eyes that reminded her of a doe's.

Giric was the shy one in the group. He could barely look directly at her when he told her his name.

"It's a pleasure to meet all of you," she announced once they'd finished.

"May I ask you a question, mi'lady?" Quinlan said.

"Yes," she answered.

"When you first saw us, you were afraid. Some of us were wondering why."

"Did you think we were going to harm you?" Aeden asked. He added a smile, indicating he found the possibility amusing. "You were praying."

"Yes, I was praying, and yes, I did believe you were going to harm me."

"But after, mi'lady," Owen said. "After you knew we meant you no harm, weren't you still afraid? I wondered why."

Hadn't any of them ever looked in a mirror? Or did they have such luxuries where they lived?

She decided it would be unkind to point out how peculiar they looked, and so she simply shrugged and didn't say anything at all.

None of them wanted to let it go. "Was it our war paint that put you on your guard?" Owen asked.

"I really don't care to answer, for I have no wish to hurt your feelings."

For some reason, her honesty made the men laugh again. She decided to be a bit more blunt then. "However, I will admit it was your war paint that put me on my guard. Yes, it was," she emphasized with a nod. "And your size, and your dress, and your manners, and your intimidating frowns, and the way my father's twelve soldiers cowered to the five of you. . . . Shall I go on?"

She could tell they'd taken her comments as compliments. She really should set them straight, she thought, and explain she hadn't been at all impressed with them—no proper English lady in her right mind would be—but then a fresh worry popped into her head, and she immediately looked at Connor.

"I'm not wearing war paint. You might as well understand that fact right this minute. It's barbaric, Connor, and you cannot expect me to . . ."

The men's laughter stopped her protest. Connor didn't laugh, of course; the man never laughed as far as she could tell, but he did smile. Her heart noticed by pounding a quick beat. He had beautiful white teeth, all of them did, and she wondered how they could put such ugly paint on their skin and take such good care of their teeth at the same time. They really were a peculiar lot, all right. Would she ever be able to understand them or find her place among them?

"Women aren't given the honor."

She didn't know what he was talking about. "What honor?"

"Paint," he explained. "The tradition belongs to warriors alone."

Connor didn't look as though he was jesting, and so she didn't dare laugh. The effort cost her, though. Her throat ached considerably from the strain of being polite.

"Have you never seen a Highlander before, mi'lady? Do you know anything at all about us?" Giric asked in a whisper. He was blushing to the roots of his freckles and, in his shyness, had directed his question to the ground.

"When I was younger, I thought I knew all about you. I even knew where you lived."

"Where did you think we lived?" Donald asked, smiling over the sparkle he'd noticed in his mistress's eyes.

"Under my bed. You came out only at night, while I was sleeping. I'd always wake up screaming, of course, and run like lightning to my parents' chamber."

She expected the men to laugh over her jest, or at the very least, smile a little. Unfortunately, none of them seemed to understand she was teasing them. Three of them looked confused; the other two looked appalled.

"Did you just insult us?" Owen asked. He sounded as though he couldn't believe such an atrocity was possible.

"No, I was jesting. For heaven's sake, couldn't you tell the difference?"

They all shook their heads. Quinlan had the most difficulty hiding his smile. "It seems your bride has been dreaming about you for years, Laird," he drawled out.

"It would seem so," he agreed.

She didn't even try to hide her exasperation. The effort to

have a decent conversation with them was making her head throb, and being polite was a wasted undertaking.

She gave up trying. "Connor, may I be excused?"

She bowed her head to the men and walked away. She had already headed for the lake with her hairbrush, fresh clothing, and her blanket in her arms before Connor got around to giving her permission. She reached the break in the pines, stopped, and then glanced back over her shoulder.

"Quinlan?"

"Yes, mi'lady?"

"They weren't dreams. They were nightmares."

They didn't laugh until she was well out of sight, but the sound of their amusement was loud enough to reach the other side of the lake. She didn't believe the soldiers had finally gotten her jest, though; they appeared to be too slow-witted for that. She assumed Connor had made an atrocious remark about something his men would find humorous, like murder and mayhem. They all seemed to have a twisted sense of humor. She'd come to her opinion when she saw them smiling like heathens after Connor had told them they could kill the English soldiers. And hadn't they pouted like boys when the order was rescinded?

Brenna was immediately nagged by guilt. She knew she shouldn't continue to judge Connor so harshly. Could he help it if he was a barbarian or that he had been raised like a wild animal? No, no, of course he couldn't. Besides, he was her husband now. She was going to be stuck with him for the rest of her life, and shouldn't she at least try to like him?

Did he expect to take her to his bed tonight? She tried to block the frightening possibility as soon as it entered her mind. That was easier said than done, however; Lord help her, she couldn't even think about Connor touching her without shaking in panic. She knew her reaction wasn't at all reasonable. She was a grown woman now, not a child, and, therefore, understood what was expected of her. Her mother had patiently explained that all husbands wanted to bed their wives as soon as the wedding festivities ended. She hadn't given her daughter any specifics though, and while Brenna understood the basics, or at least believed she did, she'd still been left guessing about the finer points. It all sounded horribly awkward and messy to her.

Brenna wouldn't worry about it. If Connor decided to bed her, perhaps God would take pity on her and let her sleep through the ordeal.

She smiled over this fanciful notion while she stripped out of her clothes. She ran into the water before she could change her mind, gritted her teeth against the chill, and hurriedly washed.

Just as she was getting out, she heard someone approach. She moved back into the water, until she was covered to her chin, and waited.

A minute or so later, Connor appeared. A plaid was draped over his arm.

"It's time to get out."

"I would have privacy when I do."

"Why?"

She couldn't believe he needed to ask. "Because I require it."

"You're going to freeze to death. Come out. Now." His hard command didn't leave room for argument.

"I will not get out. I'm not wearing anything. I really must have privacy now."

He pretended not to notice she'd shouted at him. "No one's here," he said.

"You're here, and you're standing right in the moonlight. I cannot come out until you leave."

His bride had dared to shout at him again. He shook his head over her audacity. "Don't raise your voice to me."

He sounded as though he'd run out of patience. She reminded herself she'd vowed to get along and thought that perhaps if she gave him what he wanted, he would naturally reciprocate in kind.

Her lips were getting numb from the frigid water and her teeth were chattering so, she could barely speak at all now. "All right then. I won't shout. Will you please leave now?"

"No."

Her husband obviously didn't understand how to reciprocate. She'd have to explain it all to him later, but not now. Her skin was wrinkling like old prunes, and if she didn't get out soon, she really would freeze to death.

Pride was killing her. "I cannot possibly get out."

"Why? Are you embarrassed?"

He sounded surprised by the possibility. She closed her eyes, said a fast prayer for endurance, then answered, "Of course I'm embarrassed."

"Shyness has no place between us. Do you want me to come in after you?"

"I'll drown you if you do."

The ridiculous threat made him smile. "Will it help if I take my clothes off?"

"No."

She didn't realize he was teasing her, and honest to God, if she shouted at him once more, he thought he just might go in and get her.

"Connor, will you at least turn your back while I get dressed?"

His sigh was strong enough to push her under the water. "You're being very foolish."

She didn't mind his criticism. She got what she wanted, after all. He finally turned around. She hurried up the bank and dried herself with all possible haste. Fearing there wouldn't be enough time before her impatient husband turned around, she didn't bother putting on her chemise but slipped the white cotton gown over her head.

Pink ribbons secured the thin undergown from the bottom of her waist to the top of her chin. Her fingers felt as though they were being pricked by a thousand sharp pins now, making the task terribly awkward, and try as she did, she couldn't get the delicate ribbons properly tied.

She gave up on the task for the moment. The heavy tunic she planned to put over the undergown would sufficiently cover her bare chest. The problem was getting to the thing. She'd draped the garment on a low-hanging branch so it wouldn't get dirty, but she'd have to walk around Connor to get to it. She wasn't about to let him see her in such an indecent state and was forced to ask him to please hand it to her.

He turned around instead. She started backing away from him, thinking only to put a little distance between them, but then she felt herself slipping on the wet slope. She would have fallen flat on her face or plunged back into the water, but Connor saved her from disgracing herself by pulling her back to safety.

If he hadn't looked so disgruntled, she would have thanked him for his assistance.

She pulled her gown tight over her breasts and frowned with disapproval.

"I want you to understand you have nothing to fear from me. My duty is to take care of you, not harm you."

"I don't fear you."

"You just backed away from me," he reminded her dryly. "You were obviously frightened a minute ago."

She shook her head. The ribbon holding her hair up in a lopsided knot near the top of her crown flew into the water, and the thick mass of curls dropped down around her shoulders.

Looking at her in such a disheveled state gave him a sudden rush of pleasure. She was the most provocative creature he'd ever met. A man could get lost in the magic of those big blue eyes of hers and forget all about his duties while he paused to admire the sensual grace in the way she moved.

What the hell was wrong with him? Brenna wasn't casting a spell on him, yet he was acting as though she were. He quickly became irritated. He wasn't about to let her rob him of his discipline, and damn, but she was a bother.

And a temptress. All he wanted to think about was kissing her frown away and making hard, hot love to her.

She would probably die of fright if she had any idea of his thoughts. She couldn't possibly know how alluring she was, or how his body was reacting to her near nakedness. She wouldn't be frowning up at him with such indignation if she realized how close she was to being tossed onto the nearest blanket.

"Stop shaking your head at me," he ordered in a gruff voice.

"I was merely letting you know, most emphatically, that I wasn't frightened. It's just that I didn't expect you to turn around, and I was surprised. Your manners do give me grave concerns."

He smiled. Her eyes widened in disbelief. "Manners aren't important to you?"

"No."

"No? But you should think they're important."

"Why?"

"Why?" she repeated. Her mind went blank. Heaven help her, she couldn't come up with a single reason. The way Connor was looking at her, with such warmth and tenderness in his eyes, made her forget even what they'd been talking about.

She took a step closer to him. "You are a very confusing man," she whispered. "But if I am to keep my sanity, I guess I'll have to try to understand you. You'd better be worth the bother, Connor."

Almost as an afterthought, she said, "You may let go of me now."

He didn't feel like letting go of her, and because he was accustomed to doing exactly what he wanted to do, he ignored her wishes. Her soft skin, as smooth as an angel's and the color of pale gold in the moonlight, felt good against his rough, callused hands.

How had this treasure eluded other men?

"Haven't you ever been courted by other men?"

"I was betrothed to a baron, but he died before I was old enough to marry him. I never actually met the man, or many others for that matter. Father wouldn't allow any men around his daughters, especially Rachel," she explained. "She's the pretty one."

"Did the baron to whom you were pledged die in battle?"

"In bed."

"He died in bed?"

"It was tragic," she snapped. "Not amusing."

"Only an Englishman would die in his bed."

She thought his opinion too ignorant to argue about. "Will you stop squeezing my arms now?"

He lessened his hold. "Are you still feeling embarrassed?"

"Just a little."

"I don't want you to be embarrassed at all. You will stop it now."

She started to laugh before she realized he was perfectly serious. "Do you have any idea how arrogant you sound?"

She didn't wait for him to answer her. "I'm getting cold again. If you'll let go of me, I'll finish getting dressed."

"There isn't any need to dress. We're going to bed."

It wasn't what he said, but how he said it that made her panic. He reeked with authority and looked as tense as a warrior about to go in for the kill.

She deliberately tried to misunderstand. "Together?"

"Of course."

"Now? You want to go to bed now?"

He really was beginning to hate that word. "Yes, now."

"I'd rather not."

"I'd rather so."

"You might as well know I'm dreading it, Connor. I don't want to hurt your feelings, but I must be honest with you. Surely you don't want to force your attentions on an unwilling . . . Now what are you doing?"

"Putting the MacAlister plaid around you. Will you stop backing away from me every time I reach for you? It's damned irritating. Lift your hair out of my way."

"I'd rather you left me alone."

"You're trying my patience."

Why wouldn't he understand? She tried once again to get through to him.

"Connor, I don't have any experience."

She was sure she didn't need to explain in more detail. Surely he could hear the worry in her voice, see it in her eyes, and feel it in the way she trembled. Any decent, caring man would immediately try to soothe her.

"I do."

"That's it?" she cried out. "I'm supposed to be comforted because you have experience?"

"You want me to comfort you?" He sounded appalled by the very idea.

His reaction didn't sit well with her. Her frustration mounted until she wanted to scream. She took a slow, deep breath, instead, to calm herself.

It didn't help. "Yes, I most certainly do want you to comfort me."

He was afraid she was going to say that. For the first time in a very long while, he was at a loss for words. No other woman had ever made such a strange request of him before. In the past, women had always come to him willingly and offered their bodies, and if he'd been in the mood to

79

accommodate them—which, he had to admit, was most of the time—he'd accepted. He'd been mindful of his responsibility to be gentle with them, of course, and he'd always made certain their enjoyment matched his own. None of them had been virgins, though; he wouldn't have taken them to his bed if they had been, and now that he thought about it, damned near every one of them had been well-versed in the art of pleasuring a man. In fact, they'd usually had more experience than he had.

But they'd all left smiling.

This gentle lady standing before him wasn't at all like other women. She was his bride, the woman who would carry his name and bear his children. He should respect her by doing whatever was required of him to allay her fears. Admittedly, he was completely lacking in experience when it came to meeting the emotional needs of women, but he was certain that, if he put his mind to it, he could draw from past observations.

No, no, he was wrong about that, Connor realized after contemplating the dilemma for a moment. He guessed he'd never taken the time to notice what other men did with their women, not even his brother, Alec.

Now what? He wasn't about to tell her she was out of luck. She'd probably start crying then, and he wouldn't have any idea how to get her to stop. His brother always left the hall whenever his wife wept and returned only after she'd calmed down enough to listen to reason. He wasn't going to follow Alec's example now. He'd never get her bedded if he walked away from her. Hell, she'd think she'd been given a reprieve.

There seemed to be only one way out of this mire. He was going to have to help her get over this foolish worry of hers, no matter how long it took.

He prayed for the unthinkable—understanding. "I have decided to comfort you."

"You have?" She looked thrilled.

"Yes, I have. However, you're going to have to explain this duty to me first so I'll know how to proceed. You may begin."

"This isn't the time for jests."

"I wasn't jesting."

"You're really telling me the truth?"

The scowl on his face told her he didn't like being doubted. She hurried to calm him. "Yes, of course you're telling the truth. You're a laird, for heaven's sake. You wouldn't ever lie."

"Will you get on with it?"

She nodded, but didn't say another word.

"Brenna . . ."

"I'm thinking about it," she cried. "Your impatience is making me nervous. How to give comfort is rather difficult to explain. I don't want to make a muck of it."

She lapsed into silence again for what seemed like an hour. He couldn't understand what was taking her so long. He hadn't asked her to solve an impossible riddle, for the love of God. Why was she acting as though he had? He honestly didn't know how much longer he was going to be able to stand there without touching her. Couldn't she see what she was doing to him? No, of course she couldn't. She was fully occupied thinking about comfort, of all things. She seemed to have forgotten how to speak. She'd forgotten she was half naked too, but he hadn't. The second she stopped holding her gown together over her chest, the gap in the material widened enough for him to see the gentle swell of her breasts.

It almost killed him to look away. He suddenly realized that if he didn't get her covered up at once, he was going to completely lose his sense of discipline. He would run his fingers down her smooth, enticing skin, gently, of course, and then rip the thin-as-air gown off her.

She sure as hell wouldn't be thinking about comfort then, would she?

Connor quickly wrapped the plaid around her. He draped one long end over her shoulder, spread the material wide to cover her breasts, and secured the wool with the roped belt he'd carried along. The back of his hands deliberately brushed across her bare skin, not once but twice, while he dressed her, and damned if he didn't feel as though he'd been struck by hot lightning.

Covering her up didn't make his primitive urges go away. Now all he wanted to do was tear the plaid and her gown off her.

He stared into the distance instead.

"I'm pleased you're thinking about this."

She certainly gained his full attention with her remark. "You are?"

"Yes."

He gave her a hard look. "Exactly what do you think I'm thinking about?"

"Comfort."

He didn't laugh. She wouldn't understand why he was amused, and God help him, he'd probably tell her.

"You still haven't explained what you want from me."

"When you were younger, didn't your mother . . ."

"She's dead."

"I'm sorry."

"Why?"

"Because she died. What about your father? Didn't he ever comfort you?"

"No."

"Why not?"

"He's dead. That's why not."

"Connor, wasn't there anyone you could turn to when you were a little boy?"

He shrugged. "My brother, Alec."

"Did he ever comfort you?"

"Hell, no." He was disgusted by the very idea.

"Wasn't there anyone who cared about you?"

He shrugged. "My stepmother, Euphemia, but she was in no condition to ever comfort me, or her own son, Raen, for that matter. My father's sudden death destroyed her, and she's been in mourning ever since. She cannot even bear to come back to my land. Her pain is still terrible."

"She must have loved your father a great deal."

"Of course she did," he answered impatiently. "Does comforting take long?"

How in heaven's name was she supposed to know the answer to that question?

"I don't think so," she decided. "Some husbands simply pat their wives on their shoulders as they walk past them to let them know they care about their feelings. My father did that very thing all the time, but now that I think about it, I must admit I'm not certain if he was offering my mother comfort or showing her affection."

She lifted her shoulders in a dainty shrug. Trying to make him understand was turning out to be more complicated than she'd expected. She tried to think of another example to give him. "Perhaps other husbands put their arms around their wives and . . ."

"Which do you prefer?"

"I beg your pardon?"

He repeated his question in a brisk, will-you-hurry-up tone of voice. "Do you want me to pat you or put my arms around you?"

He was hopeless. Comfort needed to come from the heart, and Connor needed to feel it before he showed it. She guessed it was also an acquired art, learned after years of being loved and cared for by family members. And if she weren't so rattled about what was going to happen to her tonight, she probably would be able to explain it all quite nicely.

She couldn't even remember her new name now. "This isn't a lesson in sword fighting. You have to be sincere, spontaneous . . . and . . ."

She didn't continue because she couldn't think of anything else to say.

"You really don't have any idea what you're talking about, do you?"

She let out a long sigh. "No, not really."

He wasn't amused. "Then why in God's name have we been standing here?"

"I didn't realize how impatient you were, and I . . . Now what are you doing?"

"Lifting your hair up from under the plaid."

"Why?"

"I want to."

"Do you always do what you want to do? You do, don't you?"

"You'd be flat on your back now if I always did what I wanted to do."

She quit trying to push his hands away. There really didn't seem to be any reason for her to continue to argue with him anyway. Admittedly, she couldn't stop him from touching her—he was at least twice her size and strength, after all—but she protected the fragments of her pride by pretending she was in control of what was happening to her.

He made quick work of his task, and his hands were surprisingly gentle when he touched the sides of her neck. A shiver of pleasure raced down her back, and though it was a nice sensation, what was even more pleasing and surprising to her was that he corrected what bothered him instead of criticizing her. She had grown up constantly being told what was wrong with her—God only knew, something always did seem to be amiss—then being ordered to correct the flaw. She knew Connor wouldn't be any different. It was only a matter of time before he got the hang of it and fell into the same routine as her parents and brothers and sisters.

Connor wasn't going to wait any longer. He took hold of Brenna's hand and started walking toward the bed he'd prepared. He was a little surprised she didn't fight him now.

"I might as well warn you now that I'm rarely put together," she suddenly blurted out.

"Your appearance doesn't matter to me."

"It doesn't?"

"Of course not."

She thought about that for a moment or two before realizing they were walking back toward camp.

"Where are we going?"

He heard the panic in her voice. God, he hated being patient. Were all virgins this impossible?

"What can I do to end this ridiculous fear of yours?"

"You could start by not snapping at me. It isn't ridiculous."

"Answer me."

"You could say something I might find . . . pleasant and hopeful about . . ."

"Mating?"

He thought of a thousand answers to give her, but all of them focused on how he would feel.

"Your hesitation worries me," she whispered.

"It won't kill you."

"It won't kill me? That's it?"

He smiled over the outrage in her voice. "You'll like it. Eventually."

She gave him a look that told him she didn't believe him. She kept walking though, and that was all he cared about at the moment.

"It's messy, isn't it?"

"No, it isn't."

"I doubt I'll like it," she whispered, for they were getting close to where his soldiers had bedded down for the night, and she didn't wish to be overheard. "I do want children, though."

"Exactly how did you plan to get them?"

She ignored the sarcasm in his voice. "Do you want children?"

"Of course. Why do you think I married you?"

"I don't know why. You promised to explain it all after we were wed."

"Later," he promised.

"Any woman could give you children. Why did you choose me?"

They stopped talking and now faced each other in the center of the clearing. She looked around, saw the other soldiers feigning sleep on their blankets, and in the center of the circle of men was an empty bed, fashioned together with yet another plaid.

She was horrified. Did he really expect her to sleep there, in the middle of the others? Yes, of course he did, she realized. Honest to God, he really didn't have any idea about the needs of women, did he?

She couldn't make a scene. His men would hear her if she started ranting at their laird, and that would only embarrass her and make him angry.

What was she going to do? She wasn't about to let him touch her with his men pretending to sleep not five feet away. Yet how could she stop him? Connor didn't look as though he would be reasonable much longer. His stance was rigid, his frown intense, and now that she thought about it, hadn't he already given her enough time to calm her worries? He had wanted to comfort her, or at least had tried to give her what she wanted, and she couldn't even imagine any other man going to such lengths to accommodate her.

The truth made her smile. Good lord, he really had comforted her, and she hadn't even realized it. She sighed. Her husband wasn't such a bad sort, after all.

It wouldn't be right for her to argue with him now. No, she would be diplomatic instead: If she was clever enough, he might not even realize she was getting her way. She reached for his hand just as he was about to take off his boots, and bent down, picked up the blanket from the ground, and then whispered, "Please come with me."

"Now what's wrong?" he demanded in a near bellow.

"Brides always prepare the wedding bed. It's a tradition in England."

She could tell he didn't believe her lie. She walked away before he could stop her, paused once at the edge of the clearing to give him what she hoped was a come-hither smile, and continued on.

Connor didn't move. He stood there with his legs braced apart and his hands on his hips, staring after her, his attention on the gentle sway of her hips as she moved. Then he started counting to ten. When he was finished, he was either going to let the impossible woman leave or go after her and make hard, passionate love to her.

"I've never heard of this tradition."

Quinlan drawled out the remark. The soldier was sitting on the ground with his back against a tree trunk and his arms folded across his chest.

Connor turned his frustration on him. "If you say another word, I swear I'll kill you."

Quinlan ignored the warning. "Don't you think you should go to bed before it's time to get up?"

Connor took a threatening step toward his friend. Quinlan immediately straightened up. "She's only wanting privacy, Connor. That's why she's moving your blankets."

"I realize that," he said. He hadn't realized it, of course, but he wasn't about to admit it to his friend.

He walked away without saying another word and caught up with Brenna near the lake. He wasn't at all amused that they'd come full circle and were now close to where they started.

"Were you planning to prepare our bed in England?"

JULIE GARWOOD

Chapter
5

"This will do," she answered.

The isolated spot she'd chosen was a flat piece of nothing squeezed in between the pines. There was barely enough room for him to roll over. She seemed to like it, though, and for what he vowed was going to be the very last time, he let her have her way. He stood behind her as he removed his boots, all the while trying to control his temper.

She spread the blanket out on the ground, and though he was sure she would try to make an hour-long project out of the simple task, she surprised him by being quick about it.

When she was finished, she removed her slippers and then stood up, facing him. She moved closer, until her toes were touching his, and stared into his eyes, holding her breath while she waited for him to touch her.

He didn't move. Tension filled the air between them, her anxiety building as she stared into those dark, inscrutable eyes of his, looking for the first sign of displeasure. Lord, she couldn't stand the silence long.

"I had thought to keep my clothes on."

He slowly shook his head. "But then I thought to take them off," she whispered.

And still he waited. She told herself she had made the decision and now it was up to her to keep her word. Her

87

hands shook as she untied the belt at her waist, and the woolen material he'd draped around her fell in a swoosh to the ground.

She thought about moving to the side before she took her gown off, because the moonlight was blocked by the tree branches there and shadows would hide her nudity from him, but then she decided to stop being such a coward.

Should she tell him she wasn't wearing anything underneath her nightgown? No, she decided, he would find out soon enough. Her heart was pounding frantically, but her anxiety had faded a little—because he wasn't attacking her, she supposed—and somewhere in the back of her muddled thoughts was the realization that Connor wouldn't deliberately hurt her. She couldn't understand why she felt that way, but she did, and oddly, her hands weren't shaking nearly as much.

She felt she was in charge of what was happening to her, and that made all the difference.

She regarded him gravely while she gathered her courage and then slowly removed her nightgown. She kept her gaze on Connor all the while, searching for a hint of displeasure or disgust because her body was so terribly imperfect. She was fully aware of her flaws. Her breasts were too large, her hips too narrow, and her legs were too long for the rest of her body. He was bound to notice, she knew, and if he so much as frowned with displeasure, she thought she would close her eyes and die of shame.

He took his time looking at her. His gaze lingered on her parted lips, her full breasts, her narrow waist, the blond curls shielding her virginity, her long legs, all the while trying to remember how to draw a breath. Dear God, he hadn't expected such beauty. He was overwhelmed by her, for he had never imagined such a woman could exist, and if he weren't a practical man, he would have thought she wasn't English at all but a goddess sent down from heaven to reward him for the vengeance he had sought in his sainted father's name.

He was fast becoming desperate to take her into his arms and plant himself firmly inside her. He didn't give in to his body's demands yet, but stood where he was and let her take the lead once again. For some reason he didn't understand, she had gotten it into her head that she should be the one making the decisions tonight. He had come to this startling conclusion when he had hesitated instead of ordering her to remove her clothes and be damned quick about it. He had shaken his head at her to let her know he didn't care for her decision to keep her clothes on, but before he could explain exactly what he wanted her to do, she changed her mind.

And he got exactly what he wanted.

The blush covering her face reflected her embarrassment. She was trying to look defiant and not afraid, but she was worried. He could see it in her eyes, in the way she stood as straight and rigid as a spear, and in her hands clenching and unclenching at her sides. Oh, yes, she really was perfect.

She must have believed he would become the aggressor now, and when he didn't reach for her, she slowly began to relax.

Why didn't he take off his clothes? She worried about that for a full minute before deciding to offer her assistance.

"I had thought you would remove your own clothes, but then I considered you might want me to assist you. Sometimes wives in England help their husbands disrobe."

She was obviously making it all up as she went along. If it helped relieve her fear, he didn't mind.

"Do you want me to undress you, Connor?"

He considered answering her, then decided what had worked before would work again, and so he simply nodded agreement.

She took another shaky breath, no doubt bracing herself for what she thought she would find, before she finally gathered enough gumption to reach for his belt. Her toes, as weightless as a butterfly's wings, brushed over his, and the second the knot was undone and his plaid began to drop to the ground, she took a quick step back.

He wasn't wearing any underclothes. She noticed that right away, God help her for being foolish enough to look, and she deliberately turned her attention to his chin until her heart calmed down. She'd only taken a glimpse below his waist before she forced herself to look away. It was still more than enough to make her want to run all the way back to England.

"Connor, are you certain this will work?"

The bewilderment in her voice amused him. God, she was innocent. And young.

He gently pulled her into his arms and held her tight against him. His head dropped down to the top of her head. "Yes," he promised.

He was a little surprised he could speak at all. The feel of her soft breasts pressed against his chest demanded his full attention, and honest to God, he was beginning to believe the unbearable wait had been worth the trouble.

He couldn't wait any longer though. Neither his body nor his mind would allow another minute to pass without fulfilling all of his urges.

Connor had fully expected to be surprised again, and that he was, because once he'd convinced her to quit hiding in the crook of his neck and tilt her head up toward him, she let him kiss her. She didn't know what she was doing, of course. Her lips were closed tight against his, but with his gentle coaxing, she began to relax. Then he told her what he wanted her to do. She didn't fight him, just gave him a look that suggested she thought he was out of his mind to want her to do such a thing, and after he'd repeated his demand, she finally conceded to him and opened her mouth.

And then he kissed her the way he'd imagined he would from the moment he'd first seen her today. His tongue quickly moved inside her sweet warmth to stroke and explore. It was much, much better than what he'd imagined it would be. God, how he liked kissing her this way.

She liked it too. She wound her arms around his neck and began to stroke him, timidly at first, then far more boldly, until she seemed as eager as he was to experience more of the erotic pleasure.

Finally, she began to whimper low in her throat and move restlessly against him.

The temptation proved to be his undoing. He wanted to take her that very moment, and it took all he had to control his own response. He'd scare the hell out of her if he thrust inside her now, hurt her far more than was necessary too, because she still wasn't ready for him. She would be, he promised himself, even if the agony of slowing down killed him.

He was being very deliberate now. He kept up his tender assault on her senses, determined to make it impossible for her to think about what was going to come. Only when she conceded to the demands building inside her would she be able to welcome his invasion without too much discomfort. He tried to overwhelm her, to flood her senses with his touch, his taste, his scent. His mouth assaulted hers again and again, until his own desperation to be inside her overrode all other considerations. His control slipped further away with each kiss they shared, each little moan she gave.

He was aroused to a fevered pitch. He didn't give her time to protest, but kept her fully occupied with his kisses while he lifted her into his arms and moved to their bed. He tried to be gentle with her, at least he thought he tried, even remembered to brace his weight with his arms so he wouldn't crush her as he came down on top of her. His body covered every inch of hers, and God, she smelled so damned good and felt so incredibly right in his arms. He buried his face in the crook of her neck, inhaled her wonderful scent, and let out a loud groan of sheer ecstasy.

She was overwhelmed by what was happening to her. She had expected it would all be over and done with by now and she would be in terrible pain. She hadn't expected to like it or crave all the glorious sensations coursing through her body. Yet she yearned for even more from him, and how was that possible? She didn't know if she was pleasing him—she hoped she was—and she wanted to ask him to tell her what he wanted her to do, so he would also be shaking from her caresses the way she shook from his.

Once his hard body came down on top of hers, thinking became too complicated. He was whispering hot, sensual words close to her ear, which only made the yearning deep inside her more demanding.

His hands were everywhere. She shouldn't let him touch her breasts, meant to tell him to stop, even as she arched up against him in silent demand for more and more and more.

She tried to stop him when his hand moved between her thighs. He wouldn't be stopped though. It was much too late for that. He needed to know if she was ready for him, God help him if she wasn't, and as soon as he felt the wet opening he most wanted to invade, the demands of his body took over.

He tried to make his invasion swift. He moved between her thighs and thrust deep with one powerful surge. She cried out in agony, and the sound echoed through the pines. Only when he was completely surrounded by her tightness did he force himself to stop and allow her time to get past the pain. He couldn't suppress his groan of male satisfaction, or was it a shout? He was too shaken by her to know exactly what he was doing now. He could only feel, and dear God, this had to be heaven, so perfect was each sensation. And new. For the first time since he'd begun to take women to his bed, he found he was consumed by passion.

She was consumed by pain. She struggled against him and demanded that he stop at once, crying all the while, but then he let out a shout and went completely still, and she wasn't certain if he was angry or as disappointed as she was.

Connor finally realized she was crying. He immediately stopped and tried to calm her. "It's going to be all right. The pain will leave."

"How do you know it will leave?"

"I know."

He sounded terribly certain. She decided to believe him, admitting that even now the throbbing wasn't quite as intense. She still didn't like it much, though, and hoped it would all be over and done with soon. She was about to ask him to please hurry up, but then he kissed her again and she was suddenly more interested in kissing him back than talking.

He continued to stroke her and kiss her until he felt her relax her grip on him.

Then he was moving, though slowly at first, vowing he would end it if she asked him to, even if it killed him. Yet instead of fighting him or making impossible demands, she put her arms around his neck once again.

He wanted more than her acceptance, however, because he'd felt her passion before he'd hurt her, and he craved to feel it again. In between hot kisses, he whispered sensual promises and praise, most of which didn't make any sense at all, but she didn't seem to notice or mind. His patience was blessedly rewarded when she began to move against him.

Connor braced his weight with his arms and lifted up to look into her eyes. There were tears there, yet there was passion as well, wasn't there? God, he hoped so. He didn't want to keep on hurting her, vowed once again to end it quickly with one hard push to give her his seed if her pain persisted, even as he wondered how he would ever find enough discipline to leave her now.

"Should I stop?" His voice was rough with emotion.

He sounded angry. She looked at his face and saw that his jaw was clenched tight, and there were beads of perspiration on his forehead. Had she done something wrong? She could barely think about it, the throbbing inside was insistent now, yet surprisingly pleasant. She shifted beneath him, drew her knees up just a little to bring him deeper inside her, and felt a burst that was far better than simply pleasant. She couldn't stop herself from moving once again.

He let out a low groan. "Have I made you angry?" she whispered.

He shook his head before repeating his question. "Do you want me to end it?"

"No," she said.

He slowly withdrew, smiling because she instinctively tightened her legs around him, trying to keep him inside, and then he pushed forward again, all the while watching her expression for the first sign of discomfort.

She squeezed her eyes shut, let out a sweet moan, and ordered him to do just that once again.

It was all the encouragement he needed. He moved again and again, more forcefully with each thrust, and oh, how he loved the way she clung to him and made those erotic sounds in the back of her throat.

He still believed he was the one in control. He knew exactly what would happen to her; she would concede everything to him soon, her body, her mind, and her heart. Her orgasm would consume her, and as she was in the midst of her climax, he would give her his seed.

He would be well served, of course. And satisfied. Just as he had always been.

He continued his pace until she was writhing in his arms. Her hips were forcefully arching up to quicken his pace, and then he became even more demanding.

She let him know how much she liked what he was doing by scoring his back with her nails and crying out with pleasure.

"Oh, God."

"Nay, lass. Connor."

She didn't understand what he was saying to her because the hot sensations overwhelming her senses were so excruciatingly wonderful; she wanted to tell him so, but her voice got lost in her cries for more.

Her need fed his own. She suddenly became the aggressor, not he, stroking and caressing, touching him in ways he'd never been touched before.

She drew him down for a long, wet, open-mouth kiss, wild now, uncontrolled with her demand, forcing him with her uninhibited response to give her everything, and he was powerless to stop what was happening to him. Her passion ignited his own, and even that part of his mind he had always held back, he willingly gave to her.

His world came apart. He thrust deep, hard, over and over again, his movements uncontrolled now, for he was overwhelmed by her, and with one last surge forward, he poured his seed into her, shouting her name, over and over again, in acceptance and surrender. In that instant when their hearts seemed to beat as one, and their souls felt as though they were entwined, she found her own fulfillment.

She clung to her husband as though her life depended upon it, terrified by what was happening to her, and then she heard him call her name, felt him tighten, and she suddenly stopped fighting her own surrender. Tremor after tremor of ecstasy poured over her, yet all the while Connor was there with her, holding her tight, telling her it was all right by simply chanting her name.

Her climax seemed to last forever, yet it was over all too soon. Weeping softly against his shoulder because it had been so incredibly beautiful, she felt exhausted, replete, and very proud of herself.

It took her several minutes to stop shaking and draw a proper breath. Connor, she noticed, was still taking deep, shuddering breaths. The entire experience had been far more demanding for him than for her, she thought, before realizing she was still taking gasping breaths too.

He continued to hold her until she began to relax in his arms and her legs dropped down to his sides; then he tried to leave her by rolling over on his side. She wouldn't let go of him. He thought about moving her arms away so he could get up, because he knew he needed time alone to figure out what had just happened to him, but then he felt her tears on his skin and decided to wait another minute or two.

He'd hurt her, yes, of course he had. She'd been a virgin, and it was inevitable that she would have difficulty accepting him, but once she had adjusted, had he continued to hurt her? Hell, he'd been rough with her all right; he should have been able to control himself, and if she hadn't been so hot and tight, he probably would have. What had she expected? She'd given herself wholeheartedly to him.

She'd been perfect. Connor suddenly realized what he was doing and had to shake his head over his own thoughts. What was wrong with him? Now he was trying to blame her for taking away his discipline and trying to claim his heart, God help him, when he had willingly given both to her.

He really needed time to recover. She wasn't going to let go of him, though, and so he decided he would have to wait until tomorrow to figure it all out. Perhaps by then he would have reclaimed some of his control. He'd given her that too. No wonder he felt so vulnerable now, and if that wasn't disgusting, he didn't know what was. His strength was gone, and he was suddenly too exhausted to think about anything important. He inhaled her wonderful feminine scent, found it mingled with his own, and if he didn't force himself to go to sleep soon, he knew he was going to get hard again and hurt her all over.

She didn't want to sleep just yet. She wanted a tender word from him so she would know he'd been pleased with her. She needed his assurance now, and only when his breathing became deep and even did she realize she wasn't going to get it.

She moved away from him, sat up, and nudged him. He didn't even open his eyes.

She didn't want to give up. The pride she'd felt just

minutes ago was quickly fading, and damn it all, she wanted to keep on feeling wonderful about what had happened, not sorry. Didn't he understand she needed praise and comfort to give her the reassurance she ached for?

No, of course he didn't know. The insensitive bear didn't even know what comfort was.

She decided to give him one last chance to redeem himself and poked him hard in his shoulder. She'd already made up her mind that as soon as he opened his eyes, she would bluntly ask him if he had been as pleased with her as she'd been with him. He'd tell her yes, of course, and she'd finally be content.

Connor still didn't open his eyes, but he did move. He rolled over, away from her.

She saw the damage she'd done to him and thought her heart might stop beating then and there. Bright red marks streaked his broad shoulders and back. She hadn't drawn blood with her nails, but the marks were vivid enough to make her think it would take a long while for them to fade away.

How could she have done such a thing? She'd acted like a wild animal, and not at all like the well-bred lady she'd been raised to be. No wonder Connor was ignoring her. He had to be disappointed in her. In truth, she couldn't blame him.

She didn't know how she was ever going to face him again. She was going to have to, of course, unless she died of embarrassment before morning.

First things first, she told herself. She would go back to the water, wash his scent away, and get dressed.

She felt better because she had something to do. She tried not to make any noise, though she was pretty certain she could step all over him and he would continue to sleep. The second she moved, she grimaced in pain. She paused to glare at Connor, because he was responsible for her discomfort, then reached for the plaid he'd given her. She saw the spots of blood on the wool right away. She didn't panic, and in fact wasn't even surprised, because her mother had told her there would be blood, and pain, but the dear woman had exaggerated about it all being over and done with as quick as a blink. Brenna had to admit that some of her discomfort was her own fault. Her mother had also instructed her to stay perfectly still throughout the ordeal, promising that if she did, it wouldn't be so terrible after all, and Brenna hadn't stayed still, now had she? When would she start listening to her elders?

Still, it hadn't been that horrible. She admitted the truth on her way back to the water. She continued to fret while she washed every spot of skin he'd touched, which meant taking another full bath, because he'd touched her everywhere, and then she got dressed. She was thankful she'd left her clothes on the bank, especially her undergarments. Yawning now from sheer fatigue, she folded his plaid into a square with the intention of giving it back to him in the morning, then put on a clean, ivory, ankle-length chainse and covered it up with her dark, midnight blue bliaut.

"I'm pathetic," she muttered in disgust.

She removed a wooden necklace from inside her right shoe, where she'd carefully hidden it, and held it gently in her hand, treating it with as much care as she would a king's crown of jewels. The round wooden medallion was a gift from her father, and though it wasn't valuable by a thief's measure, which was exactly why her father had had it made out of wood, it was more precious and valuable to her than anything else she owned because of what the disk represented. Her father had had the wooden medallions made for all of his children, even his sons, and each one of the disks had a different design etched into the wood. Brenna's was the outline of the sun. All of her sisters and brothers recognized each other's designs, her father had insisted they memorize them, and when he had given Brenna her medallion, he gave her the same instructions he'd given the others. If she was ever in trouble, she need only send the medallion to one of her brothers or sisters and he or she would immediately come to her assistance. Their loyalty was to one another, he'd explained, first and always, and her father wanted to make certain that after he and her mother had passed on, their children would look out for one another.

Brenna admitted, though only to herself, that she had a tendency to become preoccupied and misplace her possessions, and for that reason she always put the medallion in her shoe at night. She wouldn't dare be careless with her father's dear gift.

Holding the link to her family made her ache to be with them again. Suddenly it all became too much to bear, and she began to sob with heartache and loneliness. Although she tried, she couldn't make herself stop. She sat down on the slope, giving in to what she considered the inevitable after the hellish day she'd had, and stared at her treasure until her tears were spent. The precious lifeline to her family was secured by a leather necklace. She made certain it was knotted securely before slipping it around her neck and tucking it under her clothing. It rested between her breasts, directly over her heart, exactly where it belonged.

Much to her surprise, weeping had proved to be a healing balm, and though she found it quite peculiar, she actually felt better by the time she was finished. She was also able to look at her situation with more practicality and less emotion. The wooden disk represented her past, but Connor was part of her future now, wasn't he?

She should probably learn to be loyal to him, shouldn't she? Love wasn't all that important, was it? Her mother certainly hadn't thought so. Why, she hadn't truly loved their father for years and years. Eventually, her heart did soften to his hard ways, and the two of them certainly got along well enough.

Connor had already proven he would treat her kindly. The way he'd touched her, with such care and tenderness, was evidence enough. His hands fit the rest of him, she thought. They were big, callused, hard, strong, yet he'd been so very gentle when he'd caressed her.

The memory made her sigh. It was promptly followed by a loud yawn. She didn't want to avoid Connor any longer. She needed sleep and his warmth now. The tender words of assurance would have to wait until the obtuse man finally realized what a valuable asset she was. She was going to have to prove herself to him, of course, but she was up to the challenge, and God willing, she would be a good wife and mother.

She stood up when she heard Connor. He barely made any noise at all, but it was still quite enough for her to recognize where the sound was coming from. She hurriedly wiped her face dry of any remaining tears, straightened her appearance as best she could without her brush and mirror, and then started toward him.

He stopped when he reached the break in the trees. He didn't dare get any closer to her just yet, because the urge to take her into his arms and make love to her again needed to be controlled first, then discarded, before he took another step. He couldn't force himself to stop thinking about it, though. He'd tell her it had been damned inconsiderate of her to stay away from his bed for such a long while, of course, probably just a scant second before his mouth devoured hers so she couldn't start arguing with him again. He loved the way she'd tasted, the way she'd felt.

God, but she was pretty. He couldn't seem to get past the revelation. It wasn't simply her appearance he found himself drawn to like a besotted boy. No, it was far more than that. She was such a sensual woman. The graceful way she moved, the warmth in her welcoming smile, the delicate look of her, all appealed to him, but what captivated him most was the air of dignity and strength in her bearing. She made him believe she fully understood the power she would wield as his wife.

And if he ever weakened, would she wield that power over him? The thought made him frown.

The longer she stared at him, the faster her heart beat, so overwhelmed was she by the sheer beauty before her. Connor was almost completely shrouded in the thick mist gathered in the trees. She was suddenly reminded of the giants of ancient times her father had told her bedtime stories about, and surely Connor was every bit as magnificent as his ancestors were, perhaps even more so. There wasn't a fold of fat anywhere. She understood why he radiated such strength and power now. The splay of muscles in his upper arms and thighs was evidence enough. Muscles rolled under skin that glistened when he put his hand out to her.

She immediately walked forward and placed her hand in his. "I thought you were sleeping," she whispered.

"I cannot rest until you do."

"Why is that, Connor?"

He liked the way she said his name in such a familiar,

intimate way. God, he was weary tonight. He had to be exhausted to be thinking about such foolishness now.

"I'm responsible for you, that's why. What were you doing? You were gone a long time."

He knew exactly what she'd been doing, of course, the proof of her weeping still lingered in her eyes, and the only reason he'd asked the question was to see if she would admit her weakness to him.

"I was crying like a baby. Why does that amuse you?"

"I smiled because you told me the truth."

"I always try to tell the truth. Lies become too complicated. Do you always walk around without any clothes on?"

She sounded worried about the possibility. "Only when I'm chasing after inconsiderate wives," he answered.

He didn't mean to sound surly. She didn't seem to notice, however. Her mind was somewhere else. He wasn't left guessing what she was thinking about.

"Why did you marry me?"

"I'll explain tomorrow."

He started to turn, intending to drag her back to the bed, but she stopped him by tugging on his hand.

"You promised me you would explain directly after our marriage was blessed. You don't believe I'll like hearing the truth, do you? Could that be the reason you're putting it off?"

"Come back to bed. Then I'll explain."

"You'll only fall asleep before . . ." She stopped trying to explain when he lifted her up into his arms. His skin was so wonderfully warm, she wanted to press herself against him. She didn't give in to the temptation though, but put her arms around his neck and stared directly into his eyes.

"Why were you weeping?"

"I was thinking about my family."

"I'm your family now."

The gruffness in his voice actually comforted her, and she knew she had to be exhausted to have such a strange reaction. She hadn't wanted to tell him her worry, but heaven help her, the way he stared at her made her want to blurt out every little concern she had.

"I disappointed you," she whispered.

"No."

"No?"

"You didn't disappoint me."

She waited for him to explain. He didn't say another word, which really shouldn't have surprised her, as she already had noticed he wasn't one to embellish any of his remarks. The flaw obviously extended to compliments as well. She was feeling inordinately pleased with herself now, and all because she hadn't disappointed him.

Oh, yes, she was weary tonight. It had been a long, difficult day, after all, and that was why she was being so emotional.

He carried her back to his blankets and set her on her feet again. When she tried to turn away from him, he pulled her back into his arms and kissed her long and hard.

Her knees went weak, and when he let go of her she gracefully collapsed to the bed.

She regained her strength a minute later. After he'd stretched out on the blankets, she tried to kneel over him. He was having none of that. He pulled her down beside him, forced her back up against his chest, and wrapped his arms around her.

He wasn't about to let go of her. He knew she hadn't forgotten his promise to tell her exactly why he'd married her, and he wasn't at all certain how she would react to hearing a few of his reasons. He didn't want to have to get up and chase after her again. Women, he had learned, could be peculiar about matters that really shouldn't concern them. They tended to get their feelings injured quite easily; at least Alex's wife, Jamie, did. Brenna seemed to be even more emotional. Not only did she appear to get her feelings injured, she also insisted on telling Connor about it. The fact that she'd told him she believed she'd disappointed him was proof enough.

He was astounded she'd needed his reassurance. She hadn't tried to hide her vulnerability at all.

Yes, she astounded him all right, and pleased him more than he could ever have thought possible.

"Connor, you were going to tell me . . ."

"I wanted sons."

"And daughters," she reminded him.

"And daughters," he agreed. "I told you my reason earlier."

She tried to turn so she could look at him, but he tightened his hold on her, making movement impossible.

She gave up trying. She rested the side of her face on his upper arm, smiling because it felt so hard and warm against her cheek, then yawned loudly.

"But why did you marry me? You could have married any woman from the Highlands."

"You asked me."

"Please don't use that excuse. We both know you would never have held a child to her word."

"No, I wouldn't."

"Do you remember any of it? Surely you . . ."

He remembered every detail of the meeting with her father, of course. "Are you going to keep me awake all night?" he asked, irritably.

"No, of course not. I didn't mean to stray from the topic. I'm concerned your reason for marrying me has something to do with my father. Is that true?"

"No," he answered. "My feud is with MacNare. He went after Quinlan's family. He burned their home, destroyed their crops, and killed their stock. He wanted their land to add to his own. I had only just heard about this atrocity when another one of my followers came to me with a similar outrage to report."

"And because your men are loyal to you, you went to war on their behalf."

"Yes."

"There had to be another reason as well, for surely others have come to you in the past with stories of mistreatment. If you married each time, you'd have ten wives by now."

"I have another reason, but I don't wish to discuss it now."

"Someday will you explain?"

"Yes."

"All right then. Will you explain what our marriage has to do with your war?"

"It's simple, Brenna. MacNare wanted you."

"And so you took me away from him. Why didn't you just kill me?"

"I don't kill women."

"I didn't mean to insult you. You tell me you don't kill women, but you have no concerns about using them, do you?"

"When it's necessary."

"Why didn't you simply continue to war against him? Were your losses too substantial?"

"If a Highlander has vengeance in his heart, no loss is substantial. I was fortunate though. There were injuries, but none of my own died. My brother ordered me to end the feud. Alec has become what some would call a mediator in our land, and he has the power behind him to force others to do what he considers just. Marrying you was my last . . ."

"Insult?"

"It is, only if you choose to think it is."

"What would you consider an insult then?"

"Destroying a man's crops, killing good horses. Those are insults. Killing a soldier is a much more grievous matter. I think perhaps you place too much value on marriage. You think like a woman."

"I would never have gone to such lengths."

"I'm my father's son. I am also a practical man."

He had told her the truth, God help her for asking him to, and she suddenly felt like weeping again.

She tried to be practical about it all and told herself it could have been worse. She couldn't imagine how, of course. She didn't like being used. No woman did. She didn't think he would understand how she felt, though.

"In future, I will learn how to become practical," she whispered. Her voice shook, and she didn't say another word for a long while because she knew she would start crying. She thought she'd rather die than let him know the damage he'd done to her hopes and dreams. She wasn't going to let him hurt her again, and if being practical meant she must give up her feelings and her heart, then she would be more practical than he was.

It didn't take her long to realize how foolish she was being. She didn't want to live without love, and that meant she was going to have to make Connor change his attitude, and how would she ever be able to do that?

The task was disheartening and seemed to be as impossible as making it rain on a sunny day. She squeezed her eyes shut as soon as she realized how teary she was becoming and tried to concentrate on her night prayers in hopes the ritual would occupy her thoughts.

Connor sought to close his mind against the hurt he'd just caused her so that ridiculous thoughts of guilt wouldn't bother him. It wasn't until he'd told her a fragment of the full truth that he realized how cold it made him sound to a woman as emotional as Brenna. She couldn't possibly understand, and he wasn't about to explain further.

His hatred for MacNare was burning him hollow inside, and though he still hadn't found any evidence to make him culpable in Donald MacAlister's death, Connor still wanted to believe what his father had suspected, that MacNare and MacNare's father, along with their relatives, had been involved in the planning of the attack on his home. He was determined to find the proof before he killed all those he suspected of participating in the slaughter, even if it took him long years to find the truth. Until then, he would have to be content with insignificant attacks meant solely to keep them enraged.

Alec was making his duty more difficult, of course. His brother knew what Donald MacAlister had said before he died, and Alec had also tried to find proof of MacNare's treachery. When he could find nothing, he decided that the suspicion was groundless. Now he wanted the strikes against the MacNare clan to stop. Connor knew he would have to accommodate his brother, but only for a while, until Alec became reasonable again. Gaining revenge wouldn't be forgotten, and Connor's hatred wouldn't lessen, but intensify. He was, after all, his father's son.

"When did you make your decision to marry me?"

Her question jarred him back to the present. "As soon as I heard MacNare was marrying one of Haynesworth's daughters."

Would the insults never stop? "Then you didn't even know that I was the one sent to MacNare? Dear God, you didn't know, did you? The proposals had nothing to do with your decision. The jest's on you, Connor. I wasn't supposed to marry MacNare, Rachel was. She's the pretty one," she instinctively added.

"Why didn't she come?"

"The king found out and put a stop to it. He wanted Rachel to marry a baron he favored."

"And so your father substituted you."

"Yes."

He was astonished by the way things were done in England and appalled that a father could treat his daughters with such casual disregard.

"When did you find out you were going to marry him, Brenna?"

"That isn't important."

"Answer me."

"The day I left. Father told me what I was expected to do, and I took my leave a few hours later. It was wrong for you to make me think my proposals were why you came for me."

"It wasn't wrong. It will prove convenient though."

"How?"

"My brother," he answered. "He will wish to hear my reasons for marrying you."

"And you plan only to tell him I proposed? But . . ."

He interrupted her. "My brother will ask you if you did propose."

"And if I refuse to answer?"

The thought was laughable. No man, let alone a woman, had ever refused Kincaid and lived long enough to tell of it. "You won't," he assured her.

"You show me little compassion, Connor."

"Did your father show compassion when he substituted one daughter for another? Admit it, Brenna. His behavior was sinful, not mine. We don't treat our daughters with such disrespect."

"Father had his reasons. I'm certain they were very important."

"Did your king grant his permission?"

"There wasn't time enough to gain his permission. I'm certain he will be pleased."

"I'm just as certain he won't be pleased at all. Don't rail

against me or plague me with more questions, wife. I am your husband and your laird now, and you would do well to remember that. I saved you from a bleak future with a demon."

She was suddenly too furious with him to guard her words. "You have succeeded with your plan. No one will want me now. The very least you can do is let me go back home."

"Give me a son. Then you can go."

He regretted his cruelty as soon as the words were out of his mouth, but he wouldn't take them back.

And he would never let her go.

Chapter 6

She disliked him intensely until noon the following day. Then she remembered her plan to be practical. She really should try to get along with the vile man, shouldn't she? Besides, she wasn't one to wallow in misery for long periods. There were far more exciting things to think about, although admittedly, when Connor had promised her she could go back home as soon as she gave him a son, she was so outraged, she didn't believe she would ever be able to forgive him. What kind of monster was he to think she could leave her child behind?

He wasn't a monster, however. He was a man, that was all. And a stubborn, thoroughly impractical, and ignorant one as well.

Sufficient time hadn't passed to heal what she considered a grievous injury, but by afternoon she could at least look at him with less hostility.

She believed she'd come a long way in a very short while. She wasn't having murderous thoughts about her husband any longer, and she was beginning to notice he wasn't completely heartless and unfeeling. He seemed to be as concerned about Gilly as she was. He slowed their pace so her mare would be able to keep up, riding by Brenna's side

107

all the while, and every once in a while, he actually looked worried.

After they'd crossed a wide meadow carpeted in rich green clover and purple heather she thought was too lovely to tread upon, Connor slowed the pace to a walk. He called a halt a few minutes later, as soon as they reached the protection of the forest.

"Quinlan, take the others and ride ahead. Wait for us near the crest."

Brenna noticed the surprise in Quinlan's expression. He looked as if he wanted to argue with his laird, but after giving Brenna what she could only interpret as a pitying glance, he rode on ahead.

She wasn't left guessing why Quinlan was feeling sorry for her. Connor waited until his men were gone, then forced her to look at him. She imagined she saw ice chips in his eyes, so furious did he appear to be.

"You will stop frowning at me this minute."

She had to wait until he let go of her to answer. "I didn't realize I was frowning at you. Is that why we stopped?"

"No," he answered. "I wanted to ask you something."

"Yes?"

"Are you still in pain?"

She immediately lowered her gaze in embarrassment. In the blink of an eye, her face was flooded with color.

"I'm waiting for your answer."

"Must we talk about it?"

"Answer me," he ordered once again, though in a much more pleasant tone of voice.

"No, I'm not in pain."

"Was I too rough? Did I tear . . ."

"I'm fine, really. Please don't concern yourself."

"Brenna, will you get over your shyness with me soon?"

"I fervently hope so."

He found himself smiling in spite of his irritation. She'd sounded desperate.

He still wasn't completely convinced she was telling the truth about her condition, however, and therefore refused to let the subject go just yet.

"If you aren't in pain, why are you so restless in your saddle?"

She was surprised he'd noticed. He'd barely given her a glance all the while he'd ridden by her side, after all.

"I didn't realize how observant you were."

"I notice everything. So do the others, or they wouldn't be riding with me. It's one of the reasons we stay alive."

"Did you notice you broke my heart?"

He looked exasperated. "I did no such thing."

"We argued and . . ."

"We didn't argue."

"Then what did we do?"

"You asked questions. I answered them."

He really didn't understand at all. The revelation stunned her, and with it came a glimmer of hope for their future.

Perhaps Connor wasn't cruel or heartless, after all. He was just ignorant. She was blissfully relieved by her discovery.

"What else did you notice about me?" she asked.

He noticed every little thing about her, he wanted to answer her, such as the way she'd drawn her breath in when the meadow covered in a rainbow of colors first came into view, the radiant smile that came next, and then the frown when he wouldn't let her stop and explore because it would slow down his men.

"I notice you frown every time you look at me."

She let out a sigh. "I didn't understand that you didn't break my heart. I also thought we argued, but you have explained we didn't."

He nodded. "Why are you so restless in your saddle?"

He was going to make her admit her embarrassment. "There is a little tenderness," she whispered. "I've been shifting my weight to ease the discomfort."

He lifted her from Gilly onto his lap and put his arms around her. His chin dropped down on the top of her head next. "Is it better now?"

"Yes, thank you."

"I'm not going to be able to touch you tonight, am I?"

He actually sounded a little disappointed. She had trouble believing him, of course. Then she thought he might be jesting with her and looked up to see if he was smiling. His expression didn't give anything away, however, and so she asked, "You want to touch me again?"

"Of course. Why does that surprise you? I told you you didn't disappoint me, and I want children as soon as possible."

She leaned away from him. "But after we, directly after . . . You told me you weren't disappointed, but I know you weren't very happy either."

"Why would you think such a thing?"

"You rolled away and ignored me. You needn't pretend now just to make me feel better. I'm bound to improve."

"Ah, lass, you'll kill me if you do."

She turned scarlet. "Then you were happy . . . after?"

He let out a long sigh. He couldn't understand why she needed to hear him admit it.

"Yes."

"Why didn't you tell me how you felt?"

"Why would I?"

He was ignorant of women's feelings, she reminded herself so she wouldn't get angry. "You could have given me a compliment or two."

He gave her a surprised look, and she immediately recognized it. It was the same look he had given her when she'd told him she wanted to be comforted.

"I cannot guess what you want. You have to tell me, Brenna."

She shook her head at him. "I no longer have any need for compliments, so you can stop looking appalled. It only just occurred to me that I didn't compliment you either. I certainly wasn't disappointed."

"I know."

She ignored his arrogant remark. "I believe we should start over." She nodded to emphasize her conclusion before repeating it. "Yes, that's what we must do. As of this minute, we're starting all over."

What was she talking about? Start what over? If she hadn't looked so pleased with herself, and so damned happy, he probably would have demanded she explain herself.

Brenna suddenly realized how considerate it was of him to gain privacy for their intimate talk about her condition. "I'm grateful you waited until we were alone to discuss my discomfort, and I feel better because you were concerned."

"That isn't why we stopped."

She looked so disappointed, he decided to soften the truth. "It was only one of the reasons we stopped. I also wanted to talk to you about your horse."

"Gilly's worn out, isn't she?"

"Yes," he agreed. "We're going to have to leave her behind. She won't make it up the last climb," he continued on, in spite of the fact that she was vehemently shaking her head at him. His wife still didn't understand it was not proper to disagree with her husband. He hoped she'd figure that out soon.

"She's ready to collapse even now."

She knew he was right about Gilly's condition, yet she wanted him to realize what he asked of her was impossible. "My brother gave me Gilly years ago. I'm very fond of her. Surely you can understand I can't leave her behind. Couldn't we stay here until she regains some of her strength?"

"No."

"Please be reasonable."

"I am being reasonable. The horse can't possibly regain what she never had. She wasn't bred for endurance."

"But if we lingered just a little while . . . ."

"It's too dangerous to stay here. Would you put the lives of my men above those of your animal?"

Her shoulders slumped in defeat. There didn't seem to be any point in continuing to try to sway him, especially since he'd given her such a valid reason.

"I know you're right," she whispered. "I would feel terrible if something happened to your soldiers. Gilly might well injure herself if I continue to press her. I was just being selfish, I realize that now. Where should we leave her?"

"Right here is as good a place as any."

She dared to shake her head at him again. Connor was again taken aback by her defiance. In time she must learn to have faith in his judgment.

She had certainly changed since their initial meeting. 'Twas a fact she'd done a complete turnabout. She could barely speak a coherent word to him when she'd first met him, no doubt because of her fear. Now, however, she didn't

JULIE GARWOOD

seem intimidated at all. Admittedly, he wasn't sorry about
the change, for he probably wouldn't have liked being
married to a woman who trembled every time he looked at
her. He had expected Brenna to be like the other women
he'd known, and he realized now his assumption had been
wrong. She wasn't anything like the others; she was wonderfully, and exasperatingly, unique, too damned beautiful for
her own good and his peace of mind, and while he found her
boldness refreshing, he really didn't believe it was necessary
for her to tell him about every little detail in her life.

Arguing with him regarding her horse was just one
example; unfortunately there were already countless others.

"Gilly couldn't possibly survive on her own. Do pay
attention, Connor. I want you to understand. You look a bit
stunned," she added with a nod. "Have I said something to
upset you?"

He counted to ten before he answered her, hoping to calm
his rising temper. His voice still had a noticeable sting in it
when he asked, "Did you just tell me to pay attention?"

She lifted her shoulders in a dainty shrug. "I might have,"
she admitted. "And that upset you? Is that why your jaw's
clenched tight? I'll apologize if you'd like me to."

"Listen carefully," he ordered in a suspiciously soft
voice. "You do not tell your husband to pay attention." He
waited for her to nod before continuing. "I am not upset
with you, but honest to God, you do try my patience."

Because she wanted him to change his mind about Gilly,
she didn't think it would be a good idea to contradict him
now. It almost killed her to keep silent. He was such a
stubborn man, determined to have things done his way and
none other. He was also her husband, however, and so she
would try to get along with him. If he wanted to believe he
wasn't upset, she'd let him, even though it was most
apparent to her that he was. The muscle in the side of his
face was twitching, for heaven's sake, and if that wasn't a
telling sign that he was bothered, she didn't know what was.

Getting along with this impossible man was going to be
the death of her, she decided. Pride would be his downfall,
unless he learned to be less arrogant.

"Thank you for explaining," she said. She didn't sound

112

very sincere, but she didn't choke on her words either, and that had to count for something, didn't it?

"I just thought you might wish to know that Gilly is used to being pampered, and therefore won't know how to forage for food."

He was now thoroughly exasperated with her. They were talking about an animal and not a child, weren't they? His wife didn't seem to understand the difference.

He was just about to take a much firmer stand when she waylaid him by touching the side of his face. He felt as though he were being stroked by the wings of an angel. She looked like an angel too, damn it all, with those enchanting blue eyes and that innocent expression on her face. While he knew the caress had been calculated to make him forget his own thoughts, that very thing happened.

He took hold of her hand so he could concentrate. His wife was being ridiculous, of course, but he knew it would be a mistake to tell her so. She'd only increase her efforts to sway him.

Diplomacy was called for. Unfortunately, he didn't have any. "She'll be just fine," he snapped.

"She won't be fine. She'll be dead."

"You will stop arguing with me, Brenna," he said, allowing his anger to show.

She wasn't the least bit intimidated. "I'm not arguing. I'm just trying to make you understand how important Gilly is to me. She's like a member of my family. I even named her after my brother."

"He must have loved that," he said dryly.

She ignored his sarcasm. "No, Gillian didn't like it much at all, but he eventually got used to it. Can't you think of someone kind and loving to take care of her?"

"Do you think I would admit to knowing anyone kind and loving?"

She was determined not to lose her temper, no matter how much he provoked her. Gilly's welfare was at issue, after all, and she was responsible for her.

"I know of someone who might take her," Brenna offered.

"No, we aren't taking her back to England. Quinlan's

family doesn't live too far from here, but I've already replaced everything they lost. You aren't going to let this go, are you?"

"If you tell me I must, I will try. Will you at least think about your decision a little longer before you make it final?"

Connor finally conceded. "I'm not an unreasonable man, and so I have decided to think about it."

Less than a minute later, he admitted Quinlan's father would be willing to have Gilly.

She was so pleased he'd decided to cooperate, she put her arms around his neck and kissed him. She only meant to give him a quick kiss to show her gratitude, but what she meant to do and what she ended up doing were vastly different. It was all Connor's fault anyway, because he'd shown her how wonderful a kiss could be. She thought she was only following his lead, and before she could pull away or draw a proper breath, his mouth was moving over hers in a long, deep kiss that made her tremble for more in no time at all. He became more demanding and she became even more uninhibited, until her tongue was every bit as wild as his in her quest to satisfy him. The taste and texture of him mingled with his scent, and God help her, it wasn't long before she felt her control slipping away.

She forgot all about the outside world. They could have been surrounded by an army of heathens and she wouldn't have noticed, or cared. Nothing mattered but the warlord in her arms.

Fortunately, Connor didn't lose his sanity. He abruptly pulled back, then grabbed hold of her hands and forced her to stop tugging on his hair and let go of him.

He knew she didn't have any idea how shaken the kiss had left him. He told himself not to look at her mouth again until he was in complete control, but damn if he didn't look anyway. Exactly what he knew would happen did happen, of course, because he ravaged her mouth a second time to keep her from tempting him to do far more intimate things to her, and when at last he found enough strength to end it, he was furious with himself.

"You make me forget where we are, wife."

Believing he must have enjoyed the tender moments as much as she had, she smiled with pleasure.

He lost his temper then and there. "What in God's name did you think you were doing?"

The radical change in him took her breath away. "I was . . ." Lord save her, what had she been doing?

He wouldn't wait long enough for her to regain her wits. "Yes?" he demanded.

"I was showing my appreciation."

"If this is how you show your gratitude, I wonder how you were able to remain innocent until your wedding night."

She was stunned. How dare he ruin such a perfect kiss by making such a vile remark about her character?

Her temper rose to the occasion. "It's miraculous really. My father was constantly dragging me away from the men I attacked. They were all completely helpless, of course, and like you, they never kissed me back."

Her comment was laughable, given the fact that she'd been so timid and terrified on their wedding night.

Although he still thought she should learn to be more demure around him, he had to admit he continued to be impressed by her boldness in standing up to him. Didn't she understand she wasn't supposed to give him her opinion unless he asked for it? She should give him her undying loyalty and faith in everything he said or did . . . shouldn't she?

Hell, he didn't know what she was supposed to do. He'd never been married before and was basing his beliefs on observation and past experience with women he'd taken to his bed. They'd been thankful, damn it, and certainly had never shown any boldness. And he'd become bored in no time at all.

Brenna was a refreshing change from what he was used to, no doubt about it, but he didn't have the faintest idea how to get her to do what he thought she should do.

Connor wasn't certain why he tried to provoke her again, but he thought perhaps it was because he wanted to hear another of her outrageous remarks.

"Dare you try to placate me by giving me such an ignorant rebuttal?"

"Nay, Connor. I was simply trying to give you what you wanted. It was apparent to me that you were deliberately trying to make me angry. I let you succeed. You may thank me later."

His smile gave him away of course. "You really don't understand why I became irritated, do you?"

She wasn't at all happy about his amusement. "No, I don't, but I have a feeling you're going to tell me."

"It isn't proper for you to kiss me unless I have given you permission."

She could feel her spine stiffening in annoyance. "Then I won't be kissing you much in future."

"Ah, wife, you will."

The conversation abruptly ended when he shoved her face against his chest.

"Will you stop doing that?" she demanded. "It's rude."

He didn't acknowledge her demand and in fact didn't speak to her again until late that evening when they finally stopped for the night.

He waited for Brenna to notice Gilly wasn't tethered near the other horses. The woman would probably pitch a fit then and possibly weep, God help him, which he was fully prepared to stop before she started.

She didn't say a cross word to him, but after he saw the look on her face, he began to wish she were shouting at him. The sadness in her eyes was far more bothersome.

He suffered her disappointment in him throughout supper because he was determined not to explain his actions to her, but an hour later, he changed his mind. He told himself he was making this one exception because she was so fond of the mare. Hell, she'd elevated the creature to a family member.

He waited until he caught her alone near the water to talk to her.

"Brenna, I haven't betrayed you, and I want you to stop looking as though I have. It wasn't possible for me to take the time to send someone with Gilly to Quinlan's family."

"I understand." Her voice was completely devoid of emotion, and she gave her reply to the ground so she wouldn't have to look at him.

"No, you don't understand," he muttered. "MacNare and a fair number of his clan were following us, and though I would have loved a good fight, I couldn't give in to the pleasure because you would end up in the thick of it. I wasn't about to put you in such danger."

He raised his hand when she tried to interrupt him, and continued on. "However, as soon as we get home, I'll send one of my soldiers to find your mare and take her to Quinlan's father then."

"Thank you, Connor. Is our enemy close now?"

"Close enough," he answered.

"I didn't hear them."

"They weren't close enough to hear."

He was ready to dismiss the topic and turned to leave. She wasn't. "Connor?"

"Yes?"

She hurried after him, then suddenly stopped. She'd thought to kiss him on the cheek to let him know how much she appreciated his taking the time to explain the circumstances, but the memory of how he had reacted to her affection the last time was still fresh enough to hurt, and so she decided not to provoke him again.

"Thank you for confiding in me."

"Don't get used to it. It isn't customary for me to explain my actions to anyone. I doubt I'll do it again."

He seemed determined to ruin every kind moment with a nasty remark. He also had the discourteous and grating habit of walking away from her whenever he wanted to end a conversation, forcing her to chase after him.

"Are we safe now?"

"Yes."

He refused to give her any other details, such as explaining why they were safe now but hadn't been safe earlier in the day, and she was simply too worn out from trying to get along with him to attempt to coax him into giving her additional information.

She went to the creek and washed as quickly as she could. The water was much colder here than the water she'd bathed in the night before. By the time she put on fresh undergarments and stockings, even her scalp felt numb. She hadn't been able to locate the trunk filled with her gowns, but thankfully she still had two clean but wrinkled ones left in her satchel.

The cold night air was rapidly stealing what little strength she had left. She draped the shorter tunic over a bush in hopes that the damp air would ease the wrinkles out and sat down to brush her hair. She rushed through her night prayers to get them over and done with while she braided her hair, and when she was finished, she could barely find enough strength to put her shoes back on and stand up again.

She was thinking how lovely it would be to sleep in a warm bed and immediately felt guilty because poor Gilly wouldn't have a warm stable tonight. An unfamiliar noise turned her attention then. The sound had been whisper faint and seemed to come from the opposite side of the cove, although she couldn't see anything out of the ordinary. The trees were too thick, and the moon wasn't casting sufficient light down on the branches, but she was still certain she'd heard something that shouldn't have been there.

She stayed completely still, closed her eyes, and patiently waited several minutes before she heard the sound again. It was as clear as a shout to her now and very like the familiar sound of steel brushing over steel.

Men with weapons were coming their way, God help them. They weren't allies, she knew, because friends wouldn't be sneaking up on them, would they? No, of course not, she reasoned. They would shout their greeting.

She couldn't tell how many there were, but she had a feeling there were more than just a few.

She tried not to let her fear control her actions. She wanted to run as fast as her legs would carry her to warn Connor of the danger coming their way. She walked instead and tried not to make any noise at all. She'd heard them approaching, after all, and any sound she made was bound to give them her exact location.

Lord, she was scared. She called to her husband in a soft voice as soon as she reached the narrow clearing, then saw him near a cluster of trees in deep discussion with Quinlan. They obviously had sought privacy for their talk, because they stood well away from the other warriors. She could tell from their rigid stances that the issue under discussion was serious. Connor didn't like what Quinlan was telling him, as he was shaking his head every other minute in obvious disagreement.

She hurried forward and called his name again as she approached, but he put his hand up in silent command not to interrupt him and didn't even glance her way.

She couldn't wait until they finished, of course—they'd all be dead if she did—and so she braced herself for his disapproval, then reached up and pulled his hand down.

The defiant action gained his full attention. His initial irritation vanished the second he saw how frightened she was.

"What is it?"

"Soldiers are coming toward us, Connor. I couldn't see their number, but I heard them. They're trying to be quiet."

Much to her confusion, her startling announcement didn't get the reaction she'd anticipated.

Connor smiled. "You actually heard them?"

It was apparent he hadn't grasped the ramifications yet. "Yes, I heard them. I don't believe they're allies. They wouldn't care about making noise if they were, would they? We should leave with all possible haste. Why are you smiling? Don't you understand the danger we're in?"

She guessed he didn't understand when he didn't immediately move. She hadn't thought him at all slow-witted until now, and unfortunately, his friend seemed to suffer the same affliction. In fact, he was worse. He was having so much difficulty comprehending their dire situation, he laughed.

She felt like throwing her hands up in despair. She settled on wringing them together instead. "Connor, I'm . . . concerned."

"You have no reason to be concerned."

Connor usually didn't notice how a woman was groomed, but he couldn't seem to stop staring at his wife's hair now. He couldn't imagine what she'd tried to accomplish. Honest to God, he'd never seen anything quite like it.

He considered himself to be an astute man, however, and knew Brenna had extremely tender feelings, so he was careful to sound only mildly curious and not critical when he asked her to explain what she'd done. "What the hell have you done to your hair, wife? Did you mean to tie it in knots all over your head?"

She couldn't believe he wanted to talk about her appearance. "My braid? You want to discuss my braid?"

"Ah, so it's a braid," he said. "I hadn't realized."

She started backing away from him. She shook her head several times, and every time she moved, one of the knots came undone. "Can't you see how worried I am?" she cried out.

He couldn't imagine why she was worried, unless she hadn't been paying attention to him when he'd told her not to be concerned. Or had she heard and chosen not to believe him?

He wasn't going to lecture her, no matter how much she provoked him. No, he would simply help her reason it all out in her mind. She was an intelligent woman; it wouldn't take her any time at all.

"Exactly why are you worried?"

She was overwhelmed by his incomprehension and was, for the moment, rendered speechless. No one could be this obtuse, not even warlords.

Quinlan couldn't keep silent a moment longer. He felt he was far more astute than his laird in matters concerning women, and so he naturally sought to lend his counsel before his laird put his foot in his mouth and injured his lady's delicate feelings. "I believe your wife is still upset about the men she heard approaching. She might have thought we were in jeopardy."

Brenna was vigorously nodding her head in agreement when Connor denied the possibility. "No, my wife wouldn't dare insult me that way," he replied, keeping his gaze directed on her all the while. "She knows I'll protect her from harm. Isn't that so, Brenna?"

No, it wasn't so. How would she know if he was capable of protecting anyone or not? Just because he looked like a warlord from hell didn't mean he could fight like one. She didn't think it would be a good idea to tell him her thoughts, though. The way he stared at her made caution a much wiser choice, and she found herself nodding just to placate him.

The remaining knots came apart then, and her hair was once again where Connor wanted it to be, in soft curls down about her shoulders.

Brenna was just about to leave when the truth dawned on her. "You knew those men were there."

Connor looked at her, but said nothing.

"How long have you known?" she demanded.

"Since they joined us."

"They aren't your enemies."

"Of course not."

"Why didn't you tell me?" she demanded. "You should have."

"I should?"

"You're supposed to tell your wife important news."

He shook his head. Where in God's name did she come by these ideas? "I think not."

"I think so."

Connor couldn't believe she'd contradicted him. He gave her a hard stare and folded his arms across his chest.

Quinlan knew what that meant. His laird was getting angry. It was only a matter of time now before Connor said something he would later regret. Because he was Connor's friend, Quinlan couldn't let that happen. "Mi'lady, may I suggest you put your plaid on?" he asked. "Your husband wouldn't want you to catch a chill."

She looked as though she hadn't heard him and her attention remained focused on her husband. The tension between the two continued to build, for their gazes were locked on each other. Connor's was challenging, Brenna's was defiant, and neither one of them appeared willing to back down.

"The air's damp tonight," Quinlan interjected in yet another attempt to get his mistress's attention. "We're in for a fierce thunderstorm." His last comment did the trick. Quinlan felt like sighing with relief when Lady Brenna finally looked at him.

"Of course it's going to rain," she said. "It's a fitting end to a hellishly long day. Have you seen my trunk, Quinlan? I'm in need of my heavy cloak."

"You'll wear my plaid," Connor told her.

He hadn't raised his voice to her, but she acted as though he had by backing farther away from him. "My trunk, Quinlan?" she reminded the soldier.

"We left it behind with your saddle, mi'lady."

"Please go and get it for me."

Quinlan turned to Connor to judge his reaction to her request before answering.

His laird shook his head but remained stubbornly silent, much to Quinlan's consternation, leaving him to fend for himself. "It isn't possible for me to go and get it for you. We left it behind several hours ago, and we've traveled a fair distance since then, over rough terrain, if you'll remember. We had to leave it, mi'lady," he quickly added when he noticed the look in her eyes. "The wagon wouldn't have made it up the narrow climb."

"Why did you leave it behind without asking my permission first?"

"By your laird's command," he explained, thinking that important fact would end the discussion once and for all. He was mistaken. Lady Brenna wasn't ready to let it go.

"Didn't it occur to either one of you that there might be some important reason why I wanted to keep the trunk?"

If she'd given him time to think of a reply, Quinlan was sure he would have thought of something appropriate to say to her, but she didn't give him time. His mistress's outrage seemed to be gathering momentum as she continued. "My sister Joan gave me the trunk and I had planned to put my children's clothes inside. I treasure it."

Quinlan suddenly felt about as low and inadequate as an Englishman must feel every time he looked in a mirror. He turned to his laird again, willing him with his hard stare and a slight nudge to take over the battle. Damn it all, Quinlan wasn't married to the distraught woman. Connor was. Let him suffer her disappointment.

Connor continued to stay stonily silent, however. "Mi'lady, it was necessary," Quinlan said. "Isn't that right, Laird?"

Brenna didn't particularly care what her husband had to say about it. She was too disheartened to listen to anyone any longer. The injustices done to her in the past several days were taking their toll now, and she thought that if she didn't get away from her husband for a few minutes, she'd start screaming.

She didn't bother to excuse herself; she simply walked away. A sudden thought made her stop. "My saddle, Quinlan? Did you say you also left the saddle my dear sister Rachel loaned to me?"

"Did you have another one, Brenna?" Connor asked dryly.

Lord, how she hated his condescending, be-reasonable tone. "No, I didn't," she answered.

"Mi'lady, it was also necessary to leave your sister's saddle behind," Quinlan blurted out.

"I treasured it too," she whispered.

Quinlan's shoulders slumped. He had known she would say that.

"I cannot help but wonder why you didn't ask my permission first, though."

Quinlan vowed not to say another word. He stared at his laird, imitated his threatening stance by folding his arms across his chest, and simply waited.

Connor didn't take the hint fast enough to please his friend. "Wouldn't you like to answer *your wife?*" Quinlan sounded downright desperate.

Connor let his friend see his exasperation before turning to Brenna. "I wouldn't be laird if I asked permission before I made decisions, especially insignificant ones. You were merely curious, weren't you? You wouldn't show disapproval of your husband's actions in front of his followers. Isn't that right?"

She surprised him by agreeing. "Yes, I was simply curious, and no, I would never criticize you in front of your followers. Do you have the patience to endure one more question, husband?"

"What is it?"

"When do you suppose you'll leave me behind?"

Connor's mood darkened in the space of a heartbeat. He took a threatening step forward and briskly ordered her to come to him. Quinlan moved back, looked to the heavens, and began to pray for divine intervention. His mistress had never seen Connor lose his temper, and though Quinlan knew his laird would never physically harm her, or any other woman for that matter, he could do considerable damage to her heart.

He wouldn't be cruel, though, and for that reason, Quinlan didn't try to intervene. The fat was in the fire now, and she had placed it there when she deliberately provoked her husband by asking him such an atrocious question. She would have to suffer the consequences of her actions, and by moving a little distance away from the two of them, Quinlan hoped she would realize he wouldn't, and couldn't, come to her assistance.

Connor didn't have any intention of losing his temper, for he knew that his bride was worn out. The shadows under her eyes indicated her exhaustion. He was fully responsible for her condition, of course, and believed the only thing he could do about it now was force her to bed. Getting her to relax enough to sleep was going to be a little more difficult. She'd have to get rid of the tension inside her first, and perhaps arguing would serve that purpose. A good fight always left him feeling relaxed, and while he admitted he didn't know anything at all about how gentlewomen like Brenna would react, he didn't believe there was any harm in letting her rail at him. Once she was rested, she would become reasonable again, or so he hoped, and then she would beg his forgiveness.

"You're being unreasonable, Brenna."

"I believe I'm being very reasonable."

"You do? Then explain your reason for asking me such a question. Did your sainted parents leave you behind?" He fully expected a denial, of course.

She gave him the truth instead. "As a matter of fact, they did." As soon as the words were out of her mouth, she regretted them. Now Connor was going to have an even lower opinion of her dear parents.

"They didn't leave me on purpose. They just forgot. Surely you see the difference."

"Do you expect me to believe they forgot you? No parents would leave their child behind, even English parents."

"Your wife looks as though she means what she says," Quinlan interjected. "Did they leave you at home, mi'lady?"

She shook her head. "I spoke in haste."

"Then you exaggerated?" Connor asked, thinking he was being considerate because he hadn't asked her to admit she'd lied to him.

"You're making this more important than it was. I wish I'd never said a word now, because you're going to think ill of my mother and father. You just don't understand. It only happened a couple of times, and they were still loving parents. They had eight children, and with so many, they were bound to forget about one of us every now and again. It was all my own fault anyway. I should have stayed with the others."

"They left you twice?"

The bit of added information she'd mentioned had stunned him.

"You look furious, and I cannot imagine why. You weren't left behind. I was, and I assure you, it didn't bother me at all."

"Of course it bothered you," he countered. "Did they ever forget any of the others?"

"No, but I tended to wander . . ."

He wouldn't listen to any excuses. "Where did these loving parents leave you?"

The pigheaded man was never going to understand, and she was suddenly too tired to keep on trying to make him. Lord, he was a trial, and if she didn't find a little peace and quiet soon, she was going to start screaming like a madwoman.

Connor didn't look as if he was in any mood to leave, and so she decided she would.

He had other inclinations. He wasn't going to let her walk away from him until she satisfied his curiosity. "I want an answer."

"I have finished discussing this topic."

The look he gave her suggested she change her mind.

"Honestly, Connor, you're just like a flea chasing after a hound. My parents left me in the middle of the countryside. Are you happy now? Or was there something more embarrassing you wanted me to admit?"

She didn't wait around long enough to find out. She

didn't bother to ask permission to leave either, but she couldn't seem to stop herself from bowing her head to both men before she walked away. She blamed the courtesy on her mother because she'd been relentless in her attempts to turn her daughters into proper ladies.

Owen called out to his mistress as she passed him. "Mi'lady, if you're looking for water, it's in the opposite direction."

She answered the soldier, but her voice wasn't strong enough to carry across the clearing.

"Now what?" Connor muttered as soon as he saw how startled Owen looked. The soldier glanced his way before chasing after his mistress.

Quinlan didn't dare smile, though he was vastly amused by the resignation he'd heard in Connor's voice. "Owen looked surprised. Your wife must have said something to alarm him."

"Of course she did," Connor replied. "Honest to God, Quinlan, she's a damned nuisance."

In Quinlan's estimation, she was still just about perfect. Connor didn't realize his blessing yet, but Quinlan could tell from the way Connor studied his wife with such a perplexed look on his face that he was already captivated by her. He obviously didn't like the way he reacted to her if his dark mood of late was any indication. From what Quinlan had observed about his mistress, he could only conclude she was having just as much difficulty understanding her reaction to her husband.

"She's going to cause quite a disturbance at home."

"I can't let that happen."

"I'm not sure you can stop it from happening," Quinlan said. "The men will have trouble concentrating on their duties. They'll want to spend their days staring at your wife, and their women won't like it much. Have you any idea how beautiful she is, or haven't you taken the time to notice?"

"I'm not blind; of course I noticed. Her appearance is yet another flaw I must contend with."

"I don't see it as such."

"You're a shallow man. That's why you don't see it as such."

Quinlan thoroughly appreciated the insult and smiled in reaction.

"Laird?" Owen shouted. "May I have a moment of your time? It's important."

He waited for Connor's approval before coming forward. "Mi'lady told me she wasn't going to the creek. She's going to get her trunk. Then she thought she might want to walk all the way back to England. Those were her very words to me, and given with a smile, mind you. I tried to dissuade her, but she wouldn't listen to reason. Do you think she really means to try?"

Connor didn't answer the soldier. He doubted Owen would hear a word he said anyway, as Quinlan's laughter was gratingly loud. He considered shoving his friend to the ground just for the sheer hell of it, then decided he couldn't really fault him. Connor would find Brenna's independence amusing too, if he weren't married to the impossible woman; but he was married to her, and that made everything different.

Why couldn't she be more agreeable? Her impulsiveness was going to drive him to distraction. She surprised him every time he turned around, and he didn't like it at all. She should be more predictable, shouldn't she? Oh, he should have known she was going to be trouble the minute he met her. Hell, his wife was thoroughly unique. Connor wasn't a fool; he realized his good fortune. Still, he wished she would hurry up and get used to him; once she did, she'd calm down enough for him to be able to concentrate on more important matters.

He was beginning to think he would never understand how her mind worked. How could he when she was constantly changing on him? One minute she was soft and willing, and the next, she was stubborn and difficult.

He couldn't be expected to put up with a whirlwind. Most men surely wouldn't have been as patient as he'd been, but he was finished with that now. He could take only so much provocation in one day, and he had had his fill.

"I wonder if Lady Brenna realizes she's going the wrong way," Quinlan remarked. "She'll be knocking on Kincaid's door if she keeps walking through the night."

"Mi'lady knows she's going north," Owen said. "She told me she's deliberately making a wide circle so as not to disturb the soldiers patrolling the creek."

Quinlan turned to Connor. "Shouldn't you go after your wife?"

"My brother's soldiers won't let her get far."

"I believe she expects you to come after her."

"The hell with that," he muttered.

He contradicted his own decision a second later, when he shoved the two men aside and went striding after his wife.

He had to go farther than he'd expected. He found her leaning against a tree a fair distance away from the clearing. She looked defeated. He didn't like to see her like that, especially when he realized he was largely responsible. Still, he was still thankful she wasn't weeping.

She put her hand up in a silent command to stop him from coming any closer, which he completely ignored, and as soon as he reached her, he lifted her into his arms.

He expected her to fight him; she surprised him by putting her arms around his neck and resting her head against his shoulder. She was suddenly soft and willing again.

"My brother told me no woman in her right mind would marry me, and if you really meant to go after your trunk, I would have to say . . . ?"

"That I'm not in my right mind?" she responded. "If I'm demented, it's all your fault. You pushed me right over the edge, Connor."

He smiled in spite of himself. His wife said the most outrageous things to him.

"You meant to keep on walking?"

"No. I meant to have a few minutes alone. You knew that, didn't you?"

No, he hadn't known, but he decided to pretend he had. "Yes," he said.

"I was never alone, though. You knew that too, didn't you?"

"I did."

"Who are the two soldiers following me?"

"My brother's sentries. You're on Alec's land, if you'll remember."

She didn't remember any such thing. She yawned then and turned her attention to a more worrisome problem. "I seem to have misplaced my shoe. I can't imagine how it happened."

He didn't have any trouble imagining it at all. She was constantly leaving her things about. "I'll find it," he promised. "Brenna, what was it really all about back there? Do you know?"

"Do you mean to ask me if I had another reason for becoming upset?"

He had just asked her that very question, hadn't he? "Yes," he said.

She began to rub the back of his neck while she thought about how she could make him understand. Connor doubted she was even aware of what she was doing, but he found the caresses very pleasing.

"I understand now what was bothering me. I didn't understand then."

He rolled his eyes heavenward. Getting a straight answer out of her was turning into strenuous work. "And?" he prodded.

"The trunk and the saddle and my mare were all gifts from members of my family. You're trying to take them away from me, and I can't let you do that. I'm not ready to let go."

"Exactly what am I taking away?"

"My family."

"Brenna . . ."

She wouldn't let him continue. "You are trying to take them away, aren't you? And if I let you succeed, what will I have left?"

"Me."

The impact of what he said struck her, and yet she still tried to resist the truth. She didn't want him; she wanted her family.

"You have me." His voice was hard now, insistent.

She looked up at him then, and her childish resolution to cling to the old and the familiar seemed to lose its importance. The look in his eyes mesmerized her. There was such tenderness and vulnerability there.

"Do I have you, Connor?"

"Aye, lass, you do."

She smiled then, her doubts gone. He had surely spoken from his heart, or so she believed, and her own heart warmed in reaction. She had seen this side of him only once before, on their wedding night, when he'd taken her into his arms and made love to her. The warlord had vanished then, and she had embraced the man. Now he was giving her this magical gift once again. How could she resist him?

She nodded her acceptance, her mind at peace, because she finally understood that what she was doing was both holy and right, made so by the church and God himself the minute Father Sinclair had united them as husband and wife, and although she'd been telling herself she would make the best of her circumstances, she admitted now she hadn't really accepted the marriage.

It was time for her to stop fearing her future and let go of her desperate hold on her past, and as soon as she made the decision to do just that, the most wondrous thing happened to her. She willingly gave herself to him.

"You have me now, Connor MacAlister, because I have decided that you should."

She sealed her promise with a kiss, in spite of his specific order that she must never, ever kiss him without first gaining permission, and when she'd finished, she tucked her head under his chin and closed her eyes.

He was never again going to be surprised by anything she said, Connor thought. She'd decided? Aye, those had been her very words all right.

"You and I are starting over," she whispered.

Here we go again, he thought to himself. He still didn't understand what she was talking about, but if she'd asked him for his agreement, he would have given it just to make her happy. He really shouldn't have cared if she was happy or not, but he did care. He consoled himself with his hope that once she adjusted to her new life, she would stop having such peculiar ideas.

Connor leaned back against the tree and stared down at his wife. She seemed serene now, which meant he was finally going to get some peace and quiet and could figure out what in hell he would say to his brother tomorrow, and wasn't that all that mattered anyway?

"Connor?"

"Yes?" he asked.

"I'll take good care of you."

He was stunned by this promise, and though he probably should have been insulted, because it was his duty to take care of her and not the other way around, she'd sounded so sincere, he knew she meant to please him.

She fell asleep before he could set her straight. She moved closer to him until her soft mouth was pressed against the base of his neck. She tightened her hold on him as well, and he realized he liked the way she tried to get as close as she could to him. He liked the way she sighed in her sleep too. When her guard wasn't up and she wasn't trying to argue with him every other minute, she became sweet and loving. She was beginning to trust him, he knew, or she wouldn't have allowed herself to fall asleep in his arms, and with a smile. He realized he liked that most of all.

Connor didn't have any idea how long he lingered in the forest holding his wife. The sound of thunder rumbling in the distance forced him back to more practical matters, and he picked up her misplaced shoe and started back to camp.

He was in a much better mood by the time he reached the others. His men had built a tent large enough to accommodate three grown men and had covered it with thick animal skins loyal allies had given them on their way to collect Brenna. The tent had been strategically placed at the far end of the clearing, with the entrance facing the forest so that his wife would be assured of privacy when she awakened.

In one corner of the tent were the possessions Brenna had left by the creek. Connor added her shoes and stockings to the pile.

She was sleeping so soundly, she didn't stir at all while he saw to the task of removing her clothes. Too late, he realized he should have left her alone. As soon as he untied the ribbon holding the top of her undergarment together, the material parted all the way down to her waist, and a fair amount of her full breasts spilled out. It was impossible for him not to react physically. From the moment he'd awakened early that morning, he'd wanted her again; now the need consumed him. He fought his private battle for a long while, but in the middle of the night, while the storm raged around them, she moaned in her sleep, rolled over, and threw herself on top of him. He knew, then, the war wasn't finished. She couldn't even be cautious in her sleep.

His hand went to her thighs, and as he was parting them with the thought of entering her then and there, he realized what he was doing and forced himself to stop.

He jarred her awake trying to get her off of him before he hurt her. She sat up next to his side and, obviously disoriented by the pounding of the rain upon the skins, whispered his name.

"It's all right, Brenna. Go back to sleep." He sounded angry. He was sorry about that, but damn it all, he'd only just realized he had the discipline of a pig. She wasn't helping him regain his control, of course. One side of her chemise had just dropped down to her elbow, and God help him, it took all his strength not to tear the thing off her. Every time lightning streaked across the sky, light poured in through the opening, outlining her beautiful body.

She fell asleep sitting up. Had he not been observing her, he wouldn't have believed anyone could fall asleep so quickly.

"Lie down," he ordered with a gentle nudge.

He should have been more specific, he realized a scant second after she threw herself down on top of him again, hitting his chest hard enough to make him think she'd knocked herself senseless.

"Get off of me."

His gruff voice awakened her. "No," she whispered.

"No?"

"No, thank you," she corrected. "I'm cold. Shouldn't you do something about it?"

God save him, she was even telling him what to do when she was half asleep.

"What would you have me do?"

"Put your arms around me."

He felt her shivering and immediately did as she had instructed him to do.

"Did I wake you, Connor?"

"No."

"Are you cold?"

132

"No."

She began to stroke his chest, hoping her gentle touch would calm him. Perhaps then he would tell her why he was acting so prickly.

"What are you doing?"

"Soothing you."

She had to be jesting with him. Soothing? She was slowly driving him out of his mind, and he was fairly certain she was doing it on purpose.

"Stop provoking me."

"What's wrong with you? You're acting like a bear."

He didn't try to address the ludicrous comparison she'd just made, concentrating instead on making her realize what she was doing to him. "I want to be inside you again. Now do you understand why you should get the hell off me?"

She didn't move. "Do I have a say in the matter?"

"Yes."

"Do you mean to say that if I told you no, you would honor my wishes?"

Hadn't he just said he would? "If you tell me no, I won't touch you."

She started drumming her fingertips on his chest. He immediately put his hand on top of hers to get her to stop. "You'd best learn to be cautious, Brenna."

She didn't pay any attention to his instruction. "In England, wives can't deny their husbands. My mother told me so."

"Some men think the way I do."

She was amazed. She suddenly felt as though he'd given her the wondrous gift of power over her own body, and she immediately wanted more. "Regarding other matters then, do I . . ."

"No."

"Why not?"

"You cannot deny a command given to you by your laird."

She'd already done exactly that on several occasions now and had suffered no ill effects from denying her laird's orders, but she was intelligent enough not to remind him.

She couldn't stop herself from straightening out his rather twisted reasoning though.

"I didn't marry a laird. I married a man."

"It is the same."

No, it wasn't the same at all, she thought to herself. Oh, she knew what was expected of her when they were with other people, but when they were alone, he was simply her husband. She didn't believe it would be a good idea to correct his backhanded reasoning now and would wait instead until he was in a better mood.

"If I were to tell you yes, I would like you to touch me again, would it end the same way? Would you turn away from me without saying a word?"

"Of course," he replied.

"Never mind then."

He was stunned by her denial and couldn't understand why his praise had angered her.

She moved away from him, closed her eyes, and said a prayer for patience.

He rolled over on top of her, careful to brace his weight with his arms as he stared down into her eyes. "I told you I wasn't disappointed."

"You were also angry though, weren't you?"

Aye, he had been angry, though not with his wife. His fury had been self-directed, and upon reflection, he realized it was purposeful as well, for he had it as a shield to guard himself against his own vulnerability. She had dared to touch his heart, and honest to God, he still didn't know how he'd let that happen. Damn it, he didn't even like her.

Connor was quick to recognize his lie and let out a low growl of frustration. He decided then that since what had already happened couldn't be undone, as long as he stayed in control in the future, he would be content.

"Are you ever going to answer me?"

He leaned down and began to nibble on her earlobe, feeling arrogantly pleased when he noticed she shivered in reaction. "What did you ask?"

She couldn't believe he would treat her concerns so lightly. She repeated her question and added a nudge to get him to pay attention.

"I wasn't angry with you."

He could see she didn't believe him. His wife obviously needed more praise for her performance, he supposed. He wasn't sure what to say that would make her happy. He had been satisfied. And well-served, he admitted. She surely knew he never would have left her until both of them had reached fulfillment. He wasn't at all used to explaining anything to anyone, however, and perhaps that was why he wasn't any good at it, he reasoned. He needed to say something now, though, and so he decided to sum up his reactions with one word that would certainly convince her she had proven satisfactory.

"Finished."

"I beg your pardon?"

"I was finished."

Because of their close proximity, he'd naturally been considerate and spoken in a low voice. His wife wasn't as considerate. She shouted her displeasure into his ear. "You are the most pigheaded, insensitive, barbaric . . ."

He clamped his hand down over her mouth before she could finish giving him her opinion. She could have come up with another hundred remarks too, if he'd kept silent and let her think of some, but he interrupted her concentration by asking her the most appalling question, and she had to think about giving him an answer sure to destroy his pride for a full month.

"Do you want me to make love to you again?" He lifted his hand away from her mouth.

"When hell freezes over." She didn't actually shout, but her voice was still loud enough for his men to hear.

"You will not shout at me ever again. Is that understood?"

"It is," she answered.

"My hearing is never going to be the same."

"I'm sorry. What you said took me by surprise and I . . . Finished, Connor? Is that how you thought to reassure me?"

"It was a compliment. I was obviously satisfied with you or I wouldn't have been finished. I'm a man of few words, Brenna."

"I've noticed."

He turned his attention to the rewarding pleasure of kissing her.

"I don't usually feel so unsure of myself," she whispered. "But it was my first time."

"I noticed."

He kissed his way down the side of her neck.

"Why are you doing that?"

"I like the way you taste."

She shifted her position to give him better access to her shoulder. "How do I taste?"

"Like honey."

He heard her sigh in the darkness. It would have been easy for him to take her by surprise, but he would never do such a dishonorable thing. Brenna was going to have to give him permission, and if she didn't give it soon, he would have to leave her while he had enough discipline.

"Do you know what I think?" she whispered.

"No, but you're going to tell me, aren't you?"

"I don't want you to—never mind. I mean to say that I . . ." She couldn't go on, for Connor had just reached the valley between her breasts, distracting her entirely.

"You're soft everywhere. You make me burn to have you."

She thought his words were wonderfully romantic. For a man of few words, he was doing exceptionally well at giving her exactly what she longed to hear.

"Is there anything you don't like about me?"

"Aye, there is," he whispered. "You talk too much."

"You turn my head with your flowery words, husband. Make love to me now."

"I'll hurt you."

He didn't *seem* concerned about her discomfort though, for he'd already pushed her chemise down to her hips. He paused to kiss each of her knees before finishing his task of ridding her of her undergarment.

His hands were everywhere. He stroked her legs, her thighs, her hips, and her breasts. His gentle touch was maddening and made her restless for more. She wanted to caress him with the same care he was showing her and was about to demand he let go of her when he snatched the very thought right out of her mind by leaning down and kissing her breasts. His tongue brushed over one nipple, and she thought she would die from the exquisite torment, and then he began to suckle. She squeezed her eyes shut and made a sound very like a whimper.

Her stomach was just as sensitive to his touch, and then he moved lower. She couldn't imagine what he thought he was going to do, until he was there, at the junction of her thighs. She kept her legs locked together to keep him from going further. He forced them apart and continued to do what he wanted to do, and she was soon too caught up in the rush of ecstasy his mouth and his tongue evoked to be properly appalled.

He made love to her in ways she'd never, ever imagined possible. She couldn't make herself stop arching up against him. She raised her knees and cried out when she felt herself begin to tighten around him.

He couldn't wait any longer to be inside her. He knelt between her thighs then, lifted her hips, and entered her with one powerful thrust. He tried to remember to be gentle with her, but damn, his control had deserted him again and it was impossible to hold anything back. He wanted it to last all night. She wouldn't let him slow down though. She drove him on with her sweet cries and her passionate kisses. He didn't know if he was hurting her or pleasuring her. Her climax forced his own, and once he'd given her his seed, he didn't have enough strength left to keep from collapsing on top of her.

She was in much the same condition. Her breathing was uneven, her heart was pounding a frantic beat, and she was trembling all over. It took her long minutes to make herself stop sighing and start thinking again. Then she wished she hadn't bothered. Reason meant worrying, and dear God, how could she ever look at him again after what she'd begged him to keep doing to her?

She had acted like an animal in heat, hadn't she? She was suddenly desperate for reassurance before her embarrassment turned into shame. She wouldn't beg or demand he convince her that what they'd done had been all right, or let him know she was at all embarrassed now. He might say things just to appease her then, and not mean any of it.

She'd catch him by surprise, she decided, so that he wouldn't guard his reaction.

"Connor?" God help her, even her voice was trembling. "Are you dead then?"

He smiled against her neck. "No."

"Did you hurt me?"

She couldn't believe she'd asked him such an absurd question. She'd meant to tell him he hadn't hurt her, hadn't she?

It was apparent to him that she hadn't quite recovered from their lovemaking just yet. He was arrogantly satisfied, of course, because he was fully responsible for her condition.

His heat was making her drowsy. She didn't want to fall asleep before she'd gotten rid of her embarrassment and meant only to close her eyes so she could concentrate.

"Do you know what just happened?"

She smiled in anticipation, for surely he was now going to give her the reassurance she needed. She should have known better.

"Hell just froze over."

Chapter

Chapter
7

*B*renna was in a fit mood the following morning. The rain had ended, the sun was bright, and no one, not even Connor, could put a wrinkle in her happiness.

It kept getting better too. Although the men smiled while they watched her eat her morning meal, they didn't comment on her appetite, and after she returned from the creek dressed in the MacAlister plaid, Quinlan complimented her on the perfect pleats she'd made in the woolen material. He seemed to think she'd only just acquired the art.

She felt it was her duty to correct him. "My father made Rachel learn how to fashion a plaid because she was supposed to marry Laird MacNare, but Mother thought it would be a good idea for all of her daughters to master the technique. My parents did like to get as much as they could for their coins."

"Your sister was promised to MacNare?"

She nodded. "She was indeed. Connor might have ended up married to Rachel. She's the pretty one in our family," she thought to add.

Quinlan couldn't imagine there was any other woman more pleasing to the eye than his mistress. He had already noticed she wasn't vain, and her comment only confirmed his belief.

"Will it be another long day's ride?"

"No, mi'lady. We're very close to home now."

The news thrilled her. Her smile proved to be contagious, for when Quinlan glanced at the others, they were all smiling too.

She excused herself from his company as soon as she spotted Connor leading his horse across the clearing. She ran to her husband, put her arms around his neck, gave him an enthusiastic good morning kiss, and then remembered she shouldn't show him any affection in front of others. Surprisingly, he neither snapped nor growled at her. 'Twas a fact he kissed her back.

He did criticize her afterward, of course. It seemed to be a natural inclination of his, she decided and was, therefore, unperturbed.

"You are without discipline." He then lifted her up onto his horse, swung up behind her, and settled her on his thighs. "Aren't you going to argue with me?"

"It's too fine a day to argue. You are wrong, of course. I have as much discipline as you do."

"I haven't seen any yet. Stop twisting about and lean back against me."

"My rope's twisted." After explaining her problem, she pulled the necklace up, straightened the rope, and then let the wooden disk drop back down under her plaid.

"What in God's name is that thing?"

"Have you only just noticed it?"

"No. I've only just decided to ask you about it."

"The necklace is a gift from my father. I have my very own design to prove it belongs to me, and if I'm ever in trouble, I need only send the disk to one of my sisters or brothers for immediate assistance. Father had them made for all of his children."

"Get rid of it."

Her gasp was enough to upset the stallion. He reared his head up and let out a snort of indignation. She reached down and patted him. "I'll do no such thing, Connor. I plan to have one made for you too."

"You will not."

"It's a tradition."

"It's an insult to me, wife."

"We shall discuss this matter when we are home."

"We're through discussing it."

She didn't disagree with him. He was wrong about that too, she thought to herself. The man was going to listen to reason and accept the tradition, even if it took her a good week of nagging. "Why are we waiting?"

He knew she was deliberately changing the topic, but he went along just to get her to stop arguing with him. He wanted her cooperation today. She was about to meet Kincaid, and that would be unsettling for her. His brother did have a way of terrifying everyone he met. It was yet another reason why Connor so admired him.

"Owen went to the creek to collect whatever was left behind."

"That was thoughtful of him," she replied. "Still, your men shouldn't leave their things about for anyone to take."

He thought she was jesting, and he waited for her to laugh. She didn't, though, and once he realized she was sincere, he didn't explain it to her. A minute later Owen returned with his mistress's belongings. He put them in her satchel, then tied the baggage to Aeden's horse. She never noticed. Connor wasn't at all surprised, of course, for his wife seemed to walk around in a daze most of the time.

His thoughts returned to Alec then. "You will meet my brother today. He won't hurt you."

She thought his remark extremely peculiar. "I would never worry about such a thing."

"You will when you meet him. You'd best find some of this discipline you boast of having, Brenna. Do not disgrace me by crying or fainting."

She rolled her eyes heavenward. "I shall like him because he's your brother, and it's my duty to get along with all of your family. He won't intimidate me."

"Yes, he will. He isn't as pleasant as I am."

She burst into laughter. He gave up trying to caution her then and turned his attention to more important matters, such as learning how to be diplomatic before it was time to explain his actions to the man who ruled the Highlands.

A full hour passed in silence before she spoke again.

"Connor?"

"Yes?"

"Have you ever seen me cry or faint?"

"No."

"Then please explain your reason for insulting me? I'm most curious to hear it."

He didn't answer her.

If he wouldn't explain, the least he could do was apologize. She knew she would never get him to, though, because he was too stubborn to ever admit he might have misjudged her.

Proving him wrong would be enough to repair the damage he'd done to her pride. It would be easy to accomplish, for she had been properly trained and fully understood what was expected of her. She would let Connor see how unafraid she was when she greeted his brother. Surely, she would like him. He was part of her family now, after all, and God willing, if she could just remember not to speak until she was spoken to and behave with a little humility, he would like her too.

A few minutes later, the fortress came into view. Her breath caught in the back of her throat at first sight of the magnificent structure. A tall stone wall surrounded the fortress that must have taken half a century to build. Two soldiers, wearing expressions as cold and forbidding as the wall they guarded, watched them cross the drawbridge.

She thought it odd they didn't speak to Connor, then decided they were waiting for him to give them permission.

There were hundreds more of the frightening warriors inside the lower bailey. None of them welcomed Connor either.

"Is one of those men scowling at us your brother, perchance?"

"No."

"Is it always so quiet here?"

"No."

Connor wasn't in the mood to expound. She decided to follow his example and not say another word. She would have held to her decision too if she hadn't been taken by surprise when they reached the upper courtyard and she saw the beautiful flowers bordering the front of the castle.

"It's lovely here," she whispered. "Who planted the flowers?"

"Jamie."

She vowed to keep quiet. "I hope he was well rewarded for his efforts."

"Not *he, she,*" Connor corrected. "Don't step on them or you'll never hear the end of it."

"Servants may voice their opinions then?"

"Jamie isn't a servant. She's mistress here."

She would have fallen off the horse if Connor hadn't tightened his hold around her waist. "Mistress?"

"You'll like her."

She didn't even try to pray for patience. "I will not like her. You're going to have to make her leave, Connor. There can only be one mistress in my home."

"Jamie is mistress of Alec's home."

"Then why did she plant flowers for you? It was of course very thoughtful of her, but I cannot help wondering why she went to such trouble."

He finally understood what was at the root of her misconception. "This isn't my land. It's Alec's. How could you think it was?"

She felt like screaming but didn't dare speak above a whisper because of the audience watching them like hawks. "I'll tell you exactly why I thought it was your home. I was told we were going home, that's why, and since no one bothered to inform me you meant to pay a call on your brother, I naturally concluded this belonged to you."

"It doesn't."

"So I now understand," she agreed. "It would have been thoughtful of you to mention our destination."

Connor didn't respond to her veiled criticism.

The courtyard was quickly filling up with warriors. All of them were dressed in plaids with muted colors so similar to Connor's she knew she was going to get them mixed up and not be able to tell a Kincaid soldier from a MacAlister.

They were all staring at Connor and her. She straightened her spine until it felt as though it was going to snap, stared straight ahead, and tried to look serene. The welcome they were receiving was most discouraging. Was everyone who lived in the Highlands always in such a bad mood? These soldiers surely were. Their attitude was also puzzling. Connor was Alec's brother, for heaven's sake, not his enemy. Didn't the difference matter to these heathens?

Her husband dismounted first before turning to assist her. She stared into his eyes, looking for a sign that everything was going to be all right. He didn't blink or give her any indication at all of what he was thinking. She didn't squeeze herself up against him as she wanted to, but walked behind her husband with her hands down at her sides, her head held high, and her gaze fully directed on the center of his back.

Quinlan and Aeden moved to flank her on either side, while Donald, Owen, and Giric followed behind. When they reached the steps leading up to the entrance, Connor continued on, but Brenna and the others were forced by Kincaid soldiers to stay behind.

His brother obviously wanted to speak to Connor in private before she was introduced to him. She hoped they took a long, long while, as she now dreaded her audience with Alec Kincaid. The possibility that one brother might actually hurt another hadn't entered her mind. Then she heard god-awful shouting coming through the doors and she could think of nothing else.

She assumed Alec started yelling first because she didn't recognize the voice, but Connor quickly joined in, and it was soon impossible for her to understand a word of what the two of them were ranting and raving. She tried to concentrate. If they would slow down their speech or hurl their accusations in softer voices, surely she would be able to translate enough of their garbled Gaelic to understand what Alec was so furious about.

The heated discussion lasted for more than fifteen minutes. The longer Brenna was forced to wait, the more nervous she became. She moved only once in all that while. When the doors had closed behind Connor, Quinlan had deliberately brushed her arm as he turned around to face the crowd. She and Aeden had then turned with him, which she immediately regretted, of course, because she had to suffer the Kincaid soldiers' close scrutiny again.

None of them was glaring at her, though. She tried to take that as a good sign. She was careful to hide her fear from

144

them, guessing that that was what they were all searching for, but the effort was incredibly exhausting.

The wait was finally over. The doors opened, and she was summoned inside. She wanted to shake her head, pick up her skirts, and run as fast as she could in the opposite direction.

She went in instead. She was so rattled, she barely paid attention to her surroundings. The great hall was on her left. She stopped at the stone steps leading down into the huge room and waited to be called forward.

Neither Connor nor his brother had noticed her yet. She looked at her husband first to make certain he was all right. He didn't look any worse for wear, she decided, and he wasn't bleeding anywhere that she could see. He didn't look very happy, of course, but then he rarely did. He didn't look angry either, only mildly irritated.

She had delayed looking at his brother for as long as she could, and finally gathered enough courage to turn to him. She still wasn't prepared. Alec Kincaid was a ferocious-looking warrior with piercing gray eyes and a scowl on his face she was sure would make Satan shiver.

"This isn't over, Connor. I will decide what to do after I speak to the woman."

He sounded as mean as he looked. Brenna gripped her hands together behind her back and tried to get her heart to stay inside her chest. God help her, she couldn't seem to get past her initial reaction to him. 'Twas the truth, he continued to terrify her, even after he'd quit his scowl and looked at her.

She quickly bowed her head so he wouldn't be able to see her fear and hoped he took her behavior as a sign of good training. Smiling would have been impossible, however. She wasn't screaming, though, and surely that counted for something.

Alec suddenly moved toward her, and with such an arrogant swagger, she understood how Connor had learned how to be so intimidating. His brother had taught him.

"Brenna, come here." Connor gave the command in a voice tinged with exasperation. She immediately raised her head, went down the stairs, and hurried over to his side. She kept her gaze on Alec Kincaid with each step she took.

Except for their size, the two warriors didn't look at all like brothers. Connor had dark brown hair; Alec had a good deal of red in his. Connor's face looked more patrician to her, though Alec did have a fine profile too, she grudgingly admitted. The physical differences didn't end there, of course. When Connor wasn't frowning, which in her estimation was a rarity, he was somewhat handsome. Alec, on the other hand, could never ever be considered the least bit attractive.

Still, they were two thorns from the same thistle. Their tactics in terrorizing innocent ladies were identical. Their behavior was downright sinful, but what made it even worse was the fact that neither warrior seemed to realize the effect he had on others.

Brenna wondered if her hair was turning gray. She'd heard some women's did when they were subjected to a horror. She tried to calm down. He was only a man and no more threatening than Connor. Unfortunately, that simple truth didn't comfort her at all.

Her husband didn't either. She finally forced herself to stop staring at Satan's nightmare and looked up at Connor. He ignored her. It couldn't get any worse, she told herself. Then Connor shoved her behind his back. She wanted to kick him.

Alec was disappointed in Connor's bride. He couldn't imagine she would ever survive a marriage to Connor if she turned out to be the frightened little rabbit he supposed her to be. Connor would trample all over her in no time at all.

"I'm going to talk to her, Connor. Get the hell out of the way or I'll have you removed from the hall," Alec roared.

Her husband didn't even flinch. She did. She got angry too, as it was atrocious of one brother to speak to another in such a hostile tone.

"You may, of course, talk to her, Alec, but you may not raise your voice. I don't want you to frighten her."

Brenna's anger suddenly switched directions. Her wrath was now fully directed at her husband. Did he have to tell his brother he would frighten her if he raised his voice? Now Alec would think her a weakling, and what kind of a beginning was that? She nudged Connor in his back to let him know what she thought about his comment. He pulled her back to his side and gave her a frown, so she smiled just to bother him.

A woman called out to Laird Kincaid from the entrance. Connor didn't look at her. Brenna couldn't look anywhere else. The woman was so strikingly beautiful, Brenna blinked twice, thinking she might be a vision sent to comfort her through this nightmare. The woman didn't disappear. She wasn't just beautiful. She was courageous as well because she willingly walked across the hall to speak to Alec.

Laird Kincaid's reaction to the vision was a miracle. His voice turned into velvet when he granted the woman permission to come forward. He even smiled as he leaned down to listen to her. Saints be praised, he was human after all.

Unfortunately, the miracle wasn't long-lasting. Brenna stared at the vision, who bowed to them and took her leave. Brenna knew it was rude to stare, but she couldn't seem to stop, until she began to feel as attractive as last week's leftovers. Alec must think Connor was out of his mind to have married Brenna when he could have chosen one of these Highland beauties. They probably grew like heather around here.

"Connor, is your woman timid?"

"Perhaps," he allowed, wondering what his brother's game was.

"I would like to ask you a few questions, Lady Brenna. I expect you to be truthful in your replies. You have nothing to fear from me. Did you ask my brother to marry you?"

She really was going to kill Connor. How dare he tell Alec about her childish embarrassment. Granted, he had forewarned her, but she hadn't believed him because she was certain he would find it as embarrassing as she did.

"Yes, Laird. I did ask him to marry me."

"Do you have something more to say to me?" he asked, thinking she would surely explain why she'd done such a thing.

"I do."

"Say it then."

"I'm not timid."

He came close to smiling. There had been a definite note of defiance in her voice when she'd defended herself. Perhaps she wasn't such a mouse after all.

"I thought you were."

"You were mistaken."

He nodded.

"Did you ask Connor before you were promised to MacNare?"

"Yes."

"Alec, we've been over this," Connor interjected. "As I've explained several times now, she asked me three times. Now let it go," he added as he gently pushed his wife behind his back again.

Three times? He had to mention all the details, didn't he? She suddenly found herself wondering how timid Alec would think she was if he watched her throttle her husband.

"I decide when I've heard enough."

"She belongs to me now," Connor replied

"She could still be given to MacNare. Don't push me again, brother. You won't like the consequences."

"Our wedding was blessed. Brenna, stop pushing me."

"Anything can be undone," said Alec.

"You won't go against our church."

"No, I won't," Alec conceded. "There is another way I could give her to MacNare."

"She could even now be carrying my child. Damn it, wife, will you stop trying to provoke me?"

"She can still be free of you."

"How?"

"I'll kill you."

Connor was about to scoff at his brother's threat when his wife got his attention. She was suddenly standing in front of him.

"You will not kill him," she shouted at Alec.

Her anger caught both men by surprise.

"For God's sake, Brenna," Connor muttered as he moved her back behind his back again. "Stay out of this."

"Let her speak, Connor."

She was already standing in front of her husband by the time Alec finished giving his command.

"Why can't I kill him?"

"He's your brother."

"Give me a good reason."

She couldn't think of one. "You have to make the best of it."

Alec leaned back against the table, folded his arms across his chest, and stared at her. "The best of what?"

"Connor. I understand why you want to kill him. Most everyone who meets him eventually feels that way. Still, he's your brother, and if you'll only think about his virtues, you'll surely let him live."

"Name his virtues?"

"I just knew you were going to say that."

She realized she'd blurted out her thought as soon as the words were out of her mouth, and she hurried on before Connor took offense. "He has hundreds of virtues."

"Such as?"

"He's loyal."

"And?"

She threaded her fingers through her hair in agitation while she concentrated on trying to come up with another one. "His men seem to like him."

"Do you?"

"This has gone far enough, Alec. Brenna, if you continue to defend me, my brother will have me tortured before he kills me."

"I'm doing the best I can."

Alec abruptly ended the inquisition by leaving the hall. It was apparent Connor had gotten his manners from his older brother.

"What the hell just came over you, Brenna?"

"You came over me," she cried out. "You've turned me into a raving simpleton. I want to go home now."

"We can't leave until Alec comes back."

"He won't kill you, will he?"

"No, he won't kill me. I didn't realize you cared."

The laughter in his voice set her off. "I don't care."

"Then why did you try to defend me?"

He would have to turn logical on her. "If anyone kills you, it's going to be me, and I swear to God that if you try to shove me behind you again, I will. Do you have any?"

"Any what?"

"Virtues."

"I'm pleasant enough."

"I was told not to lie."

"I let you voice your opinion."

"That isn't a virtue."

He finally took mercy on her. "It's over now. I told you he wouldn't hurt you."

"It wasn't sufficient warning," she snapped. "He's coming back," she added in a whisper.

Alec wasn't alone. The vision followed her laird into the hall and waited by his side when he ordered Brenna to come to him.

Connor had to nudge Brenna to get her started. She walked over to the laird, bowed her head, and waited for him to scare the hell out of her again.

"Welcome to the family, Lady Brenna."

Chapter
8

*J*amie insisted they stay for supper so she could have a nice long visit with Brenna. Connor insisted they leave. Alec wasn't about to let his wife be disappointed, however. He ended the discussion by turning the invitation into a command.

No one bothered to ask Brenna how she felt about it. She was hungry, of course—she always was—but she wasn't about to eat anything at all in front of relatives she wanted to impress. She might do something horrid like spill her drink or eat too much once she got started, and God only knew what they would think of her then.

She'd moved close to Connor's side during the long-winded debate, but didn't realize she'd taken hold of his hand until he had to help her let go of him so he could follow his brother outside.

When he leaned down toward her, she assumed he wanted to kiss her before he took his leave. Her father had often done that when he left his wife's side, and Brenna was so appreciative that Connor was finally going to be thoughtful, she decided to beat him to the task.

He didn't expect it. Before he even had a glimmer of her intentions, her mouth touched his for a second or two, and she was finished.

She looked damned pleased with herself.

He looked thunderstruck.

He didn't make an issue of her behavior, and while he found it puzzling that she didn't seem to understand what was appropriate and what wasn't, he had to admit it didn't bother him all that much.

"Now will you let go of my hand?"

She did as he requested and clasped her hands behind her back.

Alec had already reached the top of the steps and was staring at the tapestry hanging over the mantel. The look on his face wasn't at all pleasant. Thankfully, his irritation seemed to be directed toward his wife.

"Think I wouldn't notice, Jamie?" He sounded furious.

Jamie didn't look any worse for wear, though. She frowned at her husband and called out, "Think I wouldn't notice my beloved William hanging in the stables?"

Connor nudged Brenna to get her attention, told her to stay out of trouble, and followed his brother outside.

Jamie excused herself a minute later. "Please make yourself comfortable while I go and have a word with cook about the preparations. We'll eat an hour earlier than usual so you can be home well before dark. I'll hurry back."

The minute Brenna was alone, she frantically tried to make herself more presentable. She brushed the dust off her clothes, adjusted the pleats of her plaid, shoved her hair back over her shoulders, and pinched some color into her cheeks. Unfortunately, once she was finished, she suspected she didn't look any better.

She wished she didn't feel so nervous and unsure of herself. She blamed her condition on Alec Kincaid. Why, her hands were still shaking from her introduction to Connor's brother, and how in heaven's name was she ever going to be able to sit down at the same table with the man?

She didn't want to draw any attention to herself. She was determined not to make any mistakes or talk about anything one of them might take exception to, and so she listed all the subjects she mustn't bring up. England came to mind first. Alec and Jamie probably felt the same way Connor did about her beloved country, which meant they detested it, and even though she thought such an opinion was both ignorant and foolish, she wasn't about to get into an argument with them.

The list of topics she must avoid went on and on, and it didn't take her long to realize the only safe subject left was the weather. She wanted to be perfect, knew it wasn't possible, and finally concluded her only course of action was to keep her mouth shut, her hands folded in her lap, and to speak only when she was asked a specific question.

She would also avoid standing or sitting near Jamie. Connor and Alec were bound to notice how ordinary she was in comparison to Jamie's flawlessness. Why, Alec's wife was even more beautiful than Rachel, and Brenna hadn't thought such a thing was possible.

She wanted her new relatives to believe she was worthy of Connor. She didn't understand why their acceptance was so important, and if she weren't feeling like such a nervous twit at the moment, she was sure she would be able to reason it all out. Up until the minute she'd walked into the Kincaid home, she'd believed a goat would have been worthy enough for her husband, but she doubted Alec and Jamie would appreciate hearing that opinion. They probably liked their brother, and Brenna wanted them to like her. She was in need of a friend to talk to, and there had been such kindness and warmth in Jamie's eyes, Brenna knew she would be a good ally.

Feeling inadequate made her miserable. Brenna had been taught to count her blessings and not her sorrows, and so she reminded herself of all the wondrous gifts God had bestowed on her. She had good, straight teeth, a strong back, and feet that never, ever pained her. Those were all fine assets indeed, but far more important than any physical attributes were the hidden treasures she possessed. Her mother had often told her she had a good heart. She was also a hard worker. She used to have a strong mind too, until Connor came along and turned her into a babbling half-wit.

Perhaps she wasn't completely hopeless, after all. Besides, she had a sound plan now, and that made her feel more in control. As long as she remembered to be quiet and demure, she would do just fine.

With any luck, no one would even notice she was there.

She looked about the hall with interest. Her attention was immediately drawn to the huge tapestry hanging over the mantel. She stared at it a long while, trying to figure out what had bothered Alec so much when he'd looked at it. She thought the piece was lovely. Its edges were frayed with age, but the threads were still vibrant with color.

Depicted was the likeness of a man Alec had called William, dressed in a deep royal blue robe and wearing a jeweled crown on his head, who seemed to be looking across the hall. She didn't know who William was, but she decided he must have lived a long time ago because there was a gold halo over his head, which meant he'd already been sainted. She really should have taken the time to memorize all the names and pertinent facts about the saints as her confessor had suggested, she realized, and wouldn't he be gloating now if he knew she was sorry she hadn't paid attention to his lectures? Although she was curious to find out which William it was, she wasn't going to ask Alec or Jamie to tell her, for fear they'd think she was ignorant. She would have to wait until later and put the question to Connor. She made the sign of the cross to show her respect for the saint before turning her back on him so she could look at the rest of the hall.

She was immediately captivated by the arsenal hanging on the walls on either side of the entrance. In the center of the larger wall were two magnificent swords with golden handles encrusted with jewels. The larger one had a jewel missing near the center of the cluster of gems.

It was all very impressive, she supposed, but downright peculiar too. Why would anyone want to hang their weapons in their home?

A door opened behind the balcony above the main entrance, and a little girl no bigger than a whisper came hurrying out. The child had obviously just awakened from her nap, as she was rubbing the sleep from her eyes. She was dressed in an ivory gown and had wrapped herself in a plaid that dragged on the floor around her. The little girl was in such a hurry to get downstairs, she forgot to hold the blanket away from her feet as she walked across the balcony. She had already stumbled once when Brenna started toward her to lend a helping hand.

Brenna started running when the little one tripped a second time. "Pick up your plaid and wait for me to help you down the stairs," she called out.

She didn't understand what Brenna was telling her. She didn't seem to be afraid of the stranger, just curious. She stared down at Brenna between the rails and smiled, but didn't stop.

Too late, Brenna realized her mistake in calling out to the child, because now the little one was busy watching her and wasn't paying any attention to where she was going. The child was headed for disaster. Brenna started running up the steps to stop her.

She didn't make it. The little girl reached the edge of the top step, tripped on her blanket, and catapulted herself into the air with the force of a pebble hurled from a sling.

Brenna lunged forward, caught her in her arms, and had enough wits about her to wrap herself tight around the little one and hold her close. The force of the impact made Brenna lose her footing, and as she fell backward, she tried to turn so that her shoulder, and not her head, would hit the stone wall. She didn't accomplish her goal.

Later, Jamie told her she hit her forehead twice more before she landed in a heap at the bottom, with the child still wrapped protectively in her arms.

Brenna recovered from the mishap before Jamie did, but she throbbed from her head to her toes. The top of her forehead felt as though it were on fire, but once she'd made certain the little one was all right, she was actually able to smile over her pitiful condition. Blood was streaming down her forehead; the hem of her gown was torn, and the pleats she worked so hard to straighten were gone.

Jamie was so distraught from the fright, she could barely think what to do. She sat down on the steps above Brenna, pulled her baby into her lap, and hugged her tight. "Dear God, I thought you were both going to die. Are you all right, Brenna? Don't move until I . . . What were you thinking, Grace? You know you mustn't come down the steps without . . . How many times has your father told you to call to one of us? Are you all right, Brenna? Answer me."

Jamie was sobbing, and Brenna was certain she wouldn't hear any reply she gave. She felt foolish sprawled out on the floor like a broken vase, so she forced herself to get to her feet, and once again tried to make herself presentable.

"Brenna, don't move until I make certain you haven't broken anything."

"All right, Jamie."

"Good Lord, you're standing up."

"Mama, do we got to tell Papa?"

"No, *we* don't have to tell him. You do."

Grace squirmed off her mother's lap. "When I'm ready, Mama?" she pleaded. "Not before?"

Jamie nodded. "When you're ready," she conceded. "As long as you tell him before you go to bed tonight."

"Why don't we forget it happened, Jamie. It was just an accident."

Grace must have understood a little of what Brenna suggested because she moved closer to her and nodded her agreement.

"I was so terrified, I couldn't move. I saw my baby flying through the air and my heart felt as though it had stopped. I couldn't get to her before . . ." Too upset to continue, Jamie covered her face with her hands and broke into sobs again.

Brenna patted her arm to try to calm her. "There, there. It's over now. Your daughter is as fit as ever, Jamie. She doesn't even have a scratch."

She helped Jamie stand up, put her arm around her shoulders, and led her into the hall.

Jamie had already taken her seat at the table before she came to her senses and realized what she was doing. She jumped back up, and shoved Brenna down on an adjacent stool. Landing with a thud, pain shot up from the back of Brenna's right thigh, and it took a good deal of discipline not to cry out.

Jamie finally noticed the injury on her forehead. "Good God, you're bleeding."

"It's just a little cut, nothing more. Please sit down and catch your breath. You've been through a fright, Jamie."

"No, I should be comforting you. I swear to God it's going to take me a month to recover. You're taking it all in stride, though, aren't you? Turn your head so I can get a better look. Are you bleeding anywhere else? Lord, my hands are shaking so, I can barely get your hair out of my way. Grace?"

"Yes, Mama?" The little girl came running across the hall, dragging her plaid behind her. She seemed eager to be included in the conversation until her mother told her what she wanted her to do.

"Go and get your father."

Grace dropped her blanket, climbed up on Brenna's lap, and leaned back against her. "Mama? Can I go and get Papa when I'm ready?"

Brenna burst into laughter. The sound warmed Jamie's heart and brought fresh tears into her eyes. She took Brenna's hand and squeezed. "Thank God for you. Were it not for your quickness, my daughter might have broken her neck. My husband and I are in your debt until the day we die."

Brenna colored with embarrassment. "You don't owe me anything. You are my relatives now, and I will always be willing to help you in any way I can. Besides, all of us must watch out for the little ones. Isn't that so?"

"It is so," Jamie agreed. "You and I are more than relatives, though. We're sisters. Isn't that so?"

"It is so," she whispered. "And there is always room for one more sister in my heart."

The bond between the two women was formed in that instant, and all of Brenna's worries and insecurities disappeared. Sisters, after all, didn't need to impress each other.

"Mama, don't cry anymore. I don't like it," Grace demanded in a quivering voice.

"I shall stop at once," Jamie promised. She let go of Brenna's hand, drew a deep breath, and wiped the tears away from her cheeks with the back of her hands. "I should send someone to fetch Connor. He'll want to see this."

Brenna didn't want Connor to join them any more than she wanted Alec. She simply wasn't up to a long explanation now, and if he even looked as though he blamed her for this mishap, she knew her temper would start simmering. There was also a remote chance he might show her a little sympathy, and she would be so appreciative, she might break down and cry. She couldn't think of anything more humiliating.

157

"You're being unreasonable about this. Your husband's going to demand answers as soon as he looks at you."

"I'll be happy to explain it all to him on our way home."

"Are you afraid of him?" Jamie asked, sounding stunned by the possibility.

Brenna shook her head. "Of course not. It's just that I know he'll say something I'm sure to take exception to, and I won't be able to stop myself from letting him know what I think about that, and before you know it, we'll be arguing in front of Alec. It wouldn't be at all appropriate. I want to impress the man, not infuriate him. Besides, I have vowed not to draw attention to myself. Will you please stop poking at me?"

"You saved my daughter's life. Think Alec won't be impressed with that fact? Why are you so uncomfortable with compliments, Brenna?"

"Because they're misplaced. I only did what I should have done."

"I see this embarrasses you, and so I shall let it go for now. Grace, love, go and ask one of the servants to bring fresh water and towels."

The little girl was in such a hurry to help, she forgot to take her plaid with her.

The cut was on Brenna's forehead above her left eye. After the injury had been properly cleaned, Brenna assumed Jamie was finished, and so she suggested Jamie tell her how she'd ended up married to Alec Kincaid. Jamie suggested she fetch her needle and thread first.

Brenna didn't like the sound of that. "Please don't think I'm not grateful, but I would rather you didn't go to any more trouble. I'm feeling fine, really. I barely felt it. Is Grace your only child?"

"No, I have four in all. Mary Kathleen's the oldest. She's married now and lives too far away to suit me, for I only see her twice a year. Gideon was born ten years ago, and five years later, Dillon came along. Grace is our baby."

"She's adorable. She has the face of a cherub."

"Yes, she does," Jamie agreed. "Your questions haven't changed my mind, if that was your hope. The cut is too deep to be left alone. You need to be stitched together so you may as well stop trying to be noble. We both know you're in pain."

"I wasn't being noble. I was being diplomatic."

"It's a wasted effort."

"Perhaps I wasn't specific enough for you. If you think I'm going to let you near me with a needle in your hand after you've only just told me you can't stop shaking, you're out of your mind."

"I'm determined to get my way, Brenna."

"You're demented, Jamie."

Grace's eyes had grown wide during the debate. She climbed back up on Brenna's lap and watched in fascination while the two women shouted at each other.

Jamie eventually won the battle. She was older, stronger, and had two servants on her side. Grace was Brenna's only ally. She wasn't much help, though. She giggled whenever her mama raised her voice and covered her ears whenever Brenna raised hers.

"Will you get it done before Connor and Alec come inside?"

"Yes."

Fortunately, Jamie was as good as her promise. Brenna never made a sound while Jamie cleaned the injury and sewed it together.

"You'll have a scar trailing down your forehead, but half of it can be concealed by your hair. Does that upset you?"

"No," Brenna answered. "What upsets me is the way you stop every time you want to say something to me. Please hurry up and finish."

Jamie let out a sigh. "I had no idea you were so difficult."

After making her observation, she wet a fresh towel and washed the blood off Brenna's hair. She still believed Connor would demand an explanation as soon as he looked at Brenna.

"I agree with you that he'll notice my injury, but I'm certain he won't say a word about it until we're well on our way home. He might even wait until tomorrow to bring it up. If I were to push my hair back and point to the stitches, I might get him to say something before."

The cook had joined them a few minutes before and now asked her mistress's permission to make a suggestion.

"Yes, Elyne?" Jamie asked.

"Why not make a wager?"

Brenna embraced Elyne's idea. If Connor ignored her injury, then she wanted Jamie to plant flowers in front of Connor's home to make it look as inviting as Jamie's. If Connor commented on the injury, then Jamie wanted Brenna to promise to come and see her at least once a week, no matter what the weather or schedule.

Rules were firmly set down so that neither lady would be able to sway the outcome in her favor. Elyne was given the important duty of hiding in the hallway to make certain trickery, such as hints, wasn't used.

The brothers could hear their wives' laughter from outside the entrance and smiled in reaction. Alec was pleased his wife was enjoying her visitor, and Connor was relieved Brenna wasn't as nervous with Jamie as she'd been with Alec.

Brenna heard the doors open and immediately helped Grace get off her lap. She stood up, keeping her back to her husband, and pretended concentration as she folded the plaid the little girl had discarded.

As soon as Grace spotted her father striding toward the table, she went running to the opposite end.

Alec took his place at the head of the table. Jamie sat on his left. Brenna let Connor have the stool across from Jamie and took her seat next to him. Grace was the last to sit down. She and her father faced each other at least sixteen stools apart. Once the little girl had scooted the stool up close to the table, she sat down, stacked her arms on the table, dropped her chin down on top, and stared at her father.

Connor barely glanced at Brenna. He did ask her if everything was all right, but she assumed he only wanted to know if she had stayed out of trouble as he had suggested before he left, and she gave him a quick nod in answer.

"Where are your other children?" Brenna asked Jamie.

"Alec gave them permission to stay outside with Gavin and his wife for another hour," Jamie explained before turning to her husband. "Have you told Connor the news yet?"

"No, I haven't," Alec replied with a smile.

"Is it good news?" Brenna asked.

"Oh, yes, Brenna," Jamie answered. "It's very good news."

"I've just received word, Connor, your stepmother and her son are on their way to your holding. They should reach your land late today or early tomorrow."

Brenna reacted before her husband did. She was so startled by the announcement, she jumped to her feet, almost upsetting the stool in her haste. "Now? Your mother's coming for a visit now?"

Connor gently pulled her back down by his side. "My stepmother," he corrected.

"Yes, of course, your stepmother. She's coming for a visit now?"

"Yes, *now,* according to what Alec has just told us. I see no reason to panic. Does this news upset you?"

"No, of course not. I was just taken by surprise to hear that your stepmother could now be waiting."

"She might not arrive until tomorrow," Alec suggested.

Connor turned to his wife. "What's come over you? This is good news, not bad."

"Yes, it's good news," she agreed. "And I will do everything I can to make her feel welcome."

"How long has Euphemia been away?" Jamie asked.

"Seventeen years," Connor answered. "She had only just returned to her relatives to help with an ailing uncle when my father was killed. She couldn't bear to come back once word reached her."

"You haven't seen her in all that while?" Brenna asked.

"I've seen her several times since then. Three years ago, when Alec and I were settling a dispute near the peaks, we stopped to pay our respects."

"She was still in mourning," Alec said.

"She must have loved your father a great deal," Brenna whispered.

"Of course she did," he answered.

"She should have moved on," Alec said. "Grieving for the dead won't bring them back."

"You would grieve for me, wouldn't you, Alec?" Jamie asked.

"Of course."

"How long?"

Alec wasn't about to get into a discussion about the length of time he would mourn his wife. He couldn't even think about losing her without feeling sick.

"You will not die on me. Do you understand?" he ordered in a hard, unbending voice.

Only his wife saw the panic in his eyes and hurried to put his mind to rest. "No, I won't die on you. Haven't you forgotten to tell Connor your other interesting news?"

Her husband was happy to accommodate her. He turned back to Connor and explained he had also received news from an emissary sent by a laird living on the border. Connor seemed interested and asked several questions. One topic led to another and another, and it wasn't long before Brenna and Jamie were all but forgotten.

Brenna put her concerns about pleasing Connor's stepmother aside for the moment, though she did say a quick prayer the woman wouldn't arrive before she did. Brenna wanted to get her bearings.

Her thoughts were interrupted when she heard Jamie trying to coax her little daughter to join them. Brenna quickly shook her head at her, for she feared Grace would innocently say something to prick the men's curiosity and inadvertently sway the outcome in Jamie's favor. Thus far, Brenna was winning their wager, as neither brother had said a word about her injury. She gave Jamie a sinfully gloating look before she devoured all the food that had been placed in front of her.

Alec waited until the trenchers were taken away before turning to his wife. "I've been meaning to ask why . . ."

Her laughter stopped him. He waited for her to control herself before he continued. "How can you find my question amusing when you've yet to hear it?"

"Pray forgive me, Alec. What were you going to ask?"

"Why is my daughter sitting all the way down at the end of the table? I can barely see her from here."

Everyone turned to Grace. The little girl didn't seem to be bothered by all the attention she was getting. She smiled for her papa's benefit and continued to stare at him.

"Brenna, would you like to answer Alec's question?"

"No."

"You do not deny my brother," Connor explained.

"She just did deny him," Jamie remarked before she laughed again.

Brenna believed Jamie's behavior was a direct violation of the rules they'd established because she was deliberately tempting the men's curiosity with her laughter. She wasn't about to let her get away with it. "Jamie, I believe you should go to the kitchens and thank Elyne for this meal."

"If I leave, you're coming with me."

"Neither one of you needs to get up," Connor interjected. "Elyne and two other servants are watching us from the back hallway. You can give them your praise from here."

"Will you try to control yourself?" Alec demanded when his wife was overcome with laughter again.

Brenna bounded to her feet. "Thank you for this fine meal. Will you excuse me?"

She didn't wait to gain permission. Jamie jumped to her feet next and hurried after Brenna.

Connor heard his wife accuse Jamie of cheating and almost dropped his goblet. He hoped to God Alec hadn't heard the comment. Then, when Brenna stopped in front of the hearth to make the sign of the cross before continuing, Alec was so appalled he knocked his empty goblet over.

Jamie found Brenna's show of respect hilarious. Her laughter followed her out the front doors.

Alec waited until the servants had skirted their way past the table and had hurried after their mistress before turning to Connor.

"We really should be offended."

"Yes, we should. How do you think Brenna was injured, and why in God's name are the two of them pretending nothing happened?"

"There's only one quick way to find out."

"How?"

Alec smiled. "Grace?"

"Yes, Papa?"

"Come and sit with your father."

"When I'm ready, can I come sit with you?"

"You're ready now, Grace."

The little girl kept her head down and walked as though she were on her way to a bath. Connor winked at her as she passed him.

Alec swept her up into his arms, kissed her brow, and sat her down on the edge of the table. He then ordered her to tell him what had happened.

"The lady yelled at Mama."

"Her name is Brenna, Grace. Now tell me the truth."

"She probably is telling the truth," Connor interjected.

"And what did your mother do?"

"She cried."

Alec looked at Connor. "None of this surprises you, does it?"

"No."

"Mama yelled too, Papa."

"What did you do, Grace?"

"Nothing."

Alec didn't believe that nonsense for a minute. "What more do you have to tell me?"

"The lady laughed when Mama cried again." She was so happy she'd remembered, she scrunched up her shoulders with pleasure.

"Connor, I'm going to have to address Brenna's appalling lack of respect for my wife. I mean to talk to her."

"You will not offend her, Alec."

"The lady didn't cry, Papa."

"Is that so," Alec said.

"Mama put a needle in the lady's head."

"How did Brenna hurt herself?" Connor asked.

"She fell down the steps."

"What the hell was she doing on the steps?"

"Connor, you won't get any answers from my daughter by shouting at her," Alec said. "Remember how young she is."

"I thought you said this would be quick."

"The lady Brenna told Mama she was out of her mind."

"Tell me why she was on the steps," Alec ordered.

"I love you, Papa."

The ploy didn't work. Neither did the child's attempt to wiggle out of her father's arms. "Answer me, Grace."

"She had to catch me."

Alec could picture in his mind exactly what had happened. Connor was at a disadvantage because he'd left Alec's household long before Grace was born and, therefore, didn't know about the child's history of mischief.

"I still don't understand how Brenna could have lost her footing," Connor said.

"Grace, tell your uncle how she caught you," her father instructed.

The little girl was thrilled to have both her father's and her uncle's attention. She put her feet down on his lap, stretched her arms up above her head, and tried to leap up in the air in an attempt to reenact the event.

Alec held on to his daughter and gently forced her to sit back down again.

"You're going to be the death of me, Grace," he muttered with a shake of his head.

"I know, Papa. You already told me before. Lots of times."

"She'll be the death of your dear wife too, Laird," the cook remarked as she hurried back toward the kitchens.

Alec turned to the older woman. "My daughter catapulted herself off that top step, didn't she, Elyne?"

"I didn't see it happen, Laird, but my mistress did tell me Grace came flying down the stairs, and with as much speed as a stone hurling down from the top of a tower. Lady Brenna had to jump up so she could catch her."

"They both could have broken their necks."

"Aye, they could have, Connor," Alec agreed before turning back to the loyal servant. "Explain why our wives don't want us to know what happened."

Elyne couldn't refuse her laird's command and quickly told him about the wagering.

The brothers weren't at all amused by their wives' bet. They were, however, willing to go along with them.

Jamie and Brenna joined them a few minutes later. Both husbands stood up when the ladies entered the hall, but after being ignored for several minutes, they sat back down. Alec poured wine into their goblets. He downed his drink in one long swallow.

Brenna had already gained Alec's loyalty as soon as she

married his brother. She received his devotion the minute he found out she'd saved his precious daughter from a serious injury, and she won his admiration and love when he heard her tell Jamie she must immediately remove the tapestry. Jamie vehemently refused.

"Then at least remove the yellow threads of the halo as soon as possible. You cannot saint William the Conqueror just because you think he should be a saint. It's a sacrilege."

"William will be a saint just as soon as the church gets around to it."

Brenna shook her head. "No wonder your husband looked like he was staring at the devil. Why in heaven's name would you hang the former king of England in the home of a Highlander? Even I know he doesn't belong here. You must take it down, Jamie. Good Lord, I've been making the sign of the cross every time I pass in front of him, and if that isn't a blasphemy, I don't know what is. Are there any of your kings you could hang?"

"Why would I want to?"

"Why? Because you're a Highlander, that's why."

"You don't know, do you? Brenna, I was born in England, raised there too."

Needless to say, she took the wind out of Brenna's argument with her startling revelation. Jamie laughed over the upset she'd just given her new sister.

"You sound like a Highlander, and no one told me you were . . ." Brenna paused to glare at her husband. "You could have told me."

"No, I don't suppose Connor would tell you. You might as well accept the fact that men never tell their wives anything without prodding, Brenna. My news should please you, though, not anger you."

Brenna finally managed to stop frowning at her husband. "I am pleased. No wonder I like you so much."

"You'll like Mary too. Alec, do you realize how blessed I am? I have a sister on each side of my land now."

"Aye, you do," Alec agreed.

"Connor, Brenna must meet Mary as soon as possible."

"Could we stop on our way home?" Brenna asked.

"It's too late to make another stop," Connor answered.

Determined not to let him dampen her enthusiasm, she

hurried over to the table and put her hand on his shoulder. "Another time then?"

"Yes."

She patted him to let him know how much she appreciated his cooperation. Alec turned as he stood up so Brenna wouldn't see him smile. He was pleased to see she was affectionate toward his brother, but what made him smile was the fact that he knew Connor was trying not to like it.

Connor shook his head at his brother. "Don't make more of this than it is," he remarked as he reached around his back to move his wife so he wouldn't knock her over when he stood up.

Alec nodded. "I would suggest you not make less of this than it is."

Brenna didn't have any idea what the two men were talking about. Alec abruptly changed the subject before she asked him to explain.

"You'd best keep a close lookout on your way home."

"Connor always has his guard up," she said.

"That is so," Alec agreed before issuing a second warning to his brother. "He could be waiting on your land even now."

"Ah, Alec, you do give me hope."

"Your arrogance is going to get you killed. We both know he'll want her back."

Brenna suddenly realized who the brothers were talking about. She let out a gasp, grabbed hold of Connor's arm, and whispered, "The pig MacNare?"

Her husband smiled. God love her, she was beginning to realize how fortunate she was to have married him. "Yes, the pig MacNare."

"You won't, will you?"

"I won't what?"

She leaned into his side so she couldn't be overheard. "Give me back."

His smile vanished. "What do you think?"

"You won't."

His brisk nod told her she'd made the right guess. He put his arms around her shoulders and squeezed her to let her know he approved of her answer.

She tried to hide her exasperation. It was difficult, given

the fact that her husband was now trying to defend her behavior to his brother.

"My wife meant no offense to me. She's English, if you'll remember, and therefore doesn't understand."

"What don't I understand?"

Alec answered her. "We keep what belongs to us, and we protect our wives. You don't understand your worth yet, do you, Brenna?"

"No, she doesn't," Connor answered.

"Englishmen also protect what belongs to them." She told them what should have been obvious. "The barons are just as possessive."

"Then why are you here, lass?" Alec asked. "Did your father protect you by sending you to marry MacNare?"

"One has nothing to do with the other, Laird."

"How is it different?" he asked.

Both brothers would think her father had been motivated by greed if she explained his reason, and she knew she would never be able to convince them her dear father loved his daughters.

"I'm here because I wish to be here. When I asked my husband if he would give me back, I only wanted to hear his assurance. I already knew he wouldn't," she boasted.

"Because you received the church's approval with the priest's blessing?" Alec asked.

He was already nodding when she told him no. "Connor would have gotten around to getting a priest to bless us. Many marriages begin without a blessing because there are so few confessors available."

Connor knew she was struggling to be diplomatic, and he smiled. She was about to lose her patience now, and from the way Alec was questioning her, Connor knew Alec was curious to see what she would do.

Alec was enjoying himself, and with each of her frowns and hesitant answers, he was actually finding out far more about her than she could possibly realize.

"Then how did you know Connor wouldn't give you back?" Alec persisted. "Did you understand him so well?"

"No, I didn't understand him at all. I had, of course, noticed how stubborn he was," she added when she remembered how she'd argued with Connor to get him to change his mind, and how he'd refused to listen to a word she said. "However, my parents taught all of their children to stand on their own two feet. My family, you see . . ."

Connor interrupted her. "We are your family now."

"Yes, but my sisters and brothers . . ."

He once again interrupted her. "Jamie and Alec are your sister and brother now."

"And Raen," Alec interjected.

Connor nodded. "Yes, Raen," he agreed. "It's been such a long time since I last saw him, I sometimes forget about him."

"Connor, why don't you let me talk about my family?"

"We're your family now," he gently corrected.

Alec understood exactly what his brother was doing and fully supported him. Connor wanted to help his wife become loyal to him and his followers, of course, and let go of the past, and though Alec thought Connor wasn't as subtle as he had been when he'd helped Jamie get over her homesickness, he couldn't fault his brother. 'Twas the truth, Connor still wasn't capable of being subtle.

Disheartened to realize her husband was trying to make her pretend her family didn't matter, she decided to go outside and ignore him for a few minutes and try to figure out his reason for being so cruel. She was going to have to remove Connor's arm from around her shoulders first, of course, but when she tried to do just that, she realized she was holding the Kincaid plaid she'd folded and kept on her lap through supper. She tucked the blanket under her arm with the intention of putting it down on one of the stools as soon as Connor let go of her, and then reached up to nudge him away from her.

He caught hold of her hand and held tight. She tried to pull away, but he tightened his grip. She was quite helpless now, and he knew it. She gave him a quick frown to let him know what she thought about his behavior.

He winked at her.

Alec was trying hard not to laugh. The look she'd just given Connor did amuse him, though. He recognized it too, for it was similar to the wait-until-I-get-you-alone expression his Jamie often cast him when she was dying to voice her opinion and knew she shouldn't.

JULIE GARWOOD

"You've still to appease my curiosity, Brenna," Alec told her.

She forced a smile for the laird and tried to remember what they'd been talking about. Connor had winked at her. What in heaven's name had come over him?

"Brenna, answer my brother," Connor instructed.

God help her, his eyes had turned so wonderfully warm. Why did such a handsome warrior have to be so difficult all the time? She let out a little sigh while she thought about that.

"I would be happy to answer your brother."

Both brothers waited a good long while for her to do just that. Alec took mercy on her before Connor did. He reminded her of their topic.

"You were about to explain how you knew Connor wouldn't give you to MacNare."

"It's simple, really. I wouldn't let him."

"Of course you wouldn't," Jamie interjected just to show she supported Brenna's belief.

Alec laughed. His reaction puzzled Brenna. Connor didn't laugh; he did smile, though, and she found his reaction just as bewildering.

Connor was still smiling as he pulled her behind him to the doors leading outside. He was just about to dismiss the matter from his mind when she asked him why her answer had amused him.

"I wasn't amused. I was pleased."

"All right," she agreed. "Why were you pleased?"

"Because you believe you're strong enough to enforce your decisions."

Jamie came up behind the two of them and gained Connor's full attention when she told him he was wrong. "She doesn't believe she's strong enough to enforce her wants on you. I believe she realizes she's intelligent enough to find another way to get whatever she wants."

"Our fathers didn't raise ignorant daughters, and it's your mistake to believe otherwise," Brenna said.

"Isn't that so?" Jamie asked her husband, who stood behind her.

Alec knew better than to disagree with his wife, as the issue seemed important to her. "Yes, that is so."

170

Connor held one of the doors open for his wife. Jamie gave Brenna a farewell hug, then wrapped her arms around Connor, whispered something into his ear that made him smile, and gave him a kiss on his cheek.

"Come home more often," she ordered him before moving away from the door so they could go outside.

Quinlan's eyes widened in disbelief the second he saw his mistress. She noticed his concern, shook her head at him, and pulled her hair down to hide her stitches. Quinlan didn't say anything.

They all noticed how she favored her left side coming down the steps. Connor tried to be gentle with her when he lifted her onto her horse, but she still grimaced in pain.

Connor's farewell to his brother made her forget about her discomfort. She almost laughed out loud, so amusing was his action, for instead of bowing to his brother or grasping his hand to say his good-bye, he slammed the flat of his hand against his shoulder. Alec pounded him back. Once the barbaric show of affection was finished, Connor swung up behind Brenna and put his arm around her waist.

He leaned down close to her ear and whispered, "You've only a short ride before you're home."

Alec patiently stood by their side, waiting until his wife had finished saying her good-byes and gone back inside to find Grace. As soon as the door closed behind her, he turned to Brenna. His expression showed his amusement. "My daughter has a special fondness for her plaid."

"Is that so?" she asked, wondering why he wanted to discuss Grace's blanket now.

Alec nodded. "She can tell hers from another by the scent. At least that is what my wife believes. Jamie must be right, because Grace knows when one has been substituted for another. She likes to wrap herself up in the blanket while she sleeps. She'll have need for it tonight, Brenna, or my wife and I will get little rest."

Connor could tell from his wife's puzzled expression she didn't understand what Alec was asking. "He wants you to give it back, Brenna," he said.

Her face turned the color of a sunburn in less time than it took to blink. She almost dropped the plaid when she moved her elbow away and handed it to Alec. "I can't imagine how I forgot to put it down on the stool. I did have every intention of doing just that, but I became involved in our discussion and must have . . ."

She stopped trying to come up with a logical explanation for her behavior when Alec put his hand on top of hers. He looked as though he wanted to say something important to her, and she instinctively tensed in anticipation.

"My wife will be over the first of the week to plant your flowers, Brenna."

"Thank you, Laird."

"Alec was thanking you," Connor told her.

"I realize that. I was thanking him for showing me such kindness."

"If I were not so grateful to you for coming to my daughter's assistance, I would have to take issue with you for believing Connor and I wouldn't notice anything was amiss. We notice everything."

"For two intelligent women, you both misjudged us," Connor said.

"Aye, you did," Alec agreed. He removed his hand and stepped back. "You do understand that it was our decision that allowed you to win your wager, but you need not thank us for our thoughtfulness."

She laughed again. "You believe you let me win? I think not, Laird."

He raised his eyebrow. "We deliberately pretended not to notice."

"That is so," she agreed. "And you would be right to believe you favored the outcome if *your observation* had been what we wagered about. Jamie and I knew you would notice."

"What was the wager over?" Connor asked, a hint of a smile in his voice.

"Jamie was sure you wouldn't be able to keep silent and would demand to know what happened as soon as you looked at me. I wagered you wouldn't say a word, and if my memory serves me, I do believe that is exactly what happened."

"One is the same as the other," Connor argued.

"Is it?" she asked with an innocent smile and a look that told him she thought he was wrong.

"Admit it, Connor. The victory belongs to Brenna," Alec conceded.

"It does," Connor agreed.

"Will Jamie bring Grace with her when she plants my flowers?"

"No, I don't let my children leave my land. Connor, I'll be riding with my wife. I expect you to be there."

Alec shoved him once again to show his affection, before striding back toward his home. Grace must have been waiting just inside the doors, for as soon as Alec pulled one open, she ran to him and snatched her blanket out of his hand.

Once she and Connor were on their way, Brenna made herself more comfortable by shifting her weight on his lap and wrapping her arms around his waist.

"I was sorry I didn't get to say good-bye to Grace."

"She's busy explaining her conduct to her father now."

"What will he do to her? It was an accident, Connor. Surely Alec won't hurt her tender feelings."

"She and Dillon are not allowed upstairs alone. Alec will simply remind Grace to obey his orders."

"Are the other children as carefree?"

"No. The boys are shy of strangers, but God help you once they get used to you. They're far more devilish than Grace is."

"I fear she will always be my favorite."

Connor was deliberately trying to keep up the idle conversation so Brenna wouldn't notice the number of Kincaid soldiers riding escort. He didn't want her to become concerned about Alec's reasons. She might even assume MacNare was somehow responsible for his brother's outrageously protective gesture.

He knew he was going to have to put up with his brother's interference. He wasn't happy about it, though. Neither was Quinlan, but unlike his laird, he wasn't trying to hide his irritation.

"I would not make a favorite of one of my children," she assured him.

He didn't have anything to say about that. She wanted to keep him talking, in hopes that the conversation would take her mind off the pain nagging her now. Her head was throbbing, and her thigh was once again burning something fierce.

He realized what her goal was as soon as she shifted position in his lap again.

"I had already left home before Dillon and Grace were born," he remarked. "I am closest to Mary Kathleen, as I know her better than the others. Still, I will admit I have a special fondness for Grace, but only because she reminds me of someone else."

She tried to look up at him, but he gently pushed her face against his chest so she couldn't. She pinched him to let him know how much she disliked that and then asked him to tell her who Grace reminded him of.

"A child I once held in my arms."

He wouldn't tell her anything more, but the memory of the child he'd held had pleased him. The warmth in his voice told her so.

"Are you pleased Euphemia is coming to visit?"

"Yes. You aren't, though, are you?"

"Of course I am," she argued. "I'm just a little . . . apprehensive about meeting her. It's very important to win her approval," she added. "She's your mother, after all, and it would be very upsetting if she didn't like me."

"Why?"

She couldn't believe he needed to ask. "Because there must be harmony in your household, that's why, and it's up to me to see to her wishes. While she's in your home, she's mistress. Surely you understand now."

"You worry about every little thing. She'll like you just fine."

She wasn't as certain as Connor was, but she vowed to win Euphemia's love. Several minutes passed as she thought about different ways she could please the woman, and then she put the worry aside and moved on. She tried to think about the lovely time she'd had visiting with Jamie as a means of taking her mind off the pounding her thigh was taking. It didn't work.

"It's a good day for a walk, isn't it?"

He didn't answer her. She wasn't deterred. "I believe I'd like to walk for a little while. It will be nice to stretch my legs."

"No." He softened his denial by brushing his chin across the top of her head. "Would it help if I carry you facedown across my lap?"

His suggestion horrified her. She pictured herself flung over his knees with her head hanging down on one side of the stallion and her feet dangling down on the other, and she thought she might die of mortification then and there.

What a wonderful way that would be for her to meet his followers. "I cannot imagine what you think to help with your suggestion. I'm perfectly fine, thank you. I merely thought a walk would be invigorating on such a fine day. Forget I mentioned it."

She had placed pride above comfort, just as he had expected her to do. He moved his hand under her skirts to find out for himself the extent of her injury. He considered stopping to take a look, but quickly discarded the idea. Getting her cooperation would take him an hour, and in another ten minutes, they would reach the division between the lands and be home at last.

His touch felt like a caress. Still, she didn't like it. She went completely still and whispered, "Remove your hand."

"You've got a fair-sized bruise, don't you? Does it hurt?"

"It doesn't hurt at all. Please remove your hand. It's embarrassing."

Connor conceded.

"An Englishman would give his wife a little sympathy," she muttered.

"I'm not English."

"No, you're not," she agreed. "May I ask you questions about your home?"

"Yes."

"First, please tell me when we'll reach your land."

"Look to the rise above you and you'll see my sentries watching us."

She immediately straightened her appearance. She ran her fingers through her hair to get the tangles out, bumped Connor's shoulder as she smoothed her curls behind her, fixed the pleats of her plaid to her satisfaction, and pinched color into her cheeks.

"What in God's name are you doing?"

"Pinching myself."

He told himself not to ask. He did anyway.

"Because I don't want to look pale."

He shook his head. He had never heard of anything so preposterous.

"How long before we reach your fortress?" she asked.

"Very soon."

"Do you mean to tell me we live close to Alec and Jamie?"

"Yes."

"Will I be able to visit as often as I wish?"

"Yes."

Her enthusiasm made her forget her pain. He explained he hadn't built his home in the center of his property, but near the edge of his brother's land, instead. She assumed he'd done so to please Alec.

The MacAlister soldiers let out a cheer in greeting when their laird raised his hand.

"Do they always cheer you when you return home?"

"No, only when I've been away a long time."

"How long were you away then?"

"Almost three weeks."

What had he been doing all that while? She was just about to ask him when she remembered the blue paint on his face. She promptly changed her mind. If she found out he'd been raiding, her good mood would be ruined. She'd ruin his as well because she would feel compelled to let him know what she thought about that barbaric pastime.

She noticed how the soldiers stared at her when they rode past, and even though she smiled at them, they didn't smile back. She started worrying in no time at all.

"Will your followers dislike me because I was supposed to marry MacNare?"

"No."

"None of the six soldiers we just passed smiled at me."

"Of course they didn't."

"Why not?"

"Because you're my wife. They'll honor you."

"And if I'm not worthy of their honor?"

"You are."

She thought that was a very thoughtful, kind thing to say

to her, and since Connor wasn't a thoughtful or kind man, she immediately became suspicious.

"Why?"

"Because I chose you."

"I chose you, remember?"

"You like to argue with me, don't you?"

She didn't believe his question merited an answer. "Will I like your home?"

"Of course."

"I can't wait to see it. Is it as appealing as Alec's home? I won't be disappointed if it isn't," she hastened to add. "I don't need it to be grand. Is it?"

Her enthusiasm made him smile. "Yes, it's just as appealing as my brother's home."

"You're proud of it, aren't you? I can hear it in your voice."

"I suppose I am."

"Is the hall as large as Alec's? I won't mind if it isn't."

"Because you don't need it to be as large."

"Yes."

"I cannot say for certain if it's as large. I've never taken the time to notice."

"What makes your home so appealing?"

"It's secure."

What did secure have to do with appearance? "But what does it look like?"

"Invincible," he answered.

She wasn't getting anywhere with him. She would have to wait and see for herself, she decided.

He thought he'd told her everything she needed to know. Although he felt his home was invincible, there was still work to be done on the wall. He was going to reinforce the wood with stone as his brother had suggested, and add yet another platform on the northern peak.

Brenna's excitement mounted as they rode along, and her mood was so improved, she couldn't stop smiling.

Connor's mood darkened as soon as the ruins of his father's home came into view.

"Who lived here?" she whispered as she stared at the charred remains of the vast structure.

"My father."

"Did he die there?"

"Yes."

"Did you live there with him?"

"Yes."

The coldness in his voice told her he didn't want to be questioned about his past. She had every intention of finding out everything she could about her husband so she would be able to understand how he had become such a hard, rigid man, but she knew she would have to be patient and undemanding, or he would never open his heart to her. She would first prove to him that she could be trusted, and eventually he would soften his attitude and begin to confide in her.

She couldn't stop staring at the destruction. Even after they had ridden past, she leaned into Connor's side so she could look behind him to study it.

She had seen the results of fire before, but there was something puzzling about the MacAlister ruin. It took her several minutes before she finally figured out what was missing. The burned crofter's cottage she'd once seen had quickly been overgrown by weeds. This ruin wasn't. There was a forest on three sides of it, yet not one vine had reached the hollowed-out remains. Obviously it had been carefully maintained, and perhaps that was why it seemed so eerie to her.

Why hadn't Connor ordered it torn down? Had he left it to be a reminder to himself and his followers? Patience, she reminded herself. In time she would have her answers.

She straightened up and turned around again. She slipped her hand into his free one, leaned back against him, and said a prayer for his father's soul. She added another one for his dear mother.

Her new home came into view a minute later. She started praying for herself then. She closed her eyes too, frantically hoping that what she believed she'd seen she really hadn't seen at all, but when she gathered enough courage to look again, the monstrous thing was still there, looming over her from the top of a hill like an angry gargoyle.

God really must have been furious with her to have put

her in such an ugly place. She must have caused her parents far more worry than she'd ever realized, and saying that she was sorry hadn't been enough to appease him.

Get hold of yourself, she ordered. God wasn't responsible for this fortress; Connor was.

She took a deep breath and told herself to find something nice about her new home. She would study the fortress from bottom to top, and when she was finished, by God, she would be smiling with excitement.

It was gigantic. That was nice, wasn't it? It was, if bigger was indeed better, as Connor obviously believed.

It was also tall. The fortress was at least three-stories high, perhaps even four, though it was difficult to tell because she couldn't seem to find any windows to give her hints.

Still, it was big. And tall.

She finally spotted the windows. Relieved to see them, she felt like weeping with gratitude. She wasn't going to have to live inside a tomb after all. The windows were there all right, but they'd been covered with an ugly brown fabric, which actually matched the color of dried mud rather nicely; though why in God's name anyone would want them to was beyond her. She would take them down as soon as possible, and then it wouldn't look so bad, would it?

Of course it would. Flowers weren't going to help. She would need a miracle to turn this thing into a home.

She felt ashamed of herself. She wasn't concerned only about appearances, and she must adjust her attitude at once. She would start by calling the hideous monstrosity her home.

"Brenna, is something wrong?"

"Why would you think something was wrong?"

"You're panting, like you can't catch your breath."

She said the first thing that came into her mind. Thankfully, it wasn't a lie. "Your home has taken my breath away."

She probably should add a compliment or two so that Connor would know she appreciated his efforts. He was proud of his fortress, and a good wife would at least try to feel the same.

"It's very big."

He didn't have anything to say about that.

"Why, I don't believe I've ever seen one as big. It's also tall, isn't it?"

He didn't have anything to say about that either.

"Have you finished it then?"

"Are you asking if the back of the fortress is finished?"

No, she hadn't even thought about the back of the keep. She wanted to know if he'd finished the front. "Is it?"

"Yes."

"I see," she replied for lack of anything better to say. "Your rampart is very impressive, isn't it?"

"Perhaps."

"It's at least fifteen feet high. Odd that the wood turned such a brownish color, isn't it?"

He tightened his hold around her waist, pulled her back against his chest, and leaned down close to her ear. "Brenna?"

"Yes, Connor?"

"It's going to be all right."

It took her a full minute before she could nod her agreement. She added a silent prayer next for strength and endurance and vowed to make the best of her circumstances. She had never walked away from a difficult task before, and although the idea held a certain appeal now, she wouldn't give in to her hopelessness. Nothing was impossible to achieve if she worked hard enough and used the mind God had given her.

She felt better once her resolve was back in place, and after they'd crossed the drawbridge, she looked at her new home with renewed interest. She smiled for the benefit of his followers. Like the sentries, they didn't smile back. They didn't frown or turn their backs on her, though. Perhaps they didn't quite know what to make of her, she thought. She would have to convince them through her good works that she was worthy of their respect.

"You've enclosed half the mountain, haven't you?"

"It isn't a mountain, but a hill, wife."

"Why, there must be thirty huts inside the lower bailey alone, yet room for thirty more. Do your soldiers train inside the walls?"

"Sometimes," he answered as he led the way to the upper bailey.

Brenna tried to see everything at once.

Just before they reached the courtyard Connor called a halt. He dismounted and turned to assist her while he tried to answer the questions the men called out to him.

He had only just let go of his wife when the crowd surrounded him. Holding the stallion's reins behind his back, he started up the last of the incline. He assumed Brenna was right behind him, and when the reins were taken out of his hand, he thought Quinlan or Owen had taken over the duty of leading the horse to the stablemaster, for they were the only two soldiers the temperamental stallion would let near.

Men and women pushed forward to speak to their laird. Brenna kept backing away so she wouldn't get trampled. The stallion didn't like the crowd pressing in on him any more than she did and reared up in protest. She grabbed hold of his reins before he did any damage to anyone, and forced the animal to back up with her. She was nearly lifted off her feet a couple of times, then was pushed backward as the disgruntled beast tried to charge her. The training her brothers had forced on her came to her assistance now. She refused to give in to the animal's intimidating antics, and she tightened her hold on his reins and jerked his head down hard. After one last moment of struggle, the horse understood she meant to get her way.

She patted him to let him know she appreciated his cooperation and led him toward the stables.

A soldier stood on the steps leading up to the entrance until his laird beckoned him forward.

"All's well, Connor."

An immediate hush fell over the crowd as they listened to the conversation. "I expected it would be, Crispin. 'Tis the reason you were given command while I was away."

The two warriors stood eye to eye as they faced each other in the center of the courtyard.

"I have good news for you. Your stepmother is waiting in the great hall to greet you."

Connor smiled. "That is good news."

"Lady Euphemia's curiosity to see your wife must have been the motivation she needed to come back to MacAlister land."

"I would assume so. Perhaps she sees this as a new beginning, though in truth, I thought completing a new fortress would bring her back. Is she well, Crispin?"

"She seems to be well," he answered. "Connor, do I address her as Lady MacAlister?"

"You do. She was my father's wife and hasn't married again."

"She's still mourning him, for she's dressed in black," Crispin told him. "There is one more matter I wish to tell you about."

"Can it wait until later?"

"You'll want to hear this news now," he insisted. "Laird Hugh is sending something that was left on his border. He insists you'll want to see it. Whatever it is should be here within the hour."

"Hugh sends you a gift?" Quinlan asked his laird.

Crispin answered. "It's more of a message than a gift. I wasn't able to get anything more specific out of his soldiers. They were worried, however, and insisted several times that their laird is not responsible. It was extremely important to Hugh that Connor understand this."

"This makes little sense," Quinlan muttered. "Why wouldn't they tell you who it was from?"

"They wouldn't explain," Crispin replied.

"Then we'll wait and see," Connor replied.

He then smiled at his friend and, as Connor passed him on his way inside, pounded him on the shoulder to let him know he was pleased with him. Quinlan shoved Crispin in the hopes of getting him to lose his balance. Crispin held his ground and pretended boredom, but the glint in his brown eyes gave him away.

"You missed a fine time, Crispin. Aye, you should have been there to watch me wield my sword. It was a sight to see, and you would have learned a thing or two."

Crispin laughed. "I wouldn't have needed to touch my sword, for my hands are just as effective. Besides, I taught you everything you know. Isn't that true, Connor?" he called out.

"I do not involve myself in petty disputes, though I will admit I don't understand either one of your empty boasts. 'Tis a fact I trained both of you."

Crispin fully appreciated his laird's candor. He watched Connor slowly make his way through the clan to the side of the keep so he could go up the steps. The two soldiers were expected to follow their laird, as it had become a ritual for them to sit at the table with Connor while he caught up on the latest happenings within the clan. They stayed back now so that the other followers could have a turn greeting him.

Both Crispin and Quinlan kept glancing over their shoulders every now and again. Crispin was puzzled, for he had been on the walkway above the wall when his laird rode up to the drawbridge and had seen that he wasn't alone then. Why was he now?

Quinlan couldn't stop smiling. He knew exactly why his laird was alone.

Crispin's curiosity finally got the better of him when Connor started up the steps to go inside the keep. "Was your journey successful, Laird?" he shouted.

"It was," Connor called back.

"Then you did marry?"

"I did."

"Where might your bride be?"

Connor had assumed his wife was following behind him and was now being delayed by the clan. Honest to God, he hadn't given her another thought since Crispin began his report.

He scanned the crowd, looking for his wife. He spotted Owen smiling like a simpleton at the women surrounding him. Brenna was nowhere in sight, however.

"Why aren't you at the stables tending my horse, Owen?" Connor was halfway across the courtyard by the time he finished bellowing his question.

"Another took over the duty for me, Laird," Owen explained with a nervous glance toward Quinlan.

Connor turned to his friend. "Where is my wife, Quinlan?"

"I believe you left her in the lower bailey."

The crowd scattered in every direction as their laird came striding toward the path. The look on Connor's face suggested he didn't wish to be delayed. Crispin and Quinlan followed, but unlike their laird, they weren't scowling.

"Quinlan, how were you able to tend to my stallion and return to the courtyard in such a short time?"

"I didn't tend your stallion," he answered.

"Did Davis?" Connor asked just to make certain the stablemaster had come forward to take over the duty.

"No."

"Then who . . ."

"Another more capable than Davis led your stubborn beast away."

Connor heard the laughter in Quinlan's voice and knew there was something more to be told. He stopped worrying about Brenna being left alone with his stallion because he knew Quinlan wouldn't have been so damned happy if she'd been in any real danger.

"You forgot her, didn't you, Connor?"

"I did no such thing, Quinlan. Who was more capable than Davis? No more jests," he warned. "I'm not in the mood."

"I won't jest, but you still won't believe me. Your wife took over the duty."

"I don't believe you."

Quinlan nudged Crispin. "He did forget her," he whispered.

As soon as they reached the stables, Connor pulled the doors wide before either one of his soldiers could get ahead of him to see to the duty.

The stablemaster came running. He bowed to his laird and was about to welcome him back to the keep when Connor interrupted him.

"Davis, is my stallion in his stall?"

"He is, Laird, and as content as I've ever seen."

"Then you didn't have your usual difficulty getting him to settle down?"

"I was saved from the task by your lady. She certainly has a way with animals, Laird, but I'm sure you already knew that. She soothed the anger out of the beast in no time at all. Your stallion was happy to let her lead him to his quarters."

Connor knew Davis was telling him the truth, as difficult as it was to believe.

"Where is Lady MacAlister now?"

"She spotted Ewan's wife giving their bairn the afternoon air. I'm thinking that was where she was headed."

Connor nodded and walked away. He paused once when Davis called out, "You've chosen well, Laird."

Brenna had already left Ewan's cottage, however. While the blushing mother explained she'd been thrilled to have her mistress's undivided attention, she seemed far more interested in praising Brenna than in telling Connor where she'd gone.

"She insisted on holding the baby and didn't mind at all that he hadn't had his bath yet. She has a special way with children, Laird. My little one is usually suspicious of strangers, but he took to her right away. Your wife's a dear lass, and from England, of all scandalous places. She's thoughtful as can be. She hurried over to meet Brocca when she noticed her staring out at her through the window."

His patience was nearly gone by the time he finally caught up with Brenna. She had already left Brocca's cottage and was just about to knock on another door when he stopped her.

She didn't look especially pleased to see him. He couldn't believe she dared to frown at him after she'd caused him so much trouble.

"You forgot me, didn't you?" She folded her arms and continued to frown at him.

Connor wasn't at all impressed with the way she tried to intimidate him. He moved closer so that she was forced to tilt her head back in order to look up at him, and then said, "You will not take that tone with me."

She didn't back away as he expected her to do, but she did soften her voice when she next spoke to him. "May I speak plainly, Connor?"

"No, you may not. You may follow me back to the keep now, however."

He turned to leave. She stood her ground.

"Are you defying me?" he asked.

"No, Laird, I'm not defying you. I am waiting."

"Waiting for what?"

"For you to admit you forgot me."

"I did no such thing."

"Then you do not plan to apologize?"

She saw the incredulous look that came over his face and knew the thought had never entered his mind. Dear heavens, changing Connor from a barbarian into a considerate husband was going to take every ounce of her patience. But, she had pushed him far enough today, and she didn't dare add another word of criticism until he'd recovered. In her estimation, it was a fair start.

Connor was considering tossing his wife over his shoulder and carrying her to the keep when she suddenly smiled at him and took hold of his hand. He didn't understand what had caused the transformation, but he didn't question her. He had pushed her far enough for one day, and now that he'd made her realize she must not challenge him or contradict him, he believed he'd made a fair start. He knew it was going to take him a long time to help her learn to be more disciplined.

As soon as he moved back toward the path, she noticed again the soldier standing next to Quinlan.

"Brenna, in future, don't make me chase after you."

She nodded agreement because her husband seemed to require it, then looked at Quinlan. "He did forget about me, didn't he?"

Connor squeezed her hand to let her know what he thought about her question.

"It would seem he did, mi'lady."

"Thank you for reminding him."

"I didn't," Quinlan replied, nodding to his left. "Crispin did."

She smiled at the soldier. "Thank you, Crispin." She would have officially introduced herself to the soldier, but he looked rather dazed, and she decided he was busy thinking about something more important.

Quinlan laughed at the expression on Crispin's face. His friend was looking quite stunned. "She takes your breath away, doesn't she, Crispin?"

The soldier nodded. He motioned to Quinlan to wait so that they could have a moment alone and follow at a more discreet distance.

"I've never seen Connor act this way. He doesn't usually allow any woman to make him lose his patience."

"She isn't just any woman. She's his wife. I think he likes having her around."

Crispin smiled. "I'd like having her around too, if I were married to her. She's very beautiful, isn't she? I don't think I've ever seen a woman so bonny."

"Connor doesn't notice."

The two men shared a laugh. Brenna glanced back over her shoulder to smile at them.

"Our mistress isn't easily intimidated." There was admiration in Crispin's voice when he made the remark.

"If she were the least bit timid, Connor would walk all over her. Do you remember what he told us about Isabelle?"

"He told us very little. He doesn't remember his mother."

"That is so, but he remembers every word his father said to him before he died."

Crispin nodded. "Donald called his wife his own sweet Isabelle. He loved her."

"Exactly so."

"But Donald cautioned his son not to make the same mistake."

"Connor knew he was only warning him to be careful. If you had seen the way the Lady Brenna and he looked at one another when they first met, you would conclude what I have."

"And what is that?"

Quinlan stared at Brenna as he gave his answer. "She's going to be Connor's own sweet love."

Crispin clasped his hands behind his back while he considered what Quinlan had just told him. Like his friend, he also wanted his laird to find peace and contentment. But love? He didn't know if Connor would ever let himself feel such an emotion.

"I've never heard you talk like this."

"I've never seen Connor act like this."

"Like what?"

Quinlan shrugged. "There have been sparks flying between the two of them from the very beginning. It's as though Connor were struck by a bolt. He's going to give his heart to her because he won't be able to stop it from happening. Quit frowning, Crispin. She has a good heart."

The two soldiers continued to follow behind the couple at

a leisurely pace while Crispin caught Quinlan up on the latest news. Brenna didn't realize she was being discussed by the men, and she certainly didn't know she was being watched so closely. Connor was forcing her to run in order to keep up with him, and she soon decided she had had enough. She suddenly stopped. Connor was either going to have to drag her behind him or let go of her. She would leave the choice up to him.

"Why did you stop?"

"I got tired of running."

A smile softened his expression. "Why didn't you tell me to slow down?"

"I wanted to keep up. I didn't realize I was so weary this afternoon. I'm sure I'll recover after we have our supper. Could we sit a spell until then?"

He moved back to her side. "We already ate our evening meal, remember? You cannot still be hungry."

She shrugged. There really wasn't any use in pretending with her husband that she had a dainty appetite. "I could eat a little something," she admitted. "I was a bit nervous meeting Alec and by the time we sat down at the table, I couldn't concentrate on food. I barely ate a thing. I can't imagine why you're laughing, Connor. I haven't told you a jest."

He didn't apologize, of course. She doubted he ever would. He stopped laughing, though, and she was most appreciative.

"Would it help if I carried you?"

His suggestion didn't sit well with her. "And have your followers think you married a weakling? I'll crawl first."

She straightened her shoulders, tugged her hand away from his, and tried to hurry past him. She didn't get very far. He caught her around her waist and forced her into his side. He didn't have to tell her to lean against him. She was too weary to even consider struggling. She sagged against him and let out a little sigh. She didn't dare close her eyes for even a second for fear she'd fall asleep on her feet if she did. God only knew, she'd done it before.

"You've had a difficult day."

"No, I haven't."

"Do you have to disagree with everything I say?"

"I was simply giving you my opinion. We've yet to argue, Connor. Once we do, you'll know the difference. Please let go of me as soon as we reach the courtyard. I don't want your followers to think I can't stand without assistance."

In frustration, she threaded her fingers through her hair, then grimaced as she touched her injury. "I never seem to say the right thing to you. Everything's so different here. I don't like chaos, and it seems to me that my life has been extremely chaotic since I met you. I want to live in peace."

"It's going to become much easier for you now."

She didn't look as though she believed him. "Do you promise?"

He smiled. "I promise."

She managed to smile back and relax. He didn't know if it had been his calm voice or his promise that had soothed her.

"I don't like surprises," she remarked as she moved closer to his side again. "Unless, of course, I know about them in advance."

She sounded sincere enough for him to think she didn't realize she'd just contradicted herself. "If you know in advance, it isn't a surprise."

"Exactly so," she reasoned. "Tell me how it will become easier."

"You won't have to worry about pleasing me. I'm rarely here."

"I don't worry about pleasing you now. But I don't understand why you're rarely here. This is your home."

"Yes."

"And I'm here."

"I realize that. We'll see each other now and again."

They had finally reached the courtyard proper. It was deserted.

"You mentioned you would only be here every now and again?" she asked, sorry her voice sounded so strained.

His mind was on an entirely different matter. Crispin's report that their ally to the south wanted Connor to see something that had been left at his border had made him curious, and he was guessing what the something might be. Because of the life he'd led, he was naturally suspicious and had already concluded the surprise wasn't going to be

189

welcome. He wasn't an impatient man when important issues were at stake, and so he once again decided to wait and see before he contemplated his response.

Brenna's question pulled him away from his thoughts. "Exactly how often is 'now and again'?"

"Once or twice a month."

"You're serious?"

"I am."

The more he told her, the less she wanted to hear. "A husband should be home with his wife more often than twice a month."

"I have other more important duties."

She felt as though he were abandoning her. Worse, she believed he was eager to do just that.

"Why bother to come back at all?"

He decided to ignore the anger in her voice. "Several reasons come to mind. The most compelling one is you."

A little of her irritation eased away. "Me?" she whispered, hoping he would redeem himself by giving her some praise.

"I want children."

She wanted to throttle him. "You mentioned you did."

"I'm pleased you remember."

"I remember everything you said to me: you married me to insult MacNare, and you'll be happy to take me back to England as soon as I give you a son. I doubt I'll ever forget those two important facts. Your reasons make me feel so very worthy."

"Would you rather I lied to you?"

She shook her head. "I would rather we never, ever talk about this again. You may explain your duties and your expectations the next time you happen to pass by the area. Now, if you'll excuse me, I'd like to go inside."

"I will call my followers together and introduce you to them as soon as Donald returns with the younger soldiers."

"You needn't go to any trouble, Connor. I already have one black mark against me; I might as well have another."

"What black mark?" he called out.

He stood in the center of the courtyard, his attention fully on his wife. Her behavior was most perplexing. She'd hurried on ahead of him, but hadn't gone to the steps leading inside the keep. No, she'd gone to the center of the wall and was now pacing back and forth along the front of the keep.

It was obvious he'd upset her, and while he knew he was fully responsible, he couldn't understand how it had happened. His goal had been to soothe her, yet one word had led to another, and before he realized what the outcome would be, she was getting teary eyed. He believed he'd been thoughtful by telling her he wouldn't be home very often. Yet she acted as though he'd just betrayed her. How in God's name would he ever make sense out of her?

"Explain this black mark," he ordered when she didn't immediately answer him.

"I'm English, for the love of God, and everyone knows I was on my way to marry MacNare. Surely you understand what I'm up against? Oh, and I'm clumsy too," she told her husband. "I forgot about that. What have you done with your steps? I can't seem to find them."

"They're on the side of the keep," he answered.

"I fell down Alec's steps, remember?"

Crispin had just caught up with Connor and turned to his laird. "Mi'lady fell down steps?"

"It seems she did," he replied.

Connor would have taken the time to explain if he hadn't noticed his wife was about to go around to the wrong side of the keep. "The steps are on the opposite side, Brenna."

She promptly turned around. "They're supposed to be in the center of the front, facing the courtyard. Everyone knows that is the fashion these days. I'm wanting to sleep in a bed tonight and not on the floor, Connor. Do you have beds inside?"

She finally looked at her husband so he would see her frown and realized she wasn't up to hearing any more of his plans about their future. Hearing he would stop by every once in a while was more than enough for her stomach in one day. She noticed Quinlan and Crispin were standing next to her husband and promptly changed her frown into a smile. No doubt about it, Connor was turning her into a shrew. God only knew how long his soldiers had been observing her rant and rave like a lunatic. Although it was probably too late to change their opinion of her, she decided to give it her best try.

"It's going to be a fine evening, isn't it?" she called out, pretending everything was as right as could be and she hadn't been acting like a madwoman seconds ago.

"If you think so, mi'lady," Crispin called back. "What just came over her?" he whispered to Quinlan.

"We did," he answered. "I believe she only just noticed us and doesn't want us to know her husband offended her."

"I didn't offend her."

"It would seem to me that you did."

Connor shoved his friend aside on his way to intercept his wife.

She kept on smiling, even when she reached the top of the stone steps and noticed there wasn't a landing to stand on. She backed down a step and reached forward to grasp the handle to the entrance.

The door wouldn't open. It was either bolted on the inside or reinforced with iron or steel. She put both hands to her task, added her muscle, and finally got it open a crack. It still wasn't wide enough for her to squeeze through without getting crushed.

Connor came to her assistance. He heard her muttering to herself as he came up the steps behind her. He put his arm around her waist, pulled her back against him, and reached over her shoulder to open the door with one quick flick of his wrist.

She couldn't help but be impressed by his strength. "I thought it was locked and didn't try to force it," she said so that he wouldn't think she was a weakling.

"It's open now."

He continued to wait for her to go inside. She continued to lean against him.

"Aren't you curious to see the inside?"

"Is it as grand as the outside?"

"Yes."

She had been afraid he would say that.

"What are you doing?"

Bracing myself, she admitted to herself before she told

him an altogether different tale. "I'm letting my anticipation build. Shall we go inside?"

He rolled his eyes heavenward. She hurried across the threshold and came to an abrupt stop in the center of the entrance to wait until her eyes adjusted to the darkness. She saw a soldier standing in front of double doors on her left, bowed to him, and then looked around with interest.

It was bad all right, but not as bad as she had imagined it would be. There were stone steps directly in front of her, a stone wall on her right. She assumed she was on the main floor and the bedchambers were on the floor above. She was curious to see the hall, of course, but when she turned to go through the double doors, Connor took hold of her arm to stop her.

"You won't ever go in there," he explained as he guided her toward the steps.

"Why won't I?"

"The higher ranking soldiers are inside. Do you want me to carry you upstairs?"

He didn't give her time to decide. He had lifted her into his arms and had reached the door at the top before she could answer him.

Another sentry stood guard on a landing that was so narrow, he had to come down a step in order to open the door.

Connor nodded to the soldier before striding inside. He put her down in the entrance and quickly explained where everything was located.

The great hall was to the left of the entrance and directly above the soldiers' quarters. It was quite large, though it wasn't nearly as large as Alec Kincaid's, and it was sparsely furnished.

Directly across from the entrance was a large stone hearth built into the wall. Though a fire blazed to take the chill from the air, it wasn't proving effective. Three windows covered with ugly brown fabric ran along one of the walls, and there was a long table with twin benches flanking either side.

The hall was as welcoming as a coffin. Brenna knew she was going to have to make some changes as soon as possible. She would start by placing rushes on the wooden floors and hanging several brightly colored banners and tapestries on the stark walls. A pretty cloth would hide the scarred tabletop, and cushions placed on the hard benches would make sitting more comfortable.

She pictured what the hall could look like and was suddenly eager to get started.

"May I add a few touches here and there, Connor?" In her excitement, she clasped her hands together and smiled up at him while she waited to receive his permission.

"This is your home, Brenna. You may do whatever you want to do."

"May I kiss you?"

The question caught him off guard. "Have you forgotten you're irritated with me?"

"No, I haven't forgotten, but my irritation is gone now. You do know why, don't you?"

Her voice had dropped to a whisper. He responded in kind. "No, I don't know why," he replied, a hint of a smile in his eyes.

"Because we're standing together for the first time in our home, and I realize that this is the perfect time for us to start over. You should kiss me now."

"We cannot start over whenever the mood strikes you."

She reached up to cup the back of his head in her hands and drew him down for a kiss. Her lips brushed over his in a quick, gentle caress meant to torment him. She wanted him to kiss her back, of course, and when he didn't cooperate, she brushed her lips over his once again.

"It's a new beginning," she explained in a whisper.

He continued to resist, although in truth he had stopped paying attention to what she was saying. He wanted only to benefit from his wife's arousing methods of trying to sway him.

She wasn't being at all subtle, which of course was exactly why he was enjoying himself, and as she began to tug on his lower lip to get a reaction, he knew he would soon let her win. He pulled her into his arms, pressed her body against his, and slowly shook his head at her.

"No, we can't start over."

Her eyes sparkled with devilment. "Ah, Connor, we already have."

The kiss she gave him then was altogether different from the one before. Her kiss wasn't playful now, but demanding, and the second she opened her mouth for him and began to tease him with her tongue, he took absolute possession.

He might have laughed, he couldn't remember, for this was the first time Brenna had consciously set out to tempt him. She still didn't understand the physical power she had over him, and he hoped to God she never did. She was simply tempting him to take what he would now, and in her innocent flirtation, she was actually showing him the extent of her affection for him.

He heard her low moan of pleasure, felt her tighten her hold around his neck, and was arrogantly satisfied to know that while he was completely in control of his emotions, his wife soon would not be of hers. Brenna was honest and forthright in everything she did, and in a world filled with deceit, where what wasn't said was often far more important than what was, he found himself drawn to Brenna's simplistic view.

Connor didn't consciously let himself get caught up in the moment, yet that was what happened all the same. Passion was suddenly burning inside of him, and one kiss no longer satisfied him. He wanted it all.

Just as he was making up his mind to take her upstairs and bed her, she abruptly ended the kiss by turning her face away. Her voice was a ragged whisper against his ear as she explained. "We aren't alone."

"No one would dare intrude without gaining permission," he told her as he tried to kiss her again.

"Someone's watching us, Connor. Please let go of me."

He did as she asked and then turned to confront the intruder.

Euphemia was standing on the landing above the steps leading to the bedrooms. Connor's expression changed in the blink of an eye. He smiled with true joy, and Brenna found herself smiling in reaction.

"It's good to see you again, Euphemia," he called out, his great affection for the woman apparent in his voice.

Brenna's knees almost buckled. She couldn't believe what she had just heard. Euphemia couldn't be here. She was due to arrive tomorrow, not today, but she was here now, and

195

had just observed her stepson's disgustingly undisciplined wife throwing herself at him.

Brenna considered kicking her husband because he hadn't bothered to tell her Euphemia had arrived, but didn't give in to the urge because she wanted the woman to like her, not despise her.

First impressions were often wrong. Brenna tried to keep that fact in mind as she stared up at Connor's stepmother. Euphemia appeared to be as old as the pines. She reminded Brenna of a crow, as she was dressed in black and seemed to be perched on the top step, with her shoulders hunched forward and her gaze intent, penetrating, almost piercing as she watched Connor walk toward her.

Brenna was instinctively wary of the woman, but before she could berate herself for being frightened and having such uncharitable thoughts about the elderly woman's appearance, she witnessed a startling transformation overtake Euphemia. The woman suddenly straightened up to her full height, which surely made her nearly as tall as Connor. She threw her shoulders back and glided down the steps with the grace and elegance one would expect from a queen. The smile she gave Connor softened the wrinkles at the corners of her eyes, and no one would have noticed then the maze of deep creases mapping her face. Brenna was captivated by the sincerity she saw in Euphemia's eyes.

The change in her stunned Brenna. Euphemia was still old, of course, but she wasn't any older than Brenna's own dear mother. Grieving had obviously left its cruel marks on the woman, seemingly aging her far beyond her actual years, and, oh, how she must have loved Connor's father to have been so devastated by his death. Both the gray hair and the wrinkles carved in her face gave testimony to the pain the poor woman had endured.

Brenna's heart went out to her. She wanted to help ease her sorrow in any way that she could. Connor called Brenna's name then and she hurried forward. As soon as he finished introducing her, she bowed low to Euphemia and said how pleased she was to meet her. Euphemia's smile was somewhat guarded, Brenna noticed, but Connor's wife still felt she had been found acceptable.

"The pleasure is mine," Euphemia said, surprising Brenna once again, because her voice was that of a young woman, and now that Brenna looked closely at her, she realized his stepmother had once been a very beautiful woman. She wasn't beautiful now.

"You are the reason I finally came back," Euphemia continued. "For I was quite eager to meet the woman who had at last captured Connor. I have been plaguing him for years to take a wife."

She turned to Connor once again. "Now I must work on getting Raen to marry. He's been even more resistant to the idea than you were. I fear he'll be an old man before he takes a bride."

Brenna stood by her husband's side, listening as the two of them discussed Raen's health and happiness. Connor wanted to find out who Raen was currently serving because he had heard he was no longer under Laird Ferson's command, but Euphemia skirted the issue by suggesting he speak to her son about such matters.

"Has Raen arrived yet?" Brenna asked.

"No," Euphemia answered. "My son will join me to-morrow."

Connor suggested they sit at the table and continue their conversation. Brenna followed behind her husband, smiling over the way Euphemia put her hand on Connor's arm and smiled so lovingly at him.

Euphemia continued to talk about Raen for several more minutes, and then she looked at Brenna, obviously waiting for her to say something. She blurted out the first thing that came into her head. "I'm eager to meet such a perfect man."

She realized she sounded derisive and was horrified. "You sound like my mother, Lady Euphemia. She also believes her sons are wonderful. She's right, of course, just as you are."

Euphemia nodded. "I am eager to see Raen," she said. "It's been over six months since he last visited me. He's terribly busy, and I diligently try not to meddle in his affairs."

"Was the journey difficult for you, madam?" Connor asked.

"I cannot lie and tell you it was easy," she replied. "Yet it was no worse than what I anticipated," she added, her gaze directed at Brenna now.

She thought it was sweet that Euphemia was thoughtfully including her. "How long have you been away?" she asked.

"Sixteen years, three months," she answered. "Some mornings it seems as though my Donald passed away just the day before, so overcome am I with sorrow."

Connor nodded with understanding. He noticed the tears in Euphemia's eyes and gently turned the conversation to lighter matters.

Brenna was happy to sit by her husband's side and listen. One topic led to another and another, and before Brenna realized it, a good hour had passed.

She would have been happy to sit there the rest of the night, because the look of peace on her husband's face was a worthy reward. She had never seen him this relaxed or content. He obviously loved this woman, certainly honored her, and had missed her terribly.

Her thoughts turned to her own dear mother then, and as she pictured their reunion one day in the future, tears sprang into her eyes. To stop herself from becoming melancholy, she quit thinking about her family and considered instead what she would like to eat for supper.

Euphemia pulled her back to the conversation at hand by calling her name.

"I beg your indulgence, but the journey here has left me weary. I'm not as young as I used to be, and even short rides tire me. I would like to retire for the night, if you will allow me to, and would appreciate a tray of light fare sent up to me."

Connor immediately stood up to assist his stepmother.

"May I help you get settled, Lady MacAlister?" Brenna asked.

"One of Connor's servants has already seen to the duty, child."

Brenna bowed to her and bid her good night. Connor suggested she wait in the hall for him until he returned from escorting Euphemia to her room. Brenna understood Connor's need to have a private moment with his stepmother and didn't mind at all that she had been excluded.

He was gone a long while. By the time he returned to the hall, her stomach was growling for food and she was so sleepy, she could barely hold her head up.

Her husband's manner was brisk now, and she noticed that though he'd had no difficulty whatsoever lingering during his reunion with his stepmother, he couldn't show his wife half as much consideration.

"There are four chambers upstairs, Brenna. The kitchens are in a separate building behind the hall, should you ever feel the need to go there."

He clasped hold of her hand and led her up the staircase. She was thankful the steps weren't nearly as steep as the ones leading up from the soldiers' quarters.

"Why is there a banister here and not below? Was there a reason for not building one?"

"Yes," he answered. "Are you really hungry?"

"I could eat a little something. I'm still waiting for you to tell me why there isn't a railing."

"It's easier to push soldiers down, that's why."

She thought he was jesting. When he didn't smile, she changed her mind. "That's rather impolite, isn't it?"

He didn't understand she was teasing him and apparently didn't feel her question merited an answer.

When they reached the landing, he motioned to the dark hallway behind her. "There are three chambers there. Our bedroom is on the other side of the landing, straight ahead of you."

She didn't move fast enough to suit him. He pulled her along and stopped only after they'd entered the chamber. The door slammed shut behind him with a resounding thud. It was completely dark inside. Connor crossed the chamber and pulled back the covering over the window to let the light come in.

Brenna let out a sigh of relief because the room wasn't nearly as bad as she thought it would be. There was a nice-sized hearth at one end of the chamber and a bed at the opposite end. Two low chests flanked the sides, with several candles on top of each. Other than a few hooks placed high up on the wall beside the door, there wasn't anything more to be noticed.

She hurried over to the window to see the view and

immediately wished she hadn't bothered. Straight ahead was the courtyard and then the ruins, a gloomy picture to be sure, and since she didn't want to dwell on the past now, she went to the bed to find out if it was lumpy or soft.

"It's a very nice bed," she remarked. "And so is the room. You live like a peasant, don't you, Connor, without any unnecessary luxuries?"

"Does that bother you?"

"No," she answered. "May I have a bath?"

"Tomorrow I'll take you to the lake."

"Tonight, if you please?"

He relented. "I'll have a bath prepared. You'll have to wait while the water is heated in the kitchens and carried up."

She shook her head. "I would not put your staff to such trouble. I could bathe in the kitchens, couldn't I?"

He wasn't surprised by her thoughtfulness because he'd already noticed she put the concerns of others before her own, no matter how much she was inconvenienced. Or injured, he thought to add, for she had put Grace's safety above her own.

"Yes, you may bathe in the kitchens."

"May I also eat there?"

"If you wish."

He opened the door to leave, but hesitated at the threshold, frowning as he noticed once again the dark shadows under her eyes. In the soft light they seemed more pronounced. He felt responsible for her exhaustion because he'd pushed her too hard, and while he regretted putting her through such a difficult ordeal, there really hadn't been any other choice. MacNare and his soldiers had been gaining on them, and getting her to safety far outweighed her need for sleep.

"I want you to rest."

"Will you rest beside me?"

"Yes."

"Now that Euphemia is here, are you still intent on leaving tomorrow?"

"Yes."

"Do you think she liked me?"

"Of course she liked you. You shouldn't need my reassurance."

"Will she stay with us a long while?"

"I hope so," he answered on his way out the door. "I haven't asked."

"Connor?"

"Yes?"

"Please don't forget to send one of your men to find Gilly."

"I won't forget. Any other questions?"

Neither his gruff attitude nor his frown deterred her. She hurried over to the doorway, leaned up on her tiptoes, and kissed him. She was very thorough. Connor put his arm around her waist, hauled her up against him, and kissed her a second time, far more passionately than he'd intended to and not nearly as long as he wanted. She ended the kiss by pulling away from him. She saw the bewilderment in his eyes, turned around so he wouldn't see her smile, and then thought to tell him he could now take his leave.

He was halfway down the stairs before he realized he'd been dismissed.

Quinlan had to tell him he was smiling. The soldier wanted to know why his laird was happy, leaving Connor no choice but to admit he didn't have the faintest idea.

Although it wasn't possible, the ruins of Connor's father's home seemed to have moved closer, and no matter where Brenna stood in the room, whenever she looked outside, the destruction was all she could see.

She couldn't stop staring at the depressing sight. She knew his father had died there, but had Connor witnessed his death? She hoped he hadn't because she couldn't even begin to imagine how painful it would be to watch her own dear father die.

A knock on her door was a welcome intrusion to such sad thoughts. A soldier carried in her baggage, and the minute she was left alone again, she pulled out a change of clothing, her brush and two ribbons, and hurried downstairs.

There wasn't a soul on the main floor, and not a sound could be heard coming from outside. She didn't like the silence at all. She was used to being surrounded by family, servants, and visitors, and she knew it was going to take time for her to adjust to the change.

The cook was coming to fetch her and had pushed the back door open just as Brenna was reaching for the handle. It took the woman a moment to recover from her surprise. She backed down the steps, bowed low, and introduced herself in such a low voice, it was as though she were confessing her sins to a priest and didn't wish to be overheard. Her name was Ada. She was twice Brenna's height, extremely rounded in her middle, and had enough gray in her braid to suggest she was getting on in years.

Both her gentle manner and soft voice reminded Brenna of her mother, and she took to the woman at once. Ada was just as bossy as Brenna's mother, too. Once she assisted her mistress into the steaming water, Ada refused to give her any soap until Brenna promised not to wash her hair.

The two women conversed with one another using a combination of Gaelic and gestures. Ada spoke with a brogue so thick and garbled, Brenna could catch only a word or two out of her long, rambling explanations. She finally pointed to the stitches on her mistress's forehead, frowned, and vehemently shook her head. Brenna concluded she didn't want her to get the stitches wet.

Ada didn't notice the bruise on the back of her thigh until she helped Brenna get out of the wooden tub. The older woman clucked over her like a mother hen, and in her attempt to show how sympathetic she was, she pounded so roughly on Brenna's shoulder, she very nearly sent Brenna sailing across the kitchen.

After wrapping the laird's new wife in a blanket, Ada demanded to know the story behind Brenna's injuries. Brenna tried several times to explain the circumstances, but the only words the woman understood were those conveying the fact that she'd fallen down the steps.

Brenna tried to put on the clothes she'd brought down from her baggage, but Ada wouldn't let her. She snatched the garments out of her hands and handed her new clothing instead. Brenna knew Connor was responsible for the thoughtfulness because Ada kept bowing her head and saying "Laird MacAlister" over and over again.

Ten minutes later, Brenna was dressed in a pale gold gown with a MacAlister plaid overskirt.

Ada insisted on helping her get to the kitchen's table. Telling the woman she didn't need her assistance proved useless. The woman's mind was already made up, and it was futile to argue.

Brenna didn't have any idea what it was she had been given to eat, but the flavor and the aroma were so wonderful she had to have a large second helping. Both the food and Ada's companionship invigorated her. She wasn't ready to go to bed after all and decided to explore outside until dark.

The minute she stepped outside the kitchen door, she heard men shouting. The noise seemed to be coming from the courtyard. It sounded as though quite a crowd had gathered, with everyone trying to be heard at the same time, and Brenna was curious to find out what was happening. She saw some men running up the slope toward the front of the keep, their expressions grim. Instinctively, she proceeded more cautiously.

By the time she reached the side of the keep, the courtyard was silent. She thought the soldiers must have continued on toward the crest, but when she turned the corner and saw them standing in a wide circle, she came to an abrupt stop.

As one, the soldiers stared toward the center of the circle. They seemed transfixed. Brenna noticed that three of the men were wearing plaids different from the MacAlister's. They were the only ones who moved at all. She saw their fearful expressions each time they glanced up to look at her husband. Connor was on the far side of the circle. Had he looked up, he would have seen her standing there, watching, but like the others, his attention was on the ground.

The collective mood of the men told her something was terribly wrong.

She kept her gaze on her husband as she walked forward, and hoped he would look up at her so she would know whether to come forward or turn away. His rigid stance should have been sufficient warning, yet she was still unprepared for what she was about to see.

She found an opening between two MacAlister soldiers,

moved closer, and stood up on her tiptoes trying to see over the shoulders of the men standing in front of her. Just then one of the men moved over a bit and suddenly she was able to look down at the ground and see what the others were staring at.

She saw the bloody remains of an animal with a knotted rope twisted about its neck, and at first glance she didn't understand the significance. Then she noticed what was left of the braided mane and the pretty pink ribbon tied into a perfect little bow.

The impact struck her like a blow. Bile rushed up to her throat, and with it came her low whimper of pain.

She was looking at her own sweet Gilly.

Chapter

9

Connor faced his wife in the circle and waited for her to look at him. He could tell she didn't immediately understand what she was looking at. He hoped to God she wouldn't recognize the horse, even though he knew in his heart she would. Why hadn't he taken the time to remove the damned ribbon the second he'd seen it? Surely that was the only way she would ever have known it was Gilly.

He ached for her. The pain he saw in her eyes at the moment of recognition made him come close to losing his control. It took all his willpower to stand perfectly still. She made a low sound. He was certain Hugh's soldiers would think it was just the whisper of the wind, for one man looked up at the sky before turning back to Connor.

Brenna put her hand to her throat, took a step back, and frantically sought out Connor.

He wanted to go to her, but he didn't move and, in fact, knew he couldn't show her any compassion until after the soldiers had taken their leave. Hugh's men would return to their laird to report the MacAlister's reaction, and Connor would be damned for eternity before he would let any outsider know what he thought about the message MacNare had sent him.

He was worried his wife would scream or break down in

front of the witnesses. He wouldn't blame her, for she felt great affection for her pet, but he prayed she would walk away first. He tried to help her, holding her gaze for a long moment, willing her with his silence and his mask of cold indifference to follow his lead. He knew he was asking too much of her and honestly didn't know if she could give him what he wanted. Yet, just as he made up his mind to order her back inside, he saw her hand drop down to her side and the color rush back into her face. She straightened to her full height, shuddered once, and gave him a barely perceptible nod.

She gave him far more than he'd expected. She looked at Hugh's soldiers, and honest to God, there was a faint smile on her face as though she wanted to welcome them to her home but knew she shouldn't until her laird introduced her.

Dear God, he was proud of her. She appeared to be only mildly curious as she studied each man's face, and when she finished her inspection, she glanced at Connor one last time, bowed to him, and then turned around and walked away with all the dignity and regal bearing of a princess.

Everyone watched her leave. Several servants waited by the side of the keep for their mistress, and as Brenna walked past them, one called out to her.

"Mi'lady, what are the men looking at?"

"Just a dead horse," she called out. "Nothing more."

She continued on at a leisurely pace, and only when she had disappeared around the corner did Hugh's soldiers turn back to Connor. They were staggered by the grin they saw on Laird MacAlister's face.

The senior of the emissaries addressed the laird. "Hugh is concerned you'll decide he had something to do with this."

Crispin stepped forward to answer for his laird. He towered over the soldier, forcing the man to take a hasty step back.

"Hugh has no reason to be concerned. Our laird knows who sent the message."

"You've completed your errand," Quinlan announced. "Leave now and let us get back to important matters."

Several of the MacAlister warriors nodded their agreement, and the messenger noted they were all smiling like their laird.

"Do I report your laird was inconvenienced and nothing more?"

"Report what you will," Connor answered. "It makes no difference to me."

"Do you want us to take the remains with us?"

"Leave it for our dogs," Crispin suggested.

Connor nodded before he walked away.

The messenger wouldn't forget what he had witnessed, and when he stood before his laird, he would report only that Laird MacAlister had been vastly amused by the enemy's message.

Brenna made it to the bedroom before she started gagging. She was able to keep the food in her stomach by taking deep breaths and forcing herself to block the image of Gilly.

When her nausea slowly subsided, she sat down on the side of the bed, gripped her hands together in her lap, and tried to make sense out of the horror. She didn't weep, for mourning, she believed, should be reserved for men, not animals, and it became a measure of her control that she not give in to the desire.

Poor Gilly. Her faithful mare had never done anyone any harm. The docile, obedient pet had brought Brenna such joy over the years, and should have been retired to a field of clover to die when her time came. To think that she had been mutilated and then dragged halfway up a mountain was nearly too horrible to accept.

She prayed the gentle pet had died quickly before the sadistic killers had used their knives and hatchets on her. Who would do such a vile, contemptible thing? What kind of monster would destroy one of God's gentle creatures with such malicious intent?

MacNare. He must be behind the deed. He must have been in a rage all the while he'd chased after Connor and her, and when he happened upon Gilly, he turned his wrath against her. Until today, Brenna hadn't known men were capable of such horrendous cruelty. When her father had decreed she would marry MacNare, she remembered she'd been angry and worried. But she hadn't been truly afraid of the laird.

She was terrified of him now. If this is what he would do

to an animal, what would he do to a man? The thought led to another more terrifying one. If Connor hadn't come for her when he did, she would be married to the demon now. The realization made her start gagging again.

She didn't know how long she sat on the bed thinking about what had happened, but the room was dark by the time Connor came inside. She neither looked at him nor spoke to him and was thankful for his silence, because she knew she wouldn't be able to talk about Gilly just yet.

After giving her a quick glance to make certain she was all right, he bolted the door behind him, then crossed to the hearth to start a fire blazing. He kept expecting her to shout at him, and when she remained silent, he grew even more worried. He knew she must be angry with him because he had insisted on leaving Gilly behind. He didn't want Brenna to keep her anger inside. The sooner she got it out in the open, the sooner she could sleep again.

Women, his brother had told him, had the unique ability to rid themselves of their anger simply by acknowledging it. Men weren't able to do such a thing. Anger would often fester inside the hearts of warriors for years and years, until they found a way to right the wrong done to them. Connor wouldn't have had it any other way.

"You're shivering. Come and stand by the fire."

She surprised him by obeying. As soon as she crossed the chamber, he pulled her into his arms, told her to look up at him, and then gave her permission to shout at him.

"I don't want to shout at you," she said, puzzled.

"I know you're angry with me. You'll tell me about it now and get rid of it."

"I'm not angry with you."

"I made the decision to leave your horse behind."

"Yes, but it was necessary."

She turned away from him and stared into the flames. "MacNare's responsible."

"Yes."

"He took pleasure in what he did to Gilly. Didn't he?"

"Don't think about it."

"Answer me." Her voice was sharper than she intended, but Connor didn't seem to be at all bothered by it. His response was quite mild when he agreed with her.

"Yes, I'm sure he took pleasure in mutilating the horse."

"I hope Gilly died quickly before . . . Did she?"

He looked her right in the eye while he lied to her. "Yes."

"How can you know for certain?"

"I know." He was emphatic enough for her to think he was telling her the truth.

"I shouldn't have left the braided ribbons dressing her mane. That's how he knew she belonged to a woman, isn't it?"

"They would have known anyway. She was smaller than any of ours."

Connor was taking it all in stride. She pulled out of his arms and looked up at his face again but couldn't see any anger there at all.

"You're very calm about it all, aren't you? Don't you want to shout?" she asked.

"Would such a reaction change what happened?"

She shook her head. She knew he was right. Ranting and raving wouldn't bring Gilly back to her. Still, the lack of emotion Connor was showing made her feel all the more alone with her anger and her terror.

"Why did MacNare go to such trouble to send what was left of Gilly to us?"

"He wanted me to see what he'd done. Go to bed now. You need your rest."

"Was it a message for you or for me?"

"Me."

"Gilly belonged to me."

"But you belong to me," he reasoned.

"Was it a message of what's to come?"

"Hugh's soldiers said MacNare called it a gift," he told her. He forced her closer to him again and began to remove her clothes.

She didn't resist until he tried to take her chemise off her. "I'll be cold."

He wouldn't be deterred. "I'll keep you warm tonight. I notice you're still wearing the medallion your father gave you. I told you to throw it away," he reminded her. He really didn't care what she did with the wooden disk, now that he understood her better and knew she wasn't wearing it to insult him. It seemed harmless enough.

"I didn't do it."

"Do what?"

"Throw it away."

"I can see you didn't," he said, amused. "You're really exhausted tonight, aren't you?"

"Yes. I don't think I'll be able to sleep though. I'm too angry and . . ."

"And what?"

She shook her head. She wasn't ready to admit to him how frightened she was. "Will you come to bed with me?"

"Not yet. I have one more duty to complete."

"Is it important?"

"Yes."

"Could you rest beside me for just a few minutes, please?"

She wouldn't get into bed until he agreed, so he removed his boots, stretched out on his back, and stacked his hands behind his head. He stared up at the ceiling. She stared at him.

He gave the appearance of a contented man who didn't have a worry in the world, and had she not seen him standing across from her in the courtyard, she would have thought he hadn't seen or heard about Gilly yet. His reaction didn't comfort her.

She would have preferred sleeping on the side closer to the door, but he made her take the side by the window instead. She didn't want to stare out at the ruins, but she didn't want to look at Connor either, because his cold attitude was nearly as unsettling as the view in the moonlight, and so she ended up flat on her back staring up at the ceiling, too.

She couldn't understand her husband's indifference. When he was looking down at Gilly, he'd appeared completely unconcerned, but she thought he'd been pretending so the messengers wouldn't have anything worthwhile to report. Now she wasn't so certain. Perhaps Connor hadn't been pretending at all. Could he really be so unfeeling?

The horse was her pet, yes, and though she had raised her and loved her dearly, she was still just an animal. But would Connor have behaved differently if the remains of one of his soldiers had been dragged home to him?

She found herself fervently hoping so.

Several minutes passed in silence while she thought about her husband's behavior. She thought of another question to ask him then and glanced over to make certain he was still awake first.

"Who did you say the soldiers came from?"

"Hugh."

"Is he an ally of MacNare's?"

"His soldiers would have been killed a long time ago if their laird was an ally of MacNare's."

"Is he your ally then?"

"When it's convenient for him to be," he answered. "Hugh's land borders ours to the south. I let him live in peace as long as he stays out of my way."

"I wouldn't trust him."

"I don't."

Connor watched her struggle to stay awake. She could barely keep her eyes open and was yawning every other minute now, but she was still determined to talk about what had happened instead of giving in to the inevitable. He decided to help her lose her battle. He pulled her into his arms, held her close, and began to stroke her back. The heat radiating from his body warmed her and made her drowsy in no time at all.

"MacNare's a demon, and demons don't fear anyone," Brenna said. "That makes them all the more dangerous and terrifying to others."

He closed his eyes and waited for her to tell him she was afraid of the bastard.

She took a roundabout way of admitting it. "Women, especially, would be frightened."

"But not you," he said. "You know I won't let anything happen to you, don't you, Brenna?"

"Yes," she whispered. "And you know I won't let anything happen to you, don't you, Connor?"

He was smiling when he leaned down and kissed her forehead. "MacNare isn't immortal. He has fears like everyone else. He fears one man in particular."

"You're certain of this?"

"Yes."

"Should women also fear this man?"

"No."

"Who is he?" she asked. She fell asleep waiting for her husband to give her the name of the man this demon feared.

She slept soundly for over an hour, until she was jarred awake by the clanking sound of the drawbridge being lowered.

Connor wasn't in bed with her. She knew, before her feet touched the floor, that he was leaving the safety of the fortress. She grabbed her plaid and wrapped it around her on her way to the window.

The sight was ominous. A procession of soldiers on horseback, each carrying a fiery torch in one hand and holding a rope in the other, slowly crossed the bridge, dragging a bony carcass behind them. The clipping sound the horses made didn't cover the brittle echoes of the remains banging against the wooden planks.

Connor led the way to the ruins. When the procession reached its destination, everyone dismounted. They formed an arc, and in the center, four of the men began the digging. Their muscular silhouettes glistened in the flickering light as they lifted mounds of dirt and flung them to the side.

The hole was deep. Another soldier stepped forward, reached down, and lifted each man up. The beacons were thrust into the ground then, and the soldiers moved in unison to pull on the ropes. The carcass was slowly dragged forward. It teetered on the edge of the black hole for several seconds, then plunged down. The ropes, like snakes, slithered down into the cavity as soon as the soldiers released them.

After they filled the hole with dirt, a single torch was left burning bright on top of the mound, and the other beacons moved toward the horses.

Minutes later, the procession came thundering back across the drawbridge. A single light remained behind to keep vigil over the ruins. It burned bright for several more minutes, flickered twice, and then was gone.

Brenna kept watch at the window for her husband.

When Quinlan and Crispin returned to the keep ten minutes later, she stepped back into the shadows so they wouldn't see her. The soldiers had been to the lake to wash, and she assumed her husband had gone with them.

Almost a full hour passed before he appeared on the path. The breath caught in the back of her throat at first sight of him. The fire from his torch blazed around him, and in the glow of the light, his magnificent body seemed covered with gold. She didn't sense the danger in him until he grew closer, and then she noticed the change. He was moving like a predator now. His stride was long, determined, the muscles in his shoulders and arms rolling with fluid grace under sleek skin, his gaze, watchful.

He was ready to strike. The power he radiated made her heartbeat quicken. Her hands trembled as she pulled the plaid tight around her shoulders to ward off a sudden chill. She knew she was being fanciful. He was her husband, not a stranger. Yet her instincts continued to warn her. She understood why as soon as he reached the courtyard.

She felt his rage before she saw it. His head down, he deliberately followed the grooves in the ground over which Gilly had been dragged, and when he reached the spot where the animal had lain, he stopped. He shuddered once, then drew himself up, threw his head back, and looked up at the sky. In the harsh light from the torch, the lines in his face were gray, stark, edged with fury. The vein in his clenched jaw throbbed, and his shoulders and neck became rigid.

He was consumed with anger. She stared into the cold, deadly eyes of a savage, for the rage controlled him now. He hurled the torch into the air, lifted his sword high above his head, and with both hands, plunged it deep into the bloody ground.

He was a terrifying sight. She couldn't move, couldn't breathe, couldn't cry out to him.

She looked beyond to the ruins and suddenly she understood Connor's rage. He had told her his father had died there, but she hadn't questioned him to find out who had been responsible. She wouldn't ask him now, for in her heart, she already had her answer.

She drew a long breath and turned her gaze back to her husband. He was looking directly at her. Their gazes held for a full minute before he turned away. He ripped the sword out of the ground and started back to the path.

She shouted his name. His expression was still murderous

when he looked up at her again. She should have been afraid; she wasn't. She put her hand out to him and ordered him to come home to her.

She waited in the center of the room. The sound of footsteps grew closer and closer. She kept her gaze on the door, her heart pounding with anticipation. She would take him into her arms and soothe the rage in him with gentle whispers and soft caresses.

She had witnessed the transformation from laird to savage and knew without a doubt that Connor was the one man MacNare feared.

She couldn't feel sorry for the pig.

Connor was having difficulty concentrating on his duties. Thoughts of his wife and what he'd done to her the night before kept intruding.

He'd behaved like an animal. He should have stayed at the lake until he'd gotten his anger under control, or spent the entire night there, but when she'd called out to him and beckoned him to come to her, he'd been powerless to resist her lure.

She shouldn't have touched him. If only she'd stayed on the other side of the bedroom, he might have been able to ignore her. Connor acknowledged this to be a lie as soon as he thought it. He'd had every intention of taking her from the moment he started up the steps, but he hadn't meant to take her like a savage. Had he hurt her? God help him, he didn't know. She didn't resist him, though, or ask him to stop. He would have listened to her and obeyed her wishes, of that he was certain. He remembered how she'd run to him and put her arms around him and wouldn't let go. She hadn't known what he was going to do to her then, of course. Hell, she probably would have thrown herself out the window if she'd been able to guess his thoughts.

She would never forgive him. Why should she? He'd used her shamelessly, done things to her that must have terrified her, had taken her not once but twice, and in ways she wouldn't understand. He knew exactly why he'd needed her so much. He'd been living with rage for such a long time, and she was such a gentle, loving spirit. He'd needed her to breathe, to feel . . .

"Connor, you're choking Peter." Crispin came up behind his laird and put his hand on his shoulder.

Connor shoved the soldier away. Peter staggered back, took several deep, gulping breaths, and straightened up again.

"You almost killed a man, Peter," Connor said, his voice harsh. "Had I not knocked the sword out of your hand, one of my loyal followers would be dead. I will not tolerate stupidity."

"Laird, I . . ." Peter began.

Connor silenced him by raising his hand. "Don't give me your excuses. Quinlan will decide what's to be done with you."

He waited until the soldier had taken his leave before discussing the matter with his two commanders. Crispin and Quinlan flanked his sides.

Crispin felt the soldier was hopelessly inept and should be sent home. Quinlan was in agreement, but promised he would wait until his anger had abated to make any decision.

Crispin changed the subject. "Have you decided how you're going to retaliate against MacNare?"

"I have. You and I will leave late this afternoon. Select eight or ten soldiers to ride with us."

"Will you go to Kincaid first? He did make you promise not to continue the raids."

"I should go to my brother and explain, but I'm not going to. He'll be furious, of course. However, as soon as he hears about MacNare's message, I'm certain he'll realize I should send the bastard a message of my own."

"Don't confront MacNare or kill him until it's my duty to ride with you," Quinlan requested.

"You make this same request each time we alternate responsibilities," Crispin reminded. "I'm certain Connor knows how you feel about our enemy now."

"And you put the very same request to Connor each time *I* ride with him, Crispin."

Connor stopped the rivalry by telling the soldiers they would both ride with him when the time came. "I won't kill him until I've found the evidence I need. The promise I gave my father comes above all others. Crispin, go and choose your men and be ready to leave before the sun sets.

Quinlan, walk with me back to the courtyard so that I can explain the duties I want the men to complete while I'm away."

He finished outlining the soldiers' responsibilities before they'd reached their destination and added one last request. "See that my wife is moved to another bedroom. Do it today."

"Did you and Lady Brenna disagree about the measures you're going to take against MacNare?"

"No, I haven't discussed the matter with her. Why would you think I would?"

"She's your wife, Connor."

"I'm aware of that fact."

"And it was her horse that was butchered."

"Yes," Connor agreed. "And for those reasons, you believe I should explain my intentions to her?"

Quinlan laughed when he saw how puzzled Connor was. Explaining his intentions to his wife had obviously never occurred to him.

"Most wives would like their husbands to tell them what they're feeling."

"Is that so?"

"Then your reason for moving her to another chamber was due to something else?"

"The matter doesn't concern you."

"That is so," he agreed. "But as your friend, I feel I should advise you that your wife will be injured by this decision. She won't understand. Surely you've noticed mi'lady has feelings for you."

"Of course she does, and that is precisely why I'm moving her to another room. I assure you she'll be relieved."

Connor refused to say another word on the subject. He ordered Quinlan to get started on his duties and went inside the hall.

Netta, the servant in charge of cleaning the first floor, dropped the cloth she'd been wiping a table with as soon as she saw her laird. She jumped back, bowed, and stammered out her greeting.

The servant was a jittery woman who trembled at the mere sight of him. Connor couldn't understand why. The woman had served him for over a year now, and in all that time, he'd never once raised his voice to her.

"Netta, go upstairs and tell my wife I wish to speak to her."

"Should I wake her if she's still sleeping, Laird?"

Connor shook his head. "No, it's early yet. If she doesn't immediately answer you, leave her alone. Try to be quiet," he added. "My father's widow may still be sleeping."

The servant stumbled twice in her haste to leave the hall. Connor paced about the empty room while he waited, his mind on the explanation he was going to give Brenna. He knew he should probably apologize for his conduct the night before. He wasn't going to, however, for the simple reason he knew he wouldn't make any sense. He had never, ever told anyone he was sorry, and he wasn't about to learn how to now.

Connor had only just started a fire blazing in the hearth when Netta returned with the news that Lady MacAlister wasn't upstairs. He ordered her to send servants outside to look for her and resumed his pacing again. Quinlan's remark about sharing information with his wife had surprised him, and he found himself wondering if Alec ever told Jamie how he felt about worrisome matters. No, of course he didn't. Men wouldn't . . . would they?

He shook his head with disgust. Being married complicated his life. He should have realized that before he married. It was a little late for second thoughts, however, and now that she belonged to him, he was honest enough to admit he would never give her up, and thinking about her with anyone else made him angry. Did that mean he liked being married to her? *Who was he trying to fool?* He liked her all right, more than he'd ever thought possible. Even now, he was tense in anticipation of the moment she would come into the hall.

His own admission was somewhat appalling to him. He was acting as eager as a young soldier trying to impress his commander. He had already softened toward his wife, and if he wasn't careful, he was going to fall in love with her. He was certain he knew exactly what would happen then. She would die on him.

Loving Brenna wasn't worth the heartache.

Crispin had come inside to announce Laird Kincaid's arrival. He was a little late, however, as Alec was already standing by his side. The two men watched Connor pace. When Quinlan joined them a moment later, he bowed to Laird Kincaid before turning his attention to Connor. He was amused his laird hadn't noticed his brother yet. It wasn't like Connor to be so preoccupied, but Quinlan was certain he was thinking about Lady Brenna.

Alec didn't find his brother's inattention amusing at all. Connor redeemed himself in his older brother's eyes a few seconds later. "Are you going to announce my brother or not, Crispin?"

"He was waiting for you to look at me," Alec snapped. "Turning your back on a man can get you killed."

"Turning my back on a family member is rude, Alec, not dangerous." He came forward, formally bowed to Alec, and said, "You honor me with your presence, Laird."

"Your manners still need improvement."

"I learned everything I know from you. Someone's angered you, I see. You're wearing your sword."

"I am angry," Alec replied. "My men are waiting in the lower bailey. We're going on a hunt for a man who dared to defy me, and I want you to ride with me."

"Of course."

Alec nodded, pleased that Connor had agreed without knowing the name of the man they were going to drag out of hiding. The older brother arrogantly assumed Connor's unquestioning loyalty was due in large measure to the way he had raised him.

Striding into the hall, he slapped his brother on his shoulder on his way to the table and sat down in the only tall-backed chair available. He motioned for Connor to take the adjacent bench.

"Dawson doesn't seem to understand I mean what I say. Lass, fetch me a drink of water," he called out to the servant hovering near the archway.

The servant frantically looked about her. Connor thought she was looking for a spot to place the items she was holding in her hands. Before he could tell her to put them on the steps, she came rushing across the chamber, bowed to him, and put them on the tabletop next to him.

He knew what they were before she explained. "I've sent three servants from the kitchens to search mi'lady out, Laird, but all they've found thus far are the things she dropped behind her. They're still on her trail, Laird, and after I serve Laird Kincaid, will you please tell me what I'm to do with the mistress's belongings?"

Connor was clearly exasperated with his wife and shook his head in bewilderment. "Leave them here, Netta," he instructed.

She bowed again before serving his brother. Connor noticed her hands shook when she put the goblet and pitcher down in front of Alec and he wasn't at all surprised. Women were even more intimidated by his older brother.

"You've misplaced your wife?" Alec inquired blandly.

"Of course not," he answered.

Alec wasn't through teasing his brother. He reached over and picked up a yellow ribbon. "What have we got here?"

"You can see it's a pouch, a ribbon, and a dagger. Honest to God, Alec, I don't know how she does it. Brenna can't even seem to keep her feet in her shoes as she walks along. She's constantly discarding her things and picking up others. I don't know how I will convince her to pay more attention."

Alec found Brenna's forgetfulness vastly amusing. He had a good laugh at his brother's expense before suggesting he simply put a chest in the hall for his followers to place the items that she left behind in.

"With your permission, I'll see to the task," Crispin called out from the entrance.

"Would you like me to search for your wife?" Quinlan asked.

"I'd rather both of you join us," Alec ordered. "What I have to discuss will concern both of you as well."

He waited until the two men were seated across from Connor before he began.

"We'll be away for a week or two. Dawson and his soldiers are hiding up in the mountains, and it's going to take time to drag him out."

"You don't seem to be in any hurry to get started," Connor remarked.

"Dawson isn't going anywhere. The fool thinks he's safe from me," he added with a shake of his head. "I cannot imagine where he got such an idea."

"How many are with him?" Crispin asked.

"I'm not certain of the number. Quinlan, is it your duty to guard the fortress while your laird's away?"

"Yes, Laird."

"Post double the number of sentries along the perimeter and on the walls."

"I've already given the order, Alec. You needn't concern yourself," Connor said.

"Do you expect trouble?" Crispin asked.

Connor answered the question. "Alec always expects trouble, and so do we."

"Word has it MacNare went into a rage when he found out you had taken his bride away from him. He's been convinced by her escort that she willingly went with you, and now he blames your Brenna as much as he blames you."

"She wasn't responsible," Connor said.

Quinlan looked incredulous. "Her soldiers went to MacNare instead of returning to their baron? I'm staggered by their stupidity."

"They were assisted in making their decision to go to him," Alec explained. "You can imagine MacNare's predicament. There were at least a hundred relatives and guests waiting to celebrate the wedding with him. He had expected his bride the evening before, and when she didn't arrive on schedule, he dispatched additional troops to hurry her up. I was told he was humiliated in front of the gathering. Damn it, Quinlan, don't you dare find this amusing."

"I find MacNare's humiliation humorous," Quinlan admitted.

"So do I," Connor said.

"And I," Crispin said.

Their loyalty to one another was absolute. The three of them were brothers in the heart, and while Alec understood the bond between them, he knew he should sanction them for their attitude; yet to criticize them for enjoying

MacNare's embarrassment would have made him a hypocrite. He'd had a good laugh at the laird's expense, but he wasn't about to admit that to his brother. He wanted to squelch a little of the antagonism between Connor and MacNare now, not encourage it.

"I understand how each of you feels about MacNare. I've little liking for the man, I'll admit, yet you've still to convince me that he and his father were involved in the death of your father, Connor."

He raised his hand to prevent Crispin from interrupting him before continuing. "I will remind you that until you give me adequate proof, Donald MacAlister's sword remains on my wall where I put it the day you entered my home, and none of you will kill MacNare. Have I made myself perfectly clear?"

"You have," Connor answered. "You are my laird and we will honor your wishes at all times."

"Damned right you will."

Connor was having difficulty keeping his anger under control. Although he could have given his opinion whenever he felt like it, to openly disagree with his brother in front of Quinlan and Crispin would have been wrong, as it would undermine Alec's position.

"Are you finished reminding us of our duty to you?" he asked.

Alec gave him a hard look. "I promised you a long time ago that I wouldn't kill MacNare, because if and when you find what you need to prove him culpable, that right belongs to you. However, I haven't promised to let you live, Connor. Don't push me again."

Alec waited for Connor's nod before continuing. "God has given me the impossible duty of keeping the three of you alive, and I accepted the responsibility the minute I carried each one of you inside my home. You were all half dead at the time, and kept my wife up a full week fretting over you. I still haven't forgiven you the inconvenience you caused me."

"I remember," Connor said. "You told me you wouldn't let me die."

Alec laughed. "And you ordered me to go and get the

others." He let out a long, dramatic sigh. "You've been trying to give me orders ever since. Do you remember making me promise you that Quinlan and Crispin wouldn't die either? No, of course you don't. I cannot undo the past for you, Connor, but I can do something about the present. I have some information you might find useful. One of the English soldiers told MacNare that Brenna planned your arrival. That isn't true, is it?"

"No, it isn't true."

"And you have said you didn't force her."

"No, I didn't force her."

"You left out some rather significant details when you explained you married her."

"Such as?" Connor asked.

Alec didn't immediately answer his question. "Two of MacNare's men have left with three of the English soldiers. They're headed for Baron Haynesworth's holding."

"Who is Baron Haynesworth, Laird Kincaid?" Crispin asked.

"Brenna's father," he answered.

"There were twelve soldiers escorting mi'lady," Quinlan said.

"There are three left. MacNare doesn't like hearing bad news. He holds Brenna's father responsible for raising an independent daughter and is going to demand immediate compensation. I don't know the baron, and therefore cannot predict how he will react to hearing his alliance has been broken, but I know what I would do if I had expected my daughter to marry one man and she ended up with another. I'd go after my daughter and hear the truth from her."

"In other words, you think the baron might lead his troops here."

"It's possible."

Connor shrugged. "If it happens, it happens."

"What will you do if her father challenges you?"

"No one's taking her away from me. No one." He hadn't raised his voice, but the force behind each word was just as riveting.

"Would you kill him?" Crispin asked in a voice that sounded only mildly curious.

"It would probably upset my wife if I did," Connor said.

"Probably?" Alec asked. "Of course it would upset her."

"I wouldn't let the retaliation go that far. I'll wait to see what her father does."

Alec nodded, satisfied for the moment that his brother wouldn't do anything rash.

"I wouldn't mention this to Brenna, as there seems little reason to give her such a worry. Though I find it somewhat perplexing, I have learned from watching my wife that women are inclined to worry over every little thing. Jamie was very upset to hear what MacNare had done to Brenna's horse. 'Tis the truth, I was sickened by the vile act as well. Unfortunately, Jamie insisted on hearing every detail from Hugh."

"Laird Hugh came to you?" Quinlan asked.

"He must have ridden through the night," Crispin commented.

"No, he arrived late last evening. One of my sentries led the way. Hugh was in quite a state, but once he'd had enough ale to calm him, he was able to tell me some interesting news. As you know, he has always been against joining MacNare or you. A long time ago, he came to me with his request for protection in the event one of you tried to change his mind for him by force. I assured him that my brother would never do such a thing, of course, and I'm certain I convinced him. I couldn't give him the same assurance regarding MacNare. Hugh wants to live in peace. His grandfather and his father before him both ruled that worthless little stretch of land between you and your enemy, which puts him in an untenable position, because he doesn't have nearly the number of soldiers either one of you have. Hugh has never raised his hand against any man or treated anyone unfairly, and I agreed to give him my assistance. He's an old man who means no harm, Connor, and I won't have him preyed upon."

"I offered him my protection, Alec."

"I know you did, but if he had accepted, his followers would have been slaughtered by MacNare the second you turned your back. The king has a special fondness for the old man and would also be disappointed if anything unfortunate happened to him. I explained all of this to MacNare and told him that as the king's mediator, I will make certain Hugh remains autonomous and is left alone."

"Has MacNare been pressuring him?"

"He has," Alec answered. "Hugh went to MacNare's holding because he'd been invited to attend the celebration after the wedding, but the old man didn't get out of there fast enough and therefore was forced to witness MacNare's unsavory methods in disposing of those who angered him."

"The English soldiers." It was Crispin who stated the obvious. "Were the nine men killed in the same way mi'lady's horse was killed?"

Alec held Connor's stare as he slowly nodded. "Needless to say, Hugh was shaken by what he saw. I hope Brenna never hears about the soldiers. God willing, she'll never find out."

His hope proved false, for Brenna had already heard every word they'd said. She had come in through the back door, heard Alec's voice, and immediately stopped in the hallway to straighten her appearance before she went forward to greet him. She hadn't meant to eavesdrop, until she heard her name spoken. She deliberately stayed where she was then because she wanted to find out why she was being discussed, and she knew that the minute she joined them, the conversation would stop. Neither Alec nor Connor was whispering, yet their low voices indicated the seriousness of their topic. She knew what she was doing was wrong, but at the moment, she didn't care.

She came close to giving herself away when Alec explained what had happened to nine of her father's soldiers. She was so sickened by the horror she pictured, she doubled over from the pain in her stomach. Praying for the souls of the men helped her gain a little control, and she vowed that later, when she was alone in her bedroom, she would get down on her knees and ask God to welcome them. As soon as she was finished, she would thank Him too, for sending Connor to her. If he hadn't arrived when he had, she would be married to Satan now. The thought so chilled her, her stomach lurched again.

Concentrating on the conversation in the great hall stopped her from crying out. She forced herself to pay attention by promising herself she could weep for as long as she wanted as soon as she was alone.

"Despite having survived so many years, Hugh's still hopelessly naive," Alec said. "He was in quite a state by the time he returned home, and the very next morning, one of his men came to him to tell him Brenna's horse had been left at his border with a message from MacNare requesting the remains be taken to you, Connor. Hugh felt certain you would wish to see it. Did you know MacNare called it a gift?"

"Yes," Connor answered.

"And then Hugh rode directly to you," Quinlan said with a nod.

"I would like to bring up another matter with you, Connor. It certainly isn't as important as what we've just discussed, yet I find I've been thinking about a comment Hugh made."

"What did he say?"

"Hugh heard from one of the English soldiers that Brenna was a child when she asked you to marry her. You left that out, didn't you? Now I want you to tell me again you didn't defy my command to leave MacNare alone."

Alec had just slammed his fist down on the tabletop when Brenna called out to him. "Good day, Laird Kincaid. What a pleasure it is to see you again."

As quick as a blink, Alec's expression changed from an intense frown to what she believed was a sincere smile. Quinlan and Crispin looked relieved to see her. She went directly over to Alec, gave Connor a quick glance and saw the speculative look in his eyes, and then turned back to their guest. In her enthusiasm, she grabbed hold of his hand to let him know how happy she was to see him, realized her mistake almost immediately, and quickly let go.

Alec was surprised by the gesture of affection, yet pleased all the same. He took her hand in his then. "The pleasure belongs to me, Brenna. How are you feeling today?" he asked, looking at the stitches on her forehead.

"I'm feeling very well, thank you. How could I not? It's such a fine day today."

"It's raining," Crispin reminded her.

"The rain has stopped," she answered. "Please sit down

again. Have I interrupted an important meeting? I apologize if I have. Is Jamie with you, Laird?"

Alec let go of her hand before answering. "She's home."

"I'm sorry to hear it. I do hope you bring her next time you come to see Connor."

After a second request that they take their seats, the men conceded. She went to Connor, waited until he was settled, and put her hand on his shoulder. The action wasn't meant to show affection, but to show Alec her loyalty to her husband.

"Is your wife well?" she asked.

"I will have to assume she is," Alec answered, his eyes warmed by the talk of his Jamie. "She isn't talking to me at the moment."

"Oh, dear," Brenna whispered.

"Jamie can be as stubborn as her husband," Connor remarked.

"'Tis the truth, she can," Alec admitted with a grin. "She's upset because I won't let her go attend Mary Kathleen. My daughter's time draws near," he explained for Brenna's benefit. "And because this bairn will be her first, my wife thinks her presence will make the ordeal easier for her."

"Lady Kincaid is known as a healer here," Quinlan told her.

"Laird, I cannot help but wonder why you won't let Jamie go to Mary Kathleen," Brenna said.

Connor was surprised his wife had just asked for an explanation. He knew Brenna wasn't being bold; she was simply curious, that was all. Later he would explain to his brother that she couldn't help being impetuous and certainly hadn't meant to question his decision.

Alec seemed to take it in stride, however. "That is the very thing Jamie said to me. I cannot take the time away from my other duties, and I will not let my wife go without me. She'll try to defy my orders, of course, just as soon as she realizes she can't sway me."

"My wife would never defy me," Connor announced. "Isn't that right, Brenna?"

"I'm certain you would let me go," she answered.

"No, I wouldn't."

"Well, then, for the sake of our daughter, I'm certain I would find a way to do what I needed to do without defying you, Connor."

Alec found her belief amusing. "You are that clever?"

"I like to think I am, Laird. I'm one of eight children and have learned that I must be clever if I am ever going to get anything accomplished. You think my boast is empty?" she asked when Quinlan laughed. "I did set out to marry Connor, and if you will all notice, I am now his wife."

Everyone but Connor laughed. He looked exasperated.

The tension had lifted sufficiently for her to let them get on with their meeting, but as she was about to excuse herself, Alec changed her mind.

"I've just met a friend of yours, Brenna. He was quite taken with you and considers himself your champion."

Quinlan took exception on Connor's behalf, for he felt it was insulting for any other man to think he was worthy enough to be his mistress's champion. "Connor protects his wife. Who is this man who dares to challenge him?"

"Aye, Connor's mi'lady's champion," Crispin muttered.

Brenna didn't even try to hide her vexation. "I'm quite capable of taking care of myself, thank you." For some reason, all the men found her opinion vastly amusing. She decided to pretend she wasn't offended. "Who is this friend?"

"Father Sinclair."

Quinlan looked sheepish. "If you'd mentioned it was the priest, I wouldn't have taken exception, Laird Kincaid."

Alec ignored the soldier. "He sings your praises, Brenna."

"Why did he come to you?" Connor asked.

"He'd been ordered to replace Murdock. I cannot let him stay, of course, as we are still mourning Murdock's passing. I haven't told him yet, because I was in a hurry to leave today, but I will feed him and give him a bed until I return home and then I'll send him away. It's the least I can do," he added with a shrug.

"How can you deny him, Laird?" she asked.

He looked surprised by the question. "It won't be difficult."

"But why do you want to send him away?"

"Why? Because I don't want him. I'm actually being kind. For some reason, he seems ill-at-ease with me."

"He seemed nervous with Connor too," Quinlan remarked.

"I cannot believe what I'm hearing," she stammered out. "Priests are the most powerful men in all the Highlands. Connor told me so."

"Yes, as long as they realize the power they have," Alec explained. "He, like all the other priests here, is protected and left alone."

"Then why would you send him away?"

"Because I don't want him," Alec explained a second time.

"I want him," she blurted out.

"You can't have him," Connor snapped.

"You really want a priest living here?" Alec asked.

"No," Connor answered.

"Yes," Brenna said at the very same time.

Alec grinned. "Your wish is granted, Brenna. I'll send Sinclair over as soon as Connor and I return."

"Alec," Connor warned.

"I cannot deny your wife," Alec said.

Brenna pretended not to notice her husband's frown. She thanked both brothers for giving in to her request and hurried to leave before Connor reminded her he hadn't done any such thing.

"I'll let you get back to your important discussion," she said. "With your permission, I'll go about my duties."

"You don't have any duties," Connor said.

"Oh, but I do," she said. "I have to go outside and find the perfect spot."

"The perfect spot for what?" her husband asked.

"The chapel, of course. Father will have to have one."

Too late, she realized she shouldn't mention her plan just yet. Connor looked as though he was considering throttling both her and his brother now.

He didn't tell her she couldn't go forward with her plans and, in fact, didn't say another word. He probably didn't trust his voice to speak to her yet, and she hoped by the time he finished his meeting, he would forget about it altogether

With any luck, the chapel would be completed before he remembered.

"Do you enjoy wielding your power over me, Alec?"

His brother grinned. "Immensely."

"You may leave, Brenna," Alec told her.

Brenna was halfway across the hall when Alec asked her to stop.

"Were you a clever child?"

"I was told I was."

"Were you a child when you asked my brother to marry you?"

She folded her hands together while she pretended to think about it. "I don't recall my exact age."

"Give me an approximation," he commanded.

"I was just a little older than your Grace is now. I would guess I was going on five or six. Yes, I was about that old when I asked Connor to marry me the first time, but if you'll remember, I asked him three times. I'm not only clever, Laird, I'm also tenacious. I must admit I find your curiosity intriguing, for I seem to recall having this very conversation when I was first introduced to you. I know I mentioned I wasn't forced. I'm very happy to be his wife. How could I not be? I have wanted to marry him for such a long time. Heavens, where are my manners? I should have asked you how Grace is feeling today."

"She's fine," Alec answered.

"She had quite a scare yesterday, and I hope she didn't have any nightmares last night. Do you know, it's really quite remarkable, now that I reflect upon it. God surely has grand plans in store for your daughter."

Alec's curiosity was captured. She couldn't have hoped for more.

"Why do you think so?"

"I know so," she boasted. "God made certain I was inside your home so I could get to her in time. I do believe Grace would have suffered grievous injuries if I hadn't been there to catch her. She came down those steps head first and surely would have broken her neck. You may think I'm foolish to believe God is responsible, but I believe it all the same, and I cannot help but wonder what would have happened if I had married MacNare instead of Connor.

Would Grace be feeling well today? My, listen to me going on and on, and you still have business to discuss. I trust the matter of when I proposed and all other questions about my husband's reasons for marrying me have been answered to your satisfaction."

She bowed to the laird and walked away. She couldn't resist adding one last comment, though she didn't bother to turn around. "God does work in mysterious ways. I for one would never question Him."

None of the men uttered a word for a full minute after Lady Brenna left. Each stared at the empty entrance while he pondered what she had just said.

Alec was the first to smile. "Your wife just put me in an awkward position, and do you know what I think? She did it on purpose. How much of our conversation do you suppose she overheard?"

Connor answered without a second's hesitation. "All of it."

"She shouldn't have listened in."

"No, she shouldn't have."

"I should be angry with her."

"Yes."

"Then why am I wanting to laugh? There will be no more talk about defying me, Connor, because I have decided to accept what your wife told me. You were obviously meant for each other."

"I didn't defy you, Alec. You ordered me to stop the raids, and that's what I did. You cannot hold me to my promise now that you know about Brenna's horse."

"I can," Alec argued. "But I won't. Do what you will in repayment as long as it is equal to what was done to the mare."

Alec gained his brother's agreement before leaving the hall. "You're married to a very clever woman. You'd best keep that in mind."

Connor didn't take his suggestion to heart, and it was only later, when it was too late, that he learned to regret it.

The mistake would cost him dearly.

Chapter 10

Lady Brenna didn't take the news that she had been moved into another bedroom at all well. Her husband hadn't bothered to inform her of his decision beforehand, and Quinlan fervently wished the unpleasant duty of explaining it all to her had fallen on someone else's shoulders instead of his. He had suspected she would be hurt and had tried to get her alone before explaining so that they would have privacy in the event she became embarrassed, but his mistress's worry about her missing clothes defeated his plan, and she, therefore, had to hear the news in front of Connor's step-mother.

Lady Brenna wasn't angered by Connor's command; she was clearly devastated. Quinlan felt sorry for the dear lady, of course, and it took a good deal of discipline to pretend he didn't notice her distress. His laird's callous behavior infuriated him to the point that he considered telling him that he would rather be tortured than ever give Lady Brenna such disappointing news again.

The pity she saw in his eyes made her humiliation all the more complete. Euphemia had thoughtfully turned away with the excuse that she wanted to get something from her bedroom. With effort, Brenna was able to gather herself together. "May I fetch something for you, Lady MacAlister?"

She assumed Euphemia hadn't heard her when she didn't immediately answer, and so she turned back to Quinlan again. "Thank you for explaining."

Desperate to say something to make her feel better, he blurted out the first cheerful thought that came into his mind. "So you see, mi'lady, your things weren't thrown away as you suspected. Surely you're relieved."

"Yes, of course I'm relieved. Did Connor tell you why he wanted me to move?"

"Nay, mi'lady, he didn't."

"Where is he now?"

"He went hunting with his brother."

"How long ago did he leave?"

"Both lairds left the hall just a minute or so ago."

"Then I might still catch him?"

"If you hurry."

She ran to the door to open it, but the weight was too much for her to budge without Quinlan's assistance, so he hurried to give it.

Quinlan followed her down the staircase but not across the courtyard. He naturally assumed she was going to try to change her husband's mind.

His assumption was wrong, however, as Brenna didn't have any intention of begging her husband to reconsider. She was simply going to let him know what she thought about his decision. She ran all the way to the stables, calling, "Good day to you, ladies," as she raced past mothers giving their babies a bit of fresh air.

Her pace had made her breathless, and when she noticed Alec mounted on his horse at the bottom of the hill, she waved to him instead of waiting to catch her breath so she could call a greeting.

The inside of the stables was cast in shadows. She forced a smile on her face the second she spotted her husband. Connor was standing next to the horse he'd chosen to ride, adjusting the bridle to his satisfaction, while the stablemaster tried to calm the stallion his laird usually favored. That horse was making quite a ruckus, kicking his hooves up against the back of the stall, and would soon destroy it if he wasn't stopped, but her husband didn't seem inclined to do anything about it.

Deliberately staying in the path of the doorway so he couldn't leave without walking over her, she slowly moved forward. "May I please have a moment of your time, Laird?" she asked in a voice as sweet as honeyed syrup and with a smile to match.

He didn't even bother to look at her when he answered. "Can it wait until I get back?"

"I'm not certain, Laird. Will you be back before nightfall?"

"No."

It almost did her in to keep smiling, but the stablemaster was watching her closely, and she was determined not to let him know what she was really thinking. She didn't want Connor to know either, of course, until he was ready to give her his undivided attention. She didn't want him to miss a word.

"Davis, what's wrong with my stallion?" he asked.

"I don't know what's wrong with him, Laird. He was fine until you came inside."

"I think he's upset," she called out.

"We know he's upset, Brenna."

She stiffened in response to his condescending attitude. "Yes, of course you do," she agreed. "He's upset because you aren't paying any attention to him." A reaction, she silently added, she was also experiencing at the moment. "Your stallion doesn't wish to be left behind. If you'll go to his stall and pick up his bridle, I'm sure he'll settle down."

"I would be curious to see if that works, Laird," Davis confessed as he flashed a grin toward his mistress. "Mi'lady could be right."

"I do hope I am," she replied in such a disgustingly pleasant tone she was sure she was going to be sick.

"Brenna, are you coming down with something?" Connor asked. "Your voice sounds strained."

"I'm feeling fine, Connor, though I appreciate your concern."

Her face was beginning to ache from holding on to her smile, and her only consolation was in knowing that in a few minutes, it was all going to be worth it.

"I don't have time for this nonsense," her husband muttered, which turned out to be bluster on his part because he did do what she had suggested, and just as she had predicted, the stallion immediately stopped fussing and moved forward to nudge Connor's hand for a pat of affection.

"You'll have to take him," she said. "Otherwise, you'll hurt his feelings."

"He needs to rest. Besides, horses don't have feelings."

Did he always feel the need to contradict her? She started praying in an attempt to keep herself from shouting at him.

Connor replaced the bridle on the peg, told Davis to take the horse he'd chosen outside, then leaned back against the stall, folded his arms across his chest, and finally deigned to look at her.

He didn't say a word until Davis had left the stable. "What is it you want?" he asked impatiently.

"I was wondering why you didn't say good-bye to me. Were you going to?"

The tremor in her voice was the first indication she was upset. He thought he knew why. She had expected an apology this morning, hadn't gotten one, and now, because she was an intelligent woman, realized she was never going to get one. Her conclusion would be correct, of course, as he still didn't have any intention of telling her he was sorry he'd come to her like a savage last night. Having her moved into another bedroom was his way of apologizing. A clever wife would have figured that out right away, and been thankful and relieved.

Brenna didn't appear to be either at the moment, which, he concluded, could only mean she didn't know about his magnanimous gesture yet. He wasn't going to take the time now to explain it all to her, because Alec was waiting for him. If she wanted an explanation when he returned, he would accommodate her.

"I don't usually say good-bye before I leave."

"You're married now and should always tell your wife good-bye."

"Any other instructions you wish to give me?"

"Were you planning to come back?"

"I live here, Brenna. Of course I'll come back. Is this your reason for detaining me?"

"No, I wanted to speak to you about another matter. I

would appreciate it if you wouldn't interrupt me until I'm finished."

"Will you get it said?" he demanded in vexation.

She gritted her teeth together in response to his stop-bothering-me tone of voice.

"I have only just found out you moved me into another bedroom, and I felt certain you would wish to know what I think about it. I would like your permission to speak freely first."

"You don't need to ask my permission to speak freely when we're alone. Say whatever you want to me, just be quick about it."

"Yes, I'll be quick about it," she promised in a hoarse whisper.

"Can't you wait until I return to say thank you? What the hell's wrong with your eyelid? It's twitching."

She chose to ignore her husband for a moment. She looked over her shoulder one last time to measure the distance to the doorway and safety, saw that the doorway was just behind her, and took a deep, now-you're-going-to-get-it breath. Because she was going to have to flee with all possible haste, she picked up the hem of her skirts in preparation, and only then did she give her husband her undivided attention . . . and her wrath.

She wasn't smiling now.

"I don't have any intention of thanking you, Connor. However, I do intend to tell you what I think about your decision to move me into another room. I think you are beyond contemptible. You're also a vile, despicable, arrogant, heartless, mean-spirited pig. How could you deliberately hurt me this way? After the passionate, satisfying night we shared together, for you to shame me this way makes me think I must be married to a goat. Well, you've gone and done it this time, because I'll never recover from your insult. You've broken my heart again, and I will never forgive you."

She really should have stopped while she was ahead. At the very least, she should have stopped insulting him the second she noticed his reaction to being called a pig. He clenched his jaw tight, which was a good indication to her he wasn't taking her comments at all well. She couldn't remember what other insults she threw at him, because once she got started, she couldn't seem to make herself stop, but she was pretty certain she suggested he was a horse's backside too. The hurt he'd caused her made her want to lash out at him, and even though it was childish for her to lower herself to his level, she couldn't seem to make herself care long enough to stop.

Second thoughts weren't going to do her a lick of good now, however; only distance would assure her of living another full day, as Connor's eyes had gone from wide with stunned disbelief—no doubt the mention of "pig" caused that reaction—to half-closed and burning.

He didn't even give her a head start. She turned around only to discover that someone had snuck up behind her and closed the barn doors, throwing off her timing considerably. She had to let go of her skirts so that she could push the doors open, and then Connor had hold of her hand and was pulling her back. How he'd gotten to her so quickly was beyond her comprehension. One second he was next to the stall, looking fit to be tied, and the next he was dragging her behind him toward the back of the stables.

She said a heartfelt, "God, please have mercy."

"If you must pray out loud, do so in one language. God prefers Gaelic."

Her snort of disbelief wasn't appreciated, she knew, because he tightened his grip on her hand. He dragged her to an empty stall around the corner from the others and closed the gate behind him.

She didn't start edging away from him until she saw the look in his eyes. She stopped when her back was pressed against the wall. Immediately, she realized how cowardly she must appear. She couldn't seem to make herself move away from the wall, but she was able to fold her hands together and managed to look serene while she waited to be throttled. Retreat would have been better, of course, but he blocked the only way out.

Connor seemed to be relaxed now. She knew better. She wasn't going anywhere until he was finished with her. She really needed to get hold of herself. Her husband was furious, no doubt about it, but he wouldn't ever touch her in anger. He would use words to crush her, and at the moment, that seemed to be just as horrible.

"Care to repeat what you just said to me?" he drawled out in a deceptively calm voice.

"No, thank you."

"I really insist, Brenna. I want to hear every word again." He let her know he was willing to wait, no matter how long it took, by leaning against the stall and draping one arm over the top of the gate.

She didn't like the way he was intimidating her, which, under the circumstances, was the least of her problems, and she really couldn't blame him for being angry with her since she'd said such unforgivable things to him. She wasn't about to apologize, though; for while she wasn't totally convinced he was completely heartless, he had still wounded her deeply.

"I'm afraid I won't be able to accommodate you because I seem to have forgotten most of what I said. I do recall mentioning you disappointed me," she added with a nod to prove her sincerity.

He wasn't buying it. "I remember being called a pig."

"You do?"

"You know good and well, I do. I was called a pig in two languages."

"You were?"

"I was."

"I might have spoken in haste. Yes, it is possible I might have."

"You spoke in anger."

"You gave me permission to speak freely."

His tone sharpened. "I didn't give you permission to insult me. You will never speak to me like that again, will you?"

"Will you hurt me again?"

"This is not a negotiation, woman."

She flinched in reaction to his anger and tried to think of something she could say that would appease him but not be an outright lie.

"If I remembered every word I said, I would want to take back most of what I . . . ."

He interrupted her. "I remember every word. In which language would you like for me to repeat them? Yours or mine? You couldn't seem to make up your mind during your tirade."

"I really don't wish to hear . . ."

She stopped protesting as soon as he began reciting, flinched when he repeated certain words, such as "pig" and "goat" and "horse's backside," and by the time he finished, she'd lowered her head in shame and embarrassment.

"I shouldn't have said those things to you."

"No, you shouldn't have."

"Why did you make me leave your bed?"

"Did you want to stay with me after what I did to you last night?"

"Why would you think I wouldn't want to stay?"

"Will you stop answering my questions with questions?"

"Yes, I want to stay," she cried out. "I'm your wife, not one of your camp followers."

"I hurt you." He was furious with himself now, for that reminder had once again made him realize how out of control he'd been.

"Yes, you hurt me. I already told you so several times. Haven't you been paying attention? I know you have a strong memory because you didn't have any trouble repeating every insult I gave you. How could I not be hurt? I had only just realized how much I . . ."

"How much you what?"

She shook her head. She wasn't about to admit that she was beginning to care for him, and so she substituted another remark for the one she had almost blurted out.

"It was humiliating for me to find out about your decision from Quinlan."

"What are you talking about now?" he demanded in frustration.

Her hands became fists at her sides. How dare he pretend he didn't understand? Did he think she was so naive she would be fooled so easily? Or was she so unimportant to him he had already forgotten what he'd done?

"You're deliberately trying to provoke me aren't you? Oh, I know the truth now. You've figured out I'm falling in love with you and you're trying to make me stop by hurting me this way. Well, it won't work. One way or another, I'm going to make you care about me. Yes, I am, unless your cold attitude kills me first. It's only fair, Connor. If I'm going to be miserable, by God, so are you. I am not a common wench, and I will not be treated like one. My mother would weep for a month if she knew about my humiliation. You didn't even bother to tell me; you let Quinlan do it for you, and now you're leaving and you didn't give me any warning at all. I wanted to have a medallion made for you to wear so you could send it back to me if you needed me. You wouldn't have worn it, though, would you? And all because you've gotten it into your head that needing me would be an insult. Yes, I remember exactly what you said when I showed you my medallion and told you about my family's tradition. You ordered me to throw it away because it insulted you, and what breaks my heart is that you made it quite clear that what's important to me means nothing to you."

She vowed she wouldn't say another word, yet contradicted herself less than ten seconds later. "I have only one more thing to say to you before I go back to the hall and pretend I'm not married to you. Husbands tell their wives good-bye before they leave, and they always give them proper farewell kisses."

It wasn't until she felt the tears on her face that she realized she was crying. Her own lack of control sickened her, for not only had she shamed herself by saying such terrible things to her husband—God forgive her, she'd really called him a pig—but she had also broken down in front of him.

How could she ever make him care for her if she acted like a shrew one minute and a weakling the next? She couldn't, of course, she'd already done the damage, and now nothing was ever going to be all right. Nothing.

Alec's shout saved her from further disgrace if such a thing was possible. His older brother had grown weary of waiting and had commanded Connor to hurry up.

"I've detained you long enough," she whispered.

He didn't agree or disagree with her and, in fact, didn't utter a single word. He didn't leave either; he simply stood where he was and stared at her. His expression made her imagine she had suddenly grown a pair of red devil's horns on top of her head and he didn't have the faintest idea what he was supposed to do about it.

Dear God, she'd put him into a trance. Her mind raced to remember every word she'd just said to him. She knew she'd gotten a little carried away, but she was certain, well, almost certain, she hadn't called him a pig or a goat again. Had she called him something even more offensive? She fervently hoped she hadn't; but if she had, God help her three brothers, Gillian and William and Arthur, because it was all their fault, and the next time she saw them, she was going to blister them for using crude language in front of her. They'd done it on purpose, of course, and for their own enjoyment, because they knew she was too young to understand, but old enough to repeat almost everything she heard. She was making herself crazed worrying about her possible transgression.

"Connor, if I've said something obscene to you, it must have popped out of the back of my mind where I stored it from the time I was a little girl and my older brothers . . ." She stopped as soon as she realized she was rambling and gave up her attempt to appease him. "Why don't you leave? You're looking like you're about to pounce on me, and if that is your inclination, then please get on with it. The wait is making me daft."

"You don't remember what you said?"

His question made her feel worse. "I remember some of what I said, but not all of it. I know better than to let my anger control my words, and yet I allowed it to happen anyway. I assume I said something I shouldn't have. Did I?"

Lord, that had to be an understatement. From the moment she'd walked into the stables and opened her mouth, everything she'd said had been inappropriate.

"I have to go."

"Yes," she agreed with a heartfelt sigh of relief.

After opening the gate, he motioned for her to go ahead of him.

She could feel his gaze on her as she brushed past him, but she deliberately kept her head down so she wouldn't have to look at the anger she was sure was still lingering in his eyes. And his wariness. Whatever she'd blurted out in the heat of the moment had caused that specific reaction.

She didn't want to watch him leave the fortress, knowing she would lose what thin threads of control she still had left and wail like a sinner. Wouldn't that be a fitting way for her husband to remember her?

"Good-bye," she whispered as she stopped in the center of the stables. "God keep you safe."

He didn't have any last words to say to her. He simply walked on past her and went outside. He glanced back over his shoulder once, his expression still wary. Surely he noticed how desolate she was and was probably pleased to know he was fully responsible for her misery.

And then he was gone. She stayed inside the stables while she listened to the grinding sound of the drawbridge being lowered. It was followed by the clanking noise of swords striking against their metal sheaths and horses clip-clopping across the wooden pathway to the outside. She pictured her husband taking the lead by his brother's side, smiling and laughing now over far more pleasant matters than a bothersome, never-knew-when-to-keep-her-mouth-shut wife.

After taking another minute to say a prayer to God to please watch over him while he was away from her, she made certain there weren't any tears clinging to the corners of her eyes, slapped a smile on her face, and went outside. She tried to act as though she was in a hurry so no one would bother her.

She was halfway up the gentle incline, headed toward the courtyard, when she heard the sound of thunder behind her. She glanced up at the sky, instinctively quickening her pace, but slowed down almost immediately because there wasn't a dark cloud hanging down anywhere. She was too distraught to really pay attention to what was going on around her, for she realized she had just destroyed her chances of ever living happily ever after with a husband who loved and adored her, and how could she possibly think about, or care about, anything else?

Soldiers shouted a warning to her to move out of the way, while those strolling ahead of her hurried to get off the path without being told. The thunder was still behind her, but lower to the ground now, and getting closer. If she weren't certain it was an impossibility, she would have imagined the ground was shivering under her feet.

Brenna assumed one of the horses had gotten away from Davis and was now galloping out of control up the path. She hurried toward the cluster of pine trees to get out of danger, and just in the nick of time, as the wild beast was bearing down on her now.

She didn't make it. She was taken by surprise and actually let out a startled yelp as she felt herself being plucked from the ground.

Connor swept her off her feet. He had leaned down to the side, wrapped his arm tight around her waist, and lifted her up onto his lap without bothering to slow his horse's galloping stride.

He scared the hell out of her.

He heard her cry of alarm when he lifted her off the ground, but knew the precise second she recovered. It was when she landed on his lap and realized she was in his arms. Her fear vanished. She didn't even hold on to him. With her hands at her sides, she leaned back, a carefree look on her face as enchanting as her innocence. His hand was splayed against her back. If he lightened his hold, she would be thrown to the ground. Her trust in him was absolute, however, and she left her safety up to him.

His uninhibited wife couldn't be bothered. She arched back, lifted her arms, and stretched them out as far as they would reach. With the palms of her hands facing the sun, she tossed her head back and closed her eyes in blissful surrender.

Connor was stunned. He yearned to have such sweet abandon, to take such delight in living each and every moment. And as he watched her, the laughter welled up inside him, catching him by complete surprise. Oh, how she pleased him. He slowed the horse to a walk and came to a stop at the top of the incline.

Lessening his grip around her waist, he waited for her to give him her full attention.

She wrapped her arms around his neck and leaned into him. Whispering his name, she placed a kiss near the base of his throat, her lips as soft and sweet as a butterfly's wings. He was shaken by her expression of affection. His smile disappeared, his thoughts protected by his guarded expression as he stared into her enchanting blue eyes.

A full minute passed without a spoken word. The tension and anticipation radiated between them. His gaze lowered to her mouth and stayed there as he whispered his farewell. And then he pulled her up against him, tilted her head back, and kissed her long and hard and thoroughly. It was a kiss he wanted her to remember, and one he would never forget. He made love to her with his mouth, telling her with his passion that he had forgiven her, and letting her know with his gentle touch that he meant to have her forgiveness as well.

It took Connor a considerable amount of discipline to remember Alec was waiting for him to catch up. He raised his head and realized an audience had gathered to bear witness to their laird's astonishing behavior.

None of them had ever seen him exhibit such open affection before. Most of the men were stupefied by their leader, while all but one of the women were clearly delighted because their laird was acting like a husband now. His action would surely change their own husbands' attitudes. If their laird kissed his wife farewell, the married men under his command would surely follow his example.

Connor's gaze scanned his audience, and when he noticed that Donald and the other soldiers who'd gone hunting were back and watching with ridiculous expressions of disbelief on their faces, he decided that now was as good a time as any to introduce Brenna to his clan.

He demanded their silence by raising his hand.

"Lady MacAlister is your mistress. You will take her into your hearts, protect her with your lives, and serve her as you have served me, for she is my wife."

He lowered his hand, nodded with satisfaction as the cheers of acceptance roared through the crowd, and then assisted Brenna back to the ground.

The kiss had left her dazed. She staggered back and surely would have lost her balance if two of the women hadn't steadied her.

Connor left her there staring after him and stopped again only once, to speak to Quinlan, who was waiting for him near the stables and grinning like a lunatic.

Brenna couldn't stop sighing. For the first time in a very long time, she was content.

Everything, after all, was going to be all right.

243

Chapter
11

*L*ife became a living nightmare for Lady Brenna, and it all began and ended with Raen.

Euphemia's pride and joy arrived at the holding just a few hours after Connor had made his departure to go hunting with Alec.

Because she was in the kitchens, Brenna didn't hear the drawbridge being lowered and was therefore the last to be given the news of Raen's arrival.

While all the servants were busy searching for her, Brenna sat at the kitchen table with Ada, trying to communicate. Determined to make the first meal she shared with her stepmother as perfect as any of the holiday feasts her mother had served, Brenna had already spent at least a half hour explaining, or rather, attempting to explain, what was to be served and when. Her goal was to impress Euphemia so that the woman would have no doubts Connor had indeed married well. Discussing the menu proved to be an arduous undertaking, for though the elderly woman's smile indicated her willingness to be of assistance, it was apparent she didn't understand more than a word or two of her mistress's instructions, and if Netta hadn't come to her rescue, heaven only knew what would have ended up on the

table. Netta translated Brenna's Gaelic into a twisted dialect only she and Ada and God could possibly understand.

Netta was obviously a treasure. Although the servant was
only a few years older than Brenna and had served her
laird's household only for one short year, she had lived on
MacAlister land almost as long as Connor had and therefore
knew all of the goings-on. More important, Netta knew how
to acquire necessary items for her mistress.

Once Brenna had explained what she wanted to accomplish in the great hall to make it more welcoming to
company in general, and her husband in particular, the
servant begged to take over the tasks of organizing the
household servants and volunteered to spend the afternoon
braiding rushes. She promised the floor would be cleaned
and sprinkled with rushes here and there by the middle of
the following morning.

"I would rather we keep them hidden away until I've
finished sewing the cushions for the benches and collected a
few more things for the hall. When everything is finished,
we'll make the changes all at once."

Both Netta and Ada were soon caught up in their mistress's enthusiasm. Netta was full of suggestions.

"As for the chairs you're wanting, mistress, I know for a
certainty there are two nice tall ones, close in size to the one
our laird prefers when he sits for his meals. They're in the
tanner's hut, covered up tight," she added. "Lothar's known
for scavenging out this and that from cottages that have sat
vacant for a decent interval so no one will think him a thief.
He doesn't have any use at all for the chairs—he told me so
himself—and he threatened to burn them for firewood so
he'll have room to collect more. He'd be willing and
honored to give them up to you, and might be he has other
things you'll be wanting. I'll give you fair warning, though.
Lothar's a talker, and it won't do you any good at all to
mention you're in a hurry. He won't take your hints because
he's lonely now that his wife passed on, and he likes having
company around."

"I'll be happy to sit with him for as long as he wishes,"
Brenna said.

Thrilled with the news that she could implement her

plans for the hall sooner than she'd anticipated, she asked Netta to show her where Lothar's cottage was located, but the servant happened to remember her primary reason for searching her mistress out then and hastily told her important news.

"Lady Euphemia's son is here, mi'lady."

The announcement caused her mistress to jump up and hurry to the door. If Ada hadn't given Netta a good nudge in her side, she would have forgotten the question her friend had begged her to ask.

"Mi'lady, could you spare one more minute to put Ada's mind to rest?"

Brenna paused at the door.

"Ada's started fretting you'll want to replace her because she has so much trouble understanding you. She's prone to worry . . ." The servant stopped her explanation when Lady Brenna went hurrying over to the cook and took hold of her hand.

"You'll be the mistress of the kitchens as long as you wish, Ada," she promised her, and after waiting until Netta had translated her promise, Brenna continued. "I'm the one with the problem of making myself understood, but if you'll have patience with me, I'm certain I'll improve."

Convinced her mistress meant to let her keep her important position, Ada squeezed Brenna's hand to let her know how appreciative she was and bobbed her head up and down in understanding. She was dabbing at the corners of her eyes with the cloth Netta handed her when their mistress left the kitchen.

Outside, the sky was overcast with dark gray shadows, an unwelcome sight to Brenna, who was used to being forced inside by her family whenever so much as a drip came down from the skies. She was fortunate to reach the back door before the heavy rain began.

She tried not to make any noise as she eased the door closed behind her. She didn't want to disturb the reunion between mother and son and thought only to wait by the door to the hall until there was a satisfactory lull in the conversation before she entered the room. Her plan was to quickly introduce herself, make certain both Euphemia and Raen were comfortable and had everything they needed, and then leave again so they could catch up on each other's news.

She heard Euphemia's whispered remarks and assumed she was talking to Raen.

"I don't know if Connor married well or not. Brenna's a pretty little thing, but she's barely grown and cannot possibly have acquired the skills necessary to run a household. She seems very eager to please, and from what I've observed, I would say she's already loyal to Connor. Pity she doesn't have an older woman to show her the way, but then, very soon now, that won't matter, will it? There can be only one mistress here."

"Pretty, you say? Describe her to me," Raen insisted.

"For heaven's sake, you would ask about such inconsequential things," Euphemia scolded. "Couple with camp followers if you must, but put aside any lustful thought for another man's wife. Have you learned nothing in the past few years? You would jeopardize everything if you . . ."

"Calm yourself, Mother," Raen ordered, his voice sharp with irritation. "I was merely curious. You insult me by suggesting I would even consider bedding a married woman."

"You've done it before, Raen," she reminded him. "Several times, as I recall."

"When I was too young to know any better," he said. "Connor must be pleased with his wife. Do they seem happy to you?"

"From what I've observed, I would have to conclude Connor is very unhappy. I haven't spent sufficient time with her to ascertain how she feels about him."

"If she satisfies him in bed, what more could he want? I for one wouldn't care what my wife's other skills were."

"Is mating all you ever think about?"

"Most men think of little else. I'm no different, Mother, so you can quit scowling at me with disapproval."

"I cannot know for certain, of course, but I would have to assume she doesn't satisfy him in bed either. He moved her out of his bedroom and into another earlier today. She must have gone to him and pleaded, or perhaps she reminded him she couldn't give him an heir unless he bedded her."

"Did she convince him?"

"Yes," Euphemia answered. "Just an hour past, I saw one of his men carrying her clothing back into Connor's chamber."

"You make him sound quite miserable," Raen remarked with a laugh.

"I believe he is," his mother said with conviction. "I don't feel sorry for him, of course. He married her out of spite and has no one to blame but himself. Do you know he didn't even steal the woman he went after?"

"What nonsense is this?"

"I'm telling you the truth. Brenna's father promised MacNare one daughter and sent him another."

"How very English," Raen muttered, his voice as caustic as lye.

Brenna's face felt as though it were on fire, so embarrassed was she by the conversation about Connor's physical satisfaction with her, or rather, dissatisfaction. Intimate matters between a husband and his wife should never be discussed by others. Were Connor's relatives so uneducated and crude because they lived in the barbaric land in the north and simply didn't know any better?

Although it didn't seem possible, her embarrassment had intensified a moment later when Euphemia mentioned that Connor hadn't even captured the woman he'd wanted.

His stepmother had it all wrong. Connor hadn't known or cared which sister was being sent to MacNare; he simply intended to steal the man's bride, and that's exactly what he did. But how in heaven's name had Euphemia found out what her father had done? It seemed perfectly plausible to Brenna that his stepmother would have been privy to the feud going on between the MacNares and the Mac-Alisters—everyone in the Highlands knew about it—and it was also plausible that she had heard from others that MacNare planned to marry a woman from England.

It didn't seem plausible that she would have also heard that one sister had been promised and another sent, unless Connor had told her.

Why would he have done such a thing? It wasn't like him to ever tell anyone anything he was planning, except for Alec and his two close friends, Crispin and Quinlan, of course, but they were just like Connor. They wouldn't have told Euphemia something they would consider inconsequential.

She leaned heavily against the door while she tried to come up with a reasonable explanation. She felt humiliated and worthless, but then, why wouldn't she? Her own father had treated her with callous disregard when he'd snatched her out of her warm bed and sent her to MacNare without so much as a fare-thee-well.

Had Connor been disloyal to her? She shook her head as soon as the possibility came into her mind. Granted, her husband had a considerable list of flaws that were bound to drive her daft by the time she was an old woman, yet he also had a fair number of virtues. He was above all else an honorable man, of that she was absolutely certain, and honorable men didn't deliberately embarrass their wives.

Heaven only knew how Euphemia had found out, but one day, when Brenna had won her approval and friendship, she would get up the courage to ask her.

The immediate problem facing her was proving to Euphemia that although she was young, she was still quite capable of running Connor's home. His stepmother hadn't said anything unkind about her, which gave Brenna considerable hope that she would be able to prove herself in no time at all.

Connor's family should be important to her, and in the back of her mind she knew that once he noticed how she accepted his relatives, he would realize he should give her side of the family the same consideration. At the very least, he should show some interest in listening to her talk about her brothers and sisters. He didn't even know their names now. In time he would, she vowed.

Her work was cut out for her, but she'd never backed away from a challenge before, and she wasn't about to back away now. Her ultimate goal was to turn an unfeeling, hardened warrior into a loving husband, and one way or another, she would make it happen. Training a bear to genuflect would probably be easier than teaching Connor to be thoughtful. Still, it could be done, couldn't it?

She straightened away from the door and with renewed

determination and a firm plan in her mind, she took a slow, deep breath and opened the back door. Then she slammed it shut so Euphemia and Raen would hear, forced a smile on her face, and went inside.

"Good day, Lady MacAlister," she called out from the doorway.

"Good day, Brenna. I'm happy you could join us. We've been waiting for you quite a long time now."

"I apologize if I kept you waiting. I was in the kitchens going over tonight's meal."

"Come forward, child, so I may introduce you to my son."

She felt a surge of anger at being called a child, quickly suppressed it, and did as she was asked. Raen was standing by the hearth. She intended to go to him before she curtsied, but Euphemia's son got to her first. 'Twas a fact, he actually ran, but thankfully he had enough presence of mind to stop before he ran her down. A bit unsettled by his enthusiasm, she took a quick step back to put a decent amount of distance between them.

"My son's name is Raen," Euphemia called out. "And from the look on his face, I can only conclude you've given him quite a start. Son, where are your manners?" she added in a sweet voice.

And still he didn't say a word. His close scrutiny made her uneasy in no time at all. What was the matter with him?

"It's a pleasure to meet you," she blurted out, looking up at him while she waited for him to stop gawking at her and say something in return.

She was surprised the man standing before her was related to Euphemia. They didn't look anything alike. Raen evidently favored his father's side of the family, which really wasn't all that fortunate, because they must have been rather dull-looking people.

He wasn't unpleasantly dull, just rather ordinary, with lackluster features and pale coloring and hazel eyes that couldn't decide what color to be. He was tall, nearly as tall as Connor, as a matter of fact, yet given to fat around his chest, not muscle, which meant he didn't do much strenuous work on his land.

The way he was staring at her made her horribly uncomfortable. His gaze had been centered on her mouth for surely what must have been a full minute, and then dropped to her breasts, where it lingered even now.

It wasn't appropriate behavior at all. But he was from the far north, she reminded herself, and therefore didn't know any better.

"You're a very beautiful woman, Brenna," he whispered, as he clasped her hand in his. "I hope Connor realizes your value."

"Surely you realize a woman's value isn't determined by her appearance, but what is inside her heart, and I assure you, Raen, my husband does recognize my worth. I do thank you for your compliment," she hastily added, lest he take offense because she'd just instructed him.

"Yes, of course," he agreed. He bowed low to her then, and while he was telling her how very eager he'd been to meet her, he was slowly rubbing his thumb back and forth along the palm of her hand. She couldn't understand why he would want to do such a thing. She certainly didn't enjoy it, but when she tried to pull away from him, he tightened his hold. She made up her mind then and there that she would be polite to the man, but never, ever like him.

"Come and sit with me at the table. I'm getting an ache in my back craning around to look at you," Euphemia called out.

Seizing the opportunity, Brenna jerked her hand away before turning to his mother. "Madam, wouldn't you be more comfortable sitting in the tall chair?"

"You want me to sit at the head of the table while Connor is away?"

Euphemia apparently didn't need an answer to her question, for quicker than a goblet can be tossed from the table to the floor, she took possession of the position of power. "You are very thoughtful, child."

Raen pressed against Brenna's back, and when she tried to move away, he put his hands down on her shoulders to keep her there. "Mother, Brenna isn't a child. One look at her and anyone can see she's a woman."

"Now, Raen, don't criticize me," Euphemia pleaded.

The son ignored his mother and leaned down close to Brenna's ear. "Sit by me at the table and tell me all about your wedding."

If she turned around to answer him, she knew she wouldn't be able to hide her repulsion, and so she directed her remarks to his mother instead. "I mustn't intrude upon your joyful reunion with your mother."

"Nonsense, I only left her side a week ago."

"I don't know why I assumed it had been a much longer separation," she lied, for she remembered quite well that Euphemia had insisted she hadn't seen her son in a long, long while. "But a week is still a long time to a mother, isn't that so, Lady MacAlister?"

"Not really," Euphemia answered. "Raen, you're standing entirely too close to Brenna. I'm not about to be ignored any longer. Come over here and sit close with me."

"I hadn't realized I was standing close," he said with such a tone of surprise that his mother obviously thought he was sincere. Brenna wasn't so easily fooled, however. She resisted an urge to sigh with relief as soon as he let go of her and strolled over to the table.

"Brenna, you have my permission to go about your duties. Raen, I have some interesting news to tell you."

Brenna hurried toward the entrance before Euphemia could change her mind.

Raen stopped her. "We heard thunder. Wasn't it raining when you came inside?"

"Yes, it was."

"Then why aren't your clothes wet?"

She wasn't about to admit the truth, that she had been inside several minutes before the downpour started, for then she would have to explain what she'd been doing, and they'd know she had deliberately listened to their private conversation.

"Two very thoughtful servants held cloaks over my head."

His nod indicated he accepted her lie. "I hope to God the rain lets up soon. I hate being cooped up inside."

She thought that it was rather peculiar that the rain would keep him in. Connor's soldiers went about their duties regardless of the weather. Raen wasn't at all like the other men, however. He had been overindulged and pampered by his mother and probably didn't realize what a weakling he appeared to be.

How in heaven's name was she ever going to get through supper tonight? She hoped to God she didn't have to sit next to Connor's stepbrother. The mere possibility made her lose her appetite.

She avoided the hall for the rest of the day until it was time to join her relatives for the evening meal. To her surprise, the evening turned out to be quite pleasant. Not only was Euphemia less abrasive, Raen was also somewhat charming. He sat across from her at the table, entertaining both his mother and her with amusing stories from his past. By the time she went upstairs, she was actually looking forward to sharing her next meal with him.

After spending another lovely evening with him the following night, she began to feel guilty for initially judging him so harshly. She had thought the worst of him and now realized how wrong she'd been. Granted, Raen had been overly enthusiastic at their first encounter, but not because he had lecherous intentions she decided. Perhaps he just didn't know any better. And maybe he was trying to counter his mother's uncertain attitude toward her son's wife by showing Brenna she had his complete approval.

She went to bed that night feeling she had simply overreacted and vowed to never let that happen again. Everyone deserved a second chance.

On the third morning of Connor's absence, Brenna awakened to sunshine and laughter. She threw off her covers and went to the window to look out at the glorious day. Servants were hurrying about below, and from the joy in their faces she knew they loved being outside as much as she did.

There were at least a hundred things she wanted to accomplish today, and while she knew she shouldn't put her duties aside, she meant to do just that in favor of exploring the hills.

Smiling in anticipation, she hurried to get dressed and go downstairs. The hall was deserted, and though she tried, she couldn't get the heavy door open so she could go down to the courtyard. She wasn't defeated, however, and turned to go out the back door instead.

"Good morning, mi'lady. Did you sleep well?" Netta called out from the hall.

"Yes, thank you," she answered. "Has Lady MacAlister come down yet?"

"No, mi'lady, she hasn't. Raen has already left the holding to go riding for the day. He told me he wouldn't be back until supper."

"He went outside the walls with some of Connor's soldiers?"

"No, he rode alone. He's taking a risk, isn't he?"

"He must not think so," Brenna replied with a shrug. "I wonder where he plans to go," she added.

"It wouldn't have been proper for me to ask," Netta said.

Brenna wasn't paying attention to the servant now, for she'd only just noticed the pile of items stacked on the top of the low chest in the entrance. As soon as Netta convinced her they looked familiar to her because they belonged to her, Netta helped carry everything back up to Brenna's room.

That evening, Raen returned to the holding just in time to share his evening meal with his mother and Brenna. He looked tired from his ride, but was still quite pleasant, and once again, he did nothing that was in the least inappropriate.

He was ready to go upstairs at the very same time she was. He clasped hold of her elbow and walked by her side, which was really quite gallant, and told her a humorous story that made both of them laugh. His hand brushed across her breasts as he reached for the door latch, but it was apparent from the innocent look on his face that he hadn't even realized what he had done, leaving her to wonder why she was so quick to become suspicious again.

What was wrong with her, she wondered while she prepared for bed, and finally concluded that the strain of trying to win Euphemia's approval was making her a nervous twit. 'Twas the truth, the woman could make a saint lose her temper. No wonder Brenna had her guard up all the time. Connor's stepmother was an extremely difficult woman to please, and winning her over was proving to be far more difficult than Brenna had anticipated. While

Euphemia never openly criticized her, she still managed to find fault with everything she did, and in a backhanded, condescending way that made Brenna want to clench her teeth together.

She wasn't about to give up, of course, and decided she would simply double her efforts.

The following morning, Raen had once again left the holding to go riding alone before Brenna had come downstairs. She spent a trying day seeing to Euphemia's every comfort and was worn out by supper.

The worst was yet to come, however. Brenna's evening wasn't at all delightful; it was god-awful. She tried to engage Raen in conversation, but he was in a sullen, defiant mood. Being charming must have been a strain on him, because he discarded all attempts at being the least bit polite.

He acted like a lecher again. He never took his gaze off her—or rather, her mouth—throughout the endless meal, and from the smirk on his face and the look in his eyes, she knew he was fully aware of how uncomfortable he was making her.

Euphemia chose to be oblivious to what was going on. Brenna doubted she would have done anything about it even if asked to. Her devotion to her son blinded her to his faults. She considered Raen to be perfect, which was more than evident from the way she constantly bowed to his wishes.

Up until that night, Euphemia found fault with just about everyone and everything else, though, except the meals. Brenna thought her mother-in-law was enjoying her food; she ate everything on her trencher just as she had at her previous meals, but after the table was cleared and the servants left the hall, Euphemia announced her dissatisfaction.

"Brenna, I realize you've been unprepared for company for the last several days and have obviously been in too much of a rush to go over supper arrangements thoroughly with your cook, and for that reason I have held my tongue. I cannot keep silent any longer, however, and must insist you replace the incompetent woman in your kitchen with someone more skilled. Tonight was the worst disaster yet. I swear

I ate more fat than fowl, and the tarts were so bitter and stringy I could barely get them down. Has Connor had to put up with this poor excuse for food long?"

"Mother, Brenna hasn't lived here long enough to know if he has or not," Raen snapped.

Euphemia continued to frown at Brenna. "You look flushed, dear. Have you put in a long day?"

"Yes, madam."

"Why don't you go upstairs to bed? Raen will be happy to keep me company."

She couldn't excuse herself fast enough. Unfortunately, Raen followed her to the entrance steps. He grabbed hold of her arm, told her he was escorting her, and pressed against her side. She was all but hanging over the railing in her attempt to put some distance between them.

"There isn't any need to go upstairs with me, Raen. I'm sure you have more important things to do."

"You've already taken one serious fall, and these steps are dangerously steep," he argued as he pulled her along.

"How did you hear about my fall?"

"I asked one of the servants how you injured your forehead, and she told me you fell down the stairs. I would be remiss in my duty to my brother if I didn't make certain you were kept safe while he was away."

"I fell down because I wasn't paying attention to where I was going. I am paying attention now."

He let go of her arm, giving her only a few seconds to feel relieved before he slipped his arm around her waist.

"Please let go of me," she asked.

He ignored her. "Are you eager to see Connor again? I know you must miss him, especially at night when you're in bed and you're wanting to feel him between your thighs."

"Do not dare talk to me in such a way," she ordered. She was so furious, she could barely control herself and increased her struggles to get away from him.

He shifted his grip, moving upward until his fisted hand rested just below her right breast, making it impossible for her to struggle now because, every time she moved, his knuckles rubbed against her.

He never once looked down at her or showed any reaction

at all to the pain she knew she was inflicting in his arm with her nails digging into his flesh.

"I could take care of you while he's away," he whispered. "I know how to make the ache go away. Leave your door unlatched tonight, Brenna."

Stunned by the filth he spewed, she could barely keep her wits about her. "If you don't let go of me, I swear I'll scream."

"Why in heaven's name would you want to scream?" he asked in mock astonishment, while his fingers slowly uncoiled and spread upward to squeeze her breast.

Anger gave her the strength of five men. She drove her elbow into his side and blessedly got just the reaction she wanted. He grunted in obvious pain and let go of her. She moved back against the door of her bedroom and reached for her dagger. She felt a second's panic when she touched her side and realized the knife wasn't in the pouch looped to her belt, but Raen wasn't looking at her now or trying to grab her again.

He opened the door for her, bid her good night, and strolled away. He was whistling as he went down the stairs.

Shaking with rage and terror, she ran inside, bolted the door closed behind her, and broke into sobs.

What in God's name was she going to do?

The possibility that he might try to touch her again terrified her. She slept on Connor's side of the bed that night and didn't go downstairs until later than customary the following morning. She was, however, much calmer, because she realized that Raen wouldn't dare do anything inappropriate in front of witnesses and as long as she was never alone with him, she would be safe until Connor came home.

The minute she saw her husband, she was going to tell him exactly what had happened, but until he returned and sent Raen away, it was her duty to look out for herself.

Connor should be the first to know. Raen was his stepbrother, and it wouldn't be right to tell anyone else, unless it became absolutely necessary. She wasn't about to suffer so much as an obscene look from the vile man however. If he came near her, she would banish him from the keep immediately, providing she had the power to do so, and if Quinlan told her she didn't have the authority, she would either tell him what had happened or pack her satchel and move in with the Kincaids. Alec had told her he would never deny her anything.

She walked around in a rage most of the afternoon, and at supper that evening, she ignored Raen and urged Euphemia to tell her all about herself. Connor's stepmother seemed to enjoy being the center of attention and spent over an hour complimenting herself. Brenna pretended to hang on every word. She wasn't about to leave the hall unless her stepmother was with her, which soon became apparent to Raen, because he finally went outside to stretch his legs.

He dared to ask Brenna if she would like to accompany him, in a mocking tone and with a sneer that told her he knew what her game was and found it amusing.

"No, thank you," she answered without bothering to look at him. "I would rather listen to your mother. Lady Euphemia, you've had such an interesting life."

"I've had a tragic life," Euphemia corrected.

With Brenna's encouragement, she then proceeded to tell her all about the pain she had endured over the loss of her dear parents. No one had ever suffered the way Euphemia had, and no one had ever had so many crushing disappointments.

Euphemia didn't stop talking about herself for another hour or so. Brenna stayed by her side, pretending to be fascinated, and when, at last, she announced she was going up to bed, Brenna took hold of her arm and walked by her side.

"I meant to talk to you about the evening meals, madam."

"I meant to have a word with you too. Once again, I was disappointed, Brenna. Didn't you follow my instructions and get rid of the cook?"

"Yes, of course I did," Brenna lied. "I've come up with a plan I hope you'll approve. You are far more knowledgeable than I, and I could use your counsel."

"Don't berate yourself. You don't know any better."

Brenna didn't argue, but she didn't agree either. "I have asked five women to take turns preparing your evening meals, and I will let you decide at the end of the week who is the best skilled to suit your needs."

Euphemia shrugged with indifference. "Leave it to me."

"Thank you, madam."

Managing to get to her bedroom without offending the woman, Brenna leaned against the door and let out a loud sigh.

Netta stood at the hearth, warming herself in front of the fire. "Did Lady Euphemia go along with your plan to try five different cooks?"

Brenna smiled. "Yes, she did. Be sure to remind Ada she mustn't let Euphemia see her until the end of the week."

"She knows, mi'lady, and she's most appreciative of your efforts. She's worried though that Lady Euphemia will know she prepared all the meals through the week. Are you sure you wouldn't rather have someone else . . ."

"I'm certain," Brenna replied. "Ada's a fine cook. Our laird's stepmother likes to be difficult. I've decided we aren't being disloyal to our laird with our trickery," she added. "We're simply trying to make his relatives happy, that's all."

"None of us feel tricking Lady Euphemia is disloyal. Do you have any idea how long she and her son plan to stay?"

"No, but I assure you, that will be the first question I ask my husband."

"Is there something else bothering you? I noticed you barely touched your food tonight, and when you came inside the room a moment ago, your face was terribly pale."

Brenna wasn't about to tell her about Raen, believing it was up to her, not a servant, to solve this problem. To condemn the laird's stepbrother would have severe ramifications, she imagined; God only knew, she would have been sickened if one of her own brothers' wives cried out against another brother. As Connor's wife, it was her dreaded duty to tell him, no one else.

"I wasn't very hungry tonight," she said in answer to Netta's question.

The servant left a few minutes later. After bolting the door, Brenna sat down on the bed and worked on her sewing. Ada had given her a bright saffron-colored cloth to put on the table, and Brenna was trying to embroider the colors of Connor's plaid into a square in the center of the material. Because she wanted it to be perfect, she labored well into the night, making certain each one of the stitches was straight, and if she kept to her schedule, she would be finished in just a few more days.

She didn't plan to put it on the table until she had sewn into squares the plaids she'd cut and stuffed with sheep's wool, which meant she would have to sew at least one hour every morning, but if the weather proved accommodating, she meant to sit outside with the other women and get to know them at the same time.

She wasn't going to sit about all day long though, especially when the sun was out, and so she decided to allow one hour each afternoon to go riding. Learning how to ride bareback intrigued her, and as Connor's wife, shouldn't she know how?

Besides, how difficult could it be?

Chapter 12

She almost killed herself—several times as a matter of fact—and all in the first afternoon she tried to ride bareback.

Davis swore to Quinlan that he never would have allowed his mistress to even look at their laird's stallion if he had known what she intended to do. She hadn't understood why her husband would leave the horse behind, and Davis was happy to explain that the stallion needed to rest and feed because he'd been ridden so hard. She suggested the beast needed a little pampering as well, and Davis hadn't disagreed with her.

When she asked him if she could take the stallion out for a little stroll, he made her give him every assurance she meant only to walk the black up the hill and back so he could get a little exercise and attention. The stallion had obviously taken to her. Why, the way he let her lead him to the stables on the very first day of her arrival proved he had accepted her, and hadn't her skill handling the horse been apparent to just about everyone?

Watching the docile way the animal pranced up the hill at her side had assured Davis he had made the right decision. His suspicions surely would have been aroused if Lady

Brenna had asked him for a saddle, but she hadn't asked, now had she?

"I'm not saying our mistress out and out lied to me, Quinlan. That ain't what I'm saying, or even suspecting. I'm thinking she must have changed her mind once she walked over the crest. The notion must have struck her then, and she couldn't resist giving it a try. Don't you worry though. I won't be so easily swayed again, but I'm not even thinking she might try to lie to me. I'm just saying she might get another one of her notions again. That's all."

Quinlan accepted Davis's explanation. Like the stablemaster, he wasn't concerned his mistress would ever take such a chance again, because he thought she'd finally come to her senses after the scare she had flying through the air like an eagle suddenly deprived of its wings.

And so, the very next day, while he was checking on the progress of the soldiers working on the wall, she took the stallion out for a nice stroll once again. Because she was walking with such a stiff gait, Davis didn't suffer a moment's worry.

But then, he hadn't realized his mistress was completely daft. At least that was the excuse he whispered to Quinlan, begging his forgiveness all the while because he knew he shouldn't criticize his laird's dear wife.

"She tricked me, she did," Davis told his commander. "I'm not saying she looked me right in the eye and lied to me. No, that's not what I'm saying at all. I'm thinking it though, because this time I was real specific with her, firm as I could be, and when I demanded her promise she wouldn't get up on the beast again, she answered me with a big smile, which told me she agreed with my ruling, because anyone with any sense at all knows a woman doesn't smile at you after being given an order unless she means to follow it. You don't have to be worried another minute, Quinlan. I'm on to her now, all right. She won't be fooling me again."

She did exactly that the following afternoon. Davis conveniently disappeared as soon as word reached him his mistress was once again riding the stallion.

He needn't have bothered to hide, as Quinlan finally realized he was going to have to take up the problem himself before his mistress killed herself. Davis simply wasn't up to it.

Determined to prevent disaster, the soldier had every intention of forbidding Lady Brenna to ever take such a dangerous risk again; yet as he strode through the break in the pines at the crest of the slope, he heard her laughter and began to have misgivings. A second later, he saw her sitting upright on the stallion's back. The look of joy on her face made him smile, and he stood there a long while watching her, even though he knew he should put an immediate stop to her dangerous antics.

Saints be praised, Lady Brenna managed to stay upright for several minutes before she was tossed to the ground.

Quinlan waited for her to get up. She didn't move. He started running down the incline, and he swore later to Crispin that his heart had surely stopped when, just as he was about to reach her, the stallion came charging back.

He was certain the beast would trample her. The big black nudged her instead, and quick as a wink, she rolled over, grabbed hold of the horse's reins, and burst into laughter.

He took the reins out of her hand, slapped the stallion's hindquarters to get him to move away from her, and then bent down to offer his hand. "When you didn't move, I thought you were dead."

"It's a game we play. If I stay perfectly still, Willie comes right over to my side, and I can grab hold of his reins. Otherwise, he makes me chase him."

Quinlan was too distraught to pay attention to a word she said. He kept telling himself not to raise his voice to her—she was his mistress, for the love of God, not his younger sister. "Have you lost your sense?"

"I don't think so."

"If you insist on killing yourself, do so on Crispin's watch, not mine."

After giving her his order, he pulled her to her feet, then stood back while she brushed the dust off her plaid. He wanted her full attention so there wouldn't be any misunderstandings. "You will not take such a risk again. I want your word you'll never ride without a saddle, and I assure you, a smile isn't going to work on me."

"No, you are far more clever than I am, Quinlan. I would never dare to trick you."

Somewhat placated, he reminded her she still hadn't given him her promise.

"Do you think you could manage to stop shouting at me? You're making my head pound."

Quinlan was appalled by his conduct. "I beg your forgiveness, mi'lady. I cannot imagine what came over me."

"I gave you a scare," she reminded him. "Now, tell me what I'm doing wrong. Why can't I stay very long on his back?"

"You sit too far back on the black's back," he answered. "As for your promise . . ."

She cut him off. "I certainly could have used your advice yesterday. My grip was off as well, but I have already corrected that problem. Poor Willie. For a while there, he kept tossing his head back at me, and I'm sure he thought I was daft."

The horse had more sense than his mistress did, Quinlan thought. He was still too upset to consider how uncharitable he was being. "It's amazing he didn't trample you to death," he muttered. "Willie . . . did I hear you call the black Willie?"

"Yes, but I made certain first that Connor hadn't already named him. Davis assured me he hadn't."

"No, Connor didn't name . . ." His voice trailed off into silence.

"Then I'm certain he won't mind if I call him Willie."

Quinlan's eyelid began to twitch. "Why 'Willie'?" he asked.

"It's short for William," she explained. She took the reins away from Quinlan and turned to walk back to the stables. He happened to notice she left one of her shoes behind, picked it up, and handed it to her. She thanked him while she held on to his arm so she could keep her balance slipping the shoe back on.

"I'm naming Willie after my brother. If I don't mention it to my husband, I'm sure he won't be bothered. Connor doesn't like it when I talk about my family."

"Why would you think he doesn't like it?"

"He frowns and tries to change the subject. I'm not certain why he feels the way he does. He can't dislike them, because he doesn't know them. Perhaps he just doesn't care. The topic of my family probably bores him," she added with a nod.

"I doubt that, mi'lady."

She shrugged. "Perhaps," she agreed, but not because she thought he might be right. She was just being polite.

"I would appreciate it if you wouldn't mention my name for his horse. Connor can be peculiar about some things, and even though I'm almost certain he won't be irritated, there's a slim chance he might."

"Mi'lady, are you asking me not to tell him?"

"Yes."

"I won't make a point of telling him, but if he asks, I will explain. Are you going to give me your promise you won't ride bareback again?"

"What would you do if I gave you my promise and then I deliberately broke it? I would never do such a thing, but I am curious about the consequences."

"I would have you locked in your chamber until your husband returns."

"You would do such a thing?"

"I certainly wouldn't want to, but keeping you safe would outweigh your feelings."

"Could you ever banish anyone?"

"I would never banish you," he assured her.

"But do you have the authority to banish someone else while Connor is away?"

"Yes, as long as I have valid reasons to give my laird."

"Do I happen to have the authority? Don't look so stunned. I wasn't thinking of banishing you, even if you dared to lock me in my room, which, by the way, I happen to know you would never do. I was wondering if I could send someone else away."

"If you're having difficulty with someone, then you should tell me about it, or wait until your husband comes home."

She interpreted his explanation to mean she didn't have the authority. At least now she knew what she was up against, and she certainly wouldn't threaten Raen with banishment because he would know she was bluffing. She let out a weary sigh and stared down at the ground while she walked along.

Her disappointment was softened by the recollection that she was only going to resort to such a drastic measure if Raen ever came near her again. Thankfully, she had a plan to keep him at bay.

Quinlan couldn't understand why his mistress looked so disheartened. "Did you wish to hold such a position of strength, mi'lady?"

She didn't answer him and, in fact, didn't say another word for a long while.

"If you have a problem and you cannot solve it on your own, then tell me what it is and I will be happy to take care of it."

She shook her head. "The problem is of a personal nature involving a family member."

Quinlan was relieved, and though he felt like smiling, he didn't, for fear he would injure her feelings and make her think her problem wasn't important to him.

"You're having difficulty with Euphemia, aren't you?" He didn't give her time to answer him but continued on with a suggestion he was certain would solve her worry. "It would be appropriate for you to speak to Raen about his mother. I'm certain he'll talk to her."

She shook her head again, though far more vehemently. "I should be able to solve this problem, and when Connor returns, I'll discuss it with him."

"As you wish, mi'lady."

She changed the subject then. "You know that ever since I arrived, I've been trying to understand how things are done here. There seems to be a set of regulations everyone else understands but me. I constantly fear I'll offend someone because of my lack of education about Highlanders, and I could certainly benefit from your instruction."

"I'll be happy to help in any way that I can."

"Will you and two others you select join me for the evening meal tonight? We could continue our discussion then, and I could learn about the MacAlisters. I'm one of you now and do want to fit in."

THE WEDDING

"I would be honored to join you at the table, and I'm certain the other two I choose will feel the same way."

And I'll be relieved, she thought to herself.

"I don't want to show any favoritism, however, and so, each night that Connor is away, if you would please select two other guests, then I could also become acquainted with some of my husband's followers."

"Certainly," he answered.

"When will Connor be home?"

"I cannot say for certain."

"It seems he's been away a long time. I need to talk to him."

He heard the desperation in her voice and decided then that Connor's stepmother must be giving her a very difficult time. He imagined the two women were involved in a minor power struggle and was somewhat surprised that Lady Brenna could become upset so easily. Perhaps her loneliness for her husband was making her anxious. She might even feel as though he had abandoned her. Connor had all but snatched her out of one life and put her down in the center of his.

Time was all his mistress needed to find her way. At least that was what Quinlan hoped would happen. Later that day, however, he began to think the problem was more serious than he'd first estimated. Netta caught him on his way up to the soldiers' quarters to tell him Lady Brenna was acting peculiar.

"She didn't hear me knock on her bedroom door, and when I entered, she let out a scream and jumped a foot. 'Tis the truth, she reached for her dagger. She looked terrified, Quinlan."

The cook's friend, Brocca, happened to overhear the conversation and quickly joined in. "Ada told me she's worried mi'lady might be ill. She isn't eating anything at all. It's too soon for her to be carrying a bairn," she added.

Quinlan knew there was a chance both women were exaggerating and decided to wait and see for himself. After observing his mistress push her food around on her trencher and barely eat a morsel, he realized they were right to be concerned. He decided he would take his mistress to see Lady Kincaid the following morning, believing that she

267

would surely find out what was wrong, and if his mistress was really ill, then Lady Kincaid would know how to cure her.

Brenna had no idea Quinlan was so concerned about her. For the first time in several days, she felt much more relaxed. The two soldiers he had chosen to share the honor of dining at the table were older men, who took turns telling stories about the early days. Lady Euphemia was blissfully quiet. She seemed to enjoy the conversation, though. She looked as if she was hanging on every word, and every once in a while she would actually chuckle or nod when one of the guests related a humorous incident she apparently remembered.

Raen acted like an overindulged child who wasn't getting enough attention. He pouted all through the meal and kept his gaze directed on the table. He ate quickly, and when he was finished, he gave Brenna a hard scowl, slammed his goblet down, and went storming out of the hall.

None of the soldiers seemed at all bothered by Raen's insolence. Quinlan noticed how weary his mistress looked and decided to call a halt to the evening. A good night's rest might be all she needed to get her appetite back.

One of the older soldiers offered her his arm and escorted her up the steps. He stood at the landing until she entered her room. When she turned to call out her farewell at her door, she saw Raen lurking in the shadows behind the soldier's shoulder, but before she could demand to know what he was waiting for, he turned around and hurried into his chamber.

Netta was waiting for her inside the bedroom and called out her greeting before her mistress had even entered so that she wouldn't be startled again. Before Brenna could ask her why she was waiting for her, the servant explained Euphemia had ordered her to light the candles in the woman's bedroom each night and assist her in her preparation for bed, and if Netta was going to serve her laird's stepmother, she sure as certain was going to serve her laird's wife.

"Doesn't your husband mind waiting for you to come home?"

"It's an honor that I've been chosen to work in our laird's

quarters. My Deverick is strutting around like a king, he is, telling everyone who will stop and listen how important he is because his wife has been given such a position in his laird's home."

Brenna felt blessed to have such a thoughtful woman serve her.

"You have a good heart, Netta."

"You'll turn my head with such praise, mi'lady. Would you like me to help you get ready for bed?"

"No, I'm safe now . . . I mean to say, I'm capable of taking care of myself. I do have a quick question to ask before you leave. I was wondering who would be able to make a wooden medallion for me."

"Alan's clever with his hands, and I think he's most qualified to do exactly what you're wanting. I'll be happy to take you to him tomorrow if you like."

Brenna thanked her once again, and as soon as Netta left, Brenna bolted the door. She worked on her sewing for another hour before she went to bed. She had just blown the candles out and pulled up her covers when she heard someone knocking on her door.

She didn't answer it.

Chapter

13

Connor finally returned to his holding. He felt as though he had been away much longer, and it wasn't until he crossed the drawbridge, and the tension in his neck and shoulders began to ease, that he finally acknowledged the reason he had been so anxious to get back home.

He wanted to see Brenna again. Needless to say, he wasn't at all happy with what he considered his own lack of discipline. Admitting that he had been consumed with thoughts about her only increased his agitation. What in God's name was the matter with him? Whenever he closed his eyes to rest for a few minutes, the image of his wife came into his mind. And stayed there.

Although it wasn't much of a consolation, Alec was in much the same condition; but unlike Connor, he didn't just think about his wife, he talked about her as well.

Alec had noticed Connor's restlessness on the last evening they were together. He watched Connor pace around the camp for well over an hour before finally isolating himself from the others near the break in the forest. Alec joined him a minute later. Both brothers rested their backs against tree trunks so they could eventually sleep, with one hand resting on the hilt of their swords.

Alec didn't ease into the topic he wanted to address. "I look at you and I see myself when I first married Jamie."

"And what do you see? You're going to tell me whether I want to hear it or not, aren't you?"

"Of course," he replied. "Learn from my mistakes and save yourself the aggravation."

"You sound like my father. Those were his very words to me."

"Was he talking about your mother?"

"Yes," he answered. "He called her his own sweet Isabelle."

Alec nodded. "You've fought a good battle, but the time has come for you to stop struggling. It's becoming painful to watch."

"Alec? What the hell are you talking about?"

His brother laughed. "You know good and well what I'm talking about. You're trying not to love your wife, aren't you? I understand why, of course. You're afraid."

"God help you, you've turned into an old meddlesome woman."

Alec acted as though he hadn't heard the insult. "I don't think your father's parting words about Isabelle made you more cautious than any other man. Do you remember what you told me he said?"

"I remember every word. He, too, suggested I learn from his mistakes. He loved his own sweet Isabelle and felt she betrayed him by dying. He swore he never forgave her. It was all bluster, Alec. My father was a hard man who found it difficult to speak of such emotions without sounding angry. He was trying to console me, and even as a boy, I understood. I don't understand the need for this ridiculous conversation, however."

Alec didn't say another word for a long while. He knew Connor was considering his remarks and certainly was trying to convince himself he didn't already love his wife. Ah, the foolishness of men who embraced the notion that loving would weaken them.

"I sometimes wonder, if I hadn't come so close to losing Jamie, would I even now acknowledge I love her? Hopefully, I would, because I'm older and perhaps a little wiser now. I didn't know any better back then, Connor; but you do because I have just explained it all to you. Do as I suggest and quit resisting. You'll find it's less tormenting."

"I have only been afraid of one man, Alec, and God help me the day I realize I'm afraid of a woman. You insult me by suggesting my wife has such power over me."

"Who was the man you feared?" Alec asked, curious about his earlier remark.

"You. I was afraid you wouldn't help me and my friends."

"Your father knew I would take you in. You weren't as certain, were you? Even then, you were quite cynical. Your wife isn't, however. She surprised me the way she put herself in front of you. If I hadn't known better, I would have thought she was protecting you."

"She was trying to protect me. The woman doesn't have many fears. If she lives a full year, I'll be surprised."

"She's strong, Connor, and as intelligent as my wife. There are times I think they could both be more intelligent than we are. I can see from the way you're looking at me you think I'm wrong. Answer a question for me. Where do you think our wives are sleeping tonight?"

"In our beds."

"Where are we sleeping?"

Connor laughed. "In the damp, cold forest. Get some rest, Alec, and stop hounding me with foolish talk."

His brother was in the mood to take the suggestion. "One last thing," Alec whispered after he closed his eyes and let out a loud yawn. "If you ever tell anyone about this conversation, I'll kill you."

Crispin pulled his laird away from his thoughts and back to the present. "Is something bothering you?" he asked as soon as he noticed Connor's frown.

"I'm just bone weary like you are," he answered.

"You're also just as covered with dirt and dried blood as I am. God only knows what we smell like. As soon as I see to my horse, I'm going to the lake. I assume you'll do the same."

"Is there a particular woman you want to impress?"

"Several come to mind, but I was considering how your wife will react to seeing you, Laird. She's bound to run the other way."

Quinlan caught Connor's attention then, for though it was customary to wait for his laird in front of the keep, his friend had altered his routine and was now waiting for his laird in front of the stables. The expression on Quinlan's face was one Connor had never seen before, and had he not known better, he would have thought his friend looked relieved to see him.

Crispin had the very same thought. "Whatever the problem was, it must have been exasperating."

Quinlan waited until they dismounted before coming forward. "All's well, Connor."

"I expected it would be."

"From the look on your face, I thought something was surely amiss," Crispin remarked. "You look relieved to see us."

"Relieved? If I were not a man, I swear I would be overcome with joy."

"Then there was a problem?" Crispin asked.

"I've just informed our laird there were no problems. There were, however, minor frustrating inconveniences," Quinlan added before once again addressing his laird. "Connor, I swear to God, I'm never going to get married."

"I take it, then, my wife was the cause of these inconveniences?"

"Your wife could never cause an inconvenience," he managed to say without laughing, which Quinlan personally felt had to be a rather amazing feat.

Davis and another younger soldier came outside to take the horses. The stablemaster waited until his assistant had greeted his laird and gone back inside before he took his turn.

"It's good to have you home, Laird. Your black is inside his stall, should you be wondering."

"I assumed he would be," he answered, puzzled that the old man wanted to tell him where his horse was.

"Well, now, I quit assuming that over a week ago," he said.

"Did he give you any trouble while I was gone?"

"No, he didn't, Laird, and he sure as certain didn't look me right in the eye and lie to me either."

Before Connor could ask him to explain, Quinlan

273

grabbed hold of Davis's plaid and shook him. "Your mistress didn't lie. She smiled at you. Recognize the difference."

The stablemaster nodded agreement before Quinlan released him, then bowed to his laird and hurried back inside.

"What was that all about?" Crispin asked. "Has Davis gone addled?"

"They have all gone addled," Quinlan replied. "I, however, am a much better man and didn't have any trouble at all figuring out what her game was."

Crispin was trying hard not to laugh. "Are you referring to our laird's wife?"

"I am. She is alive and well, however."

"I sure as hell hope so," Connor interjected.

Crispin lost his battle and burst into laughter.

Quinlan didn't appreciate his friend's behavior. "Laugh all you want now. Just remember, mi'lady didn't kill herself while I was on watch."

Assuming his friend was exaggerating the problems Brenna had caused, Connor shook his head to let Quinlan know he wasn't in the mood to hear about it now and started up the path toward the keep. He seemed compelled to see Brenna for a moment, just to make certain she was all right before he rode to the lake.

"I'm not interested in the paltry problems a mere woman might cause you," he remarked. "Have you anything more significant to tell me?"

"No," Quinlan answered. "As I said before, I handled the inconveniences."

"I'm curious to hear what made our friend whine like a female," Crispin remarked. "You may tell me everything, Quinlan, if it will make you feel better."

Quinlan chuckled. "Mi'lady asked me not to tell her husband, and if I can't tell him, I certainly can't tell you."

"What exactly doesn't my wife want me to hear?"

"Her surprises. She has several waiting for you and doesn't want me to ruin them. Those were her instructions, by the way, but if you insist . . ."

"No, I'll let her tell me. I'm not going to like the surprises, though, am I?"

"Perhaps," was all Quinlan would allow.

"Where is she now?"

"She's measuring."

"Meaning?"

"Father Sinclair's here for the day. Your wife requested his presence so that he could approve her dimensions for the chapel."

Connor didn't say a word for a long minute. "Where exactly is she measuring?"

Quinlan smiled as he told him. "In the courtyard."

"You're jesting."

"I'm not. She wants to put the chapel up against the keep."

Both Connor and Crispin looked incredulous. Quinlan found their reaction immensely satisfying. They were both finally beginning to understand what he had been up against.

"You put a stop to it, didn't you?" Connor asked.

"Of course. Just as soon as I found out what she was doing, I told her she had to wait and get permission from you. I would mention one other matter. I threatened to lock her in her chamber."

"Because of the chapel," Connor said with a nod.

"Actually, no, it was another matter that caused me to use such a threat."

"How did our mistress react to your warning?" Crispin asked.

"She knew I was bluffing. She misses our laird, by the way, so much so, she is easily startled. The least little sound makes her jump. She isn't eating much either. I was so concerned, I took her to Lady Kincaid. She assured me Lady Brenna was all right. She must have been correct because as soon as Sinclair arrived, she went to confession and seems much happier now. I told her word had reached us that you would be home by nightfall, and she was extremely pleased with the news."

"Did Jamie remove her stitches for her?"

"No, your wife took care of it on her own."

Connor nodded before changing the subject. "I noticed you put Ewan back on the wall. He was happy to alternate the duty with another so that he could work on his fighting skills," he reminded Quinlan.

"I had good reason."

"And that was?"

"I trusted Ewan not to be swayed by your wife. She wanted to go to the lake."

"But you didn't let her."

"No, I didn't."

"And she tried to go anyway?" Crispin asked. "Is that why you threatened to lock her away?"

Quinlan sighed. "No, that wasn't it."

"Then what . . ." Connor lost his train of thought as soon as he reached the top of the path and saw his courtyard.

There were deep holes everywhere. He was so stunned by the desecration of his land his temper ignited. Unfortunately, the woman responsible was directly across the yard. His wife. The longer he stood there staring at her, the more his throat began to throb with the need to let out a roar. Thankfully, he was able to suppress it by clenching his jaw tight and staring up at the sky.

She didn't realize her husband was there, as her back was turned to him and she was a fair distance away. Two soldiers were leaning against the wall, watching her pace. They stood at attention the second they spotted their laird.

They looked relieved to see him. Connor fully understood why.

The muscle in his jaw was beginning to ache. God help him, the longer he looked at the holes in the ground, the more infuriated he became. She didn't move for a second or two, then whirled around. She had a dagger in her hand.

She didn't scream, but from the look on her face he knew she was about to. He was taken aback by the fear he saw in her eyes. Yet as soon as she realized he was watching her, she let out a cry of joy, dropped her dagger, and came running to him.

"I told you she was acting peculiar," Quinlan remarked.

Connor nodded but kept silent as he watched his wife skirt her way around the obstacle course. He expected her to stop as soon as she reached him and was therefore surprised when she threw herself into his arms and kissed the side of his neck.

It was improper behavior, as others were watching them, yet Connor couldn't make himself care. He wrapped his arms around her and held her tight against him, feeling very like a man whose wish had finally been granted.

"I'm so happy to have you home at last," she whispered against his ear.

He gave her a squeeze and then let go of her. She continued to hold on to him for several more seconds before she could make herself step back.

"I have much to tell you."

"It seems you do," he agreed. "You will explain everything this evening. Go and wash your face now. It's covered with my dirt."

Quinlan and Crispin both watched their laird with curiosity. Connor's voice sounded strained, yet calm. He was keeping his anger hidden from his wife, and Quinlan thought that was admirable of him. Crispin knew better. His laird was simply saving his temper to take out on his weapon later when he trained with his soldiers.

"Where are you going now?" she asked.

"To the lake."

"I could go with you."

"No, you couldn't."

"But I . . ."

"Others will be there, Brenna."

"Could you please come with me inside for just a few minutes. I have a surprise for you in the great hall."

"Can't it wait?"

"I suppose it could."

He waited for her to leave. She waited for him to reconsider.

"I wonder how long you will be busy."

He wondered how long he could hide his temper from her. "Until tonight."

"Connor, are you happy to see me?"

"Yes."

His frown suggested just the opposite. She bowed to him before she started back across the courtyard. "If it's dark when you come back, be careful. The ground is full of holes."

"I noticed," he called back.

All three maintained their silence until Lady Brenna had turned the corner on her way to the kitchens.

"She remembered to pick up her dagger," Crispin remarked.

"She never forgets her knife and is constantly checking to make certain she has it with her. She still forgets everything else, though. You're to be commended, Connor," he added. "You didn't lose your temper."

"This isn't amusing, Quinlan. There are over twenty deep holes in my courtyard. Have them filled at once."

After giving his order, he and Crispin returned to the stables to get fresh horses. Connor hoped he could get over his anger before he saw his wife again. He didn't want to upset her, which he thought was damned considerate given that the demented woman was trying to squeeze a chapel up against his keep.

"She wanted to please me. I must keep that in mind every time the word chapel is spoken in my presence."

"Laird?" Quinlan called out. "Could you spare a moment of your time to speak to Father Sinclair before he returns to the Kincaids?"

Connor motioned to the priest to join him. He spoke before Sinclair had a chance. "Do you know why my wife's afraid?"

"I cannot say."

"I was told she's been acting peculiar and that after she spoke to you, she was happy again. Did she confide in you?"

Once again the priest gave him an unsatisfactory answer. "I cannot say, Laird."

"Did she go to confession?"

"Yes."

"Did she tell you what was bothering her during confession?"

"If she did, I couldn't admit it because that would be breaking my solemn promise never to acknowledge anything said during confession."

Connor nodded acceptance and didn't try to press Sinclair again.

"What did you want to speak to me about?"

"I wanted to thank you for allowing me to stay here. I won't be a bother," he promised, "and really shouldn't be here all that often. It's my duty to serve a wide area."

THE WEDDING

"You should give your appreciation to my wife, Father. She is the one who pleaded for you."

"I have already thanked her. I will forever be in her debt. She wishes me to sleep in one of the chambers inside your home, and while I appreciate her thoughtfulness, I feel I should have my own accommodations in the event any of your followers should need to speak to me in private. Is this agreeable with you?"

"It is," Connor answered. "I'll have one of the vacant cottages cleaned and readied for you. When will you be joining us?"

"As soon as Laird Kincaid grants me permission to leave. I would also mention one other matter. I return to England in a few days to explain this change to my superior. I shouldn't be away more than a week."

"I will have soldiers escort you," Connor said.

"That isn't necessary, Laird; for as long as I wear the black cassock, no one would dare harm me, even those whose souls have already been promised to Satan."

"Wild animals won't show you such consideration."

"I will stay to the main path," the priest insisted.

"As you wish."

"Was there any news you wished to send back to England?"

Connor shook his head and waited until Sinclair had left before he continued on. His thoughts were on his wife, of course. She had been very kind to the priest and was certainly concerned about the man's pride and his feelings. One day soon, Connor hoped she would learn to show him the same consideration.

She could start by leaving his damned courtyard alone.

Lord, it was good to be home.

Chapter 14

The surprises just kept on coming. Connor knew that somewhere in his wife's convoluted thoughts lurked an innocent plan to please him, yet how she ever could have imagined he would be happy to find a chapel sitting in his courtyard was beyond his ability to comprehend. He thought she might have another reason for doing such a monstrous thing, but if that was true, he would probably go to his grave still trying to figure out what it could be.

Only one truth comforted him now. It couldn't get any worse. No matter what other surprises she had ready for him, nothing could surpass the chapel.

He really should have known better.

He didn't go inside to speak to Euphemia, as he had planned, when he first arrived home, because he would have had to walk across the courtyard in order to get to her, which meant he would have to sidestep his way around the holes. Quinlan had assured him they were deep enough to cover a tall man's head, providing he was fortunate enough to fall in feet first. Getting that close to the destruction would definitely have sent his temper right over the edge. He could have gone in through the back door, of course. He didn't, though, because he needed to get away until he calmed down. His plan was to avoid the courtyard until that evening, for surely the holes would be filled by then, and he would have had enough time to get over this god-awful surprise.

After he had washed away the filth he'd accumulated over the past two weeks, he rode to the northern section of the wall to look over the progress made in fortifying the wooden posts with stone. The discovery of one problem led to another and another, and he didn't return to the keep until late that afternoon.

The sun was setting by the time he reached the stables, and as soon as he went inside, he noticed two peculiar things. The first was the fact that the black's stall was empty; the second was that Davis appeared to be sneaking out the back door.

His command stopped him cold. "Where's the black, Davis?"

"Outside, Laird."

It wasn't a satisfactory answer. He ordered the stablemaster to come forward, and then asked, "Were you trying to run out the back door?"

"I was."

"For what reason?"

"To get away from you before you noticed the black was missing."

"I see," Connor replied, his voice mild, controlled. "Exactly where is my stallion now?"

"He's getting a dose of fresh air."

"By whose order?"

Davis looked afraid to tell him. He took a hasty step back, quickly braced himself, and then said, "Your wife."

"She ordered you to take my horse out of the stall?" he asked, trying to understand what was going on and why Davis was acting so nervous.

"Well, now, she didn't exactly order me."

"Did she ask Quinlan or Crispin to take the stallion out?"

"No, she surely didn't ask either one of them. Fact is, she didn't ask me either."

Connor had to remind himself to be patient. "Help me understand, Davis, and stand still. You aren't going anywhere until I have all my questions answered. Is someone with my wife, or did she try to walk the horse on her own?"

"Quinlan's probably caught up with mi'lady by now. He usually does. I'm not understanding what you mean by walk, though. Could you explain it to me? I don't think anyone's doing any walking, least of all your black."

A sudden possibility made Connor's heart start pounding. "Is someone riding him?"

"Yes."

"Quinlan?" He resisted the urge to grab Davis by the scruff of his scrawny neck and shake the answers out of him. "Then who is riding him?"

Davis grimaced over the anger he heard in his laird's voice before answering. "Well, now, your wife might be. Then again, she might not."

He had had a feeling Davis was going to say that. If Davis hadn't already assured him that Quinlan was with her, Connor would have lost his control. As it was, he was holding on to it by threads.

What in God's name could Quinlan be thinking to let Brenna take such a risk? The high-strung stallion was difficult for most men to handle, and Connor couldn't even picture his gentle little wife trying to manage him.

"If the beast gets away from Quinlan, my wife will get trampled. Where are they?"

"Laird, I don't think you grasp what it is I'm telling you. The black can't get away from Quinlan because he isn't standing that close to him at all. He's just watching out for mi'lady."

"Dear God . . . she could be . . ."

"No harm's come to her. I know it for a fact."

Connor was nearly to the door when Davis's words stopped him. "How would you know if she's safe or not?" he asked.

"Someone in the crowd would have come looking for you if anything had happened to your dear wife."

"The crowd? What crowd?"

"The crowd watching your wife. They started gathering one at a time about six or seven days ago. No one bothers mi'lady, though; so you can rest your mind about that. And Quinlan's always standing by, looking out for her. I don't have to watch to know what's going on. All I've got to do is walk outside and listen to the sound the crowd makes, and I know right away how mi'lady's doing. When she takes a spill, they groan real loud, and when she stays upright, well then, they cheer her on, of course. Lately I've been noticing more cheering than not, which tells me mi'lady's finally catching on to how it's done."

"Where are they?"

"On the opposite side of the slope behind the kitchens. Just follow the noise," he called out when his laird took off running. "Hear that moan? Well, now, that can only mean . . ." Davis didn't see any point in continuing his explanation; his laird had already vanished over the top of the hill.

By the time Connor strode past the kitchens, he could hear the crowd's thunderous cheer, indicating his wife was safe . . . for the moment. He started breathing again, but he was so shaken that he was a little amazed he could remember how.

A moment later, he spotted the MacAlisters gathered on the side of the hill. Mothers sat on the ground with their babies perched on their laps, while fathers stood behind, talking to one another. The older women had carried along their sewing work, but they, like everyone, were too busy watching Lady MacAlister to pay any attention to anything else. All of them, from the youngest to the oldest in the crowd, were thoroughly enjoying themselves as they watched, transfixed.

Every one of them was clearly demented.

Connor finally reached the crest, a good distance away from his enraptured clan, then came to an abrupt stop and stared down in amazement at the sight before him.

Nothing could have prepared him for what he was witnessing. Not only was his wife riding the black, she was also riding bareback, and saints be praised, she seemed to be doing a fair job of it. No, no, not fair, he realized, she was actually quite remarkable. Her back and shoulders were as straight as a staff; her head was held high, and she was riding with the skill and expertise of a MacAlister warrior, yet with the grace and elegance of a deity at the same time. Her golden hair flew out behind her as she and the beast glided over the landscape, and when he heard the sound of her laughter, his heart swelled with pride over her amazing accomplishment. He knew the truth then; he was just as demented as everyone else.

He noticed the piles of hay strewn about, knew Quinlan had tried to avert disaster by putting down the cushions to ease her falls, and though Connor thought that was clever of him, he was still going to tear him limb from limb. The crowd was cheering her now, urging her on, and it wasn't until he noticed Quinlan frantically waving his hands at Brenna and vehemently shaking his head that Connor was able to pull himself out of his stupor and put an end to this madness before disaster struck.

He didn't understand, or even suspect, what she was going to do until it was too late. Connor started down the hill just as the black jumped the first mound of hay. Brenna didn't even appear to be jarred by the first leap, but she nearly went crashing to the ground with the stallion's second jump.

Connor simply couldn't take any more. He stopped, braced his legs apart, and let out a piercing whistle. The black's head immediately came up. He'd heard the command above the roar of approval from the crowd and swiftly changed directions.

Brenna couldn't understand what had come over Willie. No matter how she tried, she couldn't get the horse to turn back. He raced across the hill, turned, and began to climb.

She understood why a moment later. Connor was standing near the crest, his hands on his hips, his legs spread apart, wearing an expression that didn't leave any doubt at all as to what he thought about her performance. She immediately redoubled her efforts to go the opposite way. Heaven help her, she even begged Willie to take mercy on her.

The stubborn horse refused to obey her no matter how much she pleaded with him and pulled on his reins. He came to a rather jolting stop directly in front of his master just as she was leaning down close to the horse's ear to let him know what she thought about his behavior. "Traitor."

Connor heard. He knew better than to say a word to her now, because in his present condition, once he got started, he wouldn't be able to stop himself from crushing her feelings.

Brenna knew from the stark look in her husband's eyes, she'd given him quite a scare. She wanted to tell him everything was all right. She didn't dare. There was something in his expression that suggested she'd better not try to calm him down just yet.

She decided to pretend she didn't notice his anger. It was a bad plan, but then, she couldn't think of a better one now.

She straightened up and tried to look cheerful.

"Are you pleased with my surprise?" she asked, knowing full well he wasn't pleased at all; he was furious, and that was that. Still, there was always a hope, faint though it was, that she could bluff her way through the storm brewing inside her husband.

She expected him to pull her off Willie or start shouting. He didn't even touch the reins. He simply turned around and started walking back toward the stables.

Willie meekly followed him. Crispin suddenly appeared on her right side, looking very pale, as though he'd just seen a frightening vision; if he'd spared her a glance, she would have asked him what had happened. Then Quinlan appeared on her left side, panting from his run, but looking very, very smug. He wouldn't glance up at her either, so she couldn't ask him why in heaven's name he was so complacent.

It wasn't until they reached the stables that Connor finally spoke. He ordered Crispin to remove his wife from his stallion's back and wait by her side while he had a word with Quinlan inside.

The second the doors were closed behind them, Connor shouted to Davis. "Stay right where you are," he ordered.

"Would you like me to take your stallion off your hands?" Davis asked. "He seems a might agitated by your tone of voice."

He allowed Davis to take the reins before turning to Quinlan. "Start explaining."

"Nothing I can say can possibly justify my conduct. You have only one recourse open to you, Laird. You must remove me from this position with all possible haste."

"I'm angry, not stupid," Connor snapped. "Can't you control one woman? You damn well better learn how, because you're staying in charge when it's your turn. Now tell me, were you out of your mind to let my wife take such a risk? Everyone else seems to be. How could you let this happen?"

"Let it happen, Connor? You've got to be jesting. I would have had more success getting the rain to stop than making your wife cooperate. I've done nothing but second-guess her and try to outwit her for the last two weeks, and all my efforts were wasted."

Connor raised his hand to get Quinlan to stop when he noticed Davis was trying to stroll out the back door yet again.

"Davis," he roared. "If you go out that door, you won't die happy. Come here."

The stablemaster quickly obeyed. "I was just giving you some privacy, Laird, that was all. Did you want something more?"

"I do. I want you to answer some questions for me."

"I wouldn't ask him anything if I were you," Quinlan suggested. "You'll only end up more angry than you already are."

"That isn't possible. Now, Davis, as you know, I listen before I act."

"I do know it for a certainty," he agreed.

"Did my wife go inside the black's stall and put the bridle on him?"

"No, she didn't."

"Who did?"

"I did."

Connor's eyelid began to droop. "I see. Did you know my wife planned to take him out?"

"I did," he answered. "She's the reason I went inside with the bridle in the first place."

Connor happened to notice Quinlan's grin, shot him a hard look to let him know what he thought about that, and then directed his attention on Davis again.

Quinlan couldn't possibly stop smiling, for he knew what was coming.

"Explain why you would do such a thing so that I won't continue to believe you're demented."

"Her smile, Laird, and that's the sorry truth of it."

Connor blinked. "Her smile?"

Davis nodded. "Her smile was my reason from start to finish. It's plain trickery, I'm thinking, but I'll never say it out loud because it would sound disloyal, and I'm not at all disloyal, only honest. And her heart," he thought to add with a nod.

"Her heart?"

"Her heart is as pure as an angel's, and so is her smile, but it's her mind, you see, that's giving me trouble. I'm thinking there's something wrong with it, but I'm not coming right out and saying there is. Mi'lady isn't like all the other ladies hereabouts. She thinks like a man, a clever man, and how was I to know? She never once lied to me. No, Laird, she didn't."

"Then why did you allow her to take the black?"

"Her smile."

"You'll go around and around again the more you ask Davis. It always comes back to mi'lady's smile," Quinlan said.

"And her heart, of course, because when she smiles, I can see she's as pure as an angel . . ."

Connor cut him off. "Davis, I suggest you leave the stables immediately. Come back after I've left, not before."

The old man didn't have to be told more than once. He moved with the speed of a man who had just noticed the back of his pants were on fire.

"Am I supposed to order my wife to stop smiling?"

"It might help," Quinlan suggested with a straight face. "You'll also have to order her to stop thinking like a man."

"What in God's name does that mean?"

"She's more intelligent than Davis."

"Is she more intelligent than you, Quinlan?"

The soldier let out a sigh. "I'm not certain. She is definitely cleverer, however."

"She scared the hell out of me."

"I'm familiar with the feeling."

Neither man knew who started laughing first, but within seconds, they were overcome with amusement. Connor thought he was laughing because he was so relieved his wife hadn't killed herself. Quinlan knew exactly why he was laughing. Crispin was going to get stuck with their mistress the next time their laird left the holding, and he couldn't wait to find out what she would do under his watch.

Brenna and Crispin both heard the noise. She couldn't help but think she was the cause of their amusement, yet just as soon as Crispin noticed how crushed she looked, he casually said, "Don't be concerned, mi'lady. Neither Connor nor Quinlan would laugh at Davis, or anyone else for that matter. It would be beneath them."

"Were you worried I thought they were laughing at me? I was," she admitted before he had time to answer her. "But, it would be beneath me to think my husband or his friend would behave in such a fashion. I think I know why they're having such a fine time," she added.

"And what might that be, mi'lady?"

"Even though Connor won't admit it to me, I think he enjoyed my surprise. Just wait until he sees the other ones."

"The other ones?" Crispin asked in a hoarse whisper.

"The other surprises, of course."

For some reason she didn't understand, Crispin found her comment hilarious. She patted his arm to let him know she didn't mind and then decided that perhaps it was all the laughter coming from inside that tickled his bones so and got him started.

Of all the men, Connor was the first to gain control of himself. "I'll have a word with my wife later," he promised his friend. "Answer one last question for me before we go outside. Are there any more?"

"Any more what?"

"Surprises."

"Only one that I know of."

Connor looked as if he was going to drop to his knees. Quinlan quickly explained. "It's nothing to worry about. She made a few minor improvements in the great hall that are harmless. I saw the room this morning," he added with a nod.

"You'd better be right," his laird muttered before he reached for the door latch.

"It's going to take me a week to get over seeing my wife on the black. Every time I think about it, I shake like an old man. I keep picturing her flying across the meadow . . ."

He couldn't go on. He shook his head as if to rid himself of the thought, realized his hand was shaking even now, and let out a loud sigh in frustration.

Quinlan also pictured his mistress riding the stallion, and though he also knew it would take him a long time to recover, he also recognized the skill she'd shown.

Connor was just pulling the door open when he whispered to Quinlan, "She's good, isn't she."

JULIE GARWOOD

Chapter

15

She was in for it now.

The very first words out of her husband's mouth when he came outside the stables indicated she had crossed that imaginary line inside his mind that separated what could be touched and what couldn't. Apparently he believed the black stallion belonged to him, and only him.

She would, of course, beg to differ, but she was intelligent enough to wait until he'd gotten over his fury.

"I would like to have a word with you in private, Brenna."

"Certainly," she replied, trying her best to look mildly interested and curious, and not at all concerned. She realized almost immediately she hadn't taken the right approach, and changed her attitude to one of indignation.

"I'm glad of it, Connor. It's about time you gave your wife a private moment. When exactly would it be convenient for you to speak to me?"

Her ploy didn't work. "If you don't want me to know you're nervous, you shouldn't back away from me. I would also suggest you stop looking over your shoulder for a means of escape."

She glanced at Crispin to see how he was reacting to his laird's intimidating tactics and was thankful the soldier didn't seem to be paying any attention at all. His gaze was directed at the bottom of the hill as if he were absolutely fascinated by something he was watching there.

Quinlan, however, was hanging on Connor's every word. He still looked a little too complacent to suit her. Not only did he know she was about to catch Connor's thunder, he was glad of it. Didn't the man have anything better to do than follow her around and report her every action to her husband? Apparently he didn't. Although it was probably unkind of her, she made note of the similarity between the soldier and her old nursemaid, Elspeth, who also took delight in telling on Brenna.

"I want this private moment alone with you now," Connor announced.

He waited for her agreement before instructing Crispin and Quinlan to join him for the evening meal, then started back up the hill toward the keep with Brenna at his side.

"My surprise didn't make you happy, did it?"

His snort was all the answer she required. "Are you upset because Willie belongs to you and you don't want anyone else riding him?"

"How many times did you fall?"

Since she was almost certain Quinlan gave him a detailed accounting of her activities, she decided to be completely honest. "So many times I lost count."

"What do you think would have happened if you had been carrying my son?"

She looked thunderstruck, for the possibility had apparently never entered her mind.

"I'm not. I only just finished . . . I'm not."

"Finished what?"

"Finished realizing I can't be carrying your child yet. I would never deliberately put our baby in jeopardy."

"And you will never ride the black again, will you?"

"Not even with a saddle?"

"The horse has never had a saddle on his back, and I assure you, he wouldn't like it. It's out of the question."

"All right then. Was there anything else you wanted to mention . . . or do?"

"Don't ever call him Willie again."

She could tell he wasn't going to change his mind. "I won't," she promised before blurting out, "Do you know you haven't kissed me once since you've been back? I cannot help but wonder if you've even thought of it."

He hadn't thought about much else, but he wasn't about to admit it. "We haven't been alone. Remind me tonight, and I'll kiss you then."

She didn't realize he was teasing her. "I'll probably forget," she assured him. "It really doesn't matter to me one way or another."

"Yes, it does. Watch where you're going. Some of the holes haven't been filled yet."

"Speaking of holes . . ."

"Not yet."

"I beg your pardon?"

"I don't want to hear a word about a chapel. Not now, not ever. Understand?"

"I understand you're being very stubborn."

She knew he was still a little upset about her plan to hide the keep behind a church. Still, he hadn't told her she couldn't, giving her hope that by tomorrow he would be more willing to listen to reason. Surely by then, she would have come up with a better explanation than the blunt truth. Admitting she believed the front of his home was downright ugly would only hurt his feelings, and for that reason, she would have to think of something else to tell him.

She moved on to a far more important matter. "When we go upstairs tonight, I need to have a serious talk with you. I have something extremely important to tell you," she whispered. "You aren't going to like it."

"Tell me now."

"I would rather wait until tonight. I just wanted to prepare you in advance," she added. "My news will surely break your heart."

His laughter wasn't quite the reaction she anticipated. "It's a serious matter," she insisted.

"I assure you, no matter how serious the news is, my heart's going to stay intact. Why don't you tell me now and be done with it? You sound as though you're dreading it."

"I am dreading it. I'm still going to wait until tonight to tell you, however. You're about to see your surprise, and I don't want to ruin your happiness with bad news."

She suddenly wished she hadn't tried to prepare him, because now her stomach felt as though it were tied in knots. How could she not be upset? She was going to start a war between two brothers, God forgive her, but she didn't really have any other choice, did she?

She had asked Father Sinclair that very question during confession, and while he had firmly agreed she must tell her husband when he came home, he also felt she should tell his soldiers right away. It had taken her a long time to convince the priest how important it was that Connor hear before anyone else. Father finally gave in after she promised him she would remain cautious and avoid ever being alone with Raen.

The priest assured her he was going to come back tomorrow to find out how Connor had reacted. She suspected his real motive was to make certain she was all right, and by then, she fully expected to be able to inform him that Raen had already been banished.

Connor pulled her back to the present by telling her to pay attention to where she was walking.

"Brocca's husband is waiting to find out if you want one of his hound's pups or not," he repeated.

"Why would he want to give me a pup?"

"It's all he has to give."

"But why . . ."

"It's a gift, Brenna. You've shown his wife kindness and he wishes to repay you."

"How thoughtful of him," she replied. "Would you mind having a hound inside?"

He shook his head. "I'll tell him you'll be happy to have the pup then. Try not to lose him, all right?"

"For heaven's sake," she muttered. "You're really doing your best to put me in a bad mood, aren't you?"

He didn't bother to answer her. He surprised her when he pulled her close to his side and put his arms around her shoulders.

"You aren't disappointed it's a hound?"

She gave him a curious glance. "No, of course not. Why would you think I would be?"

His voice was filled with laughter when he answered her. "It isn't a piglet."

"You do remember meeting me," she cried out.

He opened the door for her before explaining. "Of course, I remember. I also remember holding you in my arms. You weighed less than my plaid. I think you were about Grace's age."

"No, I was much older."

"You smelled like the piglet you had rolled up in your skirts."

"I couldn't have. I had just had a bath. My sister told me so."

"You were trying to tell me what to do even when you were a baby. I really should have known then."

She was having difficulty paying attention to the conversation, for his eyes were filled with such warmth, she really couldn't think about anything else. Lord, he was handsome. "Known what?" she asked him in a breathless whisper.

"That you were going to be trouble."

She thought that was about the nicest thing he had ever said to her, and it wasn't until she had let out a loud sigh in appreciation and told him thank you that she realized he hadn't given her a compliment.

He didn't laugh at her. In fact, he pulled her into his arms, leaned down, and whispered, "You're welcome."

She didn't know he was going to kiss her until he was doing exactly that. She felt as though she was being crushed against his hard chest, so powerful and fierce was his grip, yet his mouth was surprisingly gentle against hers. His tongue thrust inside to deepen the kiss, arousing a response she didn't expect or understand until it had ended and he was pulling back away from her.

Everything was suddenly different. She wanted to hold on to him for the rest of her life, and while she wanted to believe it was only because she was so relieved to have him home again to deal with Raen, she knew there was another reason as well.

She was in love with him.

The realization didn't make her happy. It made her miserable. How had she managed to make such a foolish mistake? He didn't love her; he just put up with her, that was all, so that he could have heirs.

He watched her closely, frowning with concern over the

tears he saw in her eyes. "Mind telling me why you're crying?"

"It happened too soon," she stammered out. "I knew better, Connor, honestly I did."

"Brenna, what are you talking about? What happened too soon?"

She finally came to her senses. She wasn't about to admit she loved him and thought she'd rather stand naked in front of a church full of strangers than admit her mistake. Being vulnerable was bad enough, boasting of it would be horrible.

He wouldn't understand if she tried to explain it to him anyway. She doubted he could ever love her. So caught up was he in the past, he simply didn't have room in his heart for anything else.

"Will you answer me?" he demanded.

"I missed you," she blurted out. "I didn't want to, but I did anyway. You were gone a long time."

Her answer seemed to satisfy him. He kissed her once again, briefly yet with just as much passion, and then followed her inside and up the stairs to the main floor.

"While you were away, I gathered all the bits and pieces of information from the older men and women here and was finally able to put it all together."

"What did you put together?"

"Your past," she answered. "I know what happened to your father. I just wanted to tell you I understand why the ruins are still standing. You intend to keep them there until you've gained justice in your father's name."

"I would have explained if you'd asked."

"Then I will ask you my questions in future. Don't frown, Connor. I want you to be in a good mood when you see my surprise."

He braced himself for what he was about to see, gave her an abrupt nod to let her know he would try to be pleased, and then said, "Quinlan assures me you haven't done anything . . . damaging."

"Damaging? For heaven's sake, why would you think such a thing?" she asked before she remembered his reaction to the holes in his courtyard. "I plan to cover the mess made outside," she explained then. "After the soldiers put the posts down inside to brace the structure I thought to have constructed, and I . . ."

"Brenna?"

The warning was there in his eyes and in his voice. "Yes?"

"We aren't going to talk about it now."

"No, of course not. Smile, Connor. This is your homecoming. Besides, Euphemia may be inside, and I won't have her thinking we aren't happily wed."

His laughter surprised her. "Why does it matter what she thinks?"

How could he be so dense? "I must make her like me because she's your stepmother. You did tell me to honor her."

"I did?"

"Yes, or maybe I told you I would. It doesn't matter. She deserves our respect."

"Yes," he agreed.

Connor pulled the door open and waited for her to go ahead of him. She didn't budge. "I have one favor to ask you. Tonight, when we sit at the table together . . ."

"Yes?" he prodded.

She blushed while she blurted out the instruction to him. "Please look at me often, and don't frown at me. Try to hang on my every word, all right?"

Fortunately, she didn't require an answer, for she hurried on ahead into the entrance. A crowd of soldiers waiting for their laird bowed to her as soon as they saw her. She greeted each one by name, which surprised and pleased her husband, until he realized he was already looking at her and smiling and surely appeared to be hanging on her every word.

"Brenna, wait for me in the hall while I settle a few matters."

She bowed to him for the benefit of his followers and hurried inside. Her thought was to stand in front of the hearth so that she could see his immediate reaction to her additions.

She was halfway across the chamber before she realized everything was all wrong. She stared in disbelief, for the

JULIE GARWOOD

chamber was once again as stark and foreboding as when she'd first seen it. Even the rushes were missing from the floors.

What in heaven's name had happened? Where was the lovely cloth she'd worked so hard to finish before Connor returned?

"Mi'lady?" Netta whispered from the archway leading to the back door.

Brenna gave the entrance a quick glance, saw that Connor was still fully occupied listening to the petitions of his soldiers, and then hurried over to the servant.

"What happened, Netta? Where are all the cushions?"

"Lady Euphemia had a fit when she sat down on one. She declared it was far too uncomfortable for anyone to suffer, and after trying out each one, she ordered them removed at once. She told me to burn them, mi'lady, so you wouldn't be embarrassed in front of your husband."

"The cloth . . . what about the cloth we put on the table."

Netta shook her head. " 'Twas an accident," she whispered. "At least that is what Lady Euphemia told me. She insisted on having wine with her nooning meal. The color's red, if you'll remember, mi'lady, but she misjudged her reach for her goblet and she spilled it everywhere. She insisted the goblet knocked the pitcher over. Oh, mi'lady, it's ruined now. I know you stayed up half of every night our laird was away so you could finish the stitches, and it looked so lovely too, mi'lady. Why, even Quinlan remarked that it was."

Trying to hide her own disappointment, she patted Netta and tried to console her.

"Accidents will happen," she said. "I hadn't realized the cushions were uncomfortable, though. I tried them all and thought they were . . . all right, but if Lady Euphemia . . ."

"She said they were lumpy."

"I see. Well, then, I will try to do better next time. What about the rushes? They were all right, weren't they? And they certainly gave the room a pleasing scent. So did the flowers," she added. "They're gone too, aren't they?"

"Lady Euphemia also thought the rushes were nice, but she tripped as she tried to walk to the table and almost fell to the floor. She explained her eyesight isn't what it used to

296

be and bid me to remove the rushes as soon as possible. She was certain you would understand, mi'lady."

"Yes, of course."

"The flowers she admitted she didn't like at all."

"Did she explain why?"

"She said they reminded her of death because mourners always carry them to the graves."

Brenna's shoulders slumped. What must Euphemia think of her now? "It was thoughtless of me to put flowers on the mantel. I wasn't thinking, Netta. I never once considered she would have such a reaction. I must find a way to make up for my mistake," she added with a nod.

"Mi'lady, you couldn't have known. The chair Lothar gave you has been sent back to him. I wish now he hadn't spent half the day rubbing a shine in the wood."

"Why was it sent back?"

"Lady Euphemia confessed she was afraid to sit in it because it was so wobbly. I tried to assure her it was perfectly sound, but I couldn't sway her. She seemed to be terrified of falling. I think it's because she's getting on in years and knows her bones won't heal if she breaks one. I couldn't help but wonder if she worried about such things when she was younger. No one's bones heal well, young or old," she added with a nod to let her mistress know she spoke with authority.

"Age must make her more cautious, and we must respect that."

"There's one last thing. I hate to mention it now, after the disappointment you've suffered."

Brenna was afraid to find out what else Euphemia had found unsatisfactory, but forced herself to ask anyway. "Yes?"

"She asked me if there was anything else you meant to add to the chamber. I mentioned that you were working on a banner to hang on the wall. I boasted about how fine it was," she thought to add. "Lady Euphemia wanted to see it, of course. She seemed pleased when I told her how clever you were with your needle and thread, and how you'd labored over your task such long hours."

"Did you show it to her?"

Netta nodded. "Oh, mi'lady, she looked so disappointed

in your efforts. She clucked her tongue like a chicken would and shook her head."

Brenna could feel her face burning with embarrassment. "And what did she say to you?"

"She said the stitches were all lopsided, but she assured me she understood you didn't know any better."

"Where is my tapestry now?"

"Lady Euphemia didn't want you to be humiliated in front of your husband and his followers." Tears of sympathy had gathered in Netta's eyes, which only made Brenna's embarrassment all the more horrible.

She felt like such a failure, and yet, at the same time, she felt guilty because she was angry. Hearing that she didn't know any better each and every time she tried to please Euphemia made Brenna feel as though her mother was being attacked for failing to properly educate her daughter.

"It's gone, isn't it?" she whispered, her voice flat with defeat.

"Yes, mi'lady. Euphemia started taking the stitches out at noon, and by the time she went up to her room to wash before dining tonight, only threads were left on the floor."

Connor called her name as he strode into the hall and looked around him with interest.

Brenna let out a weary sigh and turned to go to him. Netta caught hold of her hand. "I thought everything looked lovely, mi'lady," she whispered.

The last thing Brenna needed now was pity. She smiled so that Netta's feelings wouldn't be injured, and then said, "I'll do much better with my next attempt."

The servant bowed to her mistress and then left to tell the servants that the food should be readied to be carried to the table.

"Have you finished your discussion with your soldiers?"

His wife's question made him smile. Every one of his men wanted to ask him if they could have their things returned. Connor hadn't understood what they were talking about until one of them pointed to the stack of items on the chest with the hint that one of the daggers looked very like the one his wife often used. They didn't dare accuse their mistress of deliberately stealing from them, for they knew she tended to be forgetful when she was in a hurry or having a fine time. Each soldier had actually defended Brenna to him, and for that reason he hadn't laughed.

Emmett had explained it to his laird. "When she's carefree, she forgets to pay attention," he explained. "She makes our wives feel as important as you do, Laird. They've all taken a fancy to her, of course, and would be very upset if they heard you were to sanction her because of this wee problem she seems to have in forgetting to bring things back. She leaves as many of her own things as she takes," he thought to add in Brenna's defense.

Connor promised not to criticize his wife and suggested that in future, whenever something was missing, they or their wives were simply to come inside the keep and look through the stack on the chest. They needn't ask his permission again.

"I can see from your smile that your meeting went well," Brenna remarked.

"It did," he assured her. "I solved the problem, but not the cause."

"You'll accomplish that soon enough," she replied.

His laughter echoed around the chamber. "I doubt that, but now I find I really don't want to anyway."

"Why don't you want to?"

"Because I like the cause. Don't ask me to explain. Show me your surprise instead. I've made you wait long enough."

"I can't."

"You can't wait?"

"Show you your surprise."

"Why can't you? Have you changed your mind?"

"Yes, that's it," she said. "I've changed my mind."

"Why?"

"Why?" Her mind raced for an excuse so he wouldn't know all her efforts had been found lacking. He was bound to think she was incompetent then, and she wasn't incompetent at all. She'd just been in too much of a hurry.

Fortunately, she remembered the medallion she'd had made for him. She'd meant to leave it for last anyway to give it importance.

"It's up in the bedroom. Would you like to see it now? I could go . . ."

"What would you like to do?"

"Wait," she decided.

"Then I'll wait."

"Thank you," she answered before asking him if he'd seen his stepmother yet.

"No."

"She should be coming downstairs any minute now. Have you spoken to Raen yet?"

"No, but he should be back in another hour or two according to Quinlan, and then he'll stay only one more night before he leaves for good," Connor said.

"He's leaving?"

She didn't mean to sound so blissfully happy about Raen's departure, but she couldn't help it.

He raised an eyebrow to her reaction. "He returns to his laird tomorrow."

"And where might that be?" she casually asked, hoping the man lived on the other side of England.

"A long way from here. I doubt we'll see him again for another five or ten years, Brenna, is something wrong?"

"No, no, of course not."

"Then why are you holding on to me?"

She seemed surprised, which made him shake his head in confusion. Her arms were wrapped around his waist, but she quickly moved away from him. The mere mention of his stepbrother had made her instinctively move closer to her husband. She didn't explain, of course, and ended up reminding him how much she'd missed him.

"You mentioned you did."

"Yes, but I wanted to mention it again. Will you excuse me now while I run to the kitchens and speak to the cook?"

After he granted her permission, she kissed him good-bye.

"What happened here, Connor?" Quinlan called out his question from the entrance and came striding into the hall.

Crispin followed him. "What happened where?" he asked.

"The chamber . . . it's back the way it was. What happened to all the changes mi'lady made?"

Connor didn't know what he was talking about. He stood with his hands clasped behind his back while he listened to his explanation.

"Did mi'lady tell you why it was changed back?"

Connor shook his head. "She said the surprise was upstairs."

"Why would she take the cushions and the cloth and the chair upstairs?" Quinlan asked.

"Perhaps she changed her mind," Crispin suggested.

"I told you she was acting strange. Did she take the rushes upstairs too?"

"It would seem so," Crispin replied.

"If that isn't peculiar . . ." Quinlan began

"I would appreciate it if you would stop saying that," Connor snapped. "There isn't anything wrong with my wife. She simply changed her mind, and if she didn't, there was another reason. When she's ready, she'll tell me."

The discussion ended then and there. Quinlan wanted to hear all about Dawson's capture, and while Crispin explained, Connor thought about his wife. He decided he should start paying more attention to her and to the goings-on in his home.

Euphemia joined them a few minutes later. Connor bowed to his stepmother and waited at the head of the table until she was seated before he pulled out his chair. He sat by her side for over an hour, listening to her talk about his father and the past, while Crispin and Quinlan continued their discussion over by the hearth.

Raen came in just as the trenchers were being placed on the table. Brenna and Netta entered through the back door at the very same time.

"Connor," Raen shouted. "It's about time I saw you. It's been a long time."

"It has been a long time," Connor agreed.

Raen embraced him. "You're looking fit these days. Marriage must agree with you."

After kissing his mother, Raen sat down on the opposite seat to face her. Connor was now flanked on both sides by his relatives, and though he was going to ask his stepbrother to move so that his wife could sit closer to him, he didn't make an issue out of it when Brenna hurried to the opposite end of the table, pulled up a stool, and sat down.

"I've been waiting a long time for this reunion and now feel as though my life is complete again," Euphemia announced. So overcome was the woman to have her two sons together, tears came into her eyes.

Brenna was also overcome with emotion. She wasn't overcome with joy, however, but with sadness. The affection shown by the two brothers made her want to weep. It was apparent Connor was happy to have his relatives with him, and how was she ever going to tell him what his stepbrother had done to her? Just thinking about the heartache she was going to cause made her stomach upset.

Connor spoke very little throughout the meal. He was pleased with his commanders because they chose to flank their mistress and sought to include her at every turn in the conversation.

Brenna caught her husband staring at her and quickly smiled at him, willing him with her gaze to reciprocate.

For Connor, the evening was full of revelations. Netta, he noticed, showed her affection for Brenna at every opportunity and beamed every time she received a compliment from her mistress. On the other hand, she didn't appear happy to serve Euphemia, and it was apparent she didn't like the woman.

He thought he had it all figured out and almost laughed because it had been so easy. Quinlan had mentioned that Brenna seemed to be having difficulty with Euphemia. The two women were obviously involved in some sort of tug of war as to who would give the orders. The right belonged to Brenna, of course, and while he couldn't understand why she didn't realize it, he wasn't going to interfere. He would let her solve the problem in her own way, and in her own time, because he knew, no matter how he explained it, she would end up thinking he didn't have faith in her ability.

Quinlan had been right about her lack of appetite. As soon as Crispin handed her the dagger she'd dropped in the courtyard, she thanked him because he'd thoughtfully cleaned it for her, and then moved the food around on her trencher, but didn't take one bite.

Raen was relating an amusing story that made everyone but Brenna laugh. Before he could tell another, Connor asked his wife if she was feeling well tonight.

"Yes, thank you. I am tired though. It's been a long day."

Connor suggested she go on upstairs. "I'll join you in a few minutes," he promised.

Raen also stood. "I'll be happy to escort your wife up the steps," he offered. "I understand she fell going up Kincaid's staircase," he added in the event Connor wondered why he would offer.

Brenna didn't shout her denial, but she came close. "Thank you for offering, but I wanted to have a word with Crispin," she explained, choosing him over Quinlan because he'd been so quick to stand. "If I wait until tomorrow, I might forget. Good night then," she added as she latched onto the soldier's arm to get him moving.

Crispin was honored with the duty. He kept waiting for her to explain what she wanted to talk to him about, and when they reached the door to his laird's chamber, he finally reminded her. "You mentioned you wanted a word with me, mi'lady?"

"I did say that, didn't I?" she said while she tried to think of something important to tell him. Her mind, unfortunately, went completely blank, forcing her to either tell him the truth or make him think she was a complete idiot.

"I made it up."

"You didn't wish to have a word with me?" he asked, trying to understand.

"Actually, I didn't want Raen to escort me, so I lied to get you to."

"Will you explain why you didn't want Connor's stepbrother to assist you?"

"No one needs to assist me, but since he offered, I had to think of something so he couldn't. Now do you understand?"

Crispin shook his head as he opened the door for her. "You still haven't told me why."

The soldier was just as tenacious as Quinlan. "Will you promise me you won't tell Connor what I tell you? I wish to explain it all to him first. It may take me a day or two to get up enough courage," she added. "Though I do plan to try to tell him tonight."

"Tell him what, mi'lady?"

"That I don't like his brother." She had softened the truth. Raen was as evil as MacNare, as cunning as a demon,

303

and as vile as a snake waiting to slither out of the shadows to strike. "I know Connor holds Raen in high regard. Surely you noticed how happy he was to see his brother again."

"I know Connor's quite good at hiding his true feelings. I will, of course, honor your wishes and remain silent."

"Thank you, Crispin."

"Mi'lady, will you answer a question for me?"

She had already entered the room but caught the door as it was closing behind her. "Certainly," she agreed.

"Quinlan couldn't understand why you removed all the additions you'd made to the hall. He found it very perplexing."

"Everything turned out to be unsatisfactory. That's why it was removed." She didn't give him time to ask her any other questions, bid him good night once again, and then quickly shut the door.

There was much to be done before her husband joined her. Once she'd bolted the door closed, she stripped out of her clothes in front of the fire Netta had already prepared for her, washed her entire body with rose-scented soap, and then put on her robe and slippers. While she waited for Connor, she tried to come up with an easy way to tell him about Raen without breaking his heart.

Now that the vile creature was leaving, did she really need to tell Connor anything? Brenna tried to make herself believe no harm would be done if she remained silent, yet she realized she had to let him know, no matter how much pain she caused him. By daring to touch her, Raen betrayed his own brother, and it would be wrong for her not to let Connor know.

Unfortunately, she couldn't come up with a way that would soften the truth, but she hoped the medallion would prove to him he would always have her loyalty.

The wait was torturous. Leaning against the wall helped her stay awake, though only just barely. She didn't dare get into bed, however, because she would fall asleep then. Relief that her husband was home was surely the reason she was so tired tonight. Because of her worry over Raen, she hadn't gotten any rest at all while he was away. All that was going to change now, of course.

She heard Connor's booming voice and then his heavy

footsteps as he came up the stairs. She unlatched the door and moved back to the window to wait for him. She would greet him with a kiss, help him prepare for bed, and then give him his gift.

Then she would tell him about Raen.

She ended up doing something altogether different. The second her husband stepped inside the bedroom, she ran to him, clasped the sides of his face, and kissed him with all the love and passion she possessed.

Overwhelmed by her unbridled show of affection, he wrapped her in his arms and held her tight against him. He was amazed to find he was married to such a gentle, loving woman, and when she put her arms around his neck and shyly whispered of her need to make love, he realized his own need more than equaled hers. While he had been away, an eternity it seemed to him, he had missed everything about her, intensifying his need until it had become an aching loneliness during the dark hours of the night.

"If I promise not to leave again for a long while, will you let me close the door?"

Reluctant to move away from him for even a moment, she kissed the side of his neck before finally pulling away. "Lock it against intruders," she said.

Suddenly feeling uncertain and nervous, she backed away, stopping in the center of the room to wait for him. She gazed in approval and admiration at her husband. His shoulders and chest were heavily muscled, yet she remembered how tender his touch had been each time he had reached for her.

Feeling her own pulse leap in anticipation of what was to come, she drew a shaky breath and then looked up at his face again. And found him smiling at her.

"Have you forgotten what I look like?" he asked, his left eyebrow raised only just barely. To his delight, her face flooded with color.

"It would seem so," she replied. "Your hair's dripping wet, which means you went to the lake without me again. I'll get you a cloth."

She couldn't seem to make herself move. Connor leaned against the door and patiently waited for her to get past her embarrassment. He fervently hoped she took a long time, because he was thoroughly enjoying himself watching her. Her hands were clasped behind her back, giving him an enticing glimpse of her bare chest and tiny waist. His appreciation quickly turned to desire, and within a minute or two, he was beginning to throb with his need to slide the palms of his scarred hands over her smooth, flawless skin.

Somewhat surprised by her own loss of composure, she looked up into his smoldering gray eyes, drew another shaky breath, and tried to remember what she was supposed to do.

"A cloth," she whispered, smiling anew because she hadn't completely lost her senses after all.

"You were going to get one for me."

Her laughter followed her across the chamber to the chest. No longer at a loss for words, she gave him apologies, explanations, and orders while she gracefully knelt down on the floor and carefully moved the burning candle so she could open the chest.

In the mood to do whatever she wanted him to do, he went to the side of the bed, as she had instructed, and sat down to wait for her. He knew exactly what was going to happen the second she stood close enough. He would wrap his arms around her, put her on the bed, and make passionate love to her.

She had other ideas. Standing between his thighs, she tried to dry his hair with the cloth, but found it impossible to pay attention to what she was doing once again, as he had untied the belt to her robe and was now slowly sliding his hands down her chest. He cupped her breasts with his hands, his thumbs gently brushing across her nipples, and then he leaned into her and began to drive her out of her mind with his mouth and his tongue.

He had to tell her to breathe. While he wanted to lavish her with erotic pleasure before he entered her, his own discipline vanished when she removed her robe and pushed against his shoulders to get him to drop back onto the bed.

Neither of them could bear to wait any longer to join together as one, and as he moved between her thighs and slowly entered her, he stared into her eyes to watch the pleasure overcome her and was nearly undone by the erotic sensations her reaction evoked in him.

She drew him down and kissed him, and when the

pressure inside intensified and she knew she was about to shatter apart from the splendor, she began to silently chant "I love you" until it became a desperate plea inside her heart to hear his pledge of love.

He buried his face in the side of her neck, heard her soft whisper vowing her love again and again, and was shaken and humbled that such an exquisite miracle could have happened to him. Only when he felt her tighten around him did he quicken his pace to give her fulfillment and claim his own. Emotions he had never even acknowledged before remained unspoken.

In the aftermath, they held each other, spent, satisfied. Silent now, they listened to their pounding heartbeats.

As was her endearing habit, she wept because of the sheer wonder of their lovemaking, and when she was finally able to control herself again, she flung her arms back on the bed and smiled up at him.

"It would seem I missed this most of all while you were away."

He nodded with arrogant satisfaction. "It would seem so," he agreed. He leaned down, kissed her, and then rolled onto his side. "You have my permission to give me this very same surprise tomorrow."

Her laughter pleased him. "Then it wouldn't be a surprise, would it? Besides, that wasn't it. I have something else for you."

Several kisses later, she convinced him to let her leave the bed long enough to get her gift for him, and when she returned, she wrapped the plaid around her and sat down, facing him near the foot of the bed.

He had already decided that no matter what the gift was, he would be happy to receive it, even if he had to pretend. Her feelings were at issue now, and that was all that mattered to him. Brenna had obviously gone to a considerable amount of trouble to please him, and so he decided to give the gift the importance it deserved. He sat up, propped his shoulders against the wall behind him, and then bent one leg up so that he could rest his arm on top.

"Come closer," he said.

She did as he asked and folded her legs under her before pulling the plaid up around her again.

"Closer," he repeated in a gruff voice.

She denied his request by shaking her head. "I know that look in your eyes, Connor. If I move any closer, you'll grab me."

Admitting she was right, he nodded agreement. "I have never been given a gift before, and two in one night is more than I deserve."

"Two? What other gift did you receive?"

"You don't remember what you said to me when I was inside you?"

She frowned with concentration while she thought about it. "Hurry up?" she teased.

"Besides that," he said with a grin.

"I don't recall. Did I say something else?"

Aye, you did, he thought, you told me you loved me.

Perhaps she had just been carried away by the heat of their lovemaking, unaware of the words she uttered, just the way she had prayed aloud without realizing it on the day he met her. But she had said it, which meant she'd thought it, and that was all that mattered to him.

"Why are you smiling? I haven't given you your gift yet."

"The way you wanted me tonight was all the gift I could ever want."

"But there's more."

"There will be, if you'll move closer to me."

She shook her head again. "You're going to have to wait. I'm going to tell you two stories."

"Just one," he said.

"Two," she insisted.

His sigh was deliberately exaggerated. "All right, lass."

"My first story concerns something that happened to me when I was a little girl. I was too young to remember the details, but I remember being very frightened. My father sat me on his lap and told me what had happened, and don't you dare frown, Connor; you're going to hear about my family now, like it or not."

"I'm not frowning."

"You were thinking about it."

He laughed. "I wasn't. It's all right for you to talk about your relatives now. It wasn't before."

"Why?"

Because your heart and your loyalty belong to me now, he thought. "I'll explain later," he said. "Continue with your story now."

"My father told me I was the reason for a new tradition in our family. We were on our way to an uncle's holding when we stopped for the nooning meal. Everyone wanted to stretch their legs, and when it was time to leave, my father forgot to count."

"Count?"

"There were eight children, Connor. He always counted to make certain he had all of us."

"But this time he didn't count."

"No, he didn't. He thought I was with my oldest brother, Gillian, and Gillian thought I was with Arthur, another brother," she explained. "I wasn't though. As was my habit at the time, I wandered off, got lost, and the family didn't realize they'd left me behind until they were well on their way."

Connor was frowning now. He pictured his wife around Grace's age and couldn't even begin to understand what terror she must have experienced.

"Gillian found me before the others, although I was told my wails were loud enough for the king of England to hear if he'd leaned out the window, and that very night, my father began his new tradition."

"The medallion."

She nodded. "The older brothers and sisters embraced the idea and promised to keep their medallions close at all times. Mother worried the baby and I would choke ourselves with the leather necklaces around our necks, and so I was only allowed to wear the medallion whenever we left the holding."

She held his gaze for a long minute and then took hold of his hand and turned it so that his palm was facing her. Her fingers lightly brushed across the scars puckering his skin, but he saw only sadness in her eyes now, not repulsion or pity.

"You must have been frightened," he said in an attempt to get her to look up at him instead of the marks from his past. She tightened her hold on his wrist when he started to pull back. He conceded to her wishes for the moment and waited for her to continue.

"I recovered," she whispered. "But you haven't, have you, Connor?" The sadness had moved into her voice now.

"Because it isn't finished yet," he explained. "You want me to tell you how I got the scars, don't you?"

"No."

He felt a curious mixture of relief and disappointment.

Brenna ached for the pain he had suffered and tried to think of something to say to make him realize she wasn't trying to console him now, but simply acknowledging the terrible injustices of the past so that he would know she understood.

"These scars mark your past," she whispered as she slowly lifted his hand.

Again he tried to pull away, and she resisted him a second time. "Yes," he said, angry now.

Brenna leaned down and kissed each one of the marks.

He felt the caress all the way inside his heart and his soul. Stunned by what she was doing, he closed his eyes. Her touch shattered him, yet filled him with warmth at the same time. And he was renewed. He couldn't understand how it had happened, or why, but the empty gnawing ache was gone, and only her love remained.

She didn't stop until she had kissed each palm, and then she reached down beside her and put the medallion into his hand.

He opened his eyes again and stared down at the etching carved into the wood.

"A long, long time ago, there lived a boy named David," Brenna began, quietly. "The land he and his family and friends lived in was plagued by a terrible giant named Goliath. It came to pass that David had to fight this enemy. He was too young to use a sword. He could have carried his father's sword, the way you did, but unlike you, he didn't have to crawl across burning embers. You both had tremendous courage, though, and I think he too would have dragged others to safety the way you did, because he was just as noble as you were, Connor."

Overwhelmed by what she was saying to him, he couldn't

speak. She knew everything and still felt he was courageous and noble. She didn't understand, of course. He wasn't worthy of such praise yet, because he hadn't found justice in all the years he had searched.

He shook his head at her. She nodded. And then she began to trace the outline of the figure of David with her fingertips.

"The boy only had a sling to use for his weapon, and so, when the time came for him to face Goliath, he reached for a stone," she said, pausing to trace the little circle at the bottom of David's feet. "You believe your father's sword is your strength, don't you, Connor?"

He didn't answer her. She stared into his eyes, waited no more than a few seconds, and then said, "It isn't. Your strength comes from within. It's your determination, your patience, your skill, but most of all, it's your thirst for justice. David slayed the giant and saved his people. You have already saved your followers."

"But I have still to slay the enemy."

"Look around you and see what you have accomplished. David will always represent what you were, and what you have become. You are worthy."

She lifted the medallion up so he could see it more clearly. "This is your past and your present." And then she turned it over. "And this is your future."

He recognized the symbol, for it was the same as the one on his wife's medallion. "The sun."

She was offering him her love and prayed he would give her his love in return.

He didn't say a word, or give her any other indication that he would, or could, give her what she wanted. He seemed to withdraw then, looking aloof, distant, and yet she could see the moisture in his eyes and knew that the words she longed to hear were there, inside him, locked away with his feelings.

"You have only to open your heart to accept this."

She placed the medallion in his hand again and then leaned close and kissed him.

She tried to pull back. He wouldn't let her. He wrapped his arms around her and kissed her over and over again, desperate now as he ravaged her mouth. He didn't understand or know if he was kissing her to show her how much he cared, or if he was deliberately keeping his mouth on top of hers so that she couldn't beg him to give her what he knew he couldn't.

Their lovemaking was wild, uncontrolled, savage, and it was only after he had satisfied her twice more and she had collapsed into sleep on top of him that he acknowledged his greatest weakness.

She terrified him.

Chapter 16

Connor was gone. Brenna awakened late that morning when Netta knocked on the door. She called out to her to please wait a moment, then sat up in bed and reached for her robe.

Her husband's medallion was underneath it. She felt a moment's disappointment before common sense told her he hadn't wanted to disturb her sleep searching for it, so he had simply left it behind when he'd gone downstairs. She put the medallion on the chest next to the bed and hurried to the door while she put on her robe.

Netta didn't come inside. "Father Sinclair has arrived, but you needn't hurry to greet him. He's busy hearing confession in the lower bailey now and won't make his way up here for another hour or so."

"You're certain?" Brenna asked. "I wouldn't want to keep him waiting."

"If Fionna goes through with her promise to give her confession, I'm certain. She has enough sins to keep Father busy for the rest of the day."

"Talk like that will get you a long penance, Netta," she replied with a laugh.

"I'm only telling the truth, so it can't be a sin. Would you like my help getting dressed, mi'lady?"

313

"No, thank you."

Netta looked disappointed. "I'll go on down to the hall then. I'm dreading it though, because you-know-who is sitting at the table, acting like a queen."

"Are you referring to Lady MacAlister?"

Netta nodded. Brenna immediately scolded her. "You must honor and respect her," she said. "She's your laird's stepmother, if you'll remember."

"As you wish, mi'lady."

"I do wish. Please try, Netta. I know she can be difficult."

"Aye, it is difficult, especially since she took away all your nice improvements. The cushions weren't lumpy, mi'lady. They were perfect."

Brenna thanked her for her kind opinion and sent her away so she could get dressed. While she washed, she made her list of things she must do today. First and most important, she would take her husband aside and tell him about Raen. Yes, that was the most imperative duty she had, but if there was time and opportunity, she was also going to try to find out exactly how long Lady Euphemia would be staying.

As was her custom each and every morning before she left her bedroom, she said a quick prayer for assistance in getting Euphemia to like her.

God willing, today would be the day.

Talking to Connor came first, however, and even though she would have died of embarrassment if she'd been caught, she sneaked out so that she wouldn't be delayed listening to Euphemia complain. Luck was on her side; the elder woman faced the entrance and didn't see her.

Brenna wasn't particularly worried she would run into Raen, however, because he went riding every day and stayed away from the holding until nightfall.

By tonight, he would be gone . . . forever.

Where was Connor? She searched high and low for her husband. He had promised her he wouldn't leave, and she knew he would never break his word to her. He had gone either to the lake or the ruins, she decided, and she meant to find out which from Crispin. Fortunately, she located him in the lower bailey.

She waited by the side of the path for the commander to

finish his conversation with two other soldiers, and then called out to him. "May I interrupt for just a moment, Crispin?"

"Certainly, mi'lady," he answered. He hurried over to her and bowed his head.

"I've looked everywhere for my husband. Do you know where he is?"

"He's gone, mi'lady. I'm not certain when he'll be back."

"Gone to the lake?"

"He went to Laird Hugh's holding. He should be away at least three or four days, perhaps more."

Her reaction thoroughly puzzled him. She looked as though she were going to faint dead away, and when she grabbed hold of his arm and gripped him so fiercely, he realized she was actually afraid.

"Where's Raen?" she asked. She frantically looked around her.

"He left early this morning, mi'lady. Three soldiers from Laird Finley's holding rode with him. They also were on their way back north. The higher their number, the better their protection," he added in the event she didn't understand.

She felt like weeping with relief. "Raen won't be back then, will he?"

"No, mi'lady, he won't."

"Thank God. I wanted to tell Connor, but he left, Crispin, before I could, and now I . . . Why did he leave? He told me he wouldn't."

Crispin patted her hand in an attempt to get her to let go of him. "Hugh died last night. It was important for your laird to pay his respects. Laird Kincaid will surely do the same."

It was suddenly all right again. Connor hadn't lied to her. He simply hadn't anticipated his friend's death.

"I'm sorry for Hugh's family. I hope he died peacefully."

"We were told he died in his sleep. Does this news please you, mi'lady? You're smiling."

She felt like a fool. "I'm pleased because my husband had to leave. He didn't lie to me. I'm not at all happy to hear about Hugh. I shall go and find Father and ask him to pray for his departed soul."

"Sinclair's hearing confessions. I'll send him to you as soon as he's finished."

She finally let go of the soldier. "I don't know what came over me. I was . . ."

"Afraid."

She slowly nodded. "Yes, I was. I'm not now."

She bowed to Crispin and started back up the hill. "Mi'lady? You were afraid of Raen, weren't you?"

She pretended not to hear him, but he followed her and repeated the question to her again. She turned around, smiled, and said, "I wasn't afraid."

He felt a stab of disappointment that she didn't trust him enough to tell him the truth.

"I was terrified."

He blinked. "Why, mi'lady?"

"I feel I should explain to Connor first when he returns, but I assure you, Crispin, if there was any possibility at all that Raen would be coming back before then, I would tell you everything. Do you understand?"

"I do," he replied. "Raen is Connor's stepbrother, and Connor should be the first to hear what you have to say. I'm only sorry you didn't tell him."

"I'm sorry too," she said, admitting only to herself she wouldn't have changed anything that had happened last night.

She tried to leave once again. "Mi'lady, what are your plans for today?"

It wasn't the question that made her laugh. It was the dread she heard in his voice. "Don't worry. I won't be riding the black today."

She stayed outside much longer than she'd intended, visiting with several ladies who had taken their sewing outside, and she didn't return to the keep until midafternoon. As she hurried inside, she rehearsed what she would say when she greeted Euphemia. "She best not call me a child again," she muttered.

Her bluster was short-lived, and with a sigh, she admitted the woman could call her child as often as she wanted, and she wouldn't say a word to her. Criticizing would never win her approval.

Dear heavens, how long was she going to stay? Brenna

tried to think of a way to ask Euphemia, but no matter how she phrased the question, it sounded a mite eager.

She put the problem aside when she entered the great hall. "Good afternoon, Lady Euphemia. How are you feeling today?"

"Brenna, I know I've mentioned this to you before, but it seems I must mention it again. I prefer being called Lady MacAlister. I realize you don't know any better—you're just a child, after all—but I want you to try a little harder."

She took a deep breath. "Yes, Lady MacAlister. I'll try harder."

"Did you hear the sad news about Hugh?"

"Yes."

"It's a shame, isn't it? He led such a wasted life. Never did amount to anything or do anything worth remembering."

"I'm certain his family doesn't feel that way," she replied.

"He never married. No woman would have him. Oh, heavens, I wish I had remembered to tell Connor the news Raen gave the other day. It slipped my mind. I'll probably forget again by the time he returns. Age does that to a body, Brenna. It makes one forget little things."

"Perhaps if you told me, I would remind you if you should forget," she offered.

She stood with her hands folded together, waiting for Euphemia to invite her to join her at the table. She didn't dare sit without an invitation, for Connor's stepmother had berated her for doing that very thing just two days ago. She wouldn't make the mistake again. Getting along with the woman was proving to be her greatest challenge, she decided.

"Come and join me, child, don't stand there making me look up at you. I shall tell you the news Raen heard when he was out riding yesterday. I worry when he goes out alone like that, of course, although I know he can take care of himself. Still, it isn't safe to go anywhere alone. I'm not worried about him today, though. There were three others who stopped on their way north. He'll be safe with them."

"The news, mi'lady? How did he hear news if he was riding alone yesterday?"

Euphemia needed several minutes to think about the question before she finally remembered. "As fortune would have it, he spotted a unit of soldiers on their way south. Raen knew two of the men and of course stopped to speak to them."

Brenna remembered that on her way here, Connor had avoided all of the well-trodden paths in favor of cutting through the forest, because he hadn't wanted to encounter anyone.

"I thought Connor might be interested to hear that Laird MacNare's going to get married after all. I pity the woman."

"I also pity her, mi'lady," she whispered, aching for the poor woman's future.

"I doubt he'll treat her kindly. Still, one can always hope. Now what was her name? I remember she's from England."

Where she was from really wasn't important to Brenna. All that mattered was that the poor woman would suffer a terrible fate if something wasn't done.

"Is it too late?" she asked.

"Do you mean to ask me if she's already with MacNare?"

"Yes."

"I don't believe so. The wedding won't take place for several weeks according to what Raen told me. Of course, there's always the chance MacNare will change his mind and send for her sooner."

"Then there's probably still time," Brenna said. "And MacNare might change his mind altogether and decide not to marry her," she added.

"You shouldn't get your hopes up, child. MacNare sounds like a determined man."

"Did Raen find out who the woman is?"

"Yes, but I can't seem to remember now. Age, you see." Brenna nodded. "Yes, of course."

"It was a peculiar name. I remember thinking so when Raen told me the name. Perhaps it will come to me," she added with a shrug of indifference. "It's a pity Raen left so soon. He would have wanted to pay his respects to Hugh. My son is an extremely thoughtful man. Word will reach him, of course."

"Would he turn around and come back?" Brenna asked, trying to keep the panic out of her voice.

"Perhaps, depending on when he hears the news," she answered. "He would feel it was his duty to stand by the gravesite with the other lairds, but he might be too late. If the others have all gone back home, what's the point? I do hope he hears in time, because I'm certain he'll be missed if he doesn't go."

"But Raen isn't a laird, is he?"

"He will be laird very soon now," she snapped.

"Yes," Brenna quickly agreed to placate the woman. "If he does hear about Hugh in time, would he stop here on his way?"

"It would be the thoughtful thing to do," she answered. "There wouldn't be time before the burial, but he might make time on his way back north. Do you find this possibility unsettling? You look upset."

"I was just wondering when Connor would be back. I have a problem I wish to discuss with him."

"If something is wrong, Brenna, you shouldn't bother your husband. You should come to me for counsel. Is this not so?"

She decided to test the water. "And if this problem concerns your son?"

"Then you most certainly must come to me. I'm his mother, for heaven's sake, and I could possibly settle this . . . dispute . . . before it goes any farther."

"Mi'lady, I doubt I'll ever be alone with Raen again, so the problem . . ."

Euphemia cut her off. "Alone with Raen? Explain what you mean, child. Are you afraid of my son?"

Brenna hesitantly nodded. "He has tried to, that is, he tried to take advantage of . . . by grabbing hold of me and brushing up against my . . . and when I asked him to let go of me, he wouldn't listen to me. He said very inappropriate . . ."

"Enough," Euphemia snapped. Her eyes blazed with anger, yet Brenna couldn't tell if the mother's fury was directed at her or her son.

A moment later, Euphemia's attitude underwent a radical change, and she actually looked amused. Brenna found her smile as unsettling as her anger.

"My son's smitten with you, child. It's as simple as that. Raen was always one to pity the poor unfortunates. When he was a boy, he chose the runt of the litter to raise as his own. I'm not suggesting you are an unfortunate, but Raen and I have both noticed Connor's rather cold attitude toward you. I believe that in time, once you've been properly trained to be a good wife, your husband will soften toward you. I noticed he seemed happy to have you at his table last night."

Brenna wondered what Euphemia would think if she told her she had asked Connor to act affectionate. She could understand why his stepmother would think he wasn't happy. Connor had been rather distant toward her in the past, but he had already changed his attitude, kissed her several times as a matter of fact, in plain view of all of his followers. Still, Euphemia hadn't witnessed her stepson's change of heart.

"What about Raen?" she asked.

Euphemia patted her hand. "Are you certain you aren't exaggerating this in your mind?"

"Yes, I'm not exaggerating."

Euphemia pondered the problem for a long minute before saying, "I'm sure you realize that because Raen is your husband's brother, he is just as important. I suggest you do whatever my son wants you to do. As mistress, you must see to his every request, for he is master of this keep whenever Connor is away."

Brenna was outraged. "Are you telling me I should . . ."

Euphemia interrupted her once again. "Respect his wishes at all times," she announced with a nod. "Surely you realize your value, for I find it difficult to believe women in England are treated any different by their men. You should be honored by Raen's attention. If the king of England favored you, would you turn your back on him? No, of course you wouldn't. I understand how confusing it all is to you. You're very young and tend to overreact. I wouldn't mention this to Connor, though. He would be furious if you spoke any harsh word against my son. Have faith in . . . Why, that's the woman's name. Faith. I told you it was odd . . ." Her gaze slid over to Brenna and her eyes narrowed. "I believe the girl is one of Baron Haynesworth's daughters."

"MacNare plans to marry Faith? Mi'lady, are you certain

it was Baron Haynesworth's daughter? For he is my father too."

"I am," she answered.

Brenna vehemently shook her head. "My father would have learned from his mistake by now. He wouldn't send his youngest to such a demon."

"Will that matter?" Euphemia asked. "Once a bargain's struck, it cannot be undone. MacNare won't be denied. It's rather clever of him, isn't it? He must hate you as well as Connor by now, and what better way to get even than to take something that's so precious to you? He'll take Faith by force if he must," she added with a nod. "At least that's what I would expect him to do."

"No," Brenna cried out.

Euphemia patted her hand. "It's a pity, but there really isn't anything you can do about it, is there?"

"She cannot marry him. Someone has to . . ."

"Lower your voice, Brenna. Ladies don't shout," she said, yet with the very next breath she did that very thing to get Netta to come into the hall.

"I believe she's in the kitchens," Brenna whispered.

"No, she isn't. I sent her upstairs to clean my chamber. Ah, there she is. Netta, how many times must I tell you? When I'm in the hall, you must stay near the door in the event I need you. Do you understand?"

"Yes, mi'lady," Netta answered. Her attention was riveted on her laird's wife now. "Is something wrong, Lady Brenna?"

"You can see there is. Fetch your mistress a cloth to wipe away her tears. Really, Brenna, you shouldn't cry in front of the servants. It's most unseemly. There isn't any need to carry on so. Accept that nothing can be done about it."

"Connor will put a stop to this madness," Brenna whispered.

"I doubt that, child. How can he? He's fully occupied protecting Hugh's followers at the moment. He cannot be in two places at the same time, and you cannot expect him to turn his back on defenseless men and women to go to England. Use your head."

"He went to pay his respects, not fight," Brenna argued.

She was desperately trying to concentrate on what Euphemia was telling her, but was in such a panic inside for her little sister's safety, she could barely think about anything else.

"It seems MacNare isn't paying his respects. He's waging a war to get Hugh's land before Connor does. The holding sits between the two and would give one a certain advantage over the other."

"How could you know all this?" Brenna asked.

"I heard some of the soldiers talking about the conflict. All of the MacAlisters know what's happening, even the servants, but you haven't been accepted yet, have you? Perhaps that is why you were left in the dark. Where is Netta? It's taking her entirely too long to fetch a cloth for you. If I were not preparing to leave here, I would have her replaced."

"Netta?" Brenna asked, trying to understand what she was talking about.

"Try to pay attention, Brenna. As for your sister, I think you should simply put her out of your mind. There isn't anything to be done about her."

"But Connor could talk to my father . . ."

"How can you want Connor to go to your father? Surely you realize one would have to kill the other. After all, your husband did start this when he took you away from MacNare. Your sister's fate has been sealed, and neither you nor Connor can stop the marriage. Forget about her," she added. "Or offer a prayer for her if that will make you feel better."

"Yes, I'll offer a prayer," Brenna answered.

She stood up, bowed to her stepmother, and turned to leave. Netta came running in through the back hall with the cloth Euphemia had ordered.

"I hope by the time you return, you'll be in control again," Euphemia said. "I noticed last night everyone enjoyed the food served. Will you admit now that I was right to change the cooks?"

Brenna stared at the woman in disbelief. Why in God's name did she want to talk about food now?

Netta thought Brenna didn't remember her plan to pretend to replace Ada and hurried to nudge her memory before she said something she shouldn't.

"You had Ada replaced, mi'lady. Remember?"

"Yes, I remember," she answered in a strained whisper.

"Go along now," Euphemia ordered. "It distresses me to see you in such a pitiful condition."

Brenna ran outside before she realized she should have gone up to her bedroom so that she would have complete privacy. She wasn't about to go back inside, because she knew if Euphemia said one more word to her before her panic was under control, she would start screaming and never stop.

She reached the seclusion of the trees, fell to her knees, and broke into heart-wrenching sobs.

Connor . . . Dear God, how she needed Connor. He would know what to do, and he was strong enough and powerful enough to take on the devil himself.

But how could she ask such a thing of him? Others depended upon him now for their survival. She knew Euphemia hadn't exaggerated the threat to Hugh's followers. Brenna remembered what had happened to her father's soldiers and her own sweet Gilly and knew without a doubt that MacNare would slaughter the peace-loving clan without a moment's hesitation.

If Connor was able to go, would she be sending him to his death? Or would he be forced to kill her father?

No, she couldn't send her husband. Who else could she send to stop this madness?

Greed. It all began and ended with greed. Her father had struck this bargain to gain an alliance, just as MacNare had, and neither man had considered what the ramifications would be. Consumed with lust for power, their greed controlled their minds and their hearts, leaving the innocents to be preyed upon.

But not Faith. Brenna would die before she would let MacNare touch her sister. Please, God, help me think of someone to . . . help me . . . help me.

Sobbing, she bowed her head and clasped her hands to her heart, and in that dark moment of desolation, her prayer was answered.

There was another she could send, the man who had

taken her hand and vowed to do anything she asked of him, who was even stronger than Connor.

He wouldn't deny her.

The war had begun.

Connor stood on the rise above Hugh's keep, his gaze directed on the hills beyond, his thoughts centered on the past as he once again searched for the answer that had eluded him for many years.

Quinlan joined him a few minutes later. "MacNare's playing a game with us, Connor. What's his real purpose?"

"He wants to keep us busy defending the border between his land and Hugh's until his allies join him."

"Surely he knows you've done the same thing."

"He knows. He's deliberately sacrificing the small number of soldiers he sends on each attack, knowing full well they'll all die, but this land isn't his immediate goal. He can easily claim it after he attacks me."

"Do you think the soldier was telling the truth about your wife's sister, or was that just another ploy to divide our forces?"

"Dying men usually tell the truth. It doesn't really matter though. I must still make certain Faith is protected from MacNare."

Quinlan silently agreed. "You've waited a long time for this day to come. I have a feeling you'll be able to claim your father's sword from Kincaid and end this once and for all."

Connor turned to him. "But why now? What does MacNare know that I don't? We could destroy him and his allies. He isn't a fool; he knows our numbers. Why would a coward who all these years has only provoked me with small, insignificant attacks suddenly become so aggressive?"

"I don't have an answer for you, but I do know you can't be everywhere at once. I wish to God we could end it tomorrow. Attack his holding before he attacks us."

"Be patient, Quinlan. I'm not going to put any of the MacAlisters in jeopardy. I'm taking every precaution in the meantime. God willing, any day now I will find out who the others are before I'm forced to kill MacNare."

"You think someone else is controlling MacNare?"

"I do," he answered. "Whoever he is, he's damned clever."

"What about Faith? You can't go into England now."

"No, but you can. Leave at dawn tomorrow and take ten others with you. This could be a trap," he warned.

"Of course," Quinlan agreed. "What am I to do with the woman once I have her?"

"Do whatever you wish to do, as long as she remains safe," he answered.

Connor's smile confused his friend. "What are you thinking?" he asked.

"It's about time you got married, isn't it?"

The border attacks intensified, and even though it took very little effort to maintain his position, Connor was still required to stay away from his holding much longer than he had anticipated.

He slept a few hours each day, and used the cover of darkness at night to move Hugh's followers to safety. If all continued to go according to his schedule, every man, woman, and child would be well-hidden from MacNare's clutches in just two more days. He had met with resistance from some of the older men, and only after he had promised on the soul of his father that they would all be able to return to their land as soon as the conflict was finished did he gain their cooperation.

The rest was up to his brother, Alec. Connor would wait for as long as he dared while Alec tried to find out who was in league with MacNare; yet as the days lengthened into a full week, it became apparent the truth would continue to elude him.

And it would happen all over again. Whoever was controlling MacNare wouldn't give up, and Connor's greatest nightmare was that he would die without knowing who his enemy was . . . just as his father had.

For several days Brenna tried to remain calm and keep her mind on the normal activities of the holding. She was on her way back from visiting with Lothar when Netta caught

JULIE GARWOOD

up with her. The servant immediately noticed her mistress wasn't wearing the leather necklace.

"You aren't wearing your medallion, mi'lady."

"No, I'm not."

"But you always wear it. I wouldn't have noticed if you hadn't worn your hair up today. Have you misplaced it?"

Brenna removed the ribbon from her hair and let her curls fall down around her shoulders. If Netta had noticed, Crispin would too, she reasoned, and she didn't like the idea of lying to Connor's close friend.

"The medallion will show up any day now," she said. "You needn't worry about it."

Netta wasn't quite finished discussing the matter. "I know it isn't in your room. I only just finished cleaning it, and I would have found it for you if it was there. Our laird's medallion is on the chest in the very same spot as yesterday. You never lose yours, mi'lady. Did you look on the chest in the hall?"

"Not yet," she answered before she tried to change the subject. "How did you get away from Lady Euphemia?"

"She's resting. As soon as she awakens, she wants me to pack her clothing."

"She's leaving?" Heaven help her, she couldn't contain her smile.

Netta laughed. "She told me she had decided against waiting for her stepson to come back and plans to leave tomorrow morning. I think she feels she's being ignored by our laird."

"He hasn't been ignoring her. Surely she realizes how busy he is."

"Did he send a message to you today?"

"Yes, he did. He assures me all is well and that he will be home soon."

"But that is the very same message he sends you every day."

"He is being considerate, Netta. That is all that matters to me."

"Mi'lady, may I ask a favor of you?"

"Yes, of course."

"After Lady MacAlister leaves, will you tell me why she

326

made you cry last week? I know I shouldn't ask you, but I worry about you. So does Ada. We've both become very fond of you," she added with a nod.

"I'm very fond of you too, Netta. As soon as I know the problem has been taken care of, I will tell you what she said to me."

"Thank you, mi'lady. Were you going inside?"

"Yes."

"Did you have any duties for me?"

"None that I can think of. You might as well enjoy your afternoon of freedom. I'm going to change my shoes and go riding."

"Have you warned Crispin?" Netta asked with a grin.

"He's occupied for the moment checking the work on the wall outside the holding. You needn't concern yourself that I'll ride the black. Davis hid him from me."

Netta burst into laughter. "Is Davis still closing his eyes every time you go inside his stable?"

"Yes, but he refuses to tell me why."

Brenna watched Netta run across the courtyard. Her own thoughts were on her sister as she went inside and ran up the steps to her bedroom. Waiting to hear that Faith was all right was extremely difficult, and the only way she had been able to get any sleep at all was to put the matter in God's hands. She had done everything she could. The rest was up to Him.

She swung the door open and hurried across the chamber. She spotted her dagger on the chest next to the bed and had to shake her head over her own forgetfulness. She really needed to force herself to slow down so that she wouldn't continue to lose her things. She quickly picked up the dagger to put back in its sheath.

She heard the squeak of the door as it closed behind her, assumed the wind coming in through the windows was responsible. She was just about to sit down on the bed to remove her shoes when she heard the lock clicking into place.

She knew, before she turned around, who was inside the room with her.

And then she saw him. Raen stood in front of the door,

and as her scream gathered in her throat, he slowly removed his shirt.

Crispin was informed of Raen's arrival by the soldier in charge of the drawbridge.

"He and three others came back a few minutes ago. Raen's the only one who crossed the bridge, though. His companions are waiting in the meadow below. I can see them from here," he called down. "Raen told me he had gone to pay his respects to Hugh and wanted only to tell his mother farewell before he left again. He suggested I leave the drawbridge down, which, of course, I refused to do. You'll see his horse is still wearing his saddle, Crispin, so he really means to leave soon."

Crispin left his mount with Davis and started up the hill. His mistress had told him she was afraid of Raen, and Crispin was going to stay close to her side until Connor's stepbrother left again.

The closer he got to the keep, the quicker he moved. He couldn't explain why he suddenly felt as though his mistress was in danger, but the feeling intensified until he was running to get to her.

And then he heard her scream. His heart slammed inside his chest as he reached for his sword. "Son of a bitch." He whispered the curse the first time, shouted it the second.

Everyone was running to the courtyard. The silence after such an anguished scream terrified all of them.

Crispin reached the top of the path when he heard a man's shout. Jarred, he looked up. There in the window was Raen clutching at his shoulder, teetering and swaying like a tree giving way to the ax, then plunging backward into the air. He twisted in a useless attempt to land on his feet, screaming in horror, and then crashed, face first, into the ground with a soft thud.

And on Crispin ran. Dear God, let her be alive, he prayed. He leapt over Raen, raced up to the door, and pulled it open as Brenna came charging outside.

He stopped dead in his tracks. The look on her face was more terrifying than her cry for help. Her eyes were glazed over, her face was stark white, and there was blood everywhere. Her left arm was covered in it, for the skin was splayed open from the top of her shoulder to the bottom of her wrist. More blood covered her shoulders and neck, and her clothing looked as though an animal had shredded it with its claws.

He didn't know how she was able to stand. He reached for her, but she evaded him and ran down the steps.

"Hurry, Crispin. Hurry. You have to help me," she sobbed. "We have to hide him."

A crowd of soldiers surrounded the body. They stepped back when she ran closer. Their expressions showed their shock and their outrage.

"I didn't push him out the window . . . No, no, I didn't . . . His feet got caught in his plaid when I thrust my knee into his groin . . . yes. I meant to hurt him so he wouldn't . . . He was holding me down, but the dagger was in my hand then . . . When he rolled over . . . it went . . . and he jumped, Crispin. He did, he jumped . . . and then he fell."

She grabbed hold of Crispin's hand and tried to pull him forward. "Don't you understand? We have to hide him . . . She can't see her son like this. Oh, God, I have to tell Connor . . . I couldn't let him . . . He touched me, his mouth was on my skin, Crispin . . . I couldn't let him . . . She told me I should, but I couldn't . . . No, I wouldn't," she screamed.

"Euphemia told you to submit to her son?" Crispin demanded in outrage.

"Yes, but I couldn't . . . He tried, but he fell before he could . . ."

She stopped rambling, let go of his hand, bent down to take hold of one of Raen's feet, and tried to drag him away.

"Mi'lady, let go of him. Let me help you," Crispin said.

"Yes, help me. We'll hide him before she knows he came back. All right?"

"Yes," he promised, his voice calm, his goal to reassure her. "We'll hide him."

"Mi'lady, your dagger is in his back," Owen whispered. "Do you want me to get it for you?"

"No, no," she cried out.

Crispin shook his head at Owen, telling him without words to keep his mouth closed.

"Connor will never forgive me. Oh, God, what have I done? I've killed his brother . . . No, she can't see him. Help me, Crispin. Please. I want Connor."

He slowly put his hand out to her. She frantically shook her head at him. "No, I'm not clean. He touched me with his hands and his mouth . . ."

And then she threw herself into his arms. "Take me to the lake. All right?"

"Yes, mi'lady," he lied. "I'll take you to the lake."

She patted his arm. "Thank you. I've gone and done it, haven't I?"

"Done what?"

"I killed him."

"No, he destroyed himself. He deserved to die. Connor would have killed him for you."

"Will he hate me?"

She fainted in his arms before he could answer her.

Donald moved forward, his dagger in his hand, pulled his plaid from his shoulder and sliced it into two long strips to his waist.

Crispin held Brenna in his arms and turned so that Donald could bind the injury with the material. He spoke in a low whisper when he gave his orders. "You're taking the watch for as long as I'm away. I'm taking her to Lady Kincaid. She'll need stitches," he added. "Giric, you take others, surround the three soldiers waiting for the bastard in the meadow. Bring them inside the keep and make them stay by the stables."

"What about Connor's stepmother?"

"Donald, you tell her what happened. If she wants to take his body home, let her, but not one of Connor's soldiers escorts her. Understand?"

"Yes," Donald answered.

"Aeden, find Connor and tell him what happened. Assure him his wife will be all right. Don't paint it any darker than it already is."

"Will she die?" Owen whispered, terrified by the possibility.

"No, she won't die. Donald, no one but our own comes inside the fortress until Connor, Alec, Quinlan, or I come back."

"Will you leave her with the Kincaids?" Owen asked.

"No. I'm staying with her until Connor gets to her."

"Do the three soldiers with Raen stay even if Euphemia leaves?"

"They leave with her."

Donald finished binding her injury, nodded to Crispin, and went to the stables to get his commander's horse. He called orders as he ran. He wanted a full contingent riding with his mistress, and everyone was ready to leave immediately.

"Leave the dagger in his shoulder," Crispin ordered. He was so furious now, his voice shook with rage. "She told Connor's wife to submit to her son. God help her when our laird finds out."

"Do you want me to tell him?" Aeden asked.

"Tell him everything, but make sure he understands she won't die. He has grown extremely fond of his wife."

Crispin started across the courtyard, stopped, and then turned back toward Raen and spit on him.

Blessedly, Brenna didn't awaken until they were dismounting in Kincaid's courtyard. Alec and Jamie stood in the doorway. Alec blanched when he saw Brenna's condition. Jamie began to weep. She put her hand to her mouth to keep herself from crying out.

Brenna asked Crispin to let her walk. She took hold of his arm and slowly made her way toward the steps. Crispin noticed the glazed look was still in her eyes and knew it was going to take her a long while to recover from the horror she'd endured.

Brenna stopped in front of Alec. "I killed Connor's stepbrother."

And then she turned to Jamie. In a bewildered voice, she said, "Now she's never going to like me."

Alec lifted her into his arms and carried her inside. "It's all right, Brenna. Your husband likes you, and so do we."

"Alec?"

"Yes?"

"I'm so sorry."

Chapter
17

Quinlan returned from England empty-handed. Thoroughly frustrated and bewildered, he gave his accounting to his laird.

"MacNare had already dispatched troops to England. We followed their tracks from the Lowlands on, knew their number, and exactly that many returned from Baron Haynesworth's fortress."

"How many were they?"

"Twenty-six soldiers, all fully armed."

"But they didn't have Faith with them."

"No."

"You're certain."

"We watched them leave, Connor. Yes, I'm certain."

"And what did you do to them?"

"What do you think we did?"

Connor nodded approval. "How many of my men engaged in this battle?"

"There were eleven of us."

"A fair fight then. Were any of my men injured?"

"Donovan's thigh was cut through, but his was the most serious of the injuries. The others suffered only paltry cuts. To be honest, I don't think Donovan would have made it back if it weren't for . . ."

"Weren't for what?"

"This is where it becomes a little bizarre," he said. "The baron's soldiers watched the fight from their tower, and I had only just decided to go inside the fortress to find out where Faith was when the drawbridge was lowered and a procession came out. Your wife's mother was leading the soldiers."

Quinlan paused to smile before he continued. "Her Gaelic is worse than Lady Brenna's," he said. "Her soldiers were armed, of course, but it didn't take long for me to realize they meant only to protect their mistress. I understand where your wife gets her courage. Her mother dismounted, demanded to know who was in charge, but before I could tell her, she spotted Donovan and went over to him. Needless to say, your soldier didn't want her to touch him. It didn't matter to her though. She had her supplies with her and cleaned and stitched his injury for him."

"And what were you doing?"

"Answering her questions about your wife. I assumed she was worried about her, but she insisted she wasn't worried at all. She explained that if Brenna had been in serious trouble, she would have sent her medallion to one of her sisters or brothers. Because she didn't, her mother knew she was safe. She was worried about you, though, and sent a message to you."

"What is it?"

"Treat her well or answer to her family. They had all heard what happened to Lady Brenna's escort, of course, and she assured me the baron hadn't realized what a monster the laird was. Oh, and you're going to love this. You have his gratitude for rescuing his daughter."

Connor shook his head. An Englishman's gratitude? What in thunder was he supposed to make of that?

"What about Faith?"

"She has vanished. Her mother was worried until MacNare's soldiers showed up. They had no advance warning, she explained, and they searched every corner of the keep looking for her. The mother believes someone came to her assistance. She thinks she knows who the savior is too."

"Who is he?"

"You."

"Didn't she wonder then why you were there instead of me?"

"She didn't seem to."

"What am I going to tell my wife, Quinlan? I can't continue to keep her in the dark about her sister. Eventually she'll find out from someone else. Gossip travels like the wind in the Highlands."

"You'd be right about that. In fact, it sounds as if someone heard about this situation and got to Faith before we did. I doubt it was one of her brothers. He wouldn't let his mother worry so. He'd tell her, wouldn't he?"

"I would assume so. There's only one other man I can think of who would go to such trouble on Brenna's behalf."

"Who?"

"My brother. This sounds like something he would do, doesn't it?"

"He hates England."

"But he's fond of my wife," Connor said. "I must talk to him before I tell Brenna anything. God willing, Alec has her sister tucked away somewhere. Did you have anything else to report?"

He shrugged. "Mi'lady's mother sent gifts for her daughter, and she . . ."

"And she what?" he asked, wondering over his hesitation.

"She kissed me on the cheek. I didn't want to shove her away. She's mi'lady's mother, after all, but I . . . This isn't funny, Connor. It was awkward. She told me the kiss was for her daughter and she expects me to . . . give it to her."

"She wants you to kiss my wife?" Connor wasn't laughing now.

"Yes."

"You're not going to."

"No, of course not."

The conversation ended then and there. The two warriors rode to the southwestern tip of the border where the latest attack had occurred.

Aeden arrived an hour later. Shouting at his laird, he dismounted and came running.

"Your wife is fine, Laird," he blurted out. "But there was trouble."

Connor stood perfectly still and didn't say a word until Aeden had recounted everything that had happened. The soldier also repeated every word Brenna had said, and by the time he finished, Connor was in such a rage, he was shaking with it.

"Where is my wife now?"

"With the Kincaids. Crispin's with her. He put Donald in charge of the keep."

"Is Brenna all right?"

"Yes, she is."

"You're certain?"

"I'm certain."

Connor tried to push his fear aside so he could concentrate. "And Euphemia?" he asked, his manner deadly calm now, for on the surface, he appeared to be in complete control.

"Crispin expects her to take her son's body back north for burial."

"Is Brenna . . ."

"She's fine," Aeden told him once again. "I wouldn't lie to you. She's needing stitches, and she was badly beaten, but she's going to survive. The women wanted to go with her. Donald had his hands full making them stay inside the fortress."

It took all of Connor's strength not to double over and let out a roar of anguish. He should have been with her. He should have known what was happening. The bastard. He dared to touch her.

"Laird, what would you like me to do?" Aeden asked.

Connor made himself think about the problems at hand. Aeden had to repeat his question a second time before his laird could answer him.

He called to Douglas, the senior of the soldiers guarding the border, and told him he was in charge. "Move the last of Hugh's clan tonight. As soon as you're finished, all of the MacAlisters are to return home. Aeden will assist you."

"And you, Laird?" the soldier asked.

"I'm going to my wife. Quinlan, take over the watch at home until I get back."

Quinlan stayed by Connor's side while the other soldier ran to do his laird's bidding.

Connor suddenly called out to Aeden. "She told my wife to submit to him?" he roared. He didn't wait for a second confirmation but caught hold of his horse's reins, swung up on his back, and took off at a full gallop.

Quinlan followed him. His plan was to protect his laird's back until they reached the point where he would have to turn north for home, while Connor continued on to the Kincaids.

Connor took the fastest route, cutting up along the border, and when he was well away from his other soldiers, he let out a cry that sounded like a wounded animal.

Euphemia. He couldn't even say her name without wanting to draw his sword. She would never call herself a MacAlister again, never wear the plaid she had violated, and never come near them again.

Quinlan expected his laird to turn to the east, as they were now parallel to his fortress, and was therefore taken by surprise when he stopped instead.

"Connor?" he asked as he pulled up beside him. "You're going to have to shake off your anger until after you've seen your wife. I know you feel you've abandoned her, but she'll understand you didn't have any choice. She loves you," he added with a nod. "Quit staring at the ground and look at me."

"Look down," Connor snapped.

He humored his laird and did just that. Then he let out a low expletive. "There are fresh tracks."

"Four horses . . . no, five," Connor altered. "They're going slow, in a single line. Who . . ."

"How many did Aeden tell us came back with Raen?"

"Three," Connor answered. He jerked upright then. "The bastard's mother could be on her way home now. Pity, I would have liked to talk to her."

"You'd end up killing her," Quinlan said.

Connor shook his head. "No, death would be too kind. I want her to suffer for as many years as she has left."

"If it's Raen's burial party, why would they take the opposite path? They have to know they're going the wrong way."

"I don't know."

"The tracks are fresh enough for us to catch up with them

in little time at all. We should know where they're headed, shouldn't we?"

Connor nodded. "We'll follow the tracks, but only for a few minutes. I need to get to Brenna."

"I know you do. I'd start practicing," he said as they once again goaded their mounts into a gallop.

"Practicing what?" Connor shouted.

"Telling her you love her."

Connor rode on ahead and cut through a section of the forest to shorten the distance to the rise above the slope ahead so that he could see how far away Euphemia was. When he broke through the trees, he dismounted and ran ahead to watch the procession below.

Quinlan caught up with him a minute later.

A long, narrow meadow stretched out below. It was the funeral party all right, and Raen was draped over the last horse in the line as they moved forward.

Connor's attention was drawn to the trees. Something had moved, he was sure of it. He waited, and a few minutes later, when the five reached the edge of the flat, a figure stepped out from his hiding place.

Both he and Quinlan recognized MacNare at once. Stunned and enraged, they watched Euphemia dismount and run forward to embrace her ally.

They knew who the traitor was.

He rode to the Kincaids' at a neckbreaking pace, and when he reached the courtyard, he swung down from his horse and went tearing inside.

He took the stairs two at a time to get to the balcony, frantic now to see for himself that she was going to be all right. Crispin was standing sentry outside her room. Connor raced past him, threw the door open, and charged inside.

He knew he was acting like a madman; he couldn't help it. He needed to tell her how sorry he was that he hadn't been there to protect her. If she didn't forgive him, he didn't know how he would be able to go on.

He reached the center of the room before he saw her standing by the window with Jamie. And then he came to a dead stop.

No one could have prepared him for this. His gentle little wife had been beaten so severely, he couldn't understand how she had survived. She looked as though she'd been cornered by a wild beast. Her face was blotched with purple bruises, one arm was bandaged from her shoulder to her fingers, and there were claw marks everywhere.

But she had survived. Connor repeated those words twice inside his mind in order to calm down enough to speak to her.

She wasn't dead. She wouldn't be standing if she were dead.

"No, I'm not dead," Brenna said, and only then did he realize he'd spoken his thought aloud.

On her way out, Jamie paused to whisper to Connor. "She won't stay awake long. I gave her something to make her sleep, but she's fighting it. She seems to think she has to apologize to you first. Try to get her into bed."

Connor walked closer to Brenna so he could catch her in time if she collapsed. He didn't want to frighten her. He knew he looked god-awful. There was war paint on his face and arms and a burning fury in his eyes he was helpless to conceal.

He wanted her to come to him, yet couldn't imagine why she would ever want to get near him again after what he had done to her. While he had been defending a useless piece of land, she had been left alone to defend herself against his predators.

"Do you want me to wash the war paint off? I know you don't like it," he said, his voice gruff with emotion.

"I don't mind."

"You don't?"

"I have something to tell you, Connor."

"Get into bed first."

"Jamie put something in my drink to make me sleep. She told me I won't wake up until tomorrow."

"I know," he answered.

"If I get into bed . . ."

"All right."

She didn't move. "Raen fell out the window."

"I know he did, love."

"I didn't push him. I didn't mean to stab him either. He

fell back on his blade, and if he hadn't been holding my wrist down to the floor, it wouldn't have happened. I was trying to cut his hand so he would move it away from my mouth and I could scream for help. Please believe me. I didn't mean for him to die. I just wanted him to get off me."

"I'm sorry I wasn't there to protect you."

"What would you have done?"

"Thrown him out the window for you."

Confused by what he'd just told her, she shook her head. The movement made her dizzy. "I have more to tell you before I sleep. I tried to honor and respect your mother, but I can't any longer. It's wrong for me to come between you and your family. She's part of your past, and I know how important she is to you. She'll never come back to see you again as long as I'm there. She's going to hate me, Connor, when she finds out her son is dead. Crispin was going to hide him for me. Your mother told me to do whatever Raen wanted me to do. I wouldn't, though, and I'm not sorry. It was wrong of her to think I would ever submit to him."

"Yes, it was wrong. Let me carry you to bed."

She acted as though she hadn't heard him. "She's never going to forgive me. I don't want her to anyway. I don't like her. You have to decide which of us is more important to you. I know it's wrong of me to make such a demand, but I . . ."

"Brenna . . ."

"No, I have to explain," she cried out. "I can see how angry you are, and I . . ."

She was struggling to stay awake, as the potion Jamie had given her was making her sway even now, and she could barely concentrate on what she was telling him.

The second her head fell forward, he gently lifted her into his arms and held her close. She had fallen asleep. He leaned down and kissed her forehead. He didn't move for over an hour, content to feel her warmth against him.

Jamie returned to the room to sit with Brenna. The torment she saw in Connor's face made her want to weep for him. "She needs her rest, Connor. Put her in bed now."

He wouldn't move. It took her a long while to convince him that his wife was going to be fine.

Yet still he hesitated to leave her side. "I don't want her to be alone again."

"She won't be alone," Jamie promised. "We just received word from your holding that Father Sinclair is on his way. Oh, Connor, he isn't coming to administer the last rites. Brenna isn't dying. He's her friend. He'll sit with her too."

"You'll get word to me if she needs me or if her condition changes."

"Yes, of course I will."

The fire burning inside him was raging now, and he knew that if he didn't leave the chamber quickly, he would completely lose his control.

Jamie followed him to the door. "Where are you going?"

"To finish it."

"What do I tell Brenna?"

He shook his head. He didn't want to worry his wife, and he knew if she was told he was going to MacNare, she would become afraid for his safety; yet he didn't want to lie either.

And so he simply told the truth. "I'm going to my stepmother."

His mask of composure vanished the second he stepped into the hall. Gone was the loving husband, and in its stead the savage warrior was revealed. He removed his sword from his sheath, handed it to Crispin, and went downstairs. His stride was long, purposeful; his expression cold, deadly now with his intent.

Alec watched his brother from across the hall and tensed in anticipation.

Connor didn't say a word. Rigid with fury, he stormed into the hall, reached up, and ripped his father's sword off the wall.

No command was needed. Quinlan and Crispin stepped forward and matched their laird's stride.

Alec didn't hesitate. He took up his own sword, his expression murderous, and followed his brother.

At long last, Donald MacAlister was going to gain justice.

They showed no mercy. The battle to surround MacNare's keep was hard fought, hour upon hour, their swords slicing through the air again and again as they methodically cut through the enemy's defenses from all sides. Alec's forces swarmed up from the south in a wide half-circle, while Connor and his allies swept down from the north in an impenetrable arc that joined with Alec's soldiers to make the circle complete.

It was impossible for the enemy to escape their line or their vengeance. The element of surprise was on their side.

Until the moment they attacked, MacNare was unaware his treacherous plans had been discovered. The northern clans had been told to attack Connor's fortress in two days' time, at dawn, but because of the old woman's stupidity in coming to MacNare for sanctuary earlier than planned, their timing was destroyed.

MacNare didn't engage in the fight, but hid behind closed doors inside his keep. Surrounded now on all sides in a fiery tomb, the coward frantically hurried about to gather his gold to take with him through the secret passages. Like a rat, with his razor-sharp protruding front teeth, his narrow eyes darting back and forth, he scurried about the hall to get another pouch he could fill with his treasure, while Euphemia raged against him.

"Take up the fight," she urged. "All you need do is kill Connor and Alec, and their followers will scatter."

"Silence, old woman," he screamed. "Or I'll put my sword through your belly. It was your son's lust that brought Connor here."

"He doesn't know I brought my son's body here. He thinks I've gone up north."

"Then why did he attack?"

"Your raids against Hugh's borders must have provoked him," she cried out. "Stay and fight."

"Why do you care what happens? Your precious son is dead," he scoffed. "And a dead man cannot become laird over the MacAlisters. You've already lost everything."

The outer doors were being rammed open now. The pounding noise reverberating through the hall was as terrifying to MacNare as the encroaching fire. Murky gray smoke, slithering in from under the door, was already coiling up about his feet.

"Help me fill these bags," he shouted. "Hurry, they'll be inside soon."

A resounding crash told him the barricade had been

breached. They were coming for him now. He heard the pounding of their booted feet against the stone floor outside his door, getting closer and closer and closer . . .

His hands shook so, he dropped the last bag, whimpered with regret over the spilled gold he didn't have time to collect, snatched up his sword, and ran to his escape route.

Euphemia threw herself in front of the passage. "Don't be a fool," she screamed. "Neither Alec nor Connor know the Buchanans have joined with my clan. In two days, they'll come down through the mountain passage, and attack the MacAlister fortress. You can still have your share if you stay and fight. Kill Connor for me now, or I swear I'll lead him to you."

Four warriors stood outside the entrance, listening to Euphemia's desperate pleas, and it wasn't until Alec had heard their plan that he knew the man he had called ally, the bastard Buchanan, was in league against him.

Connor reached for the door. Alec shoved him aside and thrust his shoulder against the obstacle. The bolt weakened with the first push, broke in half with the second.

He stepped back, waited until Connor had drawn his father's bloody sword from his scabbard, and then put his hand on his shoulder. "Show him as much compassion as he and the others showed your father."

Quinlan and Crispin, their weapons ready, would guard their laird when he entered the hall. Alec would protect their backs, while his army protected him.

"Get out of my way," MacNare screeched at Euphemia from within.

She refused to move. MacNare still thought he had time to make his escape. He stepped back, lifted his sword, and shoved it into her middle just as Connor walked into the chamber.

He showed no reaction to his stepmother's bloodcurdling scream and watched without emotion as MacNare ripped the sword out of her and shoved her aside. Euphemia doubled over before collapsing to the floor.

MacNare didn't realize Connor was in the hall with him. He kicked Euphemia out of his way while he frantically searched for the panel that concealed his exit.

"Going somewhere?" Connor asked.

MacNare whirled around. "You had no right to attack me, MacAlister. No right at all. Kincaid will hear of this."

"I'm part of this, you fool," Alec bellowed in rage.

MacNare's face turned white. He looked as though he were seeing Death himself walking toward him.

"I wasn't there. I had no part in your father's death, MacAlister. I was just a boy, like you were. Yes, just a boy."

"You were over twenty years old," Alec shouted back. "You were there, all right, wearing the Kaerns' plaid, you bastard. Donald MacAlister was my friend."

He nudged Connor in his back. "The sight of such refuse is foul to me. End it."

"I'll kill you first," MacNare boasted. He leapt forward, crouched down, and hurled his sword at Connor. He would have made his mark if Connor hadn't deflected the weapon with his father's sword.

"Help me, Connor," Euphemia cried out, writhing about in agony.

Connor didn't acknowledge her.

MacNare jumped up to run toward the hidden passage. As he was turning, he heard the whistle of the sword slicing through the air and dodged to his right. Connor had anticipated his reaction. Donald MacAlister's blade thrust through the center of MacNare's neck, continued on, and lodged into the wall behind. MacNare was lifted by the impact, thrown back from its force, and pinned to the passage door. It opened and began to sway back and forth.

The only sound heard was the squeaking of the panel and the low gurgling of MacNare's death rattle.

"Please help me, son," Euphemia called out again. "Have mercy on your mother."

None of the warriors acknowledged her. Crispin asked Connor if he wanted him to get his father's weapon, but his laird shook his head.

"It's where my father wanted it to be. Leave it."

"Connor," Euphemia screamed. "Please . . . please . . ."

Without a backward glance, Connor walked out of the hall, his stepmother's screams slowly fading away.

Chapter 18

Connor had made his choice. When Brenna was given her husband's message, she was overwhelmed with defeat. He had gone to Euphemia. There was little hope for a future together now, as he was clearly locked in his past, and nothing she could do would ever change that.

As soon as she saw her reaction, Jamie was sorry she'd told her. Brenna had been rapidly recovering from her injuries until she was told Connor's whereabouts. She became withdrawn then, and even though Jamie tried to get her to tell her why, she refused to say a word.

The mere mention of Connor agitated her. After trying for three full days to get Brenna to tell her what was wrong, Jamie decided she would have to wait until their husbands returned to find out what the problem was.

Time healed Brenna's body. Her appearance underwent a dramatic change in a very short while. The swelling was nearly gone from her face and shoulders; the bruises had already begun to fade, and her arm was healing nicely.

On the fourth day of her confinement, Brenna was up and dressed. Jamie looked in on her after the noon meal was served, and was pleased to see her sitting in a chair next to the window.

"How are you feeling today?" she asked.

"Much better," Brenna told her. She tried to sound cheerful, but knew she'd failed when Jamie hurried to her side and put her hand on her forehead.

"There isn't any fever," Brenna said. "I'm fine now, really."

"You're healing quickly, but we both know your heart is still aching. I have a surprise that should make you smile though. Father Sinclair has been insistent on speaking with you. If he had told me earlier that he'd spoken to your mother, I would have let him come up," she added with a laugh. "He didn't think to mention that fact until a few minutes ago."

Brenna was overjoyed. "He's here, really here?"

"Ah, finally a smile," Jamie said. "He's been here since yesterday evening. He sat with you several hours last night, but you slept through it. Shall I show him in?"

"Yes, please."

Brenna jumped to her feet the second Father Sinclair entered the chamber. "I'm so happy to see you," she cried out.

"Be happy sitting down," Jamie ordered, hovering over her patient like a mother hen.

Brenna did as she was instructed, waited until the priest had moved a second chair over to the window to face her, and then said, "Was your journey successful?"

"All is well," Father assured her with a nod.

Brenna was afraid to believe him. She clasped hold of Jamie's hand and held tight. "You're certain?"

In answer, he held up her medallion and put it in her other hand. "I'm certain."

She burst into tears.

"This isn't good news?" Jamie asked. "Are you in pain? Tell me what's wrong, please."

"She's overcome with happiness," Father said.

"Yes, I'm happy," Brenna stammered out.

"I had no idea she'd lost her medallion."

"Oh, it was never lost," the priest said.

Jamie was thoroughly confused. "Then why . . . ."

"You mustn't worry about me."

"I worry about you because I love you, sister, and so does

your husband. Now, I'm leaving the two of you alone to visit. Father, I hope you'll be able to convince her Connor hasn't forsaken her."

Before the priest could respond, Brenna shook her head. "I would much rather you sat with us and heard my news from home."

Jamie declined the invitation. "If I leave the door open, I'm certain it will be all right for me to go downstairs. Grace is hiding under the table so she won't have to take her nap. The child hasn't figured out I can see her from across the hall, of course. I'll warn you now, Brenna. I promised her she could sit with you after she rests. She seems to think you belong to her while you're here."

"I would love to see her."

After bowing to Father Sinclair, Jamie left the room.

"You must tell me everything, Father," Brenna said.

The priest nodded. "I was welcomed into your parents' home right away, and I carried with me another brown robe for Faith to wear on her journey to Gillian's fortress. I heard that he, too, was away from his home, and I'll admit I wasn't certain what I should do then. Fortunately, the abbey came to mind. I knew that the monks keep rooms available for weary travelers. Faith met me in the meadow. She put on the robe when we reached the forest, and we avoided the main path on our journey."

"How can I ever repay you?" Brenna asked.

"You needn't repay me. God watched over us, and surely that was why we didn't run into any difficulties. Your sister is a lovely young woman. I was amused by her views on several subjects," he admitted.

The priest then told her several stories about her sister. Brenna laughed with delight, and oh, how the sound warmed Father's heart.

Once again, the element of surprise was on Connor's side, and they were ready to attack when the northerners flooded down through the passage. It was a bloody battle and a fight to the death, but in just three days' time, the enemy was defeated. Tending to the wounded so that they could make the journey back home took much longer than the actual battle, and neither Connor nor Alec would leave until the last of their own was on his way.

The soldiers requiring stitches were taken to Jamie, who was kept busy from early morning until late at night repairing the damage. Stragglers continued to come across the drawbridge for three more days, and they also needed Jamie's care.

Fortunately, none of the men required last rites, which was all well and good, since Father Sinclair had left the Kincaid fortress to finish up what he told Jamie was an important matter at the Dunkady Abbey down near the Lowlands. He didn't expect to return to the MacAlisters' keep for at least two full weeks.

Because it was so chaotic, with men going and coming across the drawbridge at all hours of the day and early evening, no one noticed Brenna was missing, and it wasn't until an hour before Alec came home that Jamie realized she had vanished. Everyone searched high and low for her, of course, and all for naught.

By the time her husband came inside the hall, Jamie was beside herself with worry. Knowing how Connor was going to react, she decided to let Alec tell him.

She wouldn't even give her husband time to kiss her. She threw herself into his arms and cried out, "Oh, thank God you're home. I've lost Brenna. You have to find her."

Alec refused to believe such a thing was possible. No one could get in or out of his fortress without permission. An hour later, he wanted to kill every man who had been left behind to guard his family.

Yet, as infuriated as he was, his reaction was mild compared to Connor's. He was enraged.

"How could you lose her, Alec?" he roared.

"Could she have gone back home?"

"I stopped by my keep to get something I knew would please my wife. I sure as thunder would have noticed if she'd been there."

"I'm so sorry, Connor," Jamie said. She sat down at the table and buried her face in her hands. "I should have been watching her. I did look in every morning before I went downstairs, and I thought she was in the bed. It was too early to wake her up, and I didn't get back to the keep until late that night. I looked in her room again and thought she was sleeping. I should have pulled the covers back, and if I hadn't been so weary I would have noticed."

"Didn't one of the servants go into her room?" Connor asked.

"I told everyone not to bother her. Dear God, I don't even know how long she's been gone. I'm so sorry."

"Alec, take your wife to bed," Connor ordered. He followed his brother to the table and pulled the chair back so Jamie could get up.

"None of this is your fault, Jamie."

Alec lifted her into his arms. "You haven't had any sleep at all in the past week, have you?"

"I've been busy taking care of the wounded, Alec. I can sleep tomorrow. I have to find Brenna before . . ."

"Connor and I will find her. You're going to bed."

She was too tired to argue with him and knew she wasn't going to be very helpful anyway. She was having difficulty holding on to more than one thought at a time now. She put her head down on his shoulder. "I love you, Alec. What will you do to find her?"

"We'll start by tearing this keep apart. I'm not convinced she's gone."

Alec stopped in front of Quinlan and ordered him to keep Connor inside the hall until he came back, then carried his wife up to their bedroom.

"Don't forget to let the children know you're home," Jamie said. "And, Alec? I need to have you in our bed again. Will you wake me when you come in?"

She fell asleep before he could answer her. He removed her clothes, tucked the covers around her, kissed her forehead, and went back downstairs.

He and Connor personally went through every room in the keep. They extended their search, and when at last they reached the drawbridge, they were both convinced she had left.

Connor felt they had wasted their time. His anger quickly turned to panic.

"You know what her chances of surviving are outside the keep," Connor said. "She won't survive if she's alone, Alec. She . . ."

"She will survive," Alec snapped. "And you will soon be useless to me if you continue to think such thoughts."

By the time they returned to the hall, Connor was so scared, he couldn't think. He stormed about the room while he tried to figure out where she could have gone.

"Did you question all the men you left behind?"

"They were questioned, but not by me," Alec answered. "I've sent word for two of the men to return from sentry duty, and they will be here an hour after sunlight tomorrow."

"Tell me where they are," Connor demanded. "I'll go to them now."

"No."

Alec knew his brother well and was ready when Connor tried to leave. He blocked him with his arms.

"I'm going to order ten men to guard the doors in the event you try to leave during the night. Accept the fact that you aren't going anywhere until we figure out exactly where she is. The moon isn't providing sufficient light tonight, and you'll end up killing yourself and your horse if you leave here. You're going to be reasonable."

"You don't understand. I have to find her. She doesn't have a destination in mind."

"What does that mean?"

"Brenna only wants to get away from me. She blames me for not protecting her from Raen. I should have been there. I should have known . . . If anything happens to her, if I can't get to her before . . ."

"We'll find her," his brother insisted.

He and Quinlan stayed with Connor until the middle of the night. Alec went upstairs to sleep for an hour.

Connor wanted to begin questioning the men now, but Quinlan refused. "It would take us at least an hour to find all of them, and all have been told by their commander to be here at dawn. I know you won't sleep, but at least sit down, Connor. I know what you're going through. In your place, I would be raging inside too, but it's important that you stay clearheaded so you can find her."

Connor knew he was right. It was impossible to close his eyes, but he did eventually sit down. Quinlan fell asleep in one of the chairs near the entrance. Connor ordered him to go upstairs and sleep in one of the bedrooms. His friend didn't want to leave, of course, but as soon as the suggestion was given as an order, he was forced to obey.

For the rest of the night, Connor sat alone at the table in the darkness, waiting for dawn to arrive. He pictured every possible horror that could happen to his gentle wife until his mind rebelled and he simply couldn't take any more.

It was the longest night of his life.

The following day wasn't much better. He and Alec took turns questioning every soldier who had been left behind to guard their laird's fortress. No one knew anything that could help them.

Connor was going to leave for home to question his own people in the hope that Brenna might have said something to one of the servants that would help him find her, and as impatient as he was to get going, he also wanted to hear what each Kincaid soldier had to say.

The soldiers in charge of the drawbridge entered the hall just as Quinlan stepped forward to offer a suggestion. "Could she have gone to Faith?"

Connor rejected the possibility. "She didn't know her sister was in any danger. By the way, where did you put Faith, Alec?"

His brother didn't know what he was talking about. Quinlan explained while Connor continued to pace about the room.

Jamie came into the hall and sat at the table to listen to what the soldiers told her husband.

"Of course Brenna knew. I would know if anything happened to my sister. How she found out isn't important now. Oh, Lord, the medallion," Jamie cried out. She ran over to Connor. "I thought she lost it, but when the priest gave it back to her, he told me it had never been lost at all. Don't you understand? Brenna must have sent Father Sinclair to her sister. She gave him the medallion to show Faith so she would know she was to do whatever the priest instructed her to do. I knew Brenna was clever, but this amazes me. I know I wouldn't have thought of it."

Alec questioned his men then, a strenuous undertaking because of Connor's ranting and raving, and in little time at all they knew how Brenna'd managed to leave.

Only one priest was reported coming inside the keep under Douglas's watch, but two priests had left when Niell was in charge.

Connor weighed the damnation of his soul for eternity against the temporary pleasure he would get if he throttled a man of the cloth.

"With your permission, Laird?" Niell asked.

"What is it?"

"I don't think the priest knew she was following him. He went out first, riding his speckled gelding, and pulling the reins of a packhorse behind him. The second priest walked well behind the horses."

"And you didn't think this was peculiar behavior?" Alec roared.

"He was small, Laird. I thought he was yet to be ordained and that he was required to walk as penance."

"Now all we have to do is find out where the priest was going," Alec said.

"Dunkady Abbey," Jamie blurted out.

"You're certain?" Connor asked.

"Yes," she answered.

"If he was telling the truth," her husband said.

"For heaven's sake, Alec. He's a man of God. Of course he was telling the truth."

"I'll leave immediately," Connor said.

"I'm going with you," Alec and Jamie both announced at the same time.

Connor shook his head. "I have to do this alone."

"Not without your men, you don't," Alec warned.

Because he didn't want to waste time arguing with his brother, he told Quinlan to go to the keep and get the others. "You can catch up with me," he told him.

The monastery was only a short day's ride away by his measure. If Brenna was riding the packhorse, God only knew how long it would take her to get there.

He forced himself to block all thoughts but one. He had to get to his own sweet Brenna. He was lost without her.

Brenna was inconsolable. She couldn't eat, couldn't sleep, and couldn't stop crying long enough to make any sense to her sister.

Faith soon threw her hands up in despair. After she handed Brenna a dry cloth to wipe away her tears, she tossed the soaked square in the laundry box with the others, and then sat down next to her sister on the narrow cot in her bedroom. For what she swore was going to be the last time, she tried to get her sister to listen to reason.

"You really have to stop this mourning. We've already been thrown out of chapel because you were making so much noise."

"We weren't thrown out. We were just encouraged to go back to our rooms."

"What about dear Father Sinclair? He can't pay attention to his daily vespers, thanks to you. Why won't you listen to us? You told me you love your husband."

"Don't you understand? He made his choice when he left me. He doesn't want me or my love. He never did. She's part of his past, and he's never going to let go of what happened. No, I can't go back. It would hurt too much."

The need to blow her nose ended her protests. Faith still didn't understand. "You never used to cry. If loving someone makes a woman miserable, I swear I'm never going to fall in love. I wish I never had to get married either. For the love of God, will you stop crying? Perhaps if you went back and tried once more . . . If you told him how you feel . . ."

"He knows how I feel even though I didn't give him my declaration. He's intelligent, Faith. And so am I," she added. "I know when I'm not wanted. I can't talk about this anymore."

"What if he comes for you?"

She shook her head. "He won't."

"But what if he does?"

She let out a sigh. "I would think his pride forced him to come here. I wouldn't go back with him. Can't we talk about something else?"

Faith ignored her suggestion. "Gillian might not let you come back with us. Then what will you do? Stay in the abbey for the rest of your life, making these poor monks miserable?"

"My brother won't deny me. Did I tell you Connor doesn't even know how many brothers and sisters I have?"

"Yes, you've mentioned that fact to me about a hundred times now. You want children, don't you? If you go back . . ."

"I do want children, but I'm not about to leave them with Connor."

"Now what are you talking about? Go back to him, Brenna. Please, before it's too late. He's your husband."

"Must you nag me?"

Faith decided she had pressed enough for the moment. "Perhaps some fresh air will make you feel better. Let's go outside and stroll about the gardens."

"If we stray from the path, we aren't on sacred ground anymore."

"I don't understand."

"The path in front of the abbey. There's a wooden cross where it ends on the south side and another on the north side. If we step off the path, we aren't safe. I think we should just stay here. Besides, Gillian should be here any time now if Father Sinclair's estimation was right."

"If you insist on hiding here, then we'll hide. At least pull the fur coverings off the windows so the sun can come inside. It's like a tomb in here." Faith didn't wait for her sister to agree or disagree with her. She ran to the window, unhooked the cotton loops, and pulled the thick fur down.

Closing her eyes against the bright sun, she reached behind her head and lifted her hair away from the nape of her neck. "The breeze feels wonderful," she whispered, her face aglow with pleasure. She stayed silhouetted against the light until her arms began to ache. And then she looked out at the landscape.

"Oh . . . my . . . God . . . they're . . . they're . . . huge."

"Is something wrong?" Brenna asked.

Mesmerized by the sight before her, Faith couldn't even manage a nod. At the northern end of the abbey were giants for as far as the eye could see. Faith guessed at least forty men rode with the fierce-looking warrior who had separated himself from the others and had ridden closer to the path. Every one of the men was bare-kneed and would have been bare-chested as well if it weren't for the wide strip of material that was pulled up from one side of his waist and draped over his opposite shoulder. Some of them were scarred; others were not. All of them were in dire need of a good scrubbing, haircuts, and decent clothes.

Saints above, they were savages.

Faith whirled around. "You can't possibly go back. Thank heavens you came to your senses. No, no, you can't go back to your husband. You should live with Gillian. He'll be happy to have you. He loves you dearly. Why didn't you tell me they were . . . they were . . . Oh, Brenna, how did you ever manage to stay alive all this while?"

"What are you rambling about?"

Worried she might come to the window and see who was outside, Faith frantically shook her head. Her sister had had enough upsets to last her a lifetime. The proof was there for anyone to see. She had a scar on her forehead, and another on her arm.

In her haste to make amends because she hadn't had any idea what Brenna had been up against, she stammered out her apology. "I'm so sorry. I didn't know . . . until I saw them, I didn't know. No, it's out of the question."

"What's out of the question?" Brenna asked. She stood up to join her sister at the window.

Faith ran over to her and shoved her back down on the cot. Then she raced to the door and threw the lock into place.

"It's out of the question to . . . to go outside. Yes, it's out of the question. My, but it's gotten chilly in here. I believe I'll put the fur back up."

She went back to the window and peeked out, hoping she had only imagined the savages were there. No, they were there all right, looking just as frightening as before.

Her hands shook while she tried to rehook the loops. "Brenna, tell me what your husband looks like."

"Why?"

"I'm curious, that's all," she answered. She stared at the leader and tried to finish rehanging the fur at the same time. He really was scary.

"He's handsome."

"You're jesting."

"No, I'm not. He is handsome."

"But what exactly does he look like? Describe him for me."

354

"Dark hair and eyes, a straight nose. He's tall, and very strong. Does that satisfy you?"

"Long hair?"

"All the MacAlister men have long hair. What are you looking at?"

"Father Sinclair," she answered, which wasn't a lie, because the priest was running down the path toward the warrior in front of the other savages. Father should have been running the other way, shouldn't he? Surely he noticed they were all armed for battle.

Brenna went to the water basin to wash her face and hands. "If Father's outside, it's safe for us to go out. He won't let you wander off the path."

"Was it safe for the two of you to come here without an escort?"

"No, but it was necessary. It isn't now. Besides, I was dressed as a monk, and all the Highlanders respect men of the cloth. None would harm them. Right now, however, you are the one I'm concerned about. Once you make up your mind to do something, you do it, no matter what the risk, and if you decide to pick flowers up on the hill, I know Father won't let you."

"You taught me how to take a risk," Faith protested. "Oh, dear, the fur just fell out the window."

Leaning out, she watched the covering drop down with a *shush* to land on the stone path just a step away from the priest. Startled by the near miss, Sinclair glanced up at the window.

"I'm so sorry, Father. It slipped," she called out before she jumped back so he wouldn't lecture her in front of the savages. Besides, she knew she was going to laugh, and she really didn't want to hurt the priest's feelings.

He heard her, of course, and so did the MacAlisters. Everyone but Quinlan pretended not to notice. He grinned with obvious approval.

Curious, Crispin turned to him. "You find her amusing?"

"I find her enchanting."

Crispin shook his head to let his friend know he thought he was demented. Quinlan nodded, and then declared his intention, "I mean to have her."

"She'll run from you."

"I hope so. It wouldn't be any fun if she didn't. She's bonny, isn't she?"

"Marriage?"

"Eventually."

Connor suddenly raised his hand. His friends thought he wanted them to be silent so that he could hear what the priest was telling him. Then their laird gave the signal to let them know the enemy was near. He simply put his hand on the hilt of his sword. Englishmen were approaching.

Gillian and his soldiers were coming up the hill. From the sound their horses made, Connor estimated approximately sixty soldiers rode with their baron. Crispin and Quinlan immediately moved to flank their laird to protect him from an attack from either side.

Father Sinclair didn't notice the MacAlisters were tensed to fight. He was explaining once again that he hadn't helped Brenna leave the Kincaid holding, hadn't had the slightest inkling that she had such a plan in mind, and it was only after they had entered the forest and she called out to him that he knew she was chasing after him.

"Don't you ever look behind you?" Connor asked.

"Not when I'm on your land or Kincaid's, because I know I'm safe. I assure you I took every precaution once your wife alerted me to her presence. I tried to talk her into going back, but she wouldn't listen to me, Laird. I couldn't let her go on without me, could I?"

Connor shook his head. "You have assured me she's all right, and that's all I care about now. Tell her to come to me."

"She'll deny the request," he said. "I'll try, of course."

"She won't deny me." He took his dagger from his belt and cut the threads Jamie had used to sew the medallion to the side of his plaid. "Give her this."

The priest accepted the medallion with a nod. "And your message?"

"The medallion is my message. She'll understand. She can't deny me, Father."

"If you leave your sword at the door, you could come inside," he offered.

Connor's answer was to suggest the priest look behind him.

THE WEDDING

"Oh, Good Lord. Gillian's here. I'll hurry," he whispered. "Don't do anything rash before I return."

"We won't," Connor assured him, "unless, of course, we're provoked."

The priest picked up the hem of his robe and went racing back toward the abbey.

"You might as well stop brushing your hair, Brenna. Father's coming back inside. He's running, as a matter of fact. I wonder . . . Uh-oh."

"What's wrong?"

"Gillian's here."

Brenna dropped her brush and sat down on the cot. The time had come for her to leave the Highlands forever. Oh, God, why did it hurt so much?

Tears gathered in her eyes. She bowed her head in surrender and began to pray. "Why is this so hard?" she cried out. She doubled over and rocked back and forth, acting as though the pain were physical now instead of inside her heart.

Faith didn't know what she could say to her. "I don't know, Brenna. If I could help you, I would. Your husband might be able to make you feel better."

"No."

"He's here, Brenna."

Other than straightening up again until she was rigid, she didn't say anything or show any other reaction.

"Surely that means . . ."

"He's here because of his pride."

"I knew you'd say that," Faith said. She leaned back out the window and waved to her brother. Gillian and his men all looked so shiny and new in their hauberks and helmets. She turned then and looked at the MacAlisters again. They looked . . . "Like savages."

"Come away from the window."

"I think I should wave to your husband. It would be rude to ignore him. I already waved to Gillian, and I shouldn't slight him."

"I assure you he won't care."

She waved anyway. "He didn't wave back. Gillian did."

"Get away from there," Brenna demanded.

"Come and look."

357

"No."

A knock sounded at the door, followed by loud panting. Father Sinclair had run up the steps to get to Brenna's room.

Faith let him in. "She won't go out to him, Father. I tried to convince her, but she refuses to have anything to do with him."

The priest nodded before he rushed over to the cot. "Your husband told me you would come to him, mi'lady. He was certain this would force you to," he added as he dropped the medallion into her lap.

She stared at the wooden disk a long minute without saying a word. Faith wanted a closer look at it and reached down to pick it up. Brenna snatched it up before her sister could touch it.

She stood up and stormed over to the window. She wanted to throw the medallion out because he dared to use it now when it was too late but stubbornly refused to wear it before.

Then she saw him. "He looks tired," she whispered.

"You have to go, mi'lady. A fight's inevitable unless you let your husband know you are either going to go back with him or go with Gillian."

She stepped away from the window and walked to the door. "My brother doesn't know I'm here."

"That doesn't matter," he countered. He followed her out the door and down the steps. "Your husband knows you're here. Gillian might think he wants to take your sister."

"I have a sure way to make him go back to his fortress," Brenna said.

"Tell me," Faith demanded, running to catch up with her sister.

"I'll simply ask him if he loves me. He won't be able to say he does, and he'll realize then I should return to England."

"What if he doesn't realize it?" her sister asked.

"He won't do anything I don't want him to do as long as I tell him no."

"Have you forgotten how big your husband is? He can get whatever he wants."

"No means no to him."

"You love him, don't you, lass," Father said.

"Yes. I love him, but it isn't enough."

The priest reached for the door, yet didn't pull it open. "Faith, please go outside first. Run to your brother and stay with him so he'll know the MacAlisters aren't a threat."

"Do you think Gillian's soldiers would harm the Highlanders?"

"No, but I'm certain the MacAlisters would kill all of them without breaking a sweat. They can be ruthless when they want to be, and Lord only knows, they'll easily overpower them."

"But there are twice as many . . ."

"Number means nothing to them. I've seen them fight, and I assure you, I know what I'm talking about."

"I'll do as you say," she promised. She hurried outside, ran to her brother, and hugged him. She spent several minutes listening to him tell her how Brenna's husband had sent men to their mother to protect her from MacNare. He also added that their mother had taken a fancy to the leader of the band and actually hoped he'd come back.

Faith gave him her full attention until Brenna walked outside.

"You can tell me more after I go inside and get my clothing," she said, and though she had every intention of doing just that, she ended up following Brenna instead. Her sister looked so vulnerable and alone. Faith wanted only to protect her from further heartache, and Gillian would just have to be patient a little longer.

He could wait a few more minutes, couldn't he? "I'll be right there, Gillian," she called out. "I just want to meet Brenna's husband first."

Before her brother could deny her, she picked up the hem of her skirts and hurried toward the MacAlisters.

Father Sinclair was detained by the monks hanging out the windows on the first floor. He had to reassure each one that a battle wasn't about to be fought on sacred ground and it was perfectly all right for all of them to return to their duties.

"It's just a family reunion," he explained, and heaven help him, he told the half-truth without laughing once.

Faith didn't speak to any of the monks, but she did wave to all of them. Several, caught up in her enthusiasm, waved back. As she neared the end of the path, one of the MacAlisters caught her attention. She had the peculiar feeling he expected her to do or say something, and though he didn't motion to her, or give her any other sign, she couldn't shrug off the feeling he wanted something from her.

All of the warriors kept her brother's soldiers under close scrutiny. Brenna, she noticed, had suddenly stopped. Faith thought she was having second thoughts about talking to her husband and decided to help her make up her mind. She caught up with her, took hold of her hand, and gave her a tug to get her moving again.

Brenna wasn't paying any attention to her sister. Her gaze was on her husband. It was sheer agony for her to be so close to the man she loved and know she could never be with him again. Didn't he realize he was tormenting her by coming here? Her heart felt as though it were being shredded apart.

She stopped once again before she reached the end of the path. Faith let go of her hand and stepped behind her sister.

A full minute passed without a word being spoken while husband and wife stared at one another. Once again, Faith decided to help. She gave her sister a little shove.

Brenna ignored her. She took a deep breath, held up the medallion, and said, "This used to belong to you, Connor."

"It still belongs to me, Brenna. And so do you. Now and forever."

She shook her head. "It's too hard," she cried out.

He removed his sword, handed it to Crispin before he dismounted, and walked forward.

"I'll make it easy for you. Please don't cry. I know I hurt you."

The priest rushed forward to offer a cloth to Brenna. One look from Connor made him change his mind. He backed away, turned around, and strolled toward Gillian.

Brenna felt as though the world were intruding on her now. When he took hold of her hand and walked down the path toward the gardens, she didn't pull away from him. She kept her head down and thought to wait until they had some privacy before she said good-bye to him.

The lack of privacy didn't bother him at all. "I know I hurt you. I should have protected you from Raen. I will have to live with my mistake for the rest of my life. I don't expect you to forgive me, Brenna, but I . . ."

"You aren't responsible for what happened. I should have

told you what he was doing. I meant to, but you left before I could get up the nerve. Then he left, and I thought he wouldn't come back. It doesn't matter now anyway. You made your choice when you went to Euphemia."

He looked astonished. "Will it make you feel any better to know she's dead?"

"Good Lord, no."

"All right then," he said. "Does knowing that I didn't banish her as I intended make you realize I was considerate of your feelings?"

She turned to look at him. Connor didn't know how much longer he was going to be able to keep himself from taking her into his arms. He was determined that she willingly come to him, and he knew, if he didn't move away from her now, he would lose his battle. He let go of her hand, sat down on the stone wall, and waited for her to join him.

She moved closer, until she stood between his outstretched legs. "What happened to Euphemia?"

"I'll have to tell you about my father's legacy so that you will understand, but it's a long story. Do you want to hear it?"

There was an overwhelming sadness about him now that tugged at her heart. The strength seemed to go out of him as well. His head was down, his shoulders sagged from the weight he had borne all these many years, and she could feel the ache of his melancholy.

"Do you want to tell me?"

"Yes," he answered in desperation.

She took a step closer. "Please tell me now," she whispered.

He looked relieved. "I know that Lothar told you about the ruins, and that they would be torn down after I had avenged my father. I want to tell you how he died and what he said to me."

"He told me you were there during the massacre, and that you were just a boy. I would like you to tell me what happened, but only if you want to. Do you?"

Connor nodded.

"He didn't die easy . . ."

The past poured out of him in halting, broken sentences. He remembered all of it, remembered the fear he had felt and the hopelessness. She pictured him as a young boy, crawling over burning embers, clutching his father's heavy sword to his heart, and she was in awe of him, for he had more courage and honor than a hundred noble knights. No wonder she loved him so much.

"My father's demand to avenge him became my obsession," he ended.

She nodded to let him know she understood. "I have a question to ask you."

"Yes?"

"Would you demand from your son what your father demanded of you?"

He didn't hesitate in answering. "If there was a chance that the murderers would come back, I would warn my son to protect himself, and I would tell him to find out who they were so he would know his enemy's name. I would not want to die worrying that he and his family might one day be destroyed, but I would not ask him or demand that he avenge me, Brenna. No, I would never ask that of my son."

He didn't know that his answer had just reclaimed her future.

He put his hands out in front of him so she could see the scars on his fingers and palms. "This is my inheritance. I can't remove these marks from me, and I can't change what I am."

She took hold of his hands and kissed each palm. "Your hands are beautiful. Whenever you're overburdened or worried, you have only to look at your hands to remember that you are a man of honor and courage, for that is what these scars represent."

"A wife doesn't run away from an honorable man. I failed you."

She shook her head. "You didn't fail me. I thought you could never leave the past, and I was also afraid that you would give your son such a burden. I didn't give up hope until you went to Euphemia. I thought you chose her over me, and it became too much for me to accept. Why did you send her away?"

"Because she hurt you. Don't you have any idea how much you mean to me? When I was told what Raen did, I went into a rage. I wanted only to rid our home of the scum before you and I returned. I couldn't bear the thought of bringing such a pure heart into such a foul presence. That's why I wanted to send her away. I considered killing her."

"The MacAlisters don't kill women."

"No, we don't," he agreed. "I was going to banish her. I never wanted her to call herself a MacAlister again or dare to wear my colors. Euphemia had already left the holding, but only just barely. When I discovered her trail, I followed her so I could end it. Then I saw her embrace MacNare."

"She was the traitor," she gasped.

"Yes."

"What happened then?"

"I'll explain everything later. You told me I only had to open my heart. Do you remember?"

"I remember."

He put his hands on either side of her waist and pulled her closer. "You were asking me to love you, weren't you? I should have told you then."

"Tell me what?"

"That I love you."

She shook her head. "No, you only want . . ."

"I love you," he said again. Tears streamed down her face. He gently wiped them away for her and pulled her tight against him. "I know you love me. Why didn't you tell me? Were you afraid?"

"I didn't tell you how I felt because I knew you didn't love me. Yes, I was afraid, but you weren't afraid, were you?"

He leaned close to her. "Yes, I was. Brenna, you scared the hell out of me. If I loved you, I became vulnerable. What would happen to me if you died? And then it was too late. I couldn't protect myself from you, but once I realized I loved you, I felt reborn inside. One of us will surely die before the other, but the memories will sustain the one left behind. You know what?"

"What?" she whispered.

"I'm never going to let you go. I know you deserve far more than I can ever give you. It doesn't matter, though. You're mine."

She pushed against his chest. "You aren't going to kiss me yet. You're going to have to tell me you're sorry first."

"Because I failed to protect you." It wasn't a question but a statement of fact. He let go of her, looked into her eyes, and tried to find the words that would redeem him.

"No, you didn't fail me. You did break my heart though. How dare you tell me to give you a son and then go back to England. It was a cruel thing to say to me, and I still cannot understand why you would hurt me like that."

"You were mourning your family," he explained. "And I wanted to give you something to look forward to," he added. "And so I . . ."

"You what?" she demanded.

He had the audacity to grin while he admitted his sin to her. "I lied."

Her eyes widened in disbelief. "You lied to me?"

"You can't really believe I would let you go back to England."

"Don't you dare laugh at me. I did believe you. You shouldn't have lied. That was wrong." The sparkle in her eyes made a mockery of her attempt to make him feel guilty. "Have you lied about anything else?"

He shrugged. "Probably."

"You must stop it at once."

"I lied when I had Jamie tell you I was going to Euphemia. Actually, I guess I didn't lie. I did go to her, but only because she was with MacNare."

Her hand flew to her throat, so stunned was she by his casual remark. "You went to . . ."

"Later, sweetheart. Are you going to let me kiss you now?"

"No," she replied. "You're going to let me kiss you. Things are going to change. From this moment on, when you leave our home, you will have the good sense to tell me first. If I ever wake up again and find out you've left, I'll hunt you down, and God help you then."

"Ah, lass, you do love me, don't you?"

"You're going to wear your medallion too. I mean what I say."

"I can't wear it around my neck. It becomes a weapon then," he explained. "If you sew it into my plaid, I'll wear it. Will that satisfy you?"

His wife looked radiant. "I want you to change the doors

inside our home. It's safe for you, but I have to go out the back way because I can't open them."

"All right, I'll change them."

"I want to ride the black."

"No."

She put her arms around his neck and leaned close to him. "Will you think about it?"

"No."

She was laughing when he finally helped her remember she was going to kiss him. His mouth took absolute possession, and for long minutes, he showed her how much he loved her. She was far more aggressive than he was, and it was only when he forced her to stop that she remembered where she was.

She wept against the side of his neck while he whispered tender, loving words to her, and when at last he insisted they go home, he had to wait until she finished crying before she gave him her agreement.

He draped his arm around her shoulders and led her back to the main path.

"Will we sleep outside tonight?"

"We won't sleep," he replied. "But if you want to stay outside tonight, we will."

"Yes. You look tired."

"So do you. Brenna, don't ever put me through this torment again. Promise me you won't leave me, no matter what happens."

"I promise you. Come and meet my sister. What in heaven's name is she doing? She's entirely too close to the end of the path. None of the MacAlisters would . . ."

"Quinlan would."

"What are you saying?"

"If she steps off the path, he's got her. That's what I'm saying."

"Make him stop staring at her."

"Your sister doesn't seem to mind. She's staring back. She keeps moving closer to him too."

"Faith, come over here," Brenna shouted.

Her sister ignored her. "Connor, make Quinlan and Crispin come here."

"I can ask, but neither one of them will come. As far as

they're concerned, their duty has already been determined. They're protecting us, sweetheart. You should be proud of their restraint."

"Why should I be proud of them?"

"They want to kill the English, of course."

Dear heavens, she'd forgotten about Gillian. "You must come and meet my brother."

"No."

"If he comes to you, will you meet him then?"

He shrugged before he gave her his conditions. "If he's armed, I'll have to take him aside and discuss the insult with him."

She knew what that meant. "He won't be armed," she rushed out. "I'll go get him."

"No."

The force behind the denial told her she wasn't going to get him to change his mind. Father Sinclair came to her aid. A moment later, Gillian joined them at the center of the path. Like Connor, he was also unarmed.

Her husband didn't particularly want her to embrace her brother, but he didn't make an issue of it.

While she thanked Gillian for coming to get Faith, Father Sinclair went to fetch their sister. He got to her in the nick of time, he realized, when Quinlan winked at her. The priest grabbed her before she stepped off the path.

"You may say good-bye to the MacAlisters in a few minutes, Faith. Your sister would appreciate your help in gaining Gillian's cooperation."

"Is Brenna's husband cooperating?"

"No, no, of course not, but both Brenna and I know he will never cooperate with an Englishman. He hasn't killed him, though, and we must all appreciate the control he is showing for his wife's benefit."

Faith shook her head but quickened her step until she was running.

"I'm sorry I took so long, Gillian."

Her brother's response was to push her behind him. She took immediate exception and pushed him back. Then she ran to her sister and sat down on the wall next to her.

The two men continued to face each other as adversaries.

Brenna became impatient in no time at all. "Gillian, aren't you happy to see me?"

He finally stopped staring at Connor long enough to look at her. "Yes, of course I am. Are you coming home with me?"

"No. I'm going home with my husband. We are married, Gillian, and I assure you, I'm very happy. Tell Father I forgive him for sending me to MacNare."

"He didn't know what the bastard was capable of, Brenna. He also doesn't know you're married."

Faith explained before Brenna could ask any questions. "He thinks you're living in sin," she whispered so her sister's husband wouldn't overhear.

Father Sinclair stepped forward. "It was a proper ceremony, Gillian, with the church's blessing."

"Did you marry them?" Gillian asked.

"I did."

His blue eyes bore into the priest. It was obvious he was trying to decide if he should believe him or not.

"Gillian, please tell Mother I'm sorry she and Father weren't able to attend my wedding."

Her brother once again turned to her. "Were you married in a church?"

"We were married in one of God's most beautiful chapels. No expense was spared. There were flowers everywhere, and in every color imaginable. I entered the chapel under a canopy of green branches that were so fresh and new, dew still clung to them and sparkled like jewels against the flickering lights above. The scent of heather surrounded us while we pledged ourselves to one another. Both Connor and I were finely adorned in the most magnificent of robes, and when the ceremony was properly blessed, we attended our wedding feast."

Her eyes were misty with her recollection, and the joy her brother saw as she gave the details only a woman would remember convinced him that she had indeed been properly wed. It was also apparent that she was happy.

"The wedding was magical, wasn't it, Father?"

The priest was overcome by her recitation. He dabbed at the corners of his eyes with the edge of his sleeve, nodded several times, and said, "Aye, lass, it was magical, and meant to be. Do you realize, Baron, that if it weren't for Laird MacAlister, your sister probably wouldn't be alive today."

"Yes, I realize it."

It was all he was willing to give. Brenna found his acknowledgment satisfying. Connor couldn't have cared less. His wife's memory of their wedding had overwhelmed him, and all he wanted to do was get her alone and tell her how proud he was of her.

"Brenna, it's time to go home."

"Yes, Connor."

She stood up, went to her brother, and kissed him on his cheek. "I love you, Gillian."

"I love you too, Brenna. Make him take care of you."

"He does take good care of me. He loves me, Gillian, and I love him."

"I can see you do."

The two men stared at each other for a long silent moment. Brenna stood between them, waiting for them to acknowledge each other.

Gillian finally conceded. He bowed his head to her husband. Connor inclined his head then to him.

It was as good as it was going to get, Brenna knew, and even though they were both arrogant and stubborn, she still loved them.

Connor put his arm around his wife and turned to leave.

"Just one minute, Laird," Faith called out. She went around her brother's back so he couldn't detain her and chased after Brenna and Connor.

"Laird, do you know how many brothers and sisters your wife has?"

Brenna nudged him so he would answer. "My wife is the seventh of eight in the family. You're the youngest, aren't you?"

"Yes. Do you know their names?"

"Faith, it isn't necessary to . . ."

"Yes, it is necessary. We're important to you, and therefore we should be important to your husband, shouldn't we?"

"Come here, Faith."

She didn't even think about refusing him. She hurried forward and looked up into his eyes. "Yes?"

"Yes, Laird," Brenna corrected.

"He's my brother now. Must I still call him Laird?"

"You know perfectly well you must until he gives you permission to drop the title, which I might add, he hasn't done yet. We were raised in the same household."

Faith laughed. "Very well. My question wasn't answered yet, Laird. Would you like me to tell you the names of our brothers and sisters?"

"That isn't necessary. There's Gillian, William, Arthur, Matilda, whom you call Mattie, Joan, Rachel, my wife, and you."

"You knew . . . all the while, you knew who they were?" Brenna asked.

"Yes."

"Then why didn't you let me talk about them?"

"Because you were mourning your family. Talking about them wouldn't have made you feel any better. I also wanted your loyalty. I believe I already explained this to you."

She leaned against him. "You may explain it again when we get home. Faith, it's time to say good-bye. I'll miss you."

Her sister hugged her. "I shall miss you more. Laird, I forgot to thank you. Gillian told me you sent men to my home to protect me from MacNare."

"You sent soldiers to my parents? They went into England?" Brenna was staggered.

"Yes, he did," Faith assured her. "Mother liked the soldiers. Father wasn't there, but he was pleased when he heard the lengths your husband had gone to to protect me. I was wondering . . ."

"Yes?" Connor asked. Neither his wife nor her sister realized they were walking toward the end of the sanctuary. Quinlan certainly noticed, if his grin was a true indicator. Knowing his friend as well as he did, Connor was certain he had already counted the number of steps Faith would have to take to leave the sanctuary of the church and become fair game.

"Are the others here? I wanted to tell the man in charge thank you too, but I don't know his name."

"His name is Quinlan. He will soon be laird over his

uncle's clan, now that his duty to me has ended, and yes, he is here, Faith. He's watching you even now."

She immediately looked up at Quinlan and took another step toward him.

"My brother told me what you did. My father will want to thank you for coming to his home to protect me. I thank you too, Quinlan, with all my heart."

Her Gaelic was music to his ears, and unlike her sister's, her command of his language was remarkable.

He didn't speak to her, but he bowed his head in acknowledgment. Lord above, when she smiled, she had dimples.

"Apparently, my mother has taken quite a fancy to you. I hear that she wonders if you will ever come back."

Connor heard what she said and looked up at his friend. "She makes it almost too easy for you, doesn't she?"

Quinlan laughed. "Aye, she does."

Neither Brenna nor Faith understood what Connor had meant by his question. What would be easy?

Faith was just about to leave when Quinlan spoke to her. "Tell your mother I will be coming back. She has something I want."

She wanted to ask him to explain, but felt it would be impolite of her to question him any further. "Then perhaps I will see you again. I don't plan to marry for at least two years, no matter how much my father disagrees. I'm old enough, of course, but I've realized I'm hopelessly spoiled, and since I don't have any intention of changing, I will have to find a baron who will promise to pamper me, and that's going to take time. If I have already wed before you arrive, then please remember how thankful I am to you. Good-bye, Quinlan. I hope God watches over you."

She made a perfect curtsy to show her respect, kissed Brenna and her husband farewell, much to Connor's astonishment, then turned and went running back to her scowling brother.

"I'm going to miss Faith most of all," Brenna admitted.

"You'll probably see her again," he said.

"I doubt that," she replied. "I'm sorry Quinlan will be leaving us. Will Crispin be given command each time you're called away?"

"No, he'll go to Hugh's holding. They have asked me to assign someone to become their leader. They need Crispin, and he will be pleased as well."

He lifted his wife onto the black, swung up behind her, and then leaned down close to her ear and told her again how much he loved her.

"We're starting over again, aren't we?"

"If it makes you happy to think we are, then I won't argue with you. It will be easier, however, because I will remember always to be thoughtful."

"You already are thoughtful, and is it any wonder at all why I love you? I was wondering . . ."

"Yes?"

"I would like to ride bareback again, and if you rode with me, could I ride one of the other horses?"

"If you agree to stay inside the fortress when you ride bareback, I will grant this request. Do you see how I can be accommodating, wife?"

"Yes, I do," she agreed. "And since you're in such a wonderful mood . . ."

"Yes?"

"About the chapel . . ."

Epilogue

Sunset was a magical time. The children would be outside, running barefoot up and down the paths and shrieking with laughter while their mother kept a watchful eye on their youngest, a fiery-headed bairn with a wobble in her gait and a devilish gleam in her blue eyes, who found great sport in plucking the flowers out of the ground as soon as her mama planted them.

He would go up to his bedroom to remove his sword before joining them in their games, but he always lingered in front of the window to look out beyond the walls.

The first sprig of heather blossomed almost as soon as the ruins were torn down, and now the field was alive with rich, glorious hues, a fitting tribute, his wife believed, to the man who had gone before.

The scent of honey mingled with the sound of laughter, and, oh, what a joy it was to be home.

**Visit the Simon & Schuster
romance Web site:**

www.SimonSaysLove.com

**and sign up for our
romance e-mail updates!**

Keep up on the latest
new romance releases,
author appearances, news, chats,
special offers, and more!
We'll deliver the information
right to your inbox—if it's new,
you'll know about it.

POCKET BOOKS

2800.02